THE ORDEAL OF RILEY MCREYNOLDS

The Ordeal
of
Riley McReynolds

Michael O'Rourke

NORTH STAR PRESS OF ST. CLOUD, INC.

Author's Foreword

This is a work of fiction—a product of the author's imagination, as they say. It is not an account of actual people or real events. Nevertheless, while the story and characters are invented, attitudes and behaviors of the sort depicted in this story can be found in many large corporations. For those who doubt it, try reading the financial press for any six-month period.

Copyright © June 1, 2000, Michael O'Rourke

ISBN: 0-87839-146-0

Jacket design: Katie Murphy
Jacket art: Dan Lotts

Printed in Canada by Friesens.

Published by:
North Star Press of St. Cloud, Inc.
P.O. Box 451
St. Cloud, Minnesota 56302

To Anne Randolph

1

July 20, 1996. The mid-day sun glared full in his face as Riley drove back toward Minneapolis. He had just completed a nursing home visit near Rochester and, being in no hurry these days, he was returning by way of the scenic backroads of southeastern Minnesota.

It still weighed a little on his mind that in making these visits he was an impostor—a kind-hearted impostor, to be sure, but an impostor nevertheless. But then again he also might be an unwitting instrument of some benevolence, a carrier of some grace fashioned to reach into the crumbling chambers of Margaret's mind now ravaged by Alzheimers and a series of debilitating strokes. And so he resolved to keep coming, grateful and eager for the chance to perform this small cleansing ritual.

It was greener now. The leaves were fully in bloom and the landscape was bursting with the colors of the ripening crops spread out around him. An old barn, unstable in aspect but glowing a bright red, stood in the high fold of a distant hill. Like a man reminded of an idyllic country childhood, he felt touched by something close to nostalgia—virtual nostalgia in his case, for he had been raised in the city and had never so much as stepped foot on a farm.

As he drove past a white clapboard farmhouse snuggled against a wooded rise, he sought out the feelings that in recent weeks had so challenged the whimsical and mischievous temperament he had inherited from his father's family. Though the factual memories of those painful events were forever burned into his memory, the emotions that had so oppressed him during the closing days of June were now greatly diminished. He felt like a child who had passed through a high fever—thrilled to be recovered but still a little dazed by the experience. The chief residue of that time was a sense of wonderment, of formless surprise that, despite a series of signs and warnings, unmistakable in hindsight, he had played a significant enabling role in a cruel and unjust saga—one animated by duplicity, misplaced trust, neglected cues, and behavior of almost vaudevillian absurdity.

In his own defense, he had to say that the setting had seemed so benign, even when one took into account the stresses that were then burdening the workplace. And the inside players, though sometimes insensitive, and often foolish, had not seemed malicious or wicked. Even now he had trouble applying words of that type to Buck, for whom he held surprisingly little bitterness.

Riley had initially viewed the triggering event, the one that got everything started, as routine and easily contained. After all, he had handled much worse, and we weren't talking about murder or embezzlement or any of the sins that normally produce great suffering. All that was required, he had thought at the time, was for him to act with fairness and tact, virtues he had used to great effect all his life. And when all was said and done the company's obligations were fairly straightforward; it simply fell to him to make the right people see that. Thus, the sense of wonderment, for he could not quite get used to the fact that he had so grievously misread the motivations and vulnerabilities of the main players.

As the narrow highway rolled to the left, he turned the steering wheel gently and began a small ascent leading to the top of a high hill. When traveling the backroads he was usually a little lost, and today was no exception. He was seized with a mild sensation of Twilight-Zone-style confusion, when out of the distance a white country church appeared on the horizon, its modest form outlined against a brilliant blue sky. He now knew precisely where he was.

Shepherd of the Hills Lutheran Church, its high windows and narrow steeple reaching longingly toward heaven, stood with a quiet strength just off to his left at the crest of the hill. As he approached the church grounds, he pulled the car off onto the shoulder and slowly came to a stop. His heart raced a little as he rolled down the driver's window and stared out at the lush green churchyard, its rolling expanse broken only by a series of modest stone markers, some with flower arrangements and small flags leaning against them.

He took a calming breath in an effort to subdue the anxiety that seemed to be reawakening in his body. He did not want to be drawn back into the pain of that troubling period, still so close to the surface of his mind. The coincidence of his accidentally coming upon Shepherd of the Hills—a remote country church he couldn't have intentionally found had he been equipped with a compass and road map—scared him a little, as though some negative synchronicity might have befallen him.

But then he took several deep breaths and quietly resolved to submit to whatever unknowable processes might be at work. As he sat staring through moistened eyes at the small sacred space framed by a narrow, leafy hedge, from out of the stillness a soft breeze, hushed and forgiving, swirled off the landscape and seemed to pass gently through the car, brushing his face with a quiet absolution and with that touch came a new understanding, as certain as it was inexpressible. He felt his body go slack as it gave up its last and deepest reserves of grief and remorse. Soundless and drained, he sat in stillness for nearly half an hour.

As he pulled slowly back onto the winding country road and resumed his northerly course, memories of the last eight weeks, vivid and insistent, began to flood over him, just as they had so many times in the last several weeks. But this time there was a difference—this time he knew it was all right to surrender to their healing energies. He could replay the events from the beginning—from Monday, May 27th—without recrimination or reproach. And then he could go back to being the person he used to be.

2

May 27, 1996. The first ring of the telephone was absorbed gently and seamlessly into Riley's dream on this bright spring morning. The second ring landed disagreeably at the base of his brain. It was 7:00 A.M.

The white-haired family terrier, Tuffy, took the disturbance as permission to move from his usual spot at the end of the bed to a perch atop Riley's chest, where he stared at his master as though he were a downed pheasant.

A groggy Riley reached for the phone. "Hello," he said in a husky voice, failing in his attempt to sound professional and wide awake. Early morning phone calls always sent his mind whirling in the wrong direction. Usually up and dressed by six, he had reviewed status reports on the downsizing under way at the company until 1:20 A.M., and then tossed and turned for another hour before falling into a shallow and edgy sleep.

"Sorry to bother you, Mr. McReynolds," said a tentative, youthful voice on the other end of the line. "This is Hanson from the third-shift security detail down at work."

Young Hanson's voice trembled slightly, but Riley couldn't tell whether his fear was aroused by some actual crisis or by the understandable reluctance of a low-level security guard to wake a senior executive so early in the morning. Probably the latter, he concluded.

Sunlight pierced the east window of the bedroom, casting a yellow tint across the carpeting, up the lightly colored bedspread, and onto Riley's face, where it formed a waffle-like pattern. Tuffy sat sphinx-like upon Riley's chest, staring lovingly into his eyes, emitting a tremulous, affectionate growl, which was carried across the space between them on a wave of early-morning dog breath.

With the phone still in his hand, Riley pulled the sheet up over his face and said, "Hello, Hanson, how are you?" He couldn't bring himself to be cross with these young security guards; they occupied the bottom of the company food chain and got plenty of shabby treatment from the executive ranks as it was.

Hanson cleared his throat and said, "I never would have disturbed you, Mr. McReynolds, but I couldn't get a hold of the duty supervisor or the chief of security."

"That's all right, Hanson. Tell me what the problem is," said Riley. He peeked out at Tuffy from behind the sheet, avoiding his intense, expectant gaze and the big wet kiss he knew would be planted on his face should he make eye contact.

Hanson started in nervously, "Well, during my rounds this morning I found a locked briefcase in the men's room on the executive floor. And with all the threats and stuff we're getting because of the downsizing, I was afraid it might be a bomb or something, so I didn't dare move it." Hanson's words were picking up speed. "And because the building will start to fill with people pretty soon, I wanted to get instructions from somebody in authority. Should I call the bomb squad, Mr. McReynolds?"

Riley was now making faces at Tuffy, which caused him to fidget and growl more excitedly. The dog's blissful lack of higher consciousness fascinated Riley. Tuffy didn't give a rip if there was a bomb at company headquarters or anywhere else. He just wanted to get out to the back yard to take a pee and chase after the small animals.

"Is the briefcase ticking, Hanson?"

"No, sir, no ticking. I listened."

"Does it happen to be a large, brown accountant's briefcase with the initials RTM on the flap?"

6

After a brief silence: "Why, yes sir, it does."

"I thought so," said Riley. "That would be Bobby Morestad's briefcase. He leaves it all over the place, most often in the executive bathroom. You're new at the company, aren't you, Hanson?"

"Yes, sir, I am," Hanson replied a little dejectedly.

Riley rolled over in bed, sending Tuffy off his perch. "Don't be embarrassed, Hanson. You did just the right thing."

The downsizing was making everybody jumpy, Riley thought as he hung up and lifted himself out of bed. "Downsizing." "Rightsizing." "Reengineering." The vocabulary of the modern corporation. Cold, sterile euphemisms used to distance and objectify the firings of hundreds of good, decent human beings, all in the name of bottom-line profit and its more insidious companion, "shareholder value." Anything with the word profit in it sounded a little greedy, he thought, but shareholder value—now there was an elegant expression that could be used to conceal a host of small atrocities.

And didn't The Lindbergh Life & Casualty Company, the principal subsidiary and main revenue producer in the Lindbergh family of companies, have a long and honorable history of philanthropy and community involvement, and wouldn't that history inoculate it against public criticism for the brutalities of the downsizing now underway?

Probably not, he concluded. The Lindbergh Companies, known locally as "The Lindbergh," had expanded so dramatically and widened its product offerings so extensively in recent years that it retained little semblance to the benevolent insurance giant of former times. And though insurance still accounted for the largest portion of its revenues, it now had to compete with other products and services offered by the company, like real estate development, asset management, banking, and sales and underwriting of investment securities.

Trying to maintain the good-citizen image of the historical Lindbergh in the face of those changes—not to mention the changes wrought by the firings of thousands of local citizens—was a daunting task. And no matter how much spin control was being applied to soften the harsh realities of the mass firings, tenderhearted Minnesotans of all backgrounds and class-es were registering disgust at what they viewed to be an unnec-essarily cruel process, one that was cutting deeply into the marrow of a company that had until recently been a living symbol of corporate decency and altruism. More than any other local company, The Lindbergh had once been the insti-tutional embodiment of "Minnesota Nice," that amorphous expression used with a mixture of embarrassment and pride to describe the basic generosity and civility of the area's people.

And truth be told, Riley was himself a tenderhearted Min-nesotan, and no matter how common or accepted it was to use spin control to bolster a company's image, his participation in the process left him feeling queasy. Strangely scrupulous, per-haps, for a guy who had spent years in the criminal justice sys-tem, part of it as a defense attorney seeing to the acquittal of some pretty bad people. But at least there a higher purpose had been served: the system had operated as it was intended—presumption of innocence, due process and all that. Here there was no higher purpose, just the enrichment of a bunch of bigshots, including himself.

But he knew that, as the day wore on, after he had been up for a while, he'd be less troubled by such thoughts, thoughts which nipped away at him mostly in the early morning, when the membranes of the mind, thinned and weakened by long hours of sleep, could be easily penetrated; when the smallest negative thought could land with the force of a cancer diagnosis.

As he yawned and made his way toward the bathroom, the formal, by-the-numbers rationalization drill began. The center-piece of that drill was the self-reminder that some of the firings and cuts did have to be made, that some were absolutely neces-sary. Riley believed that, for he was a capitalist. Even a Republican—sort of. But did the firings and cost-cuttings have to be done so arbitrarily and with such apparent indifference to the human beings involved? And did there have to be so much tough-guy talk by Buck Montrowe, The Lindbergh's new chief executive officer, who was actually a pretty good guy deep down. If he would just show a little of the compassion Riley was sure he really felt, things wouldn't be so damned unpleasant.

Riley thought he understood Buck Montrowe in spite of the regional and cultural differences that separated them. Riley sprang from an Irish-Catholic breed of free-spirited northern city dwellers who worshipped a tolerant and forgiving god, while Buck had been raised amidst the dogmatism and harsh discipline of a splinter fundamentalist group in the backwoods of the Deep South. His father and grandfather had been itinerant preachers who spread hellfire and brimstone throughout Northern Florida when he was growing up.

In spite of these differences between them, and an age gap of more than a decade, Riley felt a strange affinity toward Buck. He was less wary of him than some others. Buck was a little insensitive, of course, but not evil. And, after all, he liked Riley, and that was Riley's main test for separating the good people from the bad. Buck was just insecure, he thought. That was what accounted for all the tough-guy talk. He didn't realize how he was coming off, what kind of impression he was making. The social worker in Riley was determined to fix all that, to bring out his better side.

Still . . . it was distressing the way Buck's team of paid executioners were handling the downsizing. As a result of their methods, each day in recent months had brought with it a new crisis. Managers throughout the company had been given nonnegotiable orders to eliminate a stated percentage of employees from the ranks of their work units, oftentimes without any regard for the continuing needs of those units. Apart from the pain and devastation to those losing their jobs, the survivors were left feeling shell-shocked and strangely guilty—not to mention the increased workloads they were now expected to assume, for there was rarely a decrease in the amount of work that needed doing, just fewer people to do it.

Riley thought of himself as a resilient person, even a bit of a crisis junkie, but he had to admit that this stuff was starting to wear on him. Only last week he had headed a crisis team that had to deal with an employee barricaded in his office with a shotgun to his head. The poor guy was a seventeen-year veteran with no history of instability who had taken to drink when faced with the stress of firing over half the people in his department—people he had hired, mentored, and, in violation of all managerial precepts, cared for like a loving uncle. And then one morning in boozy despair, after another night of tortured insomnia, he had locked himself in his corner office with a shotgun to his head. Riley talked him out of his plan and got him to the hospital, but his career was over.

Riley grabbed a towel out of the hall closet and headed for the bathroom, reminding himself on the way that all this, and his own discomfort, would pass when the downsizings were concluded. Then things would return to normal.

There it was, the drill was over. He stretched broadly as he entered the bathroom and looked in the mirror. He stared at the puffiness and drooping skin encroaching ever so slightly upon the upper rim of his pale blue eyes. And the boyish figure of his younger days had given way to weight concentrations in unflattering places. Even his nose seemed to be getting thicker. He used to be six-one, but when he turned forty he swore he was getting a little shorter each year, just like his grandmother Carr had. The concept of age-related height changes had been a part of his family folklore for as long as he could remember. Grandma Carr—his mother's mother—who had lived with the family when Riley was a boy, actually seemed to have shrunk about an inch every three years in her old age until you could hardly see her at the dinner table. Riley's mother eventually had to get her a booster chair.

Now he stood at the mirror, nearly fifty himself, and swore that either he was getting shorter or the sink in front of him was getting taller. At some deep-seated, inbred level, the family folklore made this conclusion plausible. Then again, it may just have been his posture (he had been slouching more since all this unhappiness at the company had started), or maybe it was the age-related disc compression he had been reading about in one of the many medical journals to which he subscribed. As the discs lost some of their elasticity, he had read, they flattened out and the spine compressed. This, he thought, must be happening to him.

Staring into the mirror, he regarded himself with a fluid curiosity, taking special note of the coarsening texture of the lightly freckled skin running from a point just above his right

10

eye to the border of dark auburn hair crossing his temple, forming a thick hairline. Seeing for the first time several gray hairs just inside the hairline, he initiated a frantic search through his scalp. To his dismay, the search yielded more areas of gray, especially just above the ears. He groaned as he looked at the aging face in the mirror and realized that to his dwindling height, he now had to add encroaching grayness.

He checked for lumps, skin lesions, and other signs of cancer. A few suspicious spots were noted, but then there had been many of these in the past. He had diagnosed them as malignant melanomas from which he had undergone spontaneous recoveries. The dermatologist, a former schoolmate, said they were freckles and age spots and that Riley was a hypochondriac. Just about everybody Riley knew said he was a hypochondriac.

Combing his thick dark hair carelessly across his forehead in the unchanging style adopted as a boy when John Kennedy was president and all good things were thought possible, he sensed that this was going to be a bad day. A small, nameless dread seemed to be taking shape in his midsection. The intuition developed during long years as a criminal lawyer—first as a prosecutor, then as a defense attorney, and then again as a prosecutor—was putting out a faint vibration, like the aura before a migraine. He tried to ignore the feeling as he sat on the edge of the bed, tying his shoes. It was just a low mood, he told himself. He'd drive through a cemetery later that day; that would cheer him up. His wife, Betsy, thought that was a peculiar way to cure a bad mood, but then she wasn't Irish. It was not for nothing that the obituaries were called the Irish sports page. Cemeteries were lush and beflowered, with gently rolling hills and birds singing cheerful tunes. And they were full of hassle-free people who used to get worked up about all kinds of things, and look where they ended up. The jumping-off spot for all human vanity. It was restful to think about.

He stood up from the bed and looked in the mirror. Throwing back his shoulders, he forced a broad smile. It was 8:05 A.M.

*****

On the main floor of The Lindbergh headquarters, through a wide entrance supported by large white pillars, the four teller stations of The Lindbergh Savings & Loan lined the east wall. Though accounting for only a tiny portion of the company's revenues, the S&L was prominently located just inside the main Lobby Court to lend the rich ambiance of a traditional banking facility to the cafeteria of retail insurance and stock brokerage units that dotted the circular borders of the building's main entryway.

The S&L's manager, Liddy Jonssen, had arrived from her suburban Minneapolis home at 7:00 A.M. The calm of the early morning hours afforded her a gentle transition into the frantic activities of the day.

Having worked her way up through a series of low-level managerial positions in the insurance and employee benefits divisions of the company, Liddy Jonssen had recently been assigned supervisory responsibility for the newly chartered S&L, which was itself a subdivision of the company's rapidly emerging Non Insurance Products Division. She was an up-and-comer within the ranks of middle management.

She wore a tan skirt that stopped just short of her thin and shapely knees and a navy blue blazer over a white blouse fastened at the neck with a simple gold medallion. She was of average height and wore her thick blonde hair in a pageboy, nicely setting off her pale blue eyes and the sharp features of her attractive Scandinavian face. Two tortoiseshell barrettes matched the frames of the glasses dangling from a holder strung around her neck. Thirty-three years of age, she looked even younger, which was primarily attributable to her slender figure and unusually soft, unblemished skin.

After checking electronic bulletins to see what had occurred overnight in world financial markets, she read e-mails and listened to voice-messages that had accumulated over the evening hours, replying on the spot to those requiring an immediate answer.

Most of the messages related to the downsizing under way

in the retail units, including hers. She noted how communications having to do with this painful subject seemed to arrive in the dead of night, apparently a practice common to downsizing programs in all industries. In her mind, it only added to the dark unpleasantness of the whole business. She longed for an end to the firings so that life and workplace relationships could return to normal.

She set about brewing coffee, which would be eagerly consumed throughout the day by the twelve employees of her unit. New to the ranks of supervisory management, Liddy had yet to develop the sense of self-importance that precluded low-status tasks like coffee-brewing, tasks generally eschewed by those of her rank. In fact, the leadership development trainers from the human resources department had recently criticized her for her seeming inability to "feel the power" inherent in her position. She recalled that criticism with a wry smile as she fiddled with the coffee pot and puzzled anew at talk of "managerial empowerment." It was a novel concept for her. A little rude and very masculine, she thought. Somehow she had gotten through other leadership challenges in her life quite nicely without recourse to muscle-flexing displays of power. Being fair and decent with people, that was her natural style.

She shook her head quizzically as she returned to her office, feeling a little guilty for compromising her "power" by making coffee for her inferiors. She was glad no leadership development trainers had been there to witness this act of managerial disempowerment.

Despite her reservations, though, she would cooperate, do her best to be a team player. After all, that was the road to advancement. And as unnerved as she was by the downsizings, she was proud of her recent promotions, and enthusiastic about the career path that lay before her.

L. I. Jonssen appeared in white letters across a black nameplate attached to the door of her office. Inside, one wall contained a large picture window through which she could watch the tellers and personal bankers she supervised conducting each day's transactions. On the credenza behind her desk stood a small glass sculpture in the shape of the

Lindbergh Tower, with lettering certifying Liddy as the April Manager of the Month at the headquarters location. The award was flanked by an arrangement of brightly colored fresh flowers. On one side of her desk sat a color portrait of her parents. Though the photograph had been taken at least fifteen years before, her mother and father looked even then to be of advanced years. The inscription on the portrait read: "To Liddy, The Joy of Our Life—Mother and Dad." On the wall behind the portrait hung a macramé design in bright colors of green and blue and red, showing a tiny spider climbing a water spout. Below the picture design were knit the words to the nursery rhyme "The Itsy, Bitsy Spider," and an inscription from her mother: "Always persevere, honey."

Liddy Jonssen had worked at The Lindbergh for nine years, having joined its management training program directly out of St. Olaf College, a small but distinguished Lutheran institution founded by pioneer Norwegians. Homecoming queen in her senior year, she was bright, athletic, and popular (president of the student council). She was the only child of Gunnar and Margaret Jonssen, a dour and serious farm couple who had married late in life, Margaret giving birth to Liddy at age forty-three after two previous miscarriages. Gunnar had died at age sixty-seven of peritonitis associated with a bleeding ulcer. Margaret was living out a confused and lonely existence (with mid-stage Alzheimer's) in a nursing home in Rochester, her sole comforts being Liddy's weekly visits and the spiritual ministrations of Pastor Einar Stensrud, chaplain to The Holy Redeemer Senior Residence. It was a disappointment to her that Liddy had so far failed to provide her with grandchildren or for that matter a good Lutheran son-in-law.

Liddy had had a good many marriage proposals from men of all, and no, religious persuasions but had yet to fall in love with the ardor she thought necessary to support a lifetime union. Though charming and fun, Liddy Jonssen's most prominent attribute was her sense of responsibility. She was a person so dependable and so admired by her friends that no fewer than nine had listed her as the designated guardian of their children should they die prematurely. It worried her

14

sometimes that if several were to die in a common accident she would find herself with a house full of orphans.

But Liddy's popularity and outward poise obscured an inner fragility unknown even to her closest friends. There had been times in life, such as when her father died, when she had been plunged into a frightening, paralyzing darkness—a darkness from which she feared she would never emerge. During prior episodes of that strange and disabling gloom she had managed, through force of will, to steel herself against its worst onslaughts until things finally returned to normal. But it was a concern to her that the stresses now being placed upon her by the cut-backs and firings in her unit seemed to be arousing some of those same frightening sensations. None of this was known to her supervisors and, if she could help it, never would be. Vulnerability was not a trait a company wanted to see in its up-and-comers, especially not in women, who automatically fell under suspicion of being temperamentally unfit for the rigors of corporate life.

Because the teller assigned to the early morning shift had been delayed in traffic, at 8:05 Liddy took up a position at the second window and began counting and sorting the cash drawer. After several minutes, a tall man with pale skin approached and stood at her station. His face was obscured by bright sunlight streaming in from a large window behind him. The disagreeable smell of sweet cologne hung thickly in the air around him.

Liddy looked up and squinted against the sun, unable to make out anything but the outlines of the man's head. She moved sideways to avoid the direct sunlight and saw that he had dark, oily hair over a thin, deeply pockmarked face. A goatee circled his chin and upper lip. The hair on his head seemed to lie unnaturally, as though it had recently been brushed forward.

Without speaking, he began counting from a pile of bills he removed from a tan folder. Liddy felt an instinctive discomfort and took a small step back to create a space between them.

After completing his counting, the man looked up at her. "Give me a cashier's check for $15,000," he demanded, pushing several piles of bills across the counter, never taking his narrow eyes from her.

Liddy had dealt with rude customers before and wasn't much put off on that account. But this was something different. She felt repulsed. She took a calming breath and, in accordance with standard policies relating to money laundering—a subject that the banking authorities and the FBI took very seriously—she said, "You can purchase a cashier's check, sir, but you should know that we are required to file a form with the government, reporting a cash transaction, or an attempted cash transaction, of ten thousand dollars or more. And we have to identify the individual involved, so I'll need some identification." She managed to appear composed but could feel fear seeping out around the edges of her words. Her heart had begun to pound.

When she reached for the stack of bills, the man slammed his hand on top of hers. She recoiled at the moist, cold touch.

Without taking his eyes from her, he shoveled the bills back into the folder. "I wouldn't be filing any reports if I were you," he said in a deep, raspy voice, his head twisting in a spastic motion. He then leaned into the counter. "And you better forget you ever saw me, or I promise you, you'll wish you had."

Out of the corner of her eye, Liddy scanned nervously for the security guard who typically stood at the desk near the end of the teller line. But he wasn't there; his job had been eliminated in the last downsizing. She stood frozen, not taking her eyes from the departing figure as he backed away from the counter and passed through the broad opening to the Lobby Court, turning again to stare at her.

It was a look, and a face, she would not forget.

3

As Riley headed downstairs, the sounds and smells of breakfast were in full swing. The kitchen TV clashed discordantly with rock music coming from the stereo in the den. Riley's wife, Betsy, and daughter, Lizzie, seemed to be engaged in a competition to see who could drown out the other. Lizzie was seventeen, a dark-haired, blue-eyed beauty with a sassy cockiness that drove her mother nearly crazy but inspired in Riley a warm fatherly pride. He thought her rebellions charming and harmless, for to him she was the living continuation of his own family of origin, a girl and four boys of such robust self-confidence that they believed the world would yield to their every wish. He had been the youngest—and mouthiest—of the boys. In his mind, Lizzie was just an extension of that bloodline. It was no wonder that he understood her better than her mother did.

Tuffy was barking wildly, running in circles, scratching at the French doors of the large, high-ceilinged den, trying to get out to the backyard to recover possession of his turf from the squirrels, chipmunks, and rabbits that trespassed each day upon his territory. The house itself sat comfortably upon nearly an acre of rolling ground that spread in a pie shape to a wooded area in the rear, and though the red-brick colonial residence and surrounding property were lush and spacious, they were less grand than those occupied by most executives of his rank. He resisted a move to more expensive housing—perhaps because of the warm memories associated with this house, or perhaps because an upgrade seemed pretentious and unnecessary.

The backyard animals maintained a studied nonchalance to Tuffy's hysterics, not even bothering to look up until Riley opened the door and Tuffy charged out at breakneck speed, in full attack mode, ears in the flaps-up position, giving off a low growl all out of proportion to his size. Even as the small animals scattered, Riley could tell from the look on their faces that they considered Tuffy to be little more than a nuisance and a bore. At eight inches tall and seven pounds wringing wet, his level of self-confidence was absurdly exaggerated. He had never caught one of his tormentors, and a good thing it was, too, for every last one of them could have kicked his ass from here to next Sunday, including the chipmunks. His only effective weapon was his breath, and it's hard to fire off a shot of bad breath when you're being mauled by a squirrel.

Riley was behind schedule, but he couldn't leave the doorway until Tuffy did his morning duty. "Go pee-pee!" he shouted into the yard at the top of his lungs three or four times until he feared that the elderly neighbors might wet their pants. Their suggestibility had been a concern to him since the horn on his car got stuck one night the previous summer and old Mr. and Mrs. Olson, mistaking it for a tornado warning, had gone to the southwest corner of their basement with a battery-powered radio. They were still there at noon the next day when their daughter, Clara, brought over the day's groceries.

Riley's shouting was doing little to speed Tuffy. He emptied his one-ounce bladder in tiny squirts across an intricate set of checkpoints discernible only to other dogs who might wander into the yard in search of combat or sex—or both. Tuffy was happy to join battle with much bigger dogs, but the sex part was a problem. His testicles had been removed the previous summer in an operation designed to get him to stop humping the guests. It hadn't work. Tuffy still humped everything that moved.

18

On the day of Tuffy's testiclectomy, Riley's seven-year-old son, Teddy, took a phone call from one of Lizzie's prospective boyfriends. In an attempt to win over the sister by buttering up the little brother, the lovesick suitor nervously asked Teddy a series of questions, including, "How's your dad?" Teddy thought he said, "How's your dog?" and replied "He had his balls cut off this morning." When Lizzie got on the phone, the boy expressed sympathy for her father's misfortune, which was a big mistake. Lizzie never felt the same about the poor kid.

Riley took a seat at the kitchen table and opened the Minneapolis and St. Paul newspapers, occasionally looking up to glimpse Betsy's small, youthful frame moving nimbly about the kitchen. After twenty-five years of marriage he still felt a small rush of gratitude when first in her presence.

He took a swallow of orange juice and turned to the metro section of the Minneapolis paper. A loud groan escaped his throat as he caught sight on the front page of a large action shot of himself being hit in the face by a ripe tomato the day before. He had been driving into the parking garage of the company headquarters when the tomato was launched from amongst a group of demonstrators protesting, among other things, the company's lack of investment in the inner city. The protesters had chosen this time to air their grievances because the bad publicity associated with the downsizing had made the company an especially easy mark.

Riley frowned painfully as he looked at the picture of himself trying unsuccessfully to duck the tomato, which had splattered rudely on the side of his face. It was not a flattering image, not one he'd have chosen to have viewed by a couple of hundred thousand readers. But he was determined to be a good sport about it—he had once been a protester himself.

Drawn by the sound of his groans, Betsy peered over his shoulder and laughed out loud. She thought the picture was hysterical.

He slugged down a cup of coffee and made for the door, hugging Teddy on the way and giving Betsy a kiss on the cheek. The kiss would have been on the lips but she was just getting over a chest cold, and if he caught it he was sure it

19

would turn into pneumonia and then tuberculosis. He had read of such cases in his medical magazines.

The spring day was bright and clear, the four-lane highway clean and dry as he made his way into morning traffic. Trees were in full bloom with thick green foliage. Thousands of Minnesotans—well scrubbed, courteous, and slightly left-of-center—were on the move from the upscale western suburbs. Two rows of fuel-efficient, nonpolluting cars sat obediently on the freeway entrance ramp, waiting for the light to flash permission to proceed.

To avoid traffic on the main 394 trunk line, he continued north on 169 to Olson Memorial Highway, where after a few minutes of easterly travel he could see off to his left the old neighborhood where his father had been raised, referred to simply as the North Side. In the early twentieth century, when his adored father, John McReynolds, was growing up, the North Side was populated largely by first and second-generation Jews with a smattering of Irish and Scandinavians, a pattern that was to greatly affect the course of his father's life. When in 1921 John was looking at a future filled with manual labor of the type endured by his Irish immigrant father and uncles, it was a Jewish merchant in the neighborhood, Saul Rosen, for whom he had worked as a delivery boy in high school, who paid his college tuition and living expenses. Saul Rosen had been nearly a saint in Riley's boyhood home, causing him to reflexively bow his head slightly whenever the name passed through his mind. John McReynolds, and later his children, had learned of tolerance and broad-mindedness from Saul Rosen, in theory and in practice. Years later, after law school and early success in business, John had declined to join the social and country clubs that excluded people because of race and color at considerable cost to his own advancement. Riley had done likewise when offered membership in those same clubs a generation later, though he was never entirely sure whether it was high-minded morality, as he liked to think, or because he hated golf.

Now in the thick of early morning traffic and drawing close to the 94E turnoff, which would take him across the river to

20

The Lindbergh headquarters in St. Paul, Riley moved in a pack of vehicles of all descriptions, representing all social classes. Bumper stickers announced the political and cultural biases of their owners. There were small cars driven by women with sensible hairdos and no makeup: THE EARTH DOES NOT BELONG TO US, WE BELONG TO THE EARTH, and MY BODY, MY CHOICE; mixed with the politically neutral: MY KID'S AN HONOR STUDENT AT GRANT MIDDLE SCHOOL; to the pickup trucks with creepy tinted windows: IF YOU WANT MY GUN, YOU'LL HAVE TO PRY IT FROM MY COLD DEAD HAND.

He squinted against the blazing sun as he turned onto the freeway, which after a brief southerly direction turned sharply east, setting a course for St. Paul. After a twenty-minute drive, and with the golden dome of the Capitol ahead on his left and the mammoth St. Paul Cathedral off to his right, the forty-story Lindbergh Tower came into view.

He left the freeway on the Tenth Street exit. As he started to slow down at the St. Peter intersection, his eyes were drawn to a late-model, green Jaguar approaching in the opposite direction. It had been traveling at an excessive rate of speed as it turned onto Tenth Street, fish-tailing widely as the driver—a young man with a car phone held to one ear—continued accelerating. As they drew close to each other, the Jag skidded out of control and crossed the center line into oncoming traffic. Riley turned sharply to the right, and, for the split second they appeared destined to collide, he and the other driver locked eyes. Under the influence of adrenaline the scene seemed to last a slow-motion eternity. The face in the other car was that of a junkie—probably speed or cocaine—one like hundreds he had seen over the years in the criminal courts; a mean, ravaged look coming from within angry, hollowed-out eyes. The rest of the mug was vintage bad guy, right out of central casting: dark greasy hair and goatee over sallow skin and pock-marked cheeks. They passed within inches of each other in a moment of fated intimacy before Riley jumped the curb of the adjoining sidewalk and the Jag spun back into its own lane and raced toward the freeway.

21

Riley's heart pounded as he came to a full stop among three or four other cars that had pulled off the road to avoid a crash. With shaking hands he dialed the police on his car phone and gave a general description of the Jag and its driver but with little expectation he'd be caught. He then looked around at his fellow survivors. They smiled nervously at each other, shaking their heads with a mixture of relief and disgust.

Heading back into the main traffic lane, he was awake in a way he hadn't been just moments before. There was nothing like a near-death experience to concentrate the senses. Maybe this had been the event foretold by the presentiment felt that morning. He smiled weakly and turned right onto St. Peter.

Ahead of him was a pickup truck driven by a muscular blue collar worker. On its back bumper was a sticker reading: MY KID BEAT THE SHIT OUT OF YOUR HONOR STUDENT.

As he turned left onto Kellogg, the Lindbergh headquarters could be seen standing with regal bearing several blocks south of the city's principal commercial institutions, its broad tan face staring southward over the river, its back facing its principal downtown competitors: The St. Paul Companies, Minnesota Mutual and First Bank. An agreeable marriage of the neoclassical and art deco, the building's first five floors were spread across the greater part of a city block, with the remaining thirty-five floors thrusting skyward in a large tower configuration. Engraved in thick Romanesque letters above the front entrance were the words THE LINDBERGH LIFE & CASUALTY COMPANY. Majestic for its time, the building reflected the quiet optimism of the company's founders, who, in spite of a looming depression and a crashing stock market, built one of the city's largest skyscrapers on a commanding site high above the Mississippi River. For more than sixty-five years the building had stood as an emblem of compassionate capitalism, of the partnership between business and the larger community. But now, as he drew closer, the great structure seemed to be tired and distressed, to be no longer flourishing, its pride and strength being drained away like that of an ailing child placed in the care of unloving relatives.

As he approached the building, he could see a mass of pro-testers stationed at the front entrance. The most animated ele-ments were blocking the sidewalk in front of the entrance to the garage, where his parking space was located. Several career radicals, adorned in outfits appropriate to their respec-tive causes, were spread across the plaza abutting the build-ing's facade. The group was preparing for a mid-morning demonstration against the many transgressions alleged against the company. Little evidence existed to support these contentions—at least in comparison with other companies in the area—but those details paled against what the protest leaders regarded as the overarching truth that American busi-ness had systematically cheated and oppressed disadvantaged classes throughout history. And what better symbol of that evil than a large insurance company undergoing a cruel and mas-sive downsizing?

The demonstrators were being shuffled about by the protest organizers like extras on a movie set, in a staged rehearsal of the upcoming spontaneous demonstration. The coalition of protest groups was known as the Southside Assembly of Social Initiatives, or SASI, for short.

As he approached the front of the building, Riley could see that even the veteran radicals looked a little bored and sullen this morning, but he knew they'd come alive like human cher-ry bombs when the cameras of the local media started to roll. Just by their presence they had succeeded in clearing the front entrance of morning pedestrian traffic, even scaring away the smokers who normally collected in an alcove off the front por-tico, huddled together in a shamed fellowship of once-cool, now scorned, drug users.

At the center of the group stood a friend of Riley's from the distant past. At six-foot-three and wearing combat boots and bib overalls, Hortense ("Tenzie") Dunseth was the tallest and most conspicuous member of the delegation, standing well above the crowd as she barked orders through a large bull-horn. Tenzie was well-known to the local business and politi-cal establishments, and her numerous detractors had a series of unkind names for her, including a county commissioner she

23

regularly criticized, who referred to her off the record as "two hundred and thirty pounds of man-hating lard." Tenzie was a fixture in the grievance community and took enormous pleasure in upsetting the well-being of politicians and business tycoons throughout the area. Riley had known her from the late sixties, when they participated together in antiwar and civil rights marches. He liked and admired her.

Determined not to be pasted with another tomato, he drove slowly past the garage entrance, making his way instead to the public ramp across the street. From there he slipped into the building through a side door. He then ducked into the freight elevator to avoid the Lobby Court, the multi-tiered, domed space consisting of glass and steel bordered on three sides by interior offices that looked down upon a central rotunda. Because a round of firings was scheduled for that morning, he wanted to steer clear of the common areas, hoping to avoid freshly butchered employees—many of them personal friends—being escorted from the building with dazed, pained expressions, carrying boxes filled with family pictures, children's drawings, and other personal items, hurriedly and unexpectedly packed.

By the time he arrived at his fourth floor office he had managed to successfully avoid encountering so much as a single human being. It was a relief, but it also made him feel like a coward.

4

An almost church-like quiet prevailed on the executive floor as Riley approached the conference room adjoining Buck Montrowe's office. He was slightly early for the weekly executive council meeting, the regular gathering of the company's most senior leadership.

In the hallway outside the conference room stood a giant stuffed alligator (the mascot of Buck's alma mater, Florida Midlands College) rearing upward in an attack posture—jaws open wide, forefeet clawing at the air, seeming to reach out for those passing by. The overall effect was one of menace, a silent warning that this was not a place for the fainthearted.

The room itself was expensive but plain, with the gray metallic ambiance broken only by a brown mahogany conference table, a dark credenza lining one wall, and a series of lightly cushioned, green, swivel chairs. The window blinds rested at uneven altitudes, giving the room a tacky quality in spite of its costly and pretentious strivings.

"Morning, Ted," he said to the only other person in the room, trying to summon a friendly air. Ted Colfax, a tall, distinguished figure dressed in a dark suit, with gold tie clip and cuff-links, was the senior executive of The Lindbergh Trust Company. A longtime employee who had come up slowly

25

through the ranks, he was known for keeping his head down during times of controversy. He concentrated exclusively on achieving high returns for the Company's fiduciary customers; and with two years left to full vesting of retirement benefits and perks, he was not about to let anything disrupt the orderly passage of that time. Though the severity and overkill of the current downsizing made him sick, he said nothing.

"Hi, Riley," said Ted Colfax, barely raising his head of thick white hair from the spreadsheet before him, a sheet that showed his unit had once again outperformed the market for the last reporting period. The Trust and Asset Management Group had succeeded—largely through the competence and likeability of Ted Colfax—in retaining fiduciary management responsibility for some of the area's oldest and most aristocratic fortunes, notwithstanding the accession of Buck Montrowe to the post of chief executive officer, a man whom no one mistook for an aristocrat.

Riley and Ted were next joined by Cole Girard, the head of the human resources department, formerly known as "personnel" but changed to human resources in one of those semantic upheavals of the 1970s, at around the same time barbers became stylists, janitors became engineers, and prostate exams became digital scrutiny. A man of medium height, with a pale, sensitive face and a head of jet-black hair, Cole Girard was the living embodiment of the HR professional, overflowing with enthusiasm, sincerity, and good works. In the 1980s, he had been active in the complex politics of Central America, holding a special fondness for the Sandinistas in Nicaragua, which he—whitebread speaker of standard American English if there ever was one—pronounced "Neek-hair-ak-waa." Riley had noticed that there was something about that word that caused wealthy suburban leftists to talk like Che Guevara.

Well intentioned and arguably correct though Cole's views may have been in relation to that struggle, as with most committed partisans his was an unnuanced point of view and one that was nearly impossible to reconcile with his own philosophy of unrestrained free enterprise here on the homefront—which may have explained why Cole confined his social-justice

26

initiatives to locations far removed from U.S. borders. Riley suspected that this highly selective approach had the added advantage of keeping Cole out of political conflict with Buck Montrowe, a stone-cold reactionary of the isolationist variety, who quite apart from his dislike of undeveloped countries generally had no earthly idea where "Neek-hair-ak-waa" was even located.

"How yaaa doin', big guy?" Cole greeted Ted Colfax, while delivering a sweeping, triple-pump, two-fisted handshake.

"Sit down, Cole," said Ted.

Cole was followed closely by M. Bryant Knox, head of the company's investment banking unit. The M. stood for Myrell, a name he never used. M. Bryant was pudgy, with a wide butt, and in conformance with the fashion protocols of the investment banking industry, wore brightly colored suspenders over a blue shirt with a highly starched white collar and slicked his thinning brown hair severely back off his forehead.

M. Bryant stopped at the credenza, and poured himself a cup of coffee. He surveyed the room carefully, and then made for a seat flanking the head of the table where Buck Montrowe usually sat, directly across the table from Garfield T. Blaisdahl, the senior executive vice president and Buck's chief of staff. In spite of Gar's impressive title, none of the others in the room—all of whom carried the slightly less pompous title of executive vice president—were in any way accountable to him.

When Gar Blaisdahl dropped from his mother's womb fifty-one years earlier, he immediately displayed the kind of simpering self-assurance one usually finds only in dysfunctional adults. The boy Gar, and the man who had now succeeded him, possessed nothing in the way of natural mirth or gaiety. At six feet tall, with plain features, dishwater blonde hair and a weak chin, he was barely noticeable in a crowd. Upon graduation from the Wharton School of Finance in 1970, he had let it be known that he wished to be referred to as "Field," rather than "Gar" or "Garfield," as had been the custom throughout his youth and young adulthood, "Field" bearing a more high-born sound. When first with The Lindbergh, twenty-five years earlier, his fellow workers tried to accommodate his wishes, but it never really took hold, instead having the unhappy effect of causing those who considered him to be an unbearable tight-ass to take to calling him "Garf" or worse yet "Garfie." Even his long-suffering wife, Marie, who drank too much, dissolved in giggles when she tried to speak the name "Field." She finally gave up and went back to calling him "Garfield," as his mother had always done.

Though he possessed the kind of homely administrative aptitudes useful to a large business enterprise, Gar Blaisdahl owed his senior status at The Lindbergh primarily to his unrestrained capacity to suck up to his superiors. He was the high-priest of what had come to be known as the "Montrowe Doctrine," which held that everything Buck Montrowe said was right, even when it was demonstrably wrong. Gar commenced most sentences with the phrase "Buck and I . . ." which gave rise to his being referred to behind his back as "Buckeye." He had heard the nickname being used, but mistakenly thought it was because he had taken his undergraduate degree at Ohio State.

By a quarter past nine the sun was easing its way past the rolls and orange juice on the side credenza, and the full executive management team, ten in number, had convened, less Buck himself, who made it a studied practice to effect a late entry to every meeting he attended, lest anyone be confused as to who was in charge. Buck thought this was one of those canny nonverbal statements that distinguished great leaders from ordinary people. Riley thought it was pure chickenshit.

Buck Montrowe had arrived at The Lindbergh six months earlier, following the previous CEO's untimely death in a late-night car accident. The company had a long and distinguished history, but its stock price had been sluggish for six consecutive quarters, and no big-time industry executives had applied for the job. The Board of Directors, therefore, dipped into the secondary ranks, with a special emphasis upon those with downsizing experience.

Buck Montrowe was not regarded as the ideal candidate, but as the former CEO of two smaller insurance companies where successful downsizings had been conducted (the last one in Indianapolis) he had achieved considerable cost savings. And though removed from one of those positions for reasons shrouded in mystery—an experience that had marked him deeply—he had established a reputation as a first-rate downsizer, and downsizing was what Wall Street was demanding.

Buck portrayed the selection process somewhat differently. After a few martinis he bragged to Riley and others that he had been selected following a rigorous evaluation of a field of top-flight candidates and that his selection had resulted not just from his superb credentials but also from a dazzling display of native, almost undefinable, charm, the centerpiece of which was a look he had developed in high school, in which he arched his right eyebrow sharply upward while turning the corners of his mouth downward in what appeared to be an upside-down smile. He thought it reminiscent of the young Gregory Peck, and its perfection accounted, in his mind, for much of his success in life and in business. Men and women alike, Buck thought, seemed to melt when he flashed the Look their way. He didn't realize that the Look was generally perceived as a sign of confusion, leaving the impression that he was unable to follow a conversation of any complexity.

When the full executive team had assembled, save only Buck, Gar Blaisdahl called the meeting to order with the I'm-in-control-here air reminiscent of Alexander Haig after the Reagan shooting. "I've brought everyone a copy of a blockbuster bestseller I found very useful in my own development as a master negotiator: *Getting To Yes; Negotiating Agreement Without Giving In.*" Snickers were heard around the table as the gathered executives were handed copies of the book to add to the collection of Gar Blaisdahl handouts previously ignored.

Gar then moved to the formal agenda. "The ticket sales for this year's employee appreciation dinner are well below previous years. We need to take steps to generate enthusiasm and spirit, so I've decided we should have a catchy slogan to get the troops fired up." Gar was given to using words and expressions like "troops" and "fired up." He had been student council vice-president in high school and had gone to Boys State at the state capitol in his senior year. "So, I propose: 'You're Our Picks in '96.' We can get out a special employee bulletin in the next few days."

After a short silence, and not expecting an answer, he asked, "Any other suggestions?"

Tom Arden, the senior executive in charge of the company's principal subsidiary, The Lindbergh Life & Casualty Company, leaned over to Riley and said in a stage whisper: "I've got a slogan. How about 'Fuck Gar Blaisdahl.'" Partially suppressed laughter rippled around the table. Gar's face darkened as though a cloud had passed between him and the ceiling lights.

Tom Arden was a veteran of the ups and downs of the insurance industry over the previous twenty-five years and the officer responsible for all life and casualty products and activities. He was of the old school, with a highly refined scorn for the pompous formulations of the bean counters, strategic planners, and touchy-feely types who had become fashionable in the industry in recent years, so nicely symbolized, he thought, by Gar Blaisdahl. At six-feet-four inches tall, with broad shoulders, a meaty build, a deep, gravelly voice, and a slashing sense of humor, he was loved by the other veterans and respected, but not loved, by most others, the latter fact causing him to swell with pride.

Never one for the snappy comeback, Gar could only sputter in tightly controlled cadences, "I suppose that's funny to someone like you, Tom," underscoring the word Tom with a tone of exaggerated patience. "But I happen to regard the morale and welfare of the ordinary employees of this company to be a serious matter." Gar had grown used to the insolence of line officers like Tom Arden, whom he considered to be his inferiors, little more than functionaries really. From his administrative perch at the holding company, he was scornful of the subsidiary executives who went into the trenches every day and generated the company's revenues.

Riley couldn't understand why Gar allowed himself to be drawn into verbal contests with the likes of Tom Arden, contests in which he inevitably got the crap kicked out of him. Normally Riley would refrain from piling on at times like this but the insufferable piety of Gar's concern for "the ordinary employees of the company" was more than he could stand. "Actually, Gar, I think what Tom means is that catchy slogans aren't a good replacement for the reduction in benefits suffered by these 'ordinary employees' over the last six months. The ones who haven't already been fired are forced to work twice as hard at frozen salary levels, and while their lunchroom has been closed, their subscriptions canceled, and a hundred other petty take-aways inflicted on them, some at the senior levels continue to live like royalty. We're putting out all this bullshit about how these painful but necessary cost reductions are being shared at all levels of the company, but they know damn well there's not a word of truth in it. Can we blame them for not wanting to go to an employee appreciation event where, by the way, they now have to buy their own tickets? Can you believe that shit?" he asked, looking around the table with an expression of disbelief. "They have to pay to get into their own appreciation dinner!"

"They're paying for their own tickets to the dinner because this is not a communist country," piped in Erving Russell, a stocky man of medium height and dark, curly hair, and the sole executive to have accompanied Buck from Indianapolis. Erving had grown up on an Iowa farm but soon abandoned his agricultural ways in favor of the world of plush offices and large stock options. He controlled all finance-related sectors of the company and was the real power behind the throne. "Do they think they're entitled to be pampered because they happen to have been with the company for a while? Hell with 'em. If they don't like it here we'll have no trouble finding replacements. There are plenty more where they came from."

Erving Russell was one of the last educated people in America to believe in a domestic communist conspiracy—a conspiracy so vast, so cunning that it reached even into the Lindbergh appreciation dinner. Although monumentally well-informed about the workings of the company, and an admirably hard worker, he was—in spite of his own sincere efforts—encumbered by an unfortunate temperament and an astonishingly poor understanding of other people. Still, his toughness and encyclopedic knowledge of the insurance business made him one of the industry's most effective executives and the ideal person to partner with the lethargic, poorly informed Buck Montrowe.

To distract attention from the fact that he was, for all practical purposes, running the company, Erving was conspicuously deferential toward Buck, a man who was protective of his image and not about to let anyone else take credit for any of the company's successes.

Gar Blaisdahl now reasserted his role as meeting leader by banging an ashtray on the table. "No, Erving, what Tom meant to say was that he has no respect for the office I hold, or for me personally."

"Actually," replied a smiling Tom Arden, "I would go a little further and say that I think you're an overpaid dipshit." This time laughter exploded around the table, even amongst those who weren't too crazy about Tom Arden.

Tom didn't care much whether he stayed on at The Lindbergh or went elsewhere. He was, ironically, possessed of more job security than anyone in the room by reason of his intimate working knowledge of the company's principal business activity and his personal credibility with state insurance regulators, who kept a close watch on the company's financial status. Beyond that, Buck Montrowe knew that Arden's inside-the-beast knowledge of the insurance industry was nearly irreplaceable. As a former salesman and claims officer, Buck felt an unspoken fellowship with Arden, of the type felt by front-line police officers. And Gar knew that this was Buck's assessment, and that there was little he could do about Arden's impudence.

"Who's quarterbacking the selection of the slogan?" asked Hedrick J. "Rick" Snelling, a muscular ex-fullback for a Division II college in South Dakota, and a great lover of sports metaphors. Rick Snelling was head of the company's charitable foundation and sat at the end of the table in the seat reserved for the lowest-status member of the group.

"I am," said Gar dismissively, not even looking in Snelling's direction. He thought all jocks were boneheads.

"Well, how about 'Thanks For A Winning Season,'" said Rick, as he rolled his shoulders and snapped a fist against his upper chest, as though straightening a pair of imaginary shoulder pads. This mannerism was the legacy of twelve years on the gridiron. Some of it without a helmet, according to Tom Arden.

"That's a terrible slogan," said Gar scornfully. "Suggestion denied!"

Rick's face reddened as he executed a partial shoulder roll. In an injured voice, he shouted, "Well, I want to pitch for the executive squad when we play the out-state agents at the afternoon softball game. I've got an arm like a fucking cannon." He looked around the table for support, but no one seemed to be paying any attention.

Without Buck Montrowe, who had yet to appear, the agenda could advance no further, so the attendees occupied themselves separately, several paging through the morning newspaper.

Riley looked about the room at the gathered executives, the company's top talent, each with a story of what brought him to the executive ranks and, perhaps more importantly, what kept him there. Talented though most of them were, they were no more so than hundreds of others spread throughout the managerial ranks. A combination of political cunning and plain dumb luck was what had elevated these people to the senior status they now enjoyed. What kept them there was their capacity, each in his own way, to stay within Buck Montrowe's psychological comfort zone. And it was that ability and that focus which accounted for the lack of social cohesiveness one would ordinarily find in a highly functioning work unit. There was little or no camaraderie. Appearances of congeniality around the table were staged and palpably false.

Still, Riley liked most of these guys. There were only two or three he couldn't stomach, one being Mr. Wade Z. Wardrick, the director of the Casualty Underwriting Division, who sat directly across the table from him. Wade was reading a newspaper article about fraud in the county welfare system and muttering angrily about "welfare queens breeding like pigeons, eating up the tax dollars of honest and hardworking people." Riley was struck anew by the irony of this familiar scene, knowing as he did that Wade was the undisputed king of the company's expense account cheats—the most blatant form of *de facto* welfare to be found anywhere in the American economy. Wade managed somehow to nearly double his base salary each year, tax free, at the expense of the shareholders and the U.S. Treasury. The son-of-a-bitch got away with more loot than all the welfare mothers Riley had ever encountered in the courts—most of whose lives had been ravaged by poverty, addiction, and partners who beat the stuffing out of them every day.

Now, as he sat in the palatial CEO's conference room, listening to the company's most dedicated practitioner of grand-larceny-by-expense-account run through his familiar litany of mindless welfare slogans, Riley took solace in recalling that the head of the Reinsurance Division, seated to the immediate left of Mr. Wade Z. Wardrick, had been screwing Mrs. Wade Z. Wardrick about twice a week for the last year, a fact known to everyone in the room save only the welfare-hating little prick muttering into his newspaper.

Riley was still smiling to himself when Buck Montrowe entered the room from stage left. He wore a get-down-to-business expression, and moved with a gait that reminded Riley of John Gotti in those FBI surveillance tapes shown over and over on TV.

Jubal Buckley Montrowe was in his early sixties, but appeared younger. He stood six feet two inches in height, with a head of curly hair dyed in rich, but uneven, reddish tones, causing some employees to crack that he had gone prematurely orange. He had a likable face, which could be described as pleasant, if not quite handsome. His complexion was florid, striking a somewhat vivid contrast with his pastel hair color. He wore large-framed, transition eyeglasses that turned a light shade of purple when in the sunlight, receding into a pale transparency when inside. A thin row of pock marks ran along his jaw line. He wore a dark suit with a slight shine to it, monogrammed cuffs, patent-leather dress shoes, transparent fingernail polish, and a heavily bejeweled Rolex wristwatch, valued at twice the annual salary of the average Lindbergh employee. The little finger of his left hand was adorned with a gold ring containing a large diamond at its center.

As Buck picked at the assorted fruits on the credenza, the sun caught the face of the Rolex, which was too large for his thin, hairy wrist, giving off a flash of light. "Who are those scumbag protesters at the front entrance?" he asked no one in particular.

"Goddamn bunch of communists, that's who," snorted Erving Russell.

Cole Girard, who in addition to human resources supervised the public relations department, looked over at Riley wearily, and then turned back to Buck. "There's really nothing to be done about them for now, Buck, if that's what you're thinking. Unless they damage property or assault someone, they have a right to be there."

Riley suppressed any mention of yesterday's incident at the side entrance, where he had been hit with a ripe tomato, and Buck had apparently not yet seen the picture in the morning newspaper. He knew Buck would use the incident as an excuse to forcibly remove the protesters, which would only make things worse. Besides, Riley was kind of amused by what had happened to him. He looked down the table at Buck and said, "The best thing to do is just let the demonstration play itself out. As long as our personnel aren't injured, we shouldn't react negatively."

A look of boyish exuberance suddenly replaced the scowl on Buck's face. "Speaking of our 'personnel,'" he said, "who's that little fox downstairs, the one with the big tits and the white panty hose—you know, the one at the desk right off the Lobby Court?"

M. Bryant Knox jumped from his seat and moved briskly through the broad portico into Buck's office, the north wall of which was all glass, affording a full view of the Lobby Court four floors below. He scanned the broad expanse in search of the woman to whom Buck had referred while three other high-status executives, each earning in excess of seven hundred thousand dollars a year—the very cream of America's business elite—ransacked their memories for the name of the little fox with the big tits.

As head of human resources, Cole Girard was sensitive to boorish behavior in the workplace, and this display caused him to shake his head in embarrassment. It clearly did not measure up to the high standards set forth in the newly released HR publication 96-9201: "Respect for Ourselves and Others—The Lindbergh Way."

"You mean Sonja Humegren, that little blond?" shouted M. Bryant, as though he had just won the Publisher's Clearing House. He seemed to glow with pride at being able to help Buck in this way. He was nearly panting as he pointed Sonja out to the three other executives who had joined him at the window, all nodding in unison.

"Right!" said Buck, his chest expanding. "That's her. She gave me one of those 'come-and-get-it' looks as I was walking to the elevator. She really wanted me. Wally noticed it too." Wally was Buck's special assistant who accompanied him everywhere he went, usually carrying his briefcase.

"Oh, man, you are a babe magnet!" said Gar Blaisdahl adoringly as he looked at Buck. He shook his head in silent recognition that some guys just have a way with women.

"Well, I don't know about that," purred Buck, now almost on fire with manly pride, "but there was no mistaking what she had in mind." He wheezed out a long, lustful laugh. It was at moments like this that Buck Montrowe felt life to its fullest.

Somebody ought to hose this guy down with saltpeter, thought Riley as he sat silently at the table. He knew Sonja Humegren, and knew that she thought Buck was a complete dweeb. Besides that, Sonja was a lesbian—but Riley didn't have the heart or the nerve to tell that to Buck.

"Could we get back to this question of morale for a minute?" Riley asked pleasantly, not intending to ruin anyone's fun.

Irritated at the change of subject, Buck looked over at him. "What about morale?" he asked.

Riley responded that the fall-off in ticket sales for the employee appreciation dinner seemed to be a result of low morale and the new policy of charging employees for admission to their own appreciation event.

36

"That's tough," said Buck gruffly, pushing aside a breakfast roll to get at the strawberries. "If they can't get used to the new culture we've established here, they should be in another company. This company has spent too much in generous giveaways to employees, and that's goin' to stop for everyone, right from the top down." He pointed to himself with a wiggling thumb when he said, "from the top down." He then seemed to relax, a faint smile crossing his face. "Besides, our employees like these take-aways because they know they're in the best interests of the company."

Gar Blaisdahl vigorously nodded his agreement.

"Amen," said M. Bryant Knox.

"Right on!" said Harold Westline, a middle-aged technology officer sitting next to Riley. Though industrious and highly focused, like most techno-whizzes Harold possessed the soul and personality of a man too long confined to the back room. His many years in the bunker had left him with a vocabulary and syntax so garbled and indecipherable that his listeners rarely had any idea what he was talking about. "We've got to reengineer an interdisciplinary de-stressing of the employeeization of the core franchise," he said with great conviction.

What these strange words meant, what they had to do with the subject at hand, Riley hadn't a clue. Nor, it seemed, had anyone else, now or at any other time Harold Westline spoke. Over the last several months Harold's lack of ordinary clarity had so confused Buck that he felt he had no choice but to declare him a genius. This he did in a memo to senior management, which said right in the opening paragraph: "Harold Westline is a genius." This came as a great surprise to the many people who had worked with Harold over the preceding five years, not to mention those who had gone to school with him.

Nodding toward Harold with a confused but admiring look, Buck said, "You bet your ass, I'm right."

"You bet your ass" was about as racy as Buck's religious upbringing would permit his language to get. Riley had noticed over the years that in spite of a ready willingness on the part of many people of Buck's fundamentalist religious background to breach most of the Ten Commandments, the one forbidding swearing was often scrupulously observed. He thought that might have been because it was essentially a freebie. They got to appear pious without really giving anything away.

Riley sat watching Buck enthroned at the head of the table, luxuriating in the power that had been bestowed upon him in the very secular world of big business. Considering the number of firings he had ordered up over the last several months, he was remarkably relaxed. Not cold or sadistic, though—just relaxed. Buck wasn't an inherently cruel person; he didn't enjoy inflicting pain. He was even soft-hearted in some ways, Riley had concluded. But when it came to bottom-line profits his more humane instincts had fought a losing battle with the lure of personal wealth. As a result he seemed to have developed an indifference, an emotional numbness, to the suffering over which he was presiding.

What bothered Riley was not that some cuts were being made—that was clearly necessary—but rather their depth and arbitrariness, the unnecessary bloodshed. And maybe more than anything else, he was disturbed by Buck's public statements about how he was suffering along with the common employees, which was obviously untrue. He was, in fact, indulging himself with every imaginable corporate perk. Riley viewed this as offensive, coming as it did from a guy who passed himself off as an unpretentious type. And everyone in that room, including him, was going along with it, pretending not to notice the greasy inconsistency of it all.

Getting back to the employee appreciation dinner, Riley shifted in his chair and cleared his throat. "Well, Buck," he said slowly, "I know there's symbolic value to some benefit reductions, as a reminder that we're going to run lean, but it seems to me that it can be done in a more evenhanded way." He then took a deep breath in preparation for the riskier part of his remarks. "We say that the pain is going to be shared equally at all levels, but I don't see these cut-backs and take-aways affecting anybody in this room. Some of us lead obscenely lavish and pampered lives. It's hypocritical and dishonest. And the employees know it."

Expressions like "some of us" were diplomatic code for Buck Montrowe. The cost of recreational trips Buck had taken at the company's expense in the last two weeks alone would have paid for the employee appreciation dinner twice over. And it was widely known that he regularly flew his beloved dogs, Butch and Fifi, and his talking parrot, Stud Boy, in the company jet. Butch and Fifi were nice, if somewhat rambunctious, dogs. But Stud Boy was a mean little bastard who shouted obscenities at anyone within hearing.

Cole Girard, who had taken off his eyeglasses and was cleaning them with his handkerchief, expressed agreement with Riley's statement. Most of the others around the table sat silently. Tom Arden looked up from a file he had opened during Gar Blaisdahl's remarks, giving a mischievous smile to Riley, and letting out a short, high-pitched squeak denoting pleasure and God only knew what else.

Buck looked down the table and fixed his gaze on Riley. He then said in a voice one might use with a mentally challenged neighbor boy: "You don't get it, do you?"

Riley took this to be a rhetorical question. "You don't get it" was an expression Buck used a lot.

Buck next turned on Cole Girard, who was still cleaning his glasses. He glared in his direction and unleashed a torrent of abuse. Small bits of the glazed doughnut he was eating sprayed into the air as he shouted, "It's HR's job to support the CEO, no matter what. You got that, pal?"

Cole Girard sat wide-eyed, stunned, looking as though he might have suffered a burst hemorrhoid. He glanced about nearsightedly, adding to the appearance of vulnerability. Most of the other executives stared vacantly at the wall as though they had missed the entire exchange. Only Tom Arden appeared openly pleased, his eyes moving expectantly from one person to the other.

Riley appreciated Cole's gesture of support, but knew that it would probably be the last time it would ever happen. Cole was a gentle soul, not a fighter. He wasn't capable of taking repeat beatings. He also had a lot to lose if he got on Buck's bad side. But then didn't they all.

To break the tension, Erving Russell cleared his throat loudly and moved to the next item on the agenda—a review of operating numbers and significant transactions over the previous two weeks. Sheets containing multicolored graphs were passed around, showing revenues in the various company sectors, which Erving explained in excrutiating detail. An hour into the review, reference was made to the recent closing of a deal with The Crosshill Real Estate Company—the largest real estate transaction in Lindbergh history. Buck proudly noted that his personal friendship with Woodward "Ward" Crosshaven, head of Crosshill, was what had gotten the deal done. "Ward really likes me," he said.

"I'm not criticizing the deal," said Tom Arden, "but I've got to say I think that guy Crosshaven is a real asshole."

Buck let a moment of uncomfortable silence pass, then he leaned forward in his chair, his face reddening. "I won't allow anybody in this room to say a bad word about Ward Crosshaven. Not even you, Tom. Ward and his family are the finest, classiest people you could find anywhere, and he's one of my closest personal friends."

Close personal friend indeed, thought Riley. The Crosshavens were the biggest snobs in the area. Ward Crosshaven wouldn't give Buck the time of day if he weren't a source of cheap funding for his many ventures. Poor Buck. His vanity and neediness made him such an easy mark for these types. And Riley wasn't so sure the Crosshavens were the model family they pretended to be. It was said that Ward kept a mistress in a penthouse down town and that the wife was actually a closet drunk. There was even a rumor among the suburban cops that one of the Crosshaven sons—Riley didn't know which—had a fairly heavy drug habit.

Tom Arden shrugged but said nothing.

Taking into account the many companies under family control and the numerous segments of The Lindbergh with which they did business, the Crosshavens were indisputably the company's largest customer. Ward Crosshaven had inherited his first ten million dollars, but made the next three hundred million by the sweat of his brow and the sharpness of his wit.

He was widely feared in the business community, and abjectly idolized by Buck, who turned into a kind of stammering sycophant whenever in his presence. Crosshaven had leveraged Buck's hero worship into some of the sweetest customer deals ever achieved from an institution the size of The Lindbergh. And though the deal under discussion was a good example of just that, Tom Arden didn't say so.

Nor did any of the others in the room. They were not about to alienate the man upon whose economic favor they had come to depend. Buck's every comment, no matter how puerile or unfactual, seemed to fall upon the ears of his listeners with the force of divine writ. Even Riley had to admit that he wasn't in any hurry to put his own status at risk—the easy money, the prestige, the perks—by being too high-minded. He couldn't bring himself to be an out-and-out suckup like some of the others, but he also didn't intend to go out of his way to jeopardize a good thing. So far he had been able to get away with a few clumsy forays into the truth without suffering any serious political damage. But he knew the day might come when he'd have to say or do things that would end it all.

The last agenda item concerned further cost-cutting steps, initiatives designed to produce what Buck called the new "No-Frills" Lindbergh—a Lindbergh free of wasteful expenses and luxuries. In pursuit of the no-frills objective, another five hundred jobs bit the dust that morning. The "Shareholder Value Analysis," a series of calculations used to determine the per share economic benefit resulting from a given cost-cutting move, showed that the loss of livelihoods and careers for those five hundred human beings—nameless and faceless to the number-crunchers in the back room—added a whopping one penny per share to annual earnings.

The bus-fare subsidy for fifteen hundred low-level employees was also discontinued, saving $45,000. Knowing that the company had just purchased an $85,000 Jaguar for Buck, this move was particularly galling to Riley. But he said nothing.

Buck closed the meeting with a not-very-funny joke about a nearsighted gynecologist. Gar and M. Bryant collapsed in laughter.

On the way down the hall after the meeting, two executives whispered their thanks to Riley for speaking up about the employee appreciation dinner. They made identical statements: "Can you believe that phony prick?" Neither offered an explanation for his own silence. These guys were survivors, and who could really blame them.

5

As Riley headed toward his office, the broad corridors of the east side of the executive floor, housing the three most senior executives, gave way to the narrower passages of the building's west side, where the six less important senior officers resided. Immune from the interior design fashions that had come and gone in the preceding sixty years, the west section retained the solid beauty of the original structure, including dark-paneled walls and tall leaded-glass windows. Over the same time period the east side, referred to as the "Sacristy," had undergone a facelift with each passing fad and each new CEO, culminating in a design made over to suit Buck's taste, a style that one observer labeled "Neo-Graceland."

Immediately adjacent to the reception area of the fourth floor, presided over by a receptionist of arresting beauty and a security guard of great bulk, was a vast, ornate, and richly paneled conference room used for formal receptions and meetings of the Lindbergh Board of Directors. Formerly known as the Board Room, it had recently been rechristened "The J. Buckley Montrowe Room." This gesture of heartstopping immodesty had been made, with a show of admirable reluctance on Buck's part, at the urging of Gar Blaisdahl.

On route to his office, Riley ducked into the men's room, taking a station at the urinal next to Tom Arden, who was relieving himself of the three cups of coffee he had consumed during the two-hour meeting.

Gar Blaisdahl then entered at a brisk pace, moving behind Tom and Riley to a stall directly behind them, which could be plainly viewed through the mirror attached to the wall above the row of urinals.

"We've had an attempted money laundering down at the S&L, Riley. Will you get down there and assess things ASAP?" said Gar as he pulled wads of toilet paper out of the wall dispenser and tossed them by the handful into the toilet bowl.

Tom shook his head, but said nothing.

Riley watched this strange ritual unfold in the overhead mirror, finally saying, "Gar, what the hell are you doing? You're going to clog the plumbing. And please close the stall door—who do you think you are, Lyndon Johnson?"

"Don't worry, smart guy, I know just how much to put in."

"But why are you doing it?"

"It stops water from splashing up on my butt. I have very sensitive rectal tissue," said Gar defensively as he took a seat on the toilet, at the same time raising a piece of tissue over his nose and mouth as though donning a surgical mask.

"What the hell is that for?" asked Riley with a look of astonishment and in an admittedly rude voice.

"It keeps the shit molecules out of my nose, stupid!" snapped Gar in an even ruder voice.

"The what?" asked Riley.

"The shit molecules, McReynolds!" Gar shouted as though he was speaking to someone who should really know better. "Didn't you ever take chemistry? If you smell something, it's because some of its airborne molecules have landed on the membranes of your nose. What do you think a fart is? It's nothing more than a gaseous cloud of shit molecules."

"Gar . . . tell me this is a joke of some kind," Riley stammered.

"The joke will be on you, McReynolds, when you walk around all day with your nose full of shit molecules."

Now quite angry, Gar slammed the door. From over the stall and accompanied by an echo, he screamed, "Just go down and talk to the goddamn teller!"

Leaning toward Riley, Tom Arden raised his eyebrows and whispered, "That is one sick puppy."

Riley zipped up and dashed for the fresh air of the hallway.

This encounter marked the beginning of what most people would have to concede was a pretty immature practice by Tom Arden, whereby in advance of any scheduled meeting that included Gar Blaisdahl he drank copious amounts of highly carbonated beverages, positioned himself upwind from Gar, and squeezed out noiseless farts for as long as his ammo lasted.

Awaiting Riley in his office was an in-basket full of RESPOND IMMEDIATELY items, including first drafts of correspondence from Buck to various people, typed up by Buck's secretary from his dictation. Riley was expected to turn Buck's verbal ramblings into intelligible English, including supplying rudimentary grammar and punctuation. The secretary, Gladys, would then retype the letters for Buck's signature, a process that often resulted in Buck congratulating himself on his accomplished writing style.

Most of the other in-basket items related to government investigations of alleged churning of life insurance policies owned by older Lindbergh customers. These investigations consumed large amounts of Riley's time, more than he found comfortable. Replacement policies sold by company agents, which were paid for from equity on existing policies, generated large revenues and sales commissions but did nothing for the customers beyond saddling them with burdensome premiums. Several officers and scores of sales agents had been fired when the company's audit department uncovered the churning. Some of those fired had been minor players, a few even unaware of the illegalities in which they were involved. As to them, Riley had recommended demotion rather than firing. But Buck had been resolute, saying, "There would be no exceptions to his policy of 'zero tolerance for misconduct.' Employees who compromised honesty in exchange for profit," he said, "would be summarily discharged."

Riley considered some of these actions to be overly punitive, but he couldn't help but be impressed by what seemed to be Buck's resolve.

Riley's office was large, high-ceilinged, and elegant, consistent with the "pillars and mahogany" style of the original building. Bookshelves filled with insurance treatises and statutes lined one wall, and heavy russet curtains framed the ten-foot-high leaded glass windows on the opposite wall. The room's only modern element consisted of plush wall-to-wall dark green carpeting. Originally built as a conference room in the 1920s, it and several other rooms on the fourth floor had been converted to executive offices when Buck arrived, it being his organizational philosophy that the company's most senior officers should work apart from ordinary employees.

Riley dropped into his chair behind a large desk on which sat stacks of files, insurance regulations, an overflowing in-basket, and a brass name-plate given to him twenty-three years before by Betsy, reading "Riley Parnell McReynolds, J.D." He waved to his secretary, a thirty-two-year-old smart aleck who saw it as her purpose in life to prevent him from adopting the airs of his high office. Eleanor Swenson went by "Skeeter," a nickname of early but unknown origin. She wore a happy, matter-of-fact expression on her attractive Scandinavian face, which was at once strong and delicate. Her thick, light brown hair was cut short and rode close to her face, giving her the look of the cheerleader she had once been. There seemed always to be a natural playfulness in her dazzling green eyes. Even her walk was sassy and irreverant.

"Okay, bigshot, I need these documents signed in the next twenty minutes, so get your fat ass in gear," she instructed, handing Riley a felt-tip signing pen.

Fat ass? thought Riley, now that hurt. She must have been talking to Betsy. He vowed he'd go on a diet soon, maybe sign up for one of those programs where they monitor everything you eat and shame you right down to your socks if you step out of line. He'd check the newspaper for a location convenient to the office. But he wouldn't tell anyone he was going to any program for the weak-willed. Skeeter and others would give him too much grief if they found out.

He looked up and said, "I'm just fine, thank you, Ms. Swenson. It's nice of you to ask, and how are you today?"

"Cut the B.S., big boy. We've got a lot to get done today, and I've got a sore throat."

"Yeah, well, that's nothing, I've got shit molecules in my nose."

She paused, shaking her head, a grimace forming on her face. "Don't even think of telling me what that means. My stomach is already a little queasy, and I'm not up for hearing about any of your imaginary illnesses." But, sensing a hint of dejection in Riley's face, she cocked her head slightly to one side. "What's the matter, is Buck wearing the tight underwear again today?"

"Oh, it wasn't too bad. He's just a little grouchy. He'll be better when he gets some self-confidence. I know he's a decent guy underneath all that stupid talk."

The fat-ass reference and the thought of a diet had made Riley hungry. When Skeeter turned her back to pick some dead leaves off the plant in the corner, he quietly eased open the second drawer on the right-hand side of his desk and plucked from a great heap of debris (which included candy bars, gum, aspirin, antacids, antihistamines, decongestants, Band-Aids, vitamin pills, antibiotic salve, stick deodorant, Rolo's, throat lozenges, and two bags of Star Burst Clusters) a bite-size Milky Way, which he tossed quickly into his mouth. When she again faced him he was relieved that she seemed not to have noticed that one cheek was bulging and that his words had been replaced with nods.

She went right on talking: "What's Buck doing in town, anyway? Were there hurricane warnings in Florida?" Like most secretaries on the executive floor, Skeeter knew just about everything about everybody, and Buck's infrequent appearances in town were an open secret among her peers.

Riley's voice, now thickened by milk chocolate, carried a hint of caution. "I hope you don't say things like that outside this office."

Skeeter didn't even look up from her busy tasks. "Are you kidding? What do I care? I can go anywhere in town and get these same wages. The only advantage to this job is that I get to ridicule you every day, and that's something you can't put a price tag on." She turned in his direction, leaned her slim, athletic body against the door frame, and crossed her arms. "And try not to drool that chocolate on your clean shirt."

Riley shook his head. "Well, I don't know what others are saying, Skeets, but I think you should be careful about what you say," he said, trying without success to be serious as he wiped the back of his hand self-consciously across his mouth.

He reached for a file marked "Money Laundering" and stuffed it into his briefcase. As he passed Skeeter on the way out the door, she awkwardly lifted one eyebrow upward and the corners of her mouth downward in a failed imitation of the Look, leaving him unsteady with laughter as he made his way down the hall.

"Shoot, where is it?" said Jeannie Kelley to herself. She was the teller at Station 4. It was mid-morning on a day of unusually large transaction volume at The Lindbergh Savings & Loan, and she was having no luck reconciling her accounts. Jeannie had been with the S&L for just under one year.

From within her office behind the teller stations, Liddy Jonssen could see, and feel, Jeannie's frustration. She got up from her desk and walked the ten steps to where Jeannie was standing.

"Let me run the numbers once to see if you might have overlooked something. Don't get discouraged, Jeannie. We all go through the same thing. I can't tell you how many times I've gotten stuck on a cash reconciliation." Liddy said this in a kind, reassuring voice. Though still upset by the unnerving encounter with the man trying to launder cash that morning, it didn't show as Liddy ran the slender, graceful fingers of her left hand down the transaction tape while entering numbers into the calculator with her right hand at what seemed to Jeannie Kelley to be an astonishing pace. It struck Jeannie as

a thing of beauty, a work of art really, that Liddy could perform this task, so difficult for her, with such ease and competence.

Relatively new to the job and freshly graduated from one of
those business schools downtown that catered to young
women just out of high school, Jeannie felt a wave of gratitude
at her good fortune in having a person like Liddy Jonssen as
her supervisor. Liddy was a mentor and a role model, and,
more important, a friend. Jeannie wanted to develop into the
kind of woman that Liddy Jonssen was. She watched adoringly as Liddy whipped through the columns of numbers that had
failed to yield to her most determined efforts just moments
before.

"There we go Jeannie. You just forgot one step," said Liddy.
Her smile projected competence mixed with affection. Another
manager might have used a haughty or scolding tone under
the same circumstances. But that was not part of Liddy
Jonssen's character; she had never in her life deliberately hurt
or embarrassed another human being.

"Thanks, Liddy. I get kinda screwed up sometimes when I'm
really hungry. I had breakfast early this morning and nothing
but coffee for the last few hours. Maybe I should have a glass
of orange juice to keep my blood sugar up. That's what they
told me at business college. They said it's amazing how many
girls have low blood sugar between meals and how it can, like,
really affect concentration. For all that money I borrowed to
pay my tuition, I suppose I oughta follow their advice."

"That might be a good idea, Jeannie," replied Liddy. "Just
remember, we appreciate all your effort. You're part of this
work family."

Jeannie adopted a quizzical look, saying, "Well, I feel like
I'm a family member in this unit because of the way you manage us and our activities, but I keep hearing that the good old
days of The Lindbergh being a real family, really caring about
its employees, are all over." She ran a brush through her plain,
brown hair, inclining her small frame toward a mirror standing
next to her purse. Then, facing Liddy but not making eye contact, her voice quivering slightly: "We didn't realize 'til we read

THE ORDEAL OF RILEY MCREYNOLDS

what Mr. Montrowe said in the newspaper that we were spoiled and expected everything to be given to us." She crossed her arms and leaned back against the wall dividing her station from the adjacent teller, looking at the ground. "I don't see why Mr. Montrowe has to say things like that. It just doesn't make much sense to me. How would he know that, anyway? Geez, I borrowed a lot of money to go to that night school for a year, and I've been working hard at every position I've had since I got here. Maybe he's a nice man; I don't know. But it just seems to me that he could come around the work areas every now and then. If he saw what we were doing, especially since all the layoffs, he might feel differently."

Liddy looked sweetly at Jeannie, even though she knew managers weren't supposed to show personal affection toward those they supervised. But she couldn't help it. She adored Jeannie Kelley and all her girlish chatter and lack of sophistication. And she knew that Jeannie worshipped her, like the sister she had never had. Still, she had to try to adhere to the company line on management issues; she would never say anything bad about Buck Montrowe or any other senior manager. "It's always upsetting when there's a management change, and you've got to try not to let it bother you. If we just go on doing our job, we'll be fine." She put one hand on Jeannie's shoulder and gave her cheek a light pinch with the other. "And don't worry about this dumb little reconciliation; we figured it out in plenty of time."

As she walked back toward her office behind the teller stations, Liddy turned and with a gentle smile said, "Why don't you just go to lunch a little early today and get some food in you."

She then strode with an air of confidence into her small office two steps above the teller line, stealing an anxious look at the entryway, half expecting to see the money launderer from that morning. Twice already he had appeared in the hallway outside the S&L, staring at her as she talked to customers. By the time security arrived, he had disappeared. Even more upsetting than his physical presence was the psychological effect she was feeling. He seemed to have taken up residence in her mind.

She took a seat at her desk and turned her attention to the in-basket sitting off to the left. She immediately noted the blue-bordered human resources envelope dreaded by all managers, containing the list of those slated for job elimination in the next round of layoffs. The downsizing consultants from Chicago had been through the S&L two weeks earlier. Well-dressed and meticulously groomed, syrupy and ghoulish, they were truly the agents of death. She wondered if they went home after work to ordinary families and lives or if, like medieval executioners, they lived in dank and joyless communities not shown on standard maps. It galled her that these outside gunslingers had been given full authority over the company's downsizing process, outranking the in-house human resources officers, whom Buck Montrowe had put in a subordinate role because he regarded them as too sentimental.

Liddy's hand trembled as she reached for the silver letter opener in her top drawer and ran it through the flap of the blue-bordered envelope. A viscous lump formed in her throat as she read the memo listing by name and social security number the people—her people—she would have to personally terminate the next day. The skin on her face started to burn, and the pace of her breathing increased. The early paragraphs of the memo were boilerplate instructions to managers to "take immediate possession from the terminated employee of keys and access cards, secure access to computers and be on alert for bizarre behaviors, such as depression, inappropriate verbalizations, denial, and hysteria."

Six names out of twelve in the unit appeared in alphabetical order in the "Downsize" column. The first name was: "Jeanne B. Kelley."

Liddy raised her body from the chair, pushing off the surface of the desk for support, and walked on hollow legs to the women's bathroom several paces down the west hallway. There she fell to one knee and while bracing herself against the sink sobbed so violently that the glasses hanging around her neck shattered as they slammed against the porcelain. "Not Jeannie," she said over and over.

51

*****

Riley turned left out of the elevator on the thirty-eight floor and inserted his access card to gain entry through the double-locked metal doors of the Corporate Security Department. Corporate Security was one of the units that reported to him, along with government relations, risk management, the corporate secretary, and Lindbergh properties, which managed the roughly one million square feet of building space occupied by Lindbergh employees throughout the company's trade territory.

Corporate Security had at one time consisted of a small army of uniformed and investigative personnel, but as a result of the recent downsizings had undergone severe cutbacks, leaving barely enough people to investigate and complete the paperwork necessary to conform to government regulations relating to money laundering, embezzlement, and workplace safety. Investigation of fraudulent insurance claims was handled in Tom Arden's division, but that unit had also been downsized.

The thirty-eighth floor was grimy and drab, with long rows of gunmetal gray workstations barely large enough for one person to crowd into. In the northwest corner of the floor was a small conference room with a tan wooden table at the center, surrounded by gray metal chairs with liver-colored vinyl seat cushions. The off-white walls were covered haphazardly with wanted posters, workplace safety checklists, and cartoons related to insurance fraud.

In the hallway, facing the door of the conference room, stood a coin-operated pop machine, and in the spot where company-paid coffee had been available in the pre-Buck era, was a large coin-operated coffee dispenser, adorned with graffiti insulting to senior management.

As he approached the conference room a man handed him a pink message slip. "You're supposed to get in touch with your secretary right away, Mr. McReynolds. She just called."

"Buck wants to talk to you," said Skeeter when Riley returned the call.

"What's he want? Did he say?"

"Yeah, he's working on his stock options again and can't figure out the vesting schedule," she said with a hint of distaste. "And he needs you to look at some personal document. A deed or something. And I've got to notarize it."

"If he calls again, tell him we'll be there as soon as we can, but that I'm in a meeting I can't get out of."

"How about if I tell him to put it in his ear?" asked Skeeter.

"I think you'd better hold off on that one . . . at least until you're working for someone else. Which may not be that long."

"When you gonna get some stones, hot shot?"

"I've got to go, Skeets. Try not to get me fired before the end of the day, okay?"

"Chickenshit," he heard her say as she hung up. God, she was a breath of fresh air. Sort of made your heart sing.

As he was putting the phone back on the receiver, Dan Thornton entered the conference room at a brisk pace. Tall, dark, meaty, and dressed like an off-duty cop, Thornton had been director of security at The Lindbergh for the past sixteen years.

"Hey, Riley," he said in a tone recognizing no distinction in rank between them, as he took a seat at the table.

"What's with the attempted money laundering that Gar Blaisdahl's all worked up about?" asked Riley.

Dan lit a cigarette, striking his match across a sign adjacent to the doorway marked: THIS IS A SMOKE FREE BUILD-ING. "It was some guy trying to convert a big wad of cash—fifteen-thousand dollars—into a cashier's check."

"So, why don't you just file a Suspicious Activity Report?" asked Riley as he slipped into one of the metal chairs.

"Well, the teller has no idea what the guy's name is. When she told him the transaction would trigger the filing of a government report, he went bullshit. Started threatening her. Sounds like he's a psycho, and probably a junkie. My gut says this one's more serious than our typical money laundering attempt."

Riley shrugged. "Can't we identify him from the security cameras?"

"Nope, the security cameras weren't on. You know, part of the cost-cutting. We don't have any film to look at."

"You're kidding?" asked an amazed Riley, his face twisted in disgust. "They turned the security cameras off to save money?"

"Yup, nobody checked with Security or Legal." The expression on Thornton's face told that he had moved beyond being surprised by anything. "Some stupid asshole was trying to earn points by saving a few bucks and just went ahead and turned off the cameras. This cost-cutting shit has made people nuts."

"Who was the teller?" asked Riley.

"Liddy Jonssen. She's actually the manager of the S&L, but was covering at the teller station when the guy came in. Do you know her?"

Riley looked at the ceiling, searching his memory. "I think she's a friend of Skeeter's. I don't know if I've actually met her. Did she give a good description?"

"Yeah, right down to a birthmark just under his hairline. And it's a good thing, too, because she's the only witness," he said, taking a pull off his cigarette. "She's got guts for turning this guy in after he threatened her. She said he was real creepy."

A short, blonde security guard with lots of makeup, in full uniform (including a gun almost as big as she was), came into the room and handed Thornton a requisition to sign. She was chewing a piece of gum in short, choppy bites.

"You know Trudi don't you, Riley?" said Thornton as he looked over the form.

Trudi looked over at Riley, giving him a quick wink.

"Oh, sure, you bet," said Riley, smiling. Trudi's wink was so snappy and natural he felt it would have amounted to a cultural rebuke not to return it. He tried to wink, but he had never been a good winker, and both eyes slammed shut in what looked more like a facial tick. Trudi suppressed a giggle as she left the room.

"Very cool, Riley. I think you really impressed her," said Thornton, deadpan.

"Yeah, thanks, prick," said Riley, his face darkening. Trying to get things back on track, he asked, "How'd Gar Blaisdahl get involved in this?"

"I ran into him in the elevator right after I found out about the cameras being turned off. I was pretty pissed, so I made a big deal about it with him."

Riley nodded. "I'll take a compliance officer and go down and talk to Liddy." He then lifted himself out of the chair. "What else is happening?"

"Not much, just the usual bullshit. We've got a zoo full of demonstrators at the north entrance. The community affairs people are out there humoring them. They insist on meeting with Buck. Fat fucking chance." Thornton expectorated this last statement amidst a husky smoker's cough.

"He'll make Gar meet with them," said Riley. "I'd like to be there to watch that."

"You may be. That big tall babe leading the demonstration says she knows you."

"Yeah, Tenzie Dunseth. She's a real gas. She'll have Gar for lunch," he said as he got up. He chuckled with delight at the thought of Tenzie doing her thing on Gar.

Dan rose from his chair and walked over to the window. With his back to Riley, he said, "While I've got your ear, I want to say for the record that I've got half the people I used to, and I'm expected to cover twice the territory. Tempers are on edge from overwork and fear of more layoffs. Scrapes between employees—even ones who have been friends for years—are happening regularly. HR keeps asking us to get involved, but we don't have the resources. There almost has to be a physical assault before we can justify diverting any of our people."

"All that security stuff was forecast in the feasibility study done by the downsizing consultant. You warned that there would be hostility among the workforce. Your ass is covered. You told them so."

"That won't help. I'll still get blamed."

Riley shrugged it off, but knew he was right. "Just do the best you can, Dan. That's all any of us can do."

A department secretary appeared at the door and signaled Dan that a call he had been waiting for had come in. He nodded to Riley and left the room.

Riley stood for a moment contemplating the decline in employee morale and the shortage of resources that had resulted from the cut-backs. He turned toward the window and looked wistfully down upon the county courthouse where he had spent so many years, first locking up the bad guys and later getting them out. In those days he and the other lawyers in the criminal justice system looked upon business types— like the ones with whom he was now associated—as a bunch of overpaid dandies, imitation tough-guys engaged in a lot of expensive paperwork. After all, the activities they took so seriously looked silly next to the drama and heartaches unfolding each day in the courthouse.

But now he was on the other side of the cultural divide and couldn't help but be amused that the business people felt their own brand of contempt for the criminal lawyers, whom they thought of as little more than unsavory thrill seekers, people to be feared and avoided—little better than the criminals they represented.

He switched windows and looked past the imposing headquarters of the Lindbergh's archrival, the St. Paul Companies, to the western horizon, on which the buildings of downtown Minneapolis were outlined in miniature, including Sacred Heart Cathedral, where he had spent eight formative years in grade school. The church building sat poised with elegance and defiance on the western edge of downtown Minneapolis, dwarfing the now-closed parish school immediately to its north. The concept of diversity had yet to be discovered in the 1950s when he was in school there, but unlike the public schools of the city, Sacred Heart was a medley of ethnicity. The student body consisted of sixty percent working-class families from the neighborhoods west and north of the parish, twenty percent from the upscale Kenwood-Lakes area, and twenty percent from the poorest, toughest areas of the inner city. Blind to social distinctions and skin color, the nuns had enforced a rigid, consecrated egalitarianism. Unsparingly democratic in the formation of young Christians, they were as likely to smack the misbehaving son of a Kenwood plutocrat as the fatherless youngster from the inner city. In those days, Sacred Heart had the distinction among area schools of sending a large share of its graduates on to prestigious colleges and a slightly larger share on to the St. Cloud State Prison.

56

He thought of the now-unused playground of Sacred Heart School and the alcove formed by the intersection of the church sanctuary and the St. Anthony Chapel, where one of his prison-bound classmates, Charles "Chasbo" Peytabohm, had explained to him in third grade what a Kotex was and, worse yet, what it was used for, leaving the eight-year-old Riley dizzy and covered with perspiration. He had spent the remainder of that day and a good part of the next offering prayers of thanksgiving for being born a boy. But this state of anxious piety was soon followed by a flurry of classroom giggles and face-making between him and Chasbo, culminating in the dispatch by Riley of a top-secret Kotex note, complete with text and hand-drawn illustrations.

The successful delivery of the note depended upon the cooperation of three classmates occupying desks between his and Chasbo's. And the note would have arrived safely had it not been for that little snitch, Mary Irene Hauptman. Riley could still see her snotty little face, turned-up nose, and blonde hair spun in cruel ringlets as she marched triumphantly up to Sister Henretta, who found Riley's drawing of a Kotex to be vulgar and unchristian.

He and Chasbo were taken by the scruff of their necks to the large office near the playground doors, where Sister St. Lillian, a school principal who could have played a prison matron in a James Cagney movie, lectured them on perversion, the general dirtiness of boys' minds, and what awaits perverts at the end of the world. The soft folds of her fleshy cheeks squeezed out like cookie dough from behind the starched white collar surrounding her large bossy face. To one side of the cleft in her chin sprouted a single white whisker of astonishing length. Riley could feel his bowels wither with shame as she glared down at him while delivering a lecture of biblical intensity.

Chasbo sat next to Riley, not scared at all. He just smirked and grunted with each new reprimand, indifferent to the consequences of the tasteless collaboration to which he had been a party. When Sister St. Lillian's scolding dragged on beyond his interest span, Chasbo implemented one of his favorite diversions, one that never failed to bring a meeting to an abrupt close. He threw up his lunch on her desk.

Chasbo was later to go to prison for a long and successful run of burglaries, where his barf-on-command capabilities spared him some of prison's most unwelcome social activities. Mary Irene Hauptman went on to become a high-ranking examiner with the Internal Revenue Service.

The jarring thud of a pop can being expelled from the Pepsi machine registered at the base of Riley's brain, causing him to glance momentarily toward the hallway, where a Lindbergh security officer nodded apologetically in his direction. His attention and memory then returned to Sacred Heart and the north side of the playground, where at age ten he had politely asked the school's biggest bully and star fullback, Igie "Mad Dog" Moriarity (the nickname coming from a local wrestling personality), who was at that time four inches taller, twenty-five pounds heavier, and a year and a half older, to stop picking on his best friend, Edgar McGuirk, the math whiz and all-around brain of the fifth grade. Riley's father had always said that inside every bully resides a coward waiting to have his bluff called. Apparently Mad Dog hadn't heard that adage. With the first punch he knocked out two of Riley's teeth.

But, in accordance with another of his father's maxims ("Once committed, don't ever retreat"), Riley refused to give up in spite of an alarming quantity of blood and swollen tissue and Mad Dog's suggestion that he just stay down on the ground. When his older brother, Ian, started to intervene, Riley waived him off.

From a distance of more than thirty years, as he stood looking out the window of The Lindbergh Tower, he could still taste the blood flowing from his broken nose, filling his mouth and throat and spilling copiously onto his standard-issue school shirt and tie, and he could feel the small gravel stones of the playground surface driving into the soft palms of his hands as he attempted to break his falls.

At the outer edge of the crowd that had gathered that day stood a lone girl, Betsy Bainbridge, in her plaid school jumper and saddle shoes, trespassing on the boy's side of the playground, sobbing for Riley (who had been her playmate and sweetheart since they took their first steps together in the small park between their homes), to stay down and stop fighting back.

But not even his friend Betsy Bainbridge could influence him in a situation like this one, and she knew it. The fight had to continue to its bloody conclusion. There were only two things he couldn't do: cry and quit. It was hard not to cry, but the thought of quitting never entered his mind. For all the pain and humiliation, it would have been much harder to quit. And he wondered with a strange detachment, even then, what drove him in that way. Was it an ethic learned at home or perhaps a centuries-old Celtic madness? Whatever it was, it was still with him as a full-grown adult. And he still hated bullies.

After the last in a series of uncounted knockdowns, Riley looked up through eyes nearly swollen shut to see his opponent strutting in a circle, hands clasped over his head in an arrogant victory salute. As Mad Dog passed by, Riley sprang from the ground onto his back and bit a slice of his ear almost cleanly off the side of his head. Just then, Sister Leonida burst through the crowd of cheering schoolboys and landed a solid right hand to Mad Dog Moriarity's head and Sister St. Agnes threw herself bodily on top of Riley. Seeing blood flow from Mad Dog's nose and what remained of his right ear as he was led away to the infirmary gave Riley a warm sense of closure. It didn't matter one little bit that he had gotten by far the worst of the fight and was bleeding lavishly from just about every place it's possible to bleed from.

From that day forward Mad Dog went out of his way to be nice to Riley, apparently fearing that he could once again find himself in a marathon blood brawl with a crazy little kid who seemed perfectly happy to take five punches for every one he landed.

For his part, Riley held no grievance against Mad Dog in spite of the beating he had taken. His friend Chasbo, on the other hand, was less forgiving. Twenty minutes before the season opener, he slipped into the boy's locker room and threw up in Mad Dog's football helmet.

"What happened to your face?" Riley's father had asked at the dinner table that night. He had barely opened his mouth during dinner in the vain hope that his mother would not notice the missing teeth. Never mind the multiple contusions and abrasions spread across his face and arms. Adhering to the family code, his brother Ian said nothing.

"I ran into a door," answered Riley, unsure of what that meant. He had heard his older brothers say it under similar circumstances.

"How does the other fella look?" asked his father.

"He looks better than I do, Pop. A lot better. But he doesn't want to fight me anymore."

His mother, now seeing the full extent of the damage to the baby of the family, let out a muffled sob as she fled the room. Maureen Carr McReynolds was the daughter of a prosperous St. Paul real estate investor and one-time professor of history at an obscure North Dakota college. Along with her four sisters—the most beautiful girls in St. Paul it was said—she had attended convent schools through twelfth grade, and Manhattanville College in New York. She spoke fluent French, played classical piano, and prior to marrying a North Side McReynolds had never been exposed to bad manners, let alone fist fights. She did have one brother, but he was a cellist. It was at times like this that she renewed her plea to send the boys to a school outside the inner city or, better yet, to move away from the crude incivilities of Minneapolis altogether, in favor of the gracious tree-lined streets of St. Paul.

The next day his father took Riley to the Fremont Avenue Gym, placing him in the care of Eddie O'Brien, a twice-removed cousin and, for twenty-eight years, the central city youth boxing director. Eddie O'Brien had also trained Riley's three older brothers in their violent rites of passage. Jamie, the oldest, and most physically gifted, had reigned for three years as the city middle-weight champion.

Now, staring out a conference room window of The Lindbergh at the Sacred Heart dome on the far horizon, Riley looked back on five years of competitive club fighting as a barbarous undertaking, detrimental in some ways to a carefree childhood but strangely beneficial to a young boy's sense of security. There was a practical sort of comfort in a young male knowing that he could drop most of the thugs and bullies of this world, even ones much bigger. He felt a lifetime ambiguity on this subject. His father, who had made his living boxing as a young man, had thought it a "manly art," so long as it was used in self-defense. The other guy had to take the first punch—that had been his hard and fast rule, a rule scrupulously observed by his four sons.

And for all its barbarities, boxing afforded a working, gut-level understanding of the primitive forces inside every man. Boxers grew to possess a visceral, almost intuitive, knowledge of what drives other men and what separates the talkers and the bluffers from the real thing. In all his years in the criminal justice system, he never saw a boxer cry or whimper at his sentencing. And he never saw a tough-talking business executive who didn't. You could almost smell their courage fail.

The Sacred Heart meditation was interrupted by a ring of the phone. "What the hell are you doing up there?" said Skeeter. "Buck's called two more times. Get your ass down here, will ya? He's buggin' the shit out of me."

6

———————

When Riley returned to his office, Skeeter was waiting at the door, holding up the morning newspaper containing his picture, a broad smile spread across her face. As he drew closer he could see himself: a large, tomato-stained object at the top of the left-hand column. Under the photograph was a cutline reading LINDBERGH EXECUTIVE RECEIVES UNFRIENDLY RECEPTION FROM SASI STRIKE FORCE. Below that was a short article about the protest, together with a quote from Tenzie Dunseth: "We want to give this arrogant and mean-spirited company a chance to make a positive contribution to the community." A balancing quote was received from Liz Bridge of the Lindbergh public relations department: "The Lindbergh has a long history of community involvement, to which the present leadership remains committed. Efforts are being made to reach an understanding with the various community groups, consistent with the best interests of our stakeholders."

Riley studied his picture with narcissistic curiosity. It closely resembled one that had appeared many years earlier where his face was undergoing a similar contortion; but in that picture in the place of the tomato was a twelve-ounce boxing glove containing the iron fist of Tommy Mulcahy, reigning welterweight champion of the Fremont Avenue Gymnasium. That caption had read: "Sacred Heart newcomer decked in first title bout." He concluded that there was something mildly heroic about today's picture. Chuckling, he autographed Skeeter's copy and gave it back to her.

"Any calls?" he asked as he dropped into the chair behind his desk.

"Just one. Some guy named Kurt McBraneman," Skeeter replied, spelling the last name as she looked at her notes. "When I asked what company he was from, he just laughed and said you'd know what business he was in."

Riley squinted, curling his mouth into an enigmatic smile. He picked up a pencil and tapped it on the desktop. After a brief silence: "Did he leave a number?"

"No, he said he'd catch you later. He had kind of a strange voice. I've never heard a voice quite like that before, kinda cold and flat." She seemed more fascinated than worried. "Do you know him?"

Riley's voice was cryptic, reserved. "Yes, I know him . . . quite well."

"Quite well?" repeated Skeeter, her voice filled with curiosity. "Tell me more."

"Let me put it this way: He's a good guy to have for a friend, but a very bad guy to have for an enemy. And he's not the guy you'd take to the senior prom."

Kurt McBraneman had a way of showing up every now and then, sometimes just to check in, sometimes for more specific reasons. Riley had first met him through his old school pal, Chasbo Peytabohm, with whom Kurt had shared a prison cell in the 1970s—Chasbo doing time for burglary, Kurt for armed robbery.

During Riley's first stint as a criminal defense attorney— between rounds with the prosecutor's office—he had, at Chasbo's request, represented Kurt on a charge of indecent liberties with a jilted girlfriend's seventeen-year-old niece, the one and only time Riley found himself on the defense side of a sex case. A conviction would have sent Kurt back to prison on a parole revocation, a fact well-known to the woman who cooked up the claim. The charges were ultimately dismissed when tape recordings of the aunt and niece rehearsing false testimony were obtained by Riley's investigator and put in the hands of the prosecutor just prior to trial. Kurt had done many naughty things in his life, but sex crimes were not among them; when Riley secured his vindication, he became to Kurt a figure of veneration, one to whom he thought he owed a great debt. That was the way Kurt's mind worked. He appointed himself Riley's "guardian angel." A guardian he clearly was, but if he was an angel, he was one of uncommon brutality.

It had always seemed odd to Riley that a man like Kurt McBraneman, who had spent the whole of his adult life in the shadows of the criminal world, a man to whom no felonious undertaking was beyond consideration, including an occasional "righteous" homicide, should be so squeamish about a mid-level misdemeanor. But to his subset of the criminal culture there was no greater disgrace, no finer insult, than to be labeled a sex offender. To him, robbery, burglary, drug-running, and worse were part of doing business. But sex crimes, never.

Kurt's single-minded devotion to the man who had secured his vindication was viewed by Riley with a kind of sentimental trepidation. Not out of fear of Kurt personally, but rather fear that Kurt's singular, almost religious belief in the debt he owed, and his determination to repay it, might result in conduct of which Riley didn't approve.

Years later, during a particularly ugly prosecution, Riley had been subjected to repeated threats from the brother of a defendant he was prosecuting for a series of gruesome assaults against women. Judging the defendant to be a special menace to the community, Riley had parlayed several related and unrelated charges into a prison sentence far exceeding the norm for the primary charge. The defendant's even more dangerous brother openly vowed a bloody revenge. Unlike the standard threats received by prosecutors and cops, this one held the solid promise of fulfillment. The usual responses—police hassling, separate criminal charges—were fruitless.

How Kurt McBraneman learned of these events was never known to Riley. He knew only that Kurt appeared out of the shadows of the parking garage under the courthouse late one evening, announcing in hushed tones that the matter had been "seen to."

"Dammit, Kurt," Riley had exclaimed. "What did you do?" Then he caught himself: "Never mind—don't answer that."

Kurt just stood there, still and ominous, patches of stubby facial hair spread in no discernible pattern across his neck and cheeks, his green army jacket stained with aging food spots below the insignia of the Special Forces unit with which he had fought half-way across the world.

"Who invited you, anyway?" Riley had sputtered, trying to fill the uncomfortable silence and experiencing a torrent of mixed emotions.

Kurt chuckled lightly as though humoring a younger brother of whom he was especially fond. "It's not up to you, man. Sleep tight. That fucker ain't goin' to hurt anybody." He said these words with an eerie, inflectionless voice and then disappeared back into the night.

Riley looked blankly at Skeeter, and went on tapping his pencil on the desktop. He wondered why the hell Kurt was calling him now. He hadn't seen him for years.

"I'll try to get back to him," he finally said to Skeeter, "but he's usually the one who does the contacting rather than the other way around. Anything else happening?"

"Yeah, we've got to go down to Buck's office, remember?"

"Right . . . the stock options."

They stood outside Buck's open door making small talk with his secretary, Gladys, a tall, thin woman in her late fifties whose great mass of graying hair sat uneasily in a giant clump atop her broad, sharp-featured face. Because the clump seemed always to be leaning to one side or the other, Riley worried that it might fall off her head at any moment, spraining her unusually thin neck. So closely did he identify with this possibility that when talking to Gladys his head unconsciously tilted in whichever direction the clump was pointing. He was listing so far to port this morning that his head was almost on Skeeter's shoulder. He brought it upright only when Gladys asked if he had recently suffered a neck injury.

The giant stuffed alligator stood sentry in the hallway outside the CEO's conference room. Buck's manservant, Wally, sat in a side office watching The Price Is Right.

Alone in his office, Buck could be heard mumbling words too indistinct to be made out in the hallway. While natively bright, he was one of those rare adults who moved his mouth when reading, pronouncing words as he went along. It was said among senior managers that he should be sent only short memos because his lips got too tired.

In the middle of Gladys's description of her recent bout with diverticulitis, Buck's mumbles exploded into a great roaring belly laugh. After pausing to gasp for breath, he discharged another roll of convulsive laughter.

"What's he doing in there?" asked Riley, leaning toward the door to try to steal a look.

"I have no idea," replied Gladys, shaking her head.

"He's probably reading his own job description," cracked Skeeter.

Riley stepped on her toe so hard she let out a painful squeak and dropped her notary seal. Gladys straightened her back and put a hand over her midsection, the site of the inflamed diverticuli, and gave a pinched-up facial grimace.

"Asshole," wheezed Skeeter as she reached down to pick up the seal.

Buck emerged from his office wiping tears from his eyes, his shoulders still rocking with laughter. He handed Gladys a cartoon from a men's magazine and instructed her to fax a copy to Hank Wallstead, lead director and senior member of the Lindbergh Board of Directors and himself the chief executive of a sizable railroad. Gladys received the cartoon between the thumb and index finger of her outstretched hand as one might hold a stranger's freshly used handkerchief.

"Hey, Riley! Skooter! Come on in," exclaimed Buck, still giggling slightly.

"Skooter?" said Skeeter a little indignantly. "My name's not Skooter." But Buck paid no attention as he strutted toward his desk.

Buck's office was large and rectangular, and commanded a sweeping view of the St. Paul skyline. A small seating area was set up in one corner, with a round table surrounded by several low-slung chairs covered in tan leather. Sitting on the table were a stack of coasters, an ash tray, that morning's edition of *The Wall Street Journal*, and, most prominently placed, an oversized, leather-bound copy of the Bible.

In meetings it was not uncommon for Buck to recite memorized passages from Scripture to bolster some point he was making, sometimes even opening the Bible to the appropriate page and reading out a supporting passage with an embarrassing theatricality. This routine was usually followed by a verbal reminder that God himself was an unseen participant in this and all other meetings. This left the attendees with the unmistakable impression that, though he spoke no audible words, God was in complete agreement with whatever position Buck had put forward. When Buck's temporal authority combined itself in this way with the force of divine providence, it took a very brave employee indeed to offer a dissenting opinion.

Adjacent to the round table, a large globe sat mounted on a mahogany stand. From a distance the globe looked to be of normal dimensions, but on closer inspection it could be seen that the State of Florida was disproportionately large. As large in fact as all the rest of the contiguous forty-seven states combined. Minnesota, along with the rest of the upper Midwest, was little more than a speck—"fly over country" as Buck referred to it.

Buck settled into his high-backed leather desk chair, which sported a tear near the head rest, from which stuffing was escaping in small puffs. He had used Wally's pocket knife to inflict the tear, which was intended to look as though the fabric had given way from overuse. It was not possible to look at Buck without noticing it.

"Gladys," Buck shouted, "I need some more stuffing."

Carrying a cellophane bag about the size of a pillow case, Gladys made her way to the desk chair and inserted a handful of cotton-like stuffing into the wound as mechanically as if she were watering the plants.

On the credenza behind Buck's desk were arrayed no less than twenty photographs of him posing with politicians,

actors, athletes, and every other species of celebrity. He took
pains to have a photographer handy at charity balls, grand
openings, premieres, and other celebrity-rich events so he
could create a photographic record of his close personal friendships with famous people. For their part, the pictured notables
showed no hint of recognition toward this man who was so vigorously shaking their hand. In one photo Buck appeared to be
trying to hug a celebrity who was rearing backwards with a
bewildered, even frightened, look on his face. Mother Theresa,
whose picture was next to Ronald Reagan's, looked as if she
were about to call security. The most prominently displayed
photo had Buck flashing the Look at a recoiling Farrah
Fawcett.

Growing up dirt-poor in the backwoods of Northern Florida
near the Georgia border had left Buck with a burning sense of
social inferiority, which he strove mightily to overcome through
association, real or photographic, with people of status. In
spite of every effort to blot out his humble origins—including
years of grueling elocution lessons to rid his speech patterns of
their backwoods inflections—he still thought of himself as
"Dogpatch" Montrowe, a nickname that had stuck with him
through college.

All this transparent striving to overcome his lowly origins
rankled most people, but it caused Riley to like him more and be
more sympathetic toward him, to be more tolerant of his relent-
less status seeking. For example, he had felt for Buck when,
freshly arrived in Minnesota as the head of one of the area's most
prestigious companies, he found himself invited to the exclusive
Grain Cities Charity Ball but with a seating assignment that
placed him conspicuously at a second-tier table, well back from
the Van Studdifords, the Wiresburys, and other local brahmins
who sponsored the event and made it the high point of the social
season. The aristocratic sponsors looked upon Buck as little
more than a common vulgarian, a peasant with money. To them,
he lacked what Seymour St. John called "the sheer restfulness of
good breeding," and—Lindbergh CEO or no Lindbergh CEO—
they were not about to admit him to their inner circle. It was a
cruel snub for a man with Buck's special vulnerabilities, and he

reacted in character. In a gesture that endeared him to Riley, he used the gold-edged response card for the Charity Ball to tell the local gentry to "Go piss up a rope."

Riley transferred his eyes from the credenza to Buck's desk. Apart from a few piles of skimmed business materials, the desk was strewn with cartoons, bottles of vitamins and minerals of every description, golf bric-a-brac, hunting magazines, and message slips. It was the desk of a hustler, a man who lived by his wits. He was like any number of guys Riley had known growing up. They were the ones in the fraternity house who hung out on the fringes of the in-crowd. Their genius for being useful to their more gifted peers was the currency with which they purchased longed-for social acceptance. They were tolerated, sometimes even liked, by their peers, in large part because of their plucky endurance and their ability to line up beer kegs and loose women for the parties. They didn't get the good-looking girls, didn't make the varsity, and never graduated with honors. But they were big winners at the poker table and were possessed of an innate cunning that would later serve them so well in the world of business. Riley had always liked those guys. But he had to admit that he never expected to see one as the CEO of a prestige, old-line company like The Lindbergh.

From one of the piles on his desk, Buck pulled out an automobile title card and looked across at Riley. "I'm transferring the BMW over to my youngest son for his eighteenth birthday. Can I use this form for a car registered in Florida?"

Irritated that he had been interrupted in an important meeting for a purely personal matter, Riley shook his head and answered, "Sure."

Buck pushed the document across the desk to Skeeter. "Put your signature and seal right there, Skooter."

"Skeeter" came the simultaneous correction, but Buck was already shouting for Gladys to fetch him another Diet Dr. Pepper.

Skeeter notarized the title card and headed for the door, her short skirt clinging handsomely to her hips. Buck leaned forward in his chair, stretching his neck to get a better view, arching his thick, rust-colored eyebrows in lusty admiration. "Not too bad," he mumbled out of the corner of his mouth while stroking his fist up and down over his lap.

Riley shook his head. "Come on, Buck, not Skeeter. She's like a member of my family. And besides that she'll cut your nuts off if she catches you looking her up and down like that."

"Yeah, right, that's what they all say. They love it—that's why they were put on earth." He wiggled his eyebrows and flashed a lecherous smile.

Wanting to change the subject, Riley asked, "What's your question on the options, Buck?"

Buck pushed a notebook across the desk. "Check this calculation for me, will ya? I can never understand these options." As Riley looked over the worksheet, Gladys put her head in the door and said that the lead director of the Lindbergh board, Hank Wallstead was on the phone. The diamond in Buck's pinkie ring reflected a ray of morning sun as he reached over and punched the speaker button on his phone panel.

"Hey, Hank, what's happening?" said Buck, looking at the speaker box as though Hank Wallstead were stuffed into its six cubic inches, gazing out through the sound holes. Buck's tone of voice changed only slightly, but the change was clearly perceptible to Riley. The "Director Tone" was equal parts sincerity and brown-nosing but also managed to communicate in its fabric and texture a sense of subtle urgency that every minute given over to casual conversation, even with someone as important as the lead director, was a minute away from the crushing burdens that had been placed upon his strong but only human shoulders.

This guy was good, thought Riley, nodding slightly without looking up from the option sheet. He couldn't help but like him. He was full of shit, but he was also full of life.

And Riley had to admit that he was fascinated by the relationship between Buck and the Lindbergh Board of Directors, that stellar cast of important personages, the area's corporate elite. All but two—a college professor and a retired major general—were CEOs, portraying to the outside world an image of dignity, prudence, and sound judgment. In fact, most of them were basically honest and well-behaved. But when Wentworth Hall, the former CEO, died in an automobile accident, leaving the company rudderless during a crucial period in its history, a collective neurosis seemed to have set in with the group. With the sudden realization that the company's mastermind was gone and that they would be held individually accountable for the company's fortunes, a stampeding panic set in, and these dignified and prudent men broke off into opposing factions, lashing out like the forces of hell at each other and at anyone close by, including a number of blameless line and staff officers, who lost their jobs during the transition. In their alarm and anxiety, they precipitously hired Buck Montrowe and were now holding their breath that things would work out.

Hank Wallstead's raspy smoker's voice sprang forth from the speaker box, "Hi, Buck. How's everything there in the executive suite? You cranking out profits for us?"

"You bet your ass," replied Buck as he winked at Riley and leaned back in his swivel chair, dislodging a tuft of stuffing, which floated gently to the ground. "There's a ton of stuff to get done, but I'm gonna work 'til I drop!"

"That's what I like to hear, man, but don't burn yourself out. We need you healthy and active," enthused Hank.

Burn himself out, thought Riley. *How dumb is this bastard? Buck hasn't worked a full day since he arrived. Are these guys completely blind, or are they just pretending? Maybe this was another one of those things he "didn't get."*

"So how'd you like the cartoon, Hank?" asked Buck, winking again at Riley as he slid a copy across the desk. In the cartoon a woman is sitting on a bar where two men are standing. The woman has her thighs wrapped around the first man's face. The second man is saying, "I think you can stop buying her drinks now."

Through partially forced laughter Hank said, "Yeah, that was hysterical. I loved it. But I've got a small request: In the future fax those to me on my home machine, will ya? Our fax operator got a little upset. She's one of those ball-busting types."

71

"Ooo," said Buck as he slapped his forehead with the palm of his right hand. "I'll tell Gladys. Sorry about that."

As Buck and Hank talked on, Riley's gaze turned to the shelves above the credenza. Perched on a ledge just above the celebrity shrine were several pictures of Buck's wife, Eileen Mornay Montrowe, a pretty and likable woman of thirty-seven, including a picture of Eileen sitting on Buck's lap at their hunting lodge, with the family dogs, Butch and Fifi, trying to pile on.

Not pictured were the first Mrs. Montrowe, who after four children (all sons) and ten years of marriage to Buck joined a religious cult in New Mexico; and the second Mrs. Montrowe, a pom-pom girl with the Miami Dolphins, who ten minutes after the expiration of the waiting period under their prenuptial agreement, moved in with one hunk of a lifeguard, taking with her half of Buck's net worth and all the household furnishings.

Buck and Eileen had met fifteen years earlier at her graduation from Florida Midlands College, also Buck's alma mater. Eileen, in her capacity as head of the Young Christian League, had offered the opening prayer at the ceremony, while Buck, one of the college's most distinguished graduates, delivered the commencement address, entitled: "You Can Accomplish Anything You Want in Life if You Are Willing to Work Hard Enough." They were immediately drawn to each other there on the platform—she tall, dark-haired, and nubile; he urbane, suave, and on his way up the corporate ladder. That very night, after a whirlwind of festivities and two pints of cherry vodka, the young Christian and the hard worker consummated their new found love in the back seat of Buck's rented Cadillac.

On the top ledge of the picture gallery was an old photo of Buck doing an Elvis impersonation at a South Georgia resort, a role at which he was a considerable hit when in his mid-twenties. A younger, thinner Buck, with a mound of natural brown hair, was rotating his groin and curling his lip sensually. The enlarged photo was a gift from Eileen and bore the inscription: "To Buck—My hunka, hunka burning love."

To the right of the Elvis photo was a large picture of Buck with his father, Reverend G. Pickett Montrowe, and his grandfather, Reverend Nathan Bedford Montrowe, the aged Bible-thumping, snake-handling founder of the Montrowe Family Traveling Salvation Show. All three were wearing diamond pinkie rings. Like his father and grandfather, the nineteen-year-old Buck was wearing the heavy, black robes of a preaching minister, even though his ordination had been a hurried and short-lived affair rigged for the sole purpose of exempting him from service in the Korean War. In the picture, Buck was flashing an odd half-smile in what Riley took to be a precursor to the Look.

Last in the sequence was a color photo of Buck with Governor George Wallace, taken during the Alabama governor's 1968 presidential campaign, in which Buck had served as a local area director.

Riley laughed softly and turned his attention back to the Hank Wallstead telephone exchange.

"How about a round of golf tomorrow?" asked Buck.

"No can do tomorrow. How about Saturday?" answered Hank.

"No, I'm going to take a couple of rest and relaxation days down in Boca Viejo," said Buck. "I've got to get out of this pressure cooker once in a while."

"Okay, Buckaroo, let's try for later in the month." Hank loved the Buckaroo line, thought it was a scream.

"Roger and out," said Buck as he punched off the speaker.

When she saw the light go off on the phone panel, Gladys allowed Art Coolidge, a lending officer in the Real Estate Investment-Loan area, to slip into the office. As a middle manager, Art got up to the Sacristy only when he had a lending document that required the CEO's signature, which wasn't very often. He nervously approached Buck's desk in short, quick steps as though he was attending a papal audience.

"Hi, Buck," Art said in a voice a full octave above his normal register.

"Hey, how ya doin'?" said Buck with a big smile. "How are things in your department? And how's the family?"

Put at ease by Buck's friendly and informal manner, Coolidge started talking at length about a troubled loan, or "investment" as they were generally known in the insurance industry. Buck nodded engagingly and, without taking his eyes from Art, scratched out a note and furtively slid it across the desk to Riley.

Riley opened the note and read: "Who is this guy?"

Equally unobtrusively Riley scratched on the bottom: "Art Coolidge—Real Estate Investment-Lending—20-year employee—wife, Arlene," and slid the note back to Buck, who was still nodding and smiling at Art.

When Coolidge's war story grew tiresome (which didn't take long), Buck got up out of his chair, threw his arm around Art's shoulder, and as he moved him toward the door said, "Great story Artie. Keep up the good work and give my best to Arlene. What a gal!"

Art Coolidge was on cloud nine as he left the room.

"Here are your option calculations," Riley said as he passed over the corrected numbers. He then stood up and said, "Say, Buck, we've had a suspected money laundering downstairs at the S&L, and we can't identify the suspect because the cameras were turned off to save costs. That's something we can't do—you know, try to save money by compromising security."

"Take it to Erving," replied Buck reflexively. He didn't like having problems brought to him.

Riley gave a resigned nod. "We also have those demonstrators at the front entrance. They're just doing their thing, but they'll probably want to meet with you at some point."

Buck really didn't like problems that required interaction with the proletariat. They made him nervous. He bristled angrily, "Talk to Gar. Do I have to do everything around here?"

Shifting on his feet, and a little taken back, Riley said, "Just a heads up, Buck. This is stuff you should be aware of—and occasionally get involved in."

"Okay, so I'm aware of it!" he snapped.

For several months Riley had speculated privately why it was that a man so affable under most circumstances would in an instant turn churlish and testy when faced with important but fairly common executive challenges—the type that CEOs faced regularly. At first he put it down to ordinary laziness. That was the reigning explanation among senior managers. But it just dawned on Riley with a rare clarity that laziness accounted for only part of Buck's disassociation from his duties. His bluster obscured the fact that he was just plain scared, insecure about his own abilities. It was as clear as it could be. He had never had these kinds of responsibilities in a large company before. He had been a salesman and a high-level claims adjuster most of his career. At Galaxy Life he had been little more than an executioner, a gun for hire. He knew next to nothing about people management or community affairs or systems operation, or any other activity outside of peddling insurance and firing people, but he was too proud to admit it. All this new responsibility provoked a fear of failure, which was understandable. And though his behavior was somewhat understandable, it was also irritating, and unhealthy for the enterprise.

But Riley didn't have time just then to address that challenge. He had more immediate concerns.

7

It was late afternoon before Riley and Gordy Moorland, the chief compliance officer, arrived at the S&L to evaluate the attempted money laundering.

"Hi," said Riley as he knocked gently on the door of Liddy's office. He and Gordy then stepped in.

Liddy, still reeling from the downsizing memo, got up from her chair, cleared her throat and extended her hand. "Hello, Mr. McReynolds," she said, with a forced smile. "Skeeter was my roommate in college, so I know who you are. It's nice to meet you." In spite of her attempts at friendliness, she looked pale and uncomfortable, and there was an uneasy feel in the room. That was often the way it was during a week of firings, and the further down the line the terminations went the more noticeable the feeling became.

Riley took a shot at lightening things up. "Yes, I know you and Skeeter are old friends. You shouldn't believe anything that mixed-up woman has to say. It's all lies."

Liddy tried to smile but lacked the power to break through her anguish.

Shortening the silence, Riley said, "This is Gordy Moorland from compliance, and please call me Riley." Gordy and Liddy nodded politely at each other, Liddy barely looking at him.

She appeared to Riley to be heartbroken about something. He felt like an intruder and thought of postponing the meeting but figured he could get the necessary information quickly and move on. "Ah, Liddy, we don't need much of your time," he said as they all sat down. "We just want to verify some facts concerning the attempted money laundering this morning."

Liddy nodded, but her swollen, bloodshot eyes seemed to focus somewhere behind them. Riley had known hundreds of Scandinavians of similar upbringing and temperament, stolid and undemonstrative, and knew from personal experience that when their composure could be seen to falter, which wasn't often, they were very near total breakdown. Not like his people, the Irish, whose cultural norm was to go nuts early in the process and then get over it.

He unconsciously adopted a softer tone. "As we understand it, Liddy, the cameras had been turned off on orders from the divisional manager—"

"Which is a regulatory violation by the way," interrupted Gordy Moorland officiously.

"—which we know was not your fault," Riley quickly added. "But we hear that you got a good look at the guy. Is that right?"

"Yes, I suppose so," she said. "I remember the height and hair color, that type of thing . . . and a birthmark on his forehead, under hair he had pulled forward, almost in bangs, like he was trying to cover it up." She pushed aside her own hair to demonstrate the location of the birthmark.

Riley was struck by the sharply chiseled, Nordic beauty of this young woman, sitting across from him so pained and vulnerable. She looked like a grief-stricken child. He wanted to ask if he could help in some way, but had long ago learned to tread lightly concerning personal matters when in the workplace, especially with an employee he hardly knew. In his household growing up, his mother and sister had been treated almost as deities. The lowest form of life, his father had taught, was the man who in any way mistreated a woman or failed to come to her aid. His old-fashioned upbringing and every instinct coded into his mind and spirit now instructed him to surface and relieve whatever problem was causing Liddy

Jonssen such unhappiness. But he knew better, knew that his father's reverence for women might have been admirable on some level, but it was at the same time contemptuous of a woman's ability to take care of herself. And besides, all the rules of the workplace had changed, some for the good and some not. Other than by-the-book business dealings, male-female interactions in the modern workplace, even when wholesome and well intentioned, were a minefield. The careful executive steered clear of anything personal.

Liddy Jonssen surely knew that. And she didn't appear to be one to step over any lines. In fact, Skeeter had described her as reserved around men. But, still, Riley felt her looking at him strangely. And though choked with upset, she didn't seem guarded or reserved toward him. She was open, almost without boundaries, in a way few women were when dealing with men they didn't know. Most women were immediately comfortable with other women, he thought, as could be seen in the small social cues, like eye contact and body language, but cautious with men—even unintimidating men like Riley. But from the beginning Liddy seemed unguarded toward him. Not, he sensed, because she was an especially open person, but because of something about him personally, something she had picked up on and was responding to. She was staring at him intently and it threw him a little off balance.

He turned away from her gaze and looked at the items on the credenza behind her. The knit design with the spider crawling up the water spout in particular caught his eye and started the lines of "The Itsy, Bitsy Spider" repeating themselves in his head.

He wanted to break the silence. "Well, Liddy, we'll only keep you for a minute. Is there anything else you can tell us that might help identify this guy?"

She shook her head weakly. "I was pretty nervous at the time. This guy was scary. In fact the whole thing's scary." She shuddered slightly. "He was threatening, seemed almost insane. Said he was going to get me if I said anything. And he showed up twice this afternoon in the hallway, just glaring at me and nodding his head as if to remind me of his warning."

She now looked up. Her eyes seemed to be reaching to him personally, as though they were old friends. She didn't even look at Gordy Moorland—it was almost as if he wasn't in the room.

Riley cleared his throat nervously and shifted in his chair. He looked down to consult a list he had scratched out on his way down. "Did it seem like he was on drugs?"

"Maybe," she replied without taking her eyes from him, "but I can't tell the difference between drug crazy and regular crazy. I've been robbed at the teller cage before, but I've never had an experience like this. This guy was different. There was something evil about him."

Gordy Moorland started to ask some detailed fact questions when Riley noticed Liddy's eyes drift over to the blue-bordered memo on her desk and saw the corners of her mouth go slack. He now understood what else was troubling her: she had people in her unit who she would have to fire the next day. He understood; he had one of those damned envelopes on his desk, too.

"Let's get this information later in the week," he said, pulling rank on Gordy Moorland. "It's getting pretty late."

Gordy stopped midsentence, shrugging as he looked over at Riley.

Riley got up from his chair. "We'll find our way out, Liddy. Thanks for the information," he said as they moved toward the door. Liddy nodded but made no sound. Her eyes followed him from the room.

When he returned to his office, Skeeter helped him through a laundry list of the days unfinished items. Her irreverence, always uplifting—or almost always uplifting—helped dispel the gloom that had attached itself to him in Liddy's office.

He leaned back in his chair and looked over at Skeeter. "This may sound really stupid, Skeets, and maybe I'm just imagining things, but your friend Liddy Jonssen seemed interested in me in some way. She was looking at me really funny." He blushed as these words came out because they conveyed a meaning he didn't intend. They sounded dumb, like something you'd have said in high school to the best girlfriend of a girl you were interested in.

Skeeter giggled and arched her eyebrows. "It's just your animal magnetism, you stud. Women are helpless in your presence."

His face reddened with embarrassment That was exactly the response he had feared. He asked for it—and he got it. Acutely embarrassed, he said, "That's not what I meant, smart ass."

Skeeter giggled impishly. "Actually, I think I know what that was about, and you'll be relieved to know it had nothing to do with your charm or sex appeal."

At that moment they were interrupted by a knock on the door which announced the presence of Bobby Morestad, the head of the Executive Services Division. Bobby was sixty-two years old, and dressed absent-mindedly in a rumpled Brooks Brothers suit, striped tie, and brown loafers. He gave the impression of being an aging ivy leaguer, which was precisely what he was. Princeton 1959, Riley thought.

Though he was on his way to the parking garage, Bobby Morestad was without his briefcase, which he had once again left in the men's bathroom.

Bobby stepped over several piles of papers arranged carelessly about the floor surrounding Riley's desk. "I haven't gotten around to organizing those files yet," said Riley apologetically, sensing an unspoken criticism on Bobby's part.

In an effort to restore the shock of hair that had once graced his head and of which he had been inordinately proud, Bobby Morestad had recently undergone a hair transplant that relocated plugs of hair from the back of his head to the front. The plugs, which bore a distinctly different shade and texture from the ones they were replacing, were planted in rows as perfect as a Midwestern corn crop across the top of his head. The bald patches on the back of his head, where the plugs had previously resided, gave him the look of a man who had recently undergone chemotherapy. Bobby Morestad was a bright and likable man of whom Riley had grown fond over the years, and he didn't have the heart to tell him he should take a leave of absence until his head no longer looked like a 4-H project. That is what any real friend would have done.

The glassy clatter of the day's coffee cups being assembled and rinsed, and the thump of drawers closing could be heard across the hall, accompanied by voices of fourth-floor secretaries preparing to leave for the day. Skeeter got up from her chair but stayed in the room.

Bobby took a seat, and while softly patting his newly planted hair said in a tone used by people who have your best interests at heart, "You know, Riley, I like you, but, frankly, I'm worried about your survival prospects around here if you keep telling Buck things he doesn't want to hear. I watched him during your exchange this morning at the executive council meeting. Even though he seems to have a special fondness for you, he's also starting to think of you as a spoiler—you know, not a team player." He now crossed his arms and his voice took on a tone of deep concern. "You've got to be a better politician, not get in his face like that. As your friend, I want you to mend your ways before it's too late. You've got to decide whether you're going to conform, and stay around, or openly criticize Buck and get punished for it. If you can't stand the heat, get off the pot."

Riley didn't even flinch at the mixed metaphor. He was used to Bobby's semantic mutilations. They were legendary within the company. Something in his brain having nothing to do with intelligence, some circuit long ago disconnected, insisted upon dismembering bits and pieces of time-worn expressions and combining them, uninvited, with other time-worn expressions. As one of the smartest and most honest members of senior management, Bobby Morestad was living proof that idiosyncrasies of speech and grooming had nothing to do with character or talent.

Skeeter, who avidly tracked Bobby's malaprops, pursed her lips tightly and scurried from the room. Riley could hear sobs of laughter coming from the copy room, to which she had fled.

"Don't you mean 'get out of the kitchen,' Bob?" said Riley.

"Whatever," said Bobby, waving his hand as if to dismiss a nuisance. "The point is that a big part of success with egomaniacs like Buck is telling them what they want to hear." One of the plugs fell directly across the center of his forehead.

To avoid staring at Bobby's head, Riley transferred his gaze to the life-size portrait of Sir Thomas More hanging on the north wall of his office. *Good God,* he wondered to himself, *what would The Man For All Seasons think of this place? Is it just me?* he thought, *or is there something really strange about a company that has a CEO who's family pets travel by executive jet, a chief of staff who thinks he's being stalked by shit molecules, and a major division head who can't distinguish between a kitchen and a toilet.*

"I'm not trying to bug you, Riley, I just want to give you the benefit of an old man's experience. You'd be well-advised to look the other way on some of these things. You're too much of a goddamn idealist." His tone was flatter now as he got out of his seat and walked toward the window.

Riley knew that Bobby was probably right. He was living proof that, if you play your cards right and duck at the right times, you can probably survive just about any political crisis without selling out your principles.

Riley rose from his desk chair. "I know you're trying to be helpful, Bob, and I appreciate the sentiment. But I've got to tell you that I don't think you or anyone else is doing Buck a favor by playing along with this stuff. Like everyone else in this world, he benefits from a little critical advice now and then. I know I can bring him around."

Bobby shook his head doubtfully.

"Listen, Bobby, he's really a pretty good guy, I feel sure of it."

"A good guy? Who are you kidding? He's a complete asshole. Everybody knows that but you. But, unlike you, they have brains enough not to criticize him."

Bobby was now standing at the window and looking down at a short line of traffic that had formed outside the entry to the parking garage. He beckoned Riley toward the window and pointed to the street. "Have you ever sat in your car, behind Buck's Jaguar, during morning rush hour, while he finishes a phone call on his car phone? He doesn't like the static that occurs when he drives into the garage, so he just sits there casually shooting the breeze on the phone, backing up rush-hour traffic for about four blocks. I tell you, the man doesn't give a shit about anyone but himself. It's sickening. How the hell do some people get to be that way? Is it just CEO disease?"

Riley winced at this reminder of the traffic jams. He could not count the number of times he had sat in a long line outside the building caused by Buck's Jag idling imperiously in an active traffic lane while he conducted a static-free conversation, his casual facial expression contrasting sharply with the angry faces of the drivers stopped for blocks behind him. Riley said nothing, but his face gave him away.

Bobby nodded knowingly, not requiring verbal confirmation. He shook his head as he headed for the door. Passing through the arch in front of Skeeter's desk, he said "I'm telling you again, no matter what he says the last thing Buck will tolerate is criticism." Bobby said this in a really serious voice, like he couldn't believe that Riley was naive enough to think otherwise.

"You may be right, Bob. I can't keep my mouth shut altogether, but maybe I can be less confrontational. That approach might be more successful."

"Okay," said Bobby. "Run it up the flagpole and see if it will hunt."

Sitting at her desk, Skeeter sprayed a mouthful of coffee on Riley's appointment calendar.

8

At 6:30 P.M. Riley finished the day's nonpostponable tasks, about equally divided between those that had been scheduled and those that arose spontaneously, like the attempted money laundering. The sounds of wastepaper baskets being dumped by the night crew and the whir of vacuum cleaners had replaced the daytime cacophony of human voices. A small Asian woman who spoke no English bowed and smiled at Riley as he stuffed the residue of the in-basket into his briefcase for sorting and review at home later that night.

All executives, save only Erving Russell, had departed the fourth floor by six o'clock. Buck had left the office, and town, and the country (fishing trip to Canada) by midafternoon. Erving, who seemed to get his most concentrated work done between six and nine o'clock at night, performed, in addition to his own assigned duties, most of the work listed in Buck's job description, remaining always careful to keep that fact hidden from the world. Should word get out, nothing short of human sacrifice would be required to assuage Buck's ego. Erving would be history.

Walking across the Lobby Court to the garage elevators, Riley navigated his way through janitorial staff cleaning up debris left by the morning demonstrators, whose devotion to the cause had spent itself shortly after the TV crews departed. He sidestepped an industrial-sized pail standing idle next to the lobby stairs, near the spot where Sonja Humegren had lusted after Buck that morning.

The stalls in the underground parking garage were arranged according to status, with the executive slots located closest to the elevators on the first level. Each executive stall was identified anonymously by an assigned number, with the exception of stall number two, which was conspicuously marked: MR. FIELD BLAISDAHL—SENIOR EXECUTIVE VICE PRESIDENT & CHIEF OF STAFF. Riley's car, moved by Skeeter from the public garage during the afternoon, was parked in stall number eight.

An overcast sky and gray mist greeted him when he pulled onto the street behind a city bus that exhaled a burst of dense, black exhaust as it bullied its way into the main traffic lane.

Rather than be stuck in the snarl at the interchange south of downtown Minneapolis, he left the freeway and headed through the southwest residential section of town, past the homes in which he and Betsy had grown up. Still a strikingly beautiful section of the city, with large and stately homes on tree-lined streets, the neighborhood had nonetheless changed considerably from their growing-up days in the 1950s, when the mansions on Lowry Hill were still occupied by the founding families of Minneapolis and General Eisenhower was in the White House providing sensible and moderate government. The sight of these large and imposing homes, with an abundance of Tudor wood and brick, fell gently on his mind. To those who had grown up and been nourished within their walls, they were like a favorite uncle. It had been as though he and the other children in that neighborhood had had a hundred sets of parents who loved and watched out for them. Especially the mothers, who, like his own mother, made him believe he was the most wonderful child who ever drew breath. He knew that the sheer goodness of these people, as seen through the eyes of a child, was what, to this day, made him see life as essentially good. He felt he had been launched into adulthood by a community of caring grown-ups, and for all he was to encounter in later years, he never lost the sense of strength and optimism imparted by that community. Of course it was all a little idealized, perhaps even a dream—but a glorious and healthy dream. He was to learn later of the pain and anguish that had played itself out in some of those houses—of alcoholism and despair and worse. But at the time, for him, it was nearly perfect, and, as he passed off Mount Curve onto Kenwood Parkway, past the sprawling, sunken park in which he had romped and played as a youngster, he could feel his eyes smart with gratitude.

In spite of an intricate series of roadblocks and one-ways constructed to discourage commuter traffic, many residents of the south suburbs took this same route home but became irritated when they encountered others doing likewise. The car in front of him as he turned right onto Dean Parkway—an older model blue Pontiac driven by a woman with agitated hair—had perched on one side of its back window a toy dog whose eyes lit up when the brakes were applied, and on the other side a plaque reading: HONK FOR JESUS. When Riley honked, the woman gave him the finger.

Fifteen minutes later, as he turned left into the shaded cul-de-sac on which his red-brick, shuttered, two-story colonial was located, Betsy scooted in front of him in her silver station wagon, throwing him a kiss from the driver's window. Her broad, happy smile was flirtatious and at the same time triumphant at having aced him out at the turn. Teddy was riding shotgun, talking a mile a minute. From the back seat Tuffy had his paws propped up on the back of Betsy's seat, trying to bite her hair. She bubbled with smiles and energy as these two small creatures competed for her loving attention. Never had Riley encountered such a naturally happy person, one whose unrestrained joy in life overflowed onto everyone around her. Betsy Bainbridge McReynolds simply threw herself onto the goodness of life, refusing entry to all that was small or mean. With her plentiful and contagious enthusiasms, she went full-speed all day and then slept like a baby at night. Even animals and flowers, to whom she talked openly, seemed to flourish in her presence.

86

What a blessing it was, he reminded himself as he pulled up to the house, that they had met while still toddlers. What other explanation could there be for such a beautiful and irrepressibly happy person falling in love with a neurotic Irish hypochondriac, who was getting shorter each year?

At the back door Riley was greeted by Tuffy, fresh from a shampoo and haircut at the Puppy Be Lovely canine beauty shop, his tail wagging like a runaway metronome. Tuffy peered up at him with that shit-for-brains look so common to small dogs, his nose quivering expectantly above a pronounced underbite. Upon confirming that Riley hadn't brought him a treat, Tuffy headed for the living room couch (where he was forbidden to go) and flopped down for a nap.

"Man, they really shaved him at the beauty shop. He looks like a fetal pig," said Riley as he gave Betsy a kiss on the lips and a pinch on the butt—the nicest little butt ever to fill a Sacred Heart jumper.

"I know," said Betsy. "He's going to need a bad-haircut support group." She was cleaning the refrigerator as she spoke. Teddy had put a can of pop in the freezer before leaving for school, and it had exploded all over everything. "I think the canine beautician was a little mad; Tuffy kept trying to hump her. For a guy with no balls he sure is frisky."

Riley nodded as he looked about the kitchen for a snack. "Maybe we could get him an inflatable girl dog at the pet store."

"I think those are just for people," said Betsy as she moved to the sink to squeeze out the sponge. "What's new with you?" she asked as Riley stood in the adjoining pantry flipping through the day's mail.

He looked up as though the question had prompted a memory. "Kurt McBraneman called me today, but I wasn't there and I don't know what he wanted."

"Kurt? Geez, you haven't seen him for a long time," said Betsy. In years past, when Kurt was at his lowest point, he had spent Christmas Day with them. That was back when Lizzie was just a tyke, and back when Kurt was on a list of the top ten local public enemies compiled by the Minneapolis Police Department, a list of felons to keep an eye on. None of this had bothered Betsy. She liked Kurt and had formed a judgment early on that, whatever his dealings with other people, whatever his crimes might have been, he was just a troubled soul and no danger to them. And for his part, Kurt was a little in love with Betsy, as so many people were. Nobody had ever been as nice to him, or as unafraid of him, as she was.

Riley walked to the refrigerator and opened it. "It's been several years since I've talked to him. I'm sure he'll call back. He knows I left practice, so I don't think he's calling about a legal matter. I'm just glad he's still alive."

"Betsy turned off the kitchen faucet and flipped the switch on the dishwasher. She then smiled impishly. "Did you remember you've got Outdoor Scouts tonight?"

Riley grimaced. "Outdoor Scouts? What's that?"

"I told you last week. I knew you weren't listening—you just gave me that brain-dead look when I went through Teddy's schedule for this week."

"What is it again?" whined Riley as he transferred a scoop of chocolate chip ice cream into a sugar cone.

"Not before dinner, Tubby," said Betsy as she returned to the refrigerator.

Tubby? Now, that hurt.

Betsy turned toward him, now with a serious look. "Outdoor Scouts is the father-son program where they go on overnight camping trips and do crafts and commune with God and nature. It's an extra-credit project for Teddy's school. You have to go to the initiation meeting tonight, so you can qualify to join the chapter before the overnight trip next weekend."

"Oh, God," said Riley in a martyred voice. "Where's the meeting?"

"It's at a different house each week. I've got the address for tonight, some people over on Wycliffe by the name of Krebsworth." Her smile told that she was greatly rewarded by the image of Riley, a man with no mechanical aptitude and an abiding hatred of everything to do with the great outdoors, on an overnight camping trip.

Lapping his ice cream cone, Riley shuffled into the den, where Lizzie was listening on headphones to the feminist manifesto: "I Will Survive." Riley couldn't hear the music, and Lizzie (who couldn't hear anything but the music) was belting out the lyrics in a flat monotone at the top of her lungs in what she believed to be perfect harmony with the singer. She didn't hit a single note. He tried to get her attention by waving to ask her to go into the other room, but her eyes were closed as she groaned out the lyrics. Her head rolled in a terrible syncopation with the sounds of her own voice, which mercifully she couldn't hear.

Betsy put a Chicken Lean Quisine and a Diet Pepsi in front of Riley and told him to chow down because he was due at Outdoor Scouts in thirty minutes. Three bites into the dinner the doorbell rang. Now on the phone, Betsy signaled for Riley to answer it. When he returned from informing two door-to-door missionaries that he didn't care whether they thought he was going to hell, Tuffy had polished off his entire dinner, including the vegetables. When he saw Riley coming, he jumped off the table like a flying squirrel and hid behind Lizzie.

Riley went upstairs for a ten-minute nap. Spread out on the bed, he retained consciousness just long enough to notice the piece of cardboard he had scotch-taped the previous week over a hole in the bedroom ceiling where a light fixture had been removed. He had painted over the cardboard, and although the tape was curling a little, his handiwork seemed to be holding up. His last thought before unconsciousness was one of pride; pride at having so easily restored the appearance of the ceiling with so little effort. And he had done it without the need for plaster, as Betsy had vehemently claimed was necessary.

At 7:30 P.M. Teddy and Riley arrived at the home of Morton Krebsworth, tax accountant by day and chief camper of Outdoor Scouts International by night. Morton was decked out in a double-knit suit of a type Riley hadn't seen since the passing of the disco era. In a good-natured attempt to break the ice, Riley quipped that with his outfit Morton might want to do a guest spot on Dance Fever. The chief camper was not amused.

The three-bedroom Krebsworth home was furnished in an early-American motif, and was loaded down with a dizzying array of high-tech gadgets and appliances. The couch on which Teddy and Riley were instructed to sit was illuminated by a crushed velvet lampshade giving off a cozy green light. Brown shag carpeting clashed uneasily with the room's centerpiece, the chief camper's Barcalounger.

Morton Krebsworth sported a mass of curly salt-and-pepper hair atop a wide, unattractive face flanked by ears so large and protuberant that Riley had to struggle not to stare at them. Though only in his mid-thirties, Morton wore a pair of thick trifocals. Inserted in his breast pocket was a shiny gray shirt protector stuffed with a wide assortment of writing instruments.

A chunky, florid little kid eating a tortilla through brightly colored braces was introduced as Morton, Jr. He munched audibly on his dinner and said nothing. Riley smiled at him but got back only a hostile stare.

Also in the chapter were an orthodontist, a divorce lawyer, and a chiropractor, together with six other father-son duos, their names spelled out on name tags. An auto mechanic, with "Vern" stitched above the pocket of his gray work shirt, sported a name tag that identified him as CAMPER OF THE MONTH.

Following fifteen minutes of chapter fellowship (which seemed to Riley to take a month and caused his facial muscles to ache from supporting a fake smile) chief camper Krebsworth donned a hunting cap with visor and ear muffs. Army surplus boots protruded from under the wide cuffs of his double-knit pants. Fastened to one side of his belt was a portable telephone and on the other a navigation unit for use in boating and hiking adventures.

At a signal from the chief camper, the father-son teams sat in a prayer circle around a simulated campfire consisting of three wooden logs crisscrossed over a lightbulb.

Morton, Sr., sat at the head of the campfire and began intoning in a low, funereal moan, "Oh, Great Spirit, we are gathered together tonight to craft and commune and ask your help for next week's overnight camping trip."

Riley lifted his eyes to see if anyone else thought all this was funny. Apparently none did, as they were all staring like zombies at the rotating aluminum foil except for Morton, Jr., who was picking food out of his teeth. When he caught Riley looking at him, he twisted his face into a noiseless snarl. Riley quickly looked back down at the camp fire but could feel a flutter building low in his abdomen, which he knew from experience signaled the beginning of an uncontrollable giggle-fit—the kind that used to overtake him and his sister in church. For the two minutes it took Morton to complete the prayer, Riley gurgled, sputtered, snorted, and eventually laughed out loud, bringing angry looks from the other campers.

The next item on the agenda called for Riley and Teddy, as part of their admission test, to assemble a tent in the Krebsworth's back yard. It appeared to be a simple task, but after the passage of the twenty minutes allowed for assembly, Riley had yet to get a single post in place. This failure alone would have been sufficient grounds for disqualification—and was in fact the official reason cited in the form sent to Teddy's school—but Riley suspected that at least as important in their rejection were his giggle-fit during the opening prayer and Morton Krebsworth's failure to see the humor in Riley's opening comment about his outfit.

Teddy turned to Riley as they drove home. "Gee, Dad, I don't think anybody's ever been turned down for Outdoor Scouts before. Nobody thought you were funny. Mr. Krebsworth was really mad. Do you think he'll call my school or anything?"

Riley looked over at his son and, mindful of his duty to set an example, said, "Mr. Krebsworth is a little prick, Teddy. Who cares what he does."

"Yeah, but Mom will think you were just trying to get kicked out. What's she going to say?" Teddy persisted, fidgeting in his seat.

"Mom's not going to know," said Riley. "For the rest of the school year we're going out every Tuesday night with our camping gear. We'll shoot pool or go to a movie."

Teddy got out of the car in the driveway and hustled into the house. Riley pulled forward into the garage, squeezing past garbage cans lining the walls.

"Hi, Sweetheart!" he said, full of cheer as he came through the back door.

Betsy was doing step calisthenics to an aerobics video in the den, wearing a black leotard, her auburn hair clipped back and up with a barrette. Riley watched her adorable little fanny bounce in perfect cadence with the background music. She clapped her hands in sync with the videotape instructor, who was herself something to behold.

Between hand claps, Betsy wheezed out, "You're back early. How'd it go?"

"Fine . . . fine," said Riley, avoiding her eyes. He dropped onto the couch, lifting the newspaper high enough to cover his face.

Without losing her count or taking her eyes from the TV, she said, "Really? I heard you got booted from the program."

"Ah, shit," he said, dropping the newspaper, looking up as though he were about to be spanked. "Teddy didn't waste any time squealing on me, did he?"

"He didn't squeal on you, he just asked me what Dance Fever was. I figured out the rest when you got home two hours early, craftless, and calling me sweetheart in that suck-up voice." Still bouncing and clapping: "You've got to apologize to Mr. Krebsworth and get admitted to the chapter."

Looking stricken, Riley muttered, "I can't go back there. We were the first rejection in the history of the program. We weren't even in before we were out on our asses."

Betsy stopped exercising and looked over at him. "I don't suppose it's possible that you smarted off and alienated somebody."

Riley gave a pouty frown. "Well, maybe. But we just can't go back there."

"The school's going to wonder where you are when it comes time to display crafts in the gymnasium. How do we get past that?"

"I don't know," he whined, "but I'll do anything not be an outdoor scout."

"Oh, all right, if it's that bad, we'll find something to say." She flicked off the video and threw a towel over her shoulder. "But you have to promise to plan some alternative activity for Tuesday nights. Teddy needs a male influence. If he keeps hanging around with Lizzie and me, he'll end up the homecoming queen."

"Oh, I will, I will!" exclaimed Riley in a voice swollen with gratitude. Expelling a deep breath, he sank into the couch as Betsy headed for the shower.

After a moment of grateful reflection, he opened his tattered briefcase and began sorting through the remainder of the day's in-basket, including budget status reports, personnel memos, performance appraisals, resumes submitted by job-seekers, and countless cover-your-ass memos—the latter items having increased five-fold since inauguration of the downsizings.

By 9:30 P.M. he had reached the trade journals and periodicals. After skimming *The Insurance Times*, his eyes fell upon *The Gopher State Business Journal*, the cover of which contained a giant picture of Buck standing coatless in the Lobby Court, feet wide apart, hands on hips, sleeves rolled up, a determined get-down-to-business look on his face. The picture was shot at an upward angle, making him look like a figure off Mt. Rushmore. Riley eagerly turned to page 73:

THE LION OF THE LINDBERGH
J. Buckley Montrowe Takes Over

When J. Buckley ("Buck") Montrowe landed at the Minneapolis-St. Paul International Airport last December on a flight from Miami, the ground temperature was 2 degrees below zero, 20 degrees below wind chill. Entering the unmarked car provided by The Lindbergh Companies Board of Directors, he remarked sharply to the driver, "Why do you people live up here. I had forgotten how cold it gets!" And so began an odyssey that surprised a lot of people, not least of all Buck Montrowe himself.

Following the untimely death in a car accident of longtime CEO Wentworth Hall in mid-1995, Lindbergh stock suffered a small drop and then dropped more when the search for a replacement CEO dragged on longer than expected.

Reacting to widespread criticism directed at them personally, The Lindbergh Board, comprised of some of the area's most distinguished business luminaries, turned the heat up on its efforts to identify a replacement for Hall, who had been lauded as one of a handful of financial wizards in the insurance business and the man who had put the sleepy Lindbergh on Wall Street's "A" list of high-growth financial stocks.

After an exhaustive nationwide search failed to generate any interest amongst the cream of the insurance world, headhunters came up with Buck Montrowe, who was one of only a handful of insurance industry executives willing to come to St. Paul for an interview. Although never a household name in the industry (he spent most of his career on the production side of the business) Montrowe gained brief fame during a short tenure as CEO of Galaxy Life when he attempted a hostile takeover of a cross-town rival, only to have the target turn around and take a counter-run at Galaxy. In the end, a "White Knight" had to come in and save Galaxy from its own folly. Montrowe lost that battle but departed the company with a hefty parachute.

Following a top-secret meeting of the Lindbergh Board's search committee at a local downtown motel an offer was made to Montrowe and he accepted. And the rest, as they say, is history.

Buck Montrowe and his wife, Eileen, together with their family pets, Butch (an Irish Setter), Fifi (a French poodle), and Stud Boy, the family parrot, left their home in Boca Viejo, Florida, and hit the northbound Interstate for the frozen tundra of Minnesota. Raised in a family of evangelical preachers in the Deep South, Buck's only other connection to Minnesota was through his first wife, who had grown up in St. Paul, where her family still lives. That connection had landed him a five-year stint in the local mutual funds industry, where he established himself as a star salesman. But when the marriage went south, so did Buck, back to his native state of Florida. An eventual return to Minnesota, especially as the head of one of the state's oldest and most prestigious companies, would hardly have crossed his mind at the time of his earlier departure.

94

But returned he is. Known for decisiveness and a no-non-sense approach to business (and life) Buck purchased a home in the exclusive North Oaks area and was at his desk in The Lindbergh's fourth floor executive suite within two days of being hired. The harried Lindbergh public relations staff, used to the gentlemanly pace that has marked the Company's long history, was caught by surprise, barely having time to get out an abbreviated press release in advance of the new CEO's arrival. The top fifty Lindbergh managers were hurriedly convened for an introduction to their new boss and left in a state of mild shell shock when, skipping all niceties, Montrowe told them bluntly that things were changing "as of yesterday," that the days of leisurely work hours were over (making it clear that he expected them to emulate his own seventy-hour work week), and that those who found this change unappealing should submit their resignations to him by the end of the day.

A visibly pleased board of directors, speaking through lead director Hank Wallstead, expressed delight at the roll-up-your-sleeves, no-nonsense CEO they had chosen to lead the Company into the next century. It is widely known and acknowledged that the board is hoping to replicate the success of other local financial institutions such as Norwest Corporation, and First Bank System. The difficulties faced by those companies in the '80s and early '90s were far more serious than those at the present-day Lindbergh.

And how has it gone in the intervening months? Well, no one can doubt the trademark Montrowe expense reductions immediately put into play, including the elimination of every fourth Lindbergh employee, a step which the new CEO calls "regrettable but necessary to maintain a competitive position in today's world." Assuming that the company's base revenue-generating capabilities aren't materially impaired by the reduction in force—and no one at this point is arguing that they have—the cost savings from personnel eliminations alone should work miracles for the bottom line. And, sure enough, Wall Street seems to have endorsed these steps, awarding the Lindbergh a whopping half-billion in added market cap since Montrowe's arrival.

Other cost savings have been implemented with equal dispatch. In addition to across-the-board salary freezes, the employee cafeteria in the downtown St. Paul headquarters, which provided a line of healthy if unglamorous food to thousands of Lindbergh employees each month at affordable prices for the average worker, simply shut down one day, with a plain paper notice taped to the doorway directing employees to a new set of cash vending machines. A money-losing perk for low-level employees was thus transformed into a small profit center. Likewise, the longtime Lindbergh practice of providing a small cash subsidy for the purchase of mass transit bus passes was junked in favor of a memo from the human resources department explaining how to start a car pool—which, it said, would help build teamwork and strong morale among the workforce.

When asked about the cost-cutting, Buck Montrowe said that he had lived in a low-cost environment his whole life, including a long career in the insurance industry at a succession of companies noted for tight cost controls. "It is objectively right in the modern corporation to squeeze costs down to the bare essentials," said an enthusiastic Montrowe, "as long as the pain and the rewards are shared at all levels, right up through the CEO. That, in a nutshell, is my philosophy." While speaking, Montrowe swept his arm in a wide arc, inviting this reporter to note the austere furnishings spread about the room.

"See my desk chair?" said Montrowe (while flashing a curious facial expression that was frankly a little hard to interpret), "it's twelve years old, and the stuffing is popping out from all the use it's gotten. The board wanted me to get a new one—said it was beneath the status of a CEO—but I refused. If the ordinary employees of this company are going to suffer, by God I'm going to suffer right along with them!" And, indeed, there was stuffing exuding from his high-backed desk chair.

One couldn't help but be struck by the ferocious commitment of this hard-driving man, a man whom one executive referred to as the company's "alpha male," or as he has come to be known in the broader community, the Lion of the Lindbergh.

But Montrowe himself modestly deflects attention from his power status. "I'm a simple, straightforward guy," he says. "And I don't believe in company politics. With me, what you see is what you get. I put in 70 hours a week at that desk before even starting the social and community commitments that take up another 30 to 40 hours each week. I believe in leading by example." Now on his feet and pacing the room with frenetic energy, he continued: "I haven't had a vacation in three years. Luxuries and executive trappings are completely foreign to me. I keep my lifestyle like that of the common employees, to whom I am devoted. No big-shot stuff for me."

On the subject of morale and employee relations generally, Montrowe says The Lindbergh is really like a close-knit family. Standing at the window, striking a Lincolnesque pose, he said in a voice filled with emotion, "I think our new company motto, which I created, pretty much says it all: IN THAT SPIRIT OF HONOR AND WARM FELLOWSHIP THAT BINDS US ALL AS ONE, WE MOVE BOLDLY INTO THE FUTURE."

"An inspiration to me personally," is how Cole Girard, Wayzata resident and director of human resources, describes Montrowe. Sitting in his spacious fourth-floor office, Girard (who gained local fame a few years back as head of the Anti-Fascist League For A Free Nicaragua) says: "I've never worked for a man for whom I had greater admiration."

"He's a man's man," according to Garfield T. (he insists upon "Field") Blaisdahl, the holdover senior executive vice president and current chief of staff, and an obvious Montrowe enthusiast. Sitting at an ornate mahogany desk, an industrial-size air purifier whirring in the background, Blaisdahl says: "I think absolute genius would be the best way to describe him. Oh, he's tough, no doubt about that; but he's also fair. He doesn't believe in double standards; he works harder than anyone in the company at any level. And he has no time—excuse my French—for butt kissers or phonies."

These sentiments seem to be widely shared among executive management. Head of the prestigious executive services division, Robert C. ("call me Bobby") Morestad expresses a special appreciation for Montrowe's intolerance of substandard performance by employees: "With Buck, if you don't pass mustard you're out of here."

"Buck has worked out a strategic plan, which is being followed very carefully," says Erving Russell, the chief financial officer and sole executive to have accompanied Montrowe from his last assignment and the man rumored in some quarters to be the real brains and energy behind The Lindbergh's current success (a rumor he vigorously denies).

And according to Rick Snelling, who directs The Lindbergh Charitable Foundation, "We were looking at fourth down and long yardage. Buck Montrowe came into the game and called the plays that will take this hummer over the goal line."

While visiting informally after completion of the interview, this reporter noted an impressive array of photographs bearing witness to the high-powered relationships Buck Montrowe has forged over his long career. Modestly declining to discuss those friendships, he commented that "folks are just folks" no matter what their accomplishments. Some of his best friends are poor people, he volunteered. As he spoke, he stroked the cover of a large, leather-bound Bible, which sets forth, he said, the core values by which he lives.

Although no one dropped by during the interview, Montrowe couldn't resist highlighting a practice, uncommon among big time CEOs, that he calls his "Open Door Policy." That policy encourages any employee to stop by his office at any time to discuss his or her concerns. "They can say anything they want to me without fear of retribution, and they know it," he said proudly. "In the end, employees are just yearning to be heard and respected. I don't mean to brag, but I'm especially good at that—it's a gift the Lord has given me."

So there you have it. A lion is loose at The Lindbergh, and things are moving like never before. Whatever the future might hold, the new Lindbergh, with J. Buckley Montrowe running things, will never be the same.

Stay tuned, Minnesota. It should be exciting.

By: George Phimster
Staff Reporter

Not knowing whether to laugh or cry, Riley closed his brief-case, and raised himself from the couch. *Good God,* he thought, *about the only true statement in that article was that it's cold in Minnesota in the winter.* Discouraged, he turned off the lights and trudged upstairs. "Just try not to think about it," he muttered to himself while undressing.

As she slept on her side of the bed, Betsy's left hand and arm stood in a rigidly upright position, the book she was reading when she lost consciousness locked high in the air in a vice-like grip. This was the way he found her almost every night: frozen in a reading pose, her glasses crunched diagonally across her face. She looked like one of those volcanically preserved figures found in the ruins of Pompeii. Surrounding her on the bed were no less than ten books and writing pads. Tuffy was cuddled in the V created by the bend in her knees, giving his private parts a good scrubbing. The unwatched TV blared out the late-night talk show that had succeeded whatever had been on when sleep overtook her.

Riley pried the book from her frozen fingers, shut off the TV, and got into bed. When he turned off the light on his side, Betsy rolled over and nestled her buns up against his midsection. When he tried to cop a little feel, Tuffy sat up on his haunches and growled a low, steady, pre-attack warning. Too tired to deal with a deranged canine, Riley rolled over on his back and closed his eyes.

Apparently feeling bad about his rude behavior, Tuffy climbed up on Riley's chest and with the same tongue he had just used to clean his private parts gave Riley a big kiss, right on the mouth.

9

In that spirit of honor and warm fellowship that binds us all as one, on the following Tuesday Buck ordered the firing of another thousand members of the close-knit Lindbergh family. And he issued the order from a golf course in Boca Viejo.

Yearning to be heard and respected, several managers whose units had been decimated beyond recognition tried, under the open-door policy, to set an appointment with Buck to discuss the decision. They were told, by phone, to quit whining or they'd find their own asses out on the street.

Riley should probably have been relieved that only five employees reporting directly to him had to be fired this time around, and that of those two were eligible for generous retirement packages, and one other was happy to accept six month's salary and benefits on the way out of a company he had come to loathe. This left only one middle manager and one administrative assistant he would have to fire face-to-face.

The termination sessions were scheduled in fifteen-minute segments on Wednesday. The instructions in the blue-bordered envelope included a word-for-word script to be followed, without deviation, by the "terminating manager" when dealing with the "outbound units," as the employees slated for termination were labeled. Riley had committed the speech to memory: "(NAME OF OUTBOUND UNIT), I have some bad news for you today. As you know, the company has had to embark on a reduction-in-force, and your position is one of those being eliminated. The company has valued your services over the last (NUMBER OF YEARS OF SERVICE), and you should not interpret this job elimination as suggesting that your performance has been inadequate in any way. (NAME OF HR OFFICER), from Human Resources, is here to escort you to the Out-Placement Center on the third floor, where you will be provided additional information concerning severance pay and benefits and out-placement services. There is no need for you to return to your work station, and you should not do so. Your HR officer will collect your personal items and get them to you at the Out-Placement Center."

Unwilling to witness human suffering, especially when she knew the humans involved, Skeeter the coward stayed home with a one-day illness. Two HR "Termination Team" members, a woman (Dorothy) and a man (Arnold), showed up ten minutes before the first "termination transaction" was to begin. Both human resource veterans, they didn't enjoy participation in these "transactions" either, but had, by reason of their daily experience over the previous six months, developed a shell that pretty much deadened any feelings of tenderness or sympathy that might be aroused by scenes such as the one about to unfold. Beyond that, they were professionals, experts in human interaction, and should any compassion well up in their bosoms, it would be easily suppressed. Bearing the countenance of the neighborhood mortician, who wears a mournful expression while at the same time admiring the artistry of the embalming staff, they had compartmentalized their emotions and behaviors, knowing what manner and mood to adopt in each situation.

For the two employees about to be terminated, Dorothy had brought brightly colored cloth sacks labelled "Memory Bags," which contained pens, T-shirts, and other memorabilia of the employee's time with the company. Also included in the bag were a disposable camera for last photos of old friends and a tribute book in which other employees could, in the fashion of a high school yearbook, write short parting messages. Lastly, was an eight-by-ten glossy of a smiling Buck, autographed, and bearing a short inscription bidding a fond farewell to the person about to be canned.

"You pull that bag of sick trinkets out while I'm terminating these people, and I'll have your jobs before the end of the day," hissed Riley, nervous and unable to conceal his disgust. "Memory Bags, my ass. Those are body bags"

He knew, though, that it wasn't their fault, Arnold and Dorothy. They were probably almost as sickened by the whole thing as he was. He apologized nervously.

It was a sad, stormy day, with rain pounding against the tall stately windows as the players took their seats around the conference table. Arnold, who was tall and bald, and Dorothy, who was short with dark hair down to her waist, delivered a ten-minute tutorial on how to remain calm and detached through-out the "transaction" and how to avoid "entering into the pain of the outbound units." Riley had seen to the incarceration of hundreds of criminals in his days as a prosecutor—arsonists, armed robbers, women beaters, murderers—and had never had a problem with entering into the pain of the jailbound units. But this was different. He knew and liked these people, and they hadn't done anything wrong. Their sentences were unearned, unjust. And all the helpful tips in the world from these trained ghouls wouldn't make this duty any less odious.

And he couldn't shake off the sickening irony of these five employees—hardworking, decent human beings with families and dogs and mortgages—being sacrificed for a savings of $175,000 a year while so much more was being squandered on executive luxuries like rarely used country clubs and luxury automobiles. Or the hunting trips having nothing to do with business that Buck and a small group of accomplices took on a regular basis. Like the one the previous fall when his band of sportsmen ventured manfully into the wilderness (on the corporate jet), fortified by a quart of whiskey and armed with high-powered rifles, and blasted eight furry deer to kingdom come—all expenses paid by the "no frills" Lindbergh Life & Casualty Company.

At 10:00 A.M. sharp, with rain now pelting the windows, Don Washington tapped on the door and was invited to take a seat at the conference table. If Arnold and Dorothy were trying not to telegraph the purpose of the meeting, they had failed miserably. The grave, almost funereal tone with which they greeted Don, and the insipid, piteous smiles on their faces, could only have been interpreted one way. (In a Robspierrean irony, after eight and one-half months of faithfully carrying out the company's dirty work, Arnold and Dorothy were themselves axed in the next downsizing).

Don's facial muscles drooped, and his hands trembled as his fingers ran repetitively over a pin in the lapel of his suit jacket. The pin was a miniature of the Lindbergh logo. "What's up, Riley?" he asked, the quiver in his voice impeaching a brave exterior. Sixty-three years old, he had joined the company when Riley was still a college student. Prior to this morning, when he had gotten the unexplained call to come to Riley's office, it had never occurred to Don Washington that The Lindbergh would not see him through to retirement. But as he looked around the table he knew with a crushing certainty that the unexpected, the unthinkable, was about to happen.

Striving to avoid eye contact, Riley spoke the words of the prepared termination script as though reciting the requiem high mass. The slightest departure from the script, the most subtle expression of compassion, brought scolding looks from Arnold and Dorothy. As it turned out there wasn't much to talk about beyond the words of termination anyway, for Don Washington had slumped into a benumbed silence. When Dorothy helped him out of his chair for the journey to the outplacement center, he offered no resistance, expressed no anger or resentment. As their eyes met on his way out the door, Don's expression recalled the look Riley's mother had given him the day he left her at the nursing home in Minneapolis—the pleading look a child might give his parents when boarding a bus for the first day of school.

Rather than calming down, Riley was growing more rattled with each passing minute. So as not to prolong the ordeal, he determined to move as quickly as possible. Instead of waiting for Arnold to return from his stop at the bathroom, he called the receptionist on the twelfth floor and told her to have Donna come to his office. Donna arrived promptly and took a seat at the conference table with a confused look on her face. Unable to even look at Donna, his eyes glued to the ground, Riley launched into the scripted remarks: "Donna, I have some bad news for you today—" At this point Arnold walked into the room and, nodding to Donna, took a seat behind and to the right of her. After consulting the file folder before him, he tried to get Riley's attention by clearing his throat loudly.

Oblivious and with his eyes cast downward as he paced nervously, Riley continued: "As you know, the company has had to embark on a reduction in force—"

From his seat behind Donna, Arnold was now waving his hands in the air in a desperate attempt to get Riley's attention. Donna just stared at Riley with an intense, perplexed look.

"—and your position is one of those being eliminated," Riley pressed on.

Having at last caught Riley's eye, Arnold was excitedly slicing the index finger of his right hand across his throat while silently mouthing words that Riley couldn't make out. Arnold's lips moved in frantic, exaggerated motions.

Riley snapped, "What are you doing, Arnold?"

Donna turned in her chair to look at Arnold's ashen face.

"This is the wrong person, Riley! You're supposed to be talking to Jennifer."

Riley now saw for the first time that it was Donna, not Jennifer. A few seconds of throbbing silence passed, followed by Riley saying, "Donna . . . I am so sorry. I just terminated Don Washington, and I had the name Don on my mind, and I was so nervous I asked for Donna instead of Jennifer."

"Hell of a deal, Riley," said a shaken Donna. "My first near-death experience."

Arnold sat with his eyes closed, wiping moisture from his forehead.

Riley went over and sat next to her. "Donna, we've been friends a long time . . . please don't tell anyone about this. I'd never hear the end of it."

As she left the room Donna said, "Okay, Riley, but for God's sake lighten up, will ya, you're too damn nervous. You're going to make us all crazy." She shook her body as though experiencing a chill.

Arnold called upstairs for Jennifer as Riley leaned against the wall taking deep, heaving breaths.

A few minutes later Jennifer entered the room, took a seat at the conference table, and said matter-of-factly: "Hey, Riley, I hear you fired the wrong person."

Liddy Jonssen carried out the executions assigned to her in exact conformance with the termination script and associated materials provided by Human Resources. And she did it, by all appearances, with the iron will and unwavering sense of duty that characterized the dispassionate Scandinavian tradition. For all its unpleasantness, this was the job she had to do, and she wouldn't fail in her duty.

But it didn't feel so tidy or logical. There was something grotesque and ugly and unfair about it all. There were no slackers in her unit, no deadwood, no costly inefficiencies; those had been eliminated in the first two downsizings. The survivors were now going to have to work well beyond a full work week to cover the duties of those being terminated and at pay levels that not only didn't increase but actually lost ground through ordinary inflation. Unlike senior executives, whose workloads hadn't increased and who were awarded large stock options that became immediately more valuable as a result of the cost reductions, the ordinary employees of the company picked up all the back-breaking work and none of the rewards. And the fallout from screw-ups and angry customers that inevitably followed upon arbitrary decreases in employee resources would befall the surviving employees, making for even more tension and stress—not to mention the visceral certainty the surviving employees now possessed regarding their own expendability should the opportunity present itself to the planners on the fourth floor, who endlessly mouthed clichés about "running lean." How would they know? There were no "reductions in force" on the fourth floor. Buck Montrowe just mindlessly ordered across-the-board cuts without any regard for the effect on the employees down on the front lines—the ones who kept the company in business day after day.

And if she lived to be a hundred she would never forget the look on Jeannie Kelley's face, like she was being abandoned to an orphanage by an older sibling. Very little was actually said. Jeannie just stared at her. In that stare Liddy saw the three nights a week of "business college" and the early arrivals and late departures day after day, and the extra efforts for customers who liked her so much. But most of all she saw Jeannie's conviction, for which there were no words, that somehow, some way, Liddy could have kept her name off the execution list if she had cared enough—cared the way Jeannie thought she had.

In truth, Liddy had cared more deeply for her adored young friend than for perhaps anyone else in the world. But there was nothing she could have done; at least not anything honest and above board. So she acted on principle. But, oh, what a price.

It wasn't until after Jeannie left with her HR escort, having barely said a word, that Liddy closed the door and, gasping for breath, cringed in the corner of her office, near the bookcase, out of sight of the interior window, and sobbed uncontrollably. In a seizure of tears, her heart slammed against her chest and her legs became so weak she could barely maintain her balance. She wanted to call her mother, but there was no point in that. Margaret Jonssen was past understanding. And the phone number that kept passing through her mind was the family's nearly twenty years before when she was a girl, when her father was still alive.

Only the sound of people outside the door forced her to summon the composure needed to emerge from her corner and make for the desk. Through the window facing the teller stations she could see an HR staff person securing Jeannie's cash drawer and computer and gathering together her personal affects—purse, hair spray, photos of her niece, a small crucifix, a greeting card from the other tellers marking her one-year

106

anniversary with the group.

It was as though Jeannie had perished in an automobile accident, and her family was there collecting the small tokens of her life. A death chord sounded through Liddy's mind and body, hauntingly similar to that time in college when Vonnie Bjorndahl, barely eighteen and newly installed in the freshmen dormitory, was killed in a freak car accident on her way to a band concert in Faribault. A junior at the time, Liddy was the upper division resident advisor to the freshman dorm, and she had taken an immediate liking to the rosy-cheeked, giggly Vonnie. It fell to her (who only four months before had visited with and provided reassurance to Vonnie's parents, who would be separated from their only child for the first time) to help those same stricken parents clean out Vonnie's room.

As she watched Jeannie's purse and the precious remnants of her small work space being thrown impersonally into a cardboard box, she reexperienced to the smallest detail the dreadful sensations that accompanied Vonnie Bjorndahl's death, augmented here by a heartsinking sense of personal responsibility. An ordinary suspicion of some nameless guilt on her part was being transformed by her fatigued and overheated imagination into an absolute certainty that she was somehow responsible for this life-changing wound inflicted on Jeannie Kelley, a young woman who had loved and trusted her. She felt herself sinking into a terrifying despair. My God, why did life, existence, consciousness, have to be so painful?

As he passed through the richly appointed reception area of the executive floor, Riley was still smarting from his screw-up that morning. Off to his left he noticed Judy Goodrich, a good-hearted young woman with bad skin and no taste in clothes, sniffling quietly as she dropped personal items from the receptionist's desk into her gunnysack-style purse. A cartoonish cat's face with giant whiskers was sewn on the front of the purse.

Judy was the part-time receptionist on the fourth floor, where she filled in as necessary for the elegant and well-spoken Renee

Douglas, the highly paid, eye-catching beauty normally found at the front desk welcoming important persons arrived to see fourth-floor executives. When not backing up Renee the beautiful, Judy supported other fourth-floor secretaries in need of temporary help. She was kind of a roving girl Friday.

Judy's tears surprised Riley, as he had been led to understand that, consistent with the double standard rigorously applied in previous downsizings, the fourth floor would be untouched by this latest reduction.

Leaning over the marble ledge of the receptionist's station where he and Goodie (as she was known by her friends) had shared many a giggle over the previous two years, not a few of which related to the boyish mischief of Teddy McReynolds, he said, "Goodie, I'm so sorry you've been caught up in this thing. It surprises me. I thought the fourth floor was immune."

Dabbing the corners of her eyes with tissue pulled from a small container next to the phone panel, she turned her head toward Riley and in a quivering voice said, "I didn't get laid off, Riley, I got fired. It had nothing to do with the downsizing."

After a brief, confused silence, Riley asked, "Who fired you, Goodie?"

"Mr. Blaisdahl," she replied through tears.

"For what reason?" he asked. Riley knew the decorous Mr. Blaisdahl had always been offended and a little embarrassed by the frumpy and unlovely presence of Judy Goodrich at the fourth-floor reception desk, a location that he thought called for style and sophistication.

"He found out I had made a few long-distance calls to my aunt in Connecticut from this phone, and he said it was 'thievery' and 'a violation of the company's code of conduct.'" As she collapsed into her desk chair, her sniffling grew into short gasping sobs, making her words hard to make out. "God, Riley, I'm so ashamed. It was only three times—and they were short conversations. I know it was wrong, and I offered to reimburse the twelve-dollars. But he wouldn't take it—he just kept saying 'stealing can't be tolerated.' It's . . . so mean to call me a thief . . ."

Riley felt his body begin to shake as the blood rushed from under his collar and up his neck. Leaning over the ledge so that

his eyes were even with hers he said in slow, distinctly pronounced words combining anger with reassurance: "Goodie,
you're no thief. Take your personal things and leave them under
Skeeter's desk. Then go home for the rest of the day. Do *not* sign
any resignation or exit forms no matter who asks you to. I'll call
you at home tonight and let you know what to do next."

Her face was covered with displaced eye makeup running in
thin streams down her cheeks. One line of dark eye shadow,
carried along by a flow of tears, navigated around a nostril and
disappeared into the corner of her mouth. The expression on
Riley's face as he moved closer to her demanded confirmation
that she would trust him and follow his instructions. Goodie
nodded a tearful concurrence.

In his office, Riley dialed Gar Blaisdahl's number without
sitting down.

"Office of senior executive vice president and chief of staff
Field Blaisdahl," answered Nancy Park, Gar's administrative
assistant.

"Nancy, let me talk to Gar," said Riley.

"Hi, Riley," she groaned. "He's not taking any calls." Nancy
was a good egg, a pal of Skeeter's.

"Why not?" asked Riley.

"He's taking a nap," she replied.

"A *nap!* I'm coming over there."

"Well, I'm not supposed to let anyone in . . . but if you just
walked in, I suppose there'd be nothing I could do about it,"
she said.

When Riley simultaneously knocked and entered Gar
Blaisdahl's palatial Sacristy suite, he caught him stretched out
on a long couch at the far end of his oversized office.

"What the hell do you think you're doing, barging in here
without permission?" shouted Gar as he scrambled to his feet
like an adolescent boy caught in an impure act.

"Gar, tell me how Judy Goodrich came to be fired this
morning," said Riley as he moved toward the now wide awake
Mr. Blaisdahl.

Straightening his tie nervously and scurrying to a position
behind his giant mahogany desk, Gar replied, "That fatso has

109

never fit in here. Not a good fit. Just doesn't project the image we're looking for." He dropped into his plush leather desk chair. "Just not a good fit," he repeated while fidgeting with his tie clip. "Not that it's any of your business, McReynolds."

"Not a good fit, Gar?" said Riley as he moved toward the desk. "You've been cutting her up behind her back ever since she arrived on the floor. Didn't anybody ever tell you that being homely is not grounds for termination?"

Gar commenced puttering self-consciously with a pile of papers in his in-basket. Not looking up and trying to strike a pose of indifference: "I don't have to explain anything to you. You don't run this place, McReynolds. But it might interest you to know that you're defending a thief."

"A thief! You mean three long distance phone calls in four months. $12.00 worth!"

"Stealing is stealing," said Gar in a voice bloated with virtue and far too controlled to be sincere. "And stealing has to be routed out, wherever it is found."

"This doesn't have anything to do with stealing, and you know it. This is about you not wanting a plain woman desecrating your image of the Sacristy. And you're willing to brand a decent human being a 'thief' to cover up your own appalling elitism. You're a snob, Gar. And worse yet, you're a bully." He now moved closer to Gar's desk, his face flushed a dark red. "I hate bullies, Gar."

Garfield Blaisdahl now shriveled protectively behind his desk. "Think whatever you want, Riley, but stealing is still stealing," he said as he turned a page of the document he was pretending to read, in what he hoped would be seen as a sign of composure. But Riley could see his mouth tighten and one of his cowlicks straining to break loose.

Taking a seat next to the desk, Riley put his face close enough to Gar's to cause him to lean back in his leather swivel chair. "Well then, senior executive vice president and chief of staff Field Blaisdahl, I'm going to join your crusade for moral rectitude, and before the sun sets on another day I'm going to 'rout' out all forms of larceny and corruption in this company, and I'm going to start with your phone records for the last three years. And when I'm done with those, I'm going to fly-speck your expense reports for the same period. And you better hope I don't find any improper charges, or I'm going to rout your sorry ass right out the front door." He got out of the chair and moved toward the door. "And you better pray that I don't find thousands of dollars worth of wrongful charges—of any description—or I may go across the street and visit my old pal, the County Attorney, in which event you may be spending the better part of the next five years breathing shit molecules up at the state prison. Think about it, Field."

Gar leaped from his chair and advanced angrily toward Riley, his face flushed, his fists clenched.

This was what Riley was hoping for. He turned his body to face Gar, a make-my-day smile lighting up his face. *Please, God, let him throw a punch . . . just one small punch*, he prayed as his right hand curled into a fist and his eyes sparkled with anticipation.

When he moved his left foot slightly forward into a preparatory stance, Gar stopped dead in his tracks and then back-pedaled rapidly toward his desk.

Riley relaxed his hands and shook his head. "You're a real piece of shit, Gar. You know that, don't you?"

Gar said nothing. He just stood behind his desk shaking and pointing at the door.

As Riley passed Nancy Park's desk (her eyes like saucers, hands over her mouth) Gar could be heard shouting hysterically, "Your attitude has been noticed, ya know. Oh, yes, it's been noticed, and not just by me! You'll see, McReynolds!"

10

Giving a weary look to the hot rollers on the beige marble counter in her bathroom, Liddy marveled at the precipitous freefall her spirits had taken from the time she awoke barely fifteen minutes before. If only she could avoid thinking, put off any mental activity, for a longer period each morning. At least until she picked up the rhythms of the day. Just long enough to marshal her depleted emotional resources, get some nourishment, maybe, and enter into the distractions of the job before her mind started serving up dark scenarios— some real, some imagined.

She had worked until ten o'clock the night before just to close out the day's essential tasks. The downsizings had left her with the work of two, not a good thing for a person with perfectionist tendencies. She had ceased liking the company, at least insofar as it was embodied by the new senior management, having come to view it as cold and mean. But it was a job she knew how to do, and it paid a living wage. And in her weakened state how could she possibly move anywhere else? The very thought of moving made her heart sink. That was one of the grim paradoxes of downsizing. It wasn't masochism. It was a creeping form of paranoia and vulnerability inherent in the process. She felt locked into a sick dependence on the company, like that of a battered spouse on her abuser.

The snappy banter of her favorite radio talk show, which used to have her in stitches by this time each morning, now fell flat upon her ears. She could no longer see the humor in their wisecracks. And yet she knew that, objectively speaking, they must be as funny now as they were a few months before. It had to be her. In this new dark, unlit frame of reference, these once-funny people seemed foreign to her, out of place. Like jesters in a sick room.

She looked back wistfully, even nostalgically, at her un-made bed. These feelings didn't make sense. How could she feel nostalgia for an experience less than fifteen minutes old? The rumpled bed sheets and toasty comforter beckoned her back. But even if she had the time (which she clearly did not), her sleep cycle had run its full course. That cycle, she had noticed, was getting shorter and shorter in recent weeks. Getting back into bed now, with her obsessive thinking and anxiety level climbing skyward, would be unbearable. She had tried that once last week, but her heart had pounded so force-fully that she could feel her body actually causing the mattress to shake.

An aching, swirling despondency seemed to be drawing her down into a deep hollow. She felt like a wounded bird fallen from a tree, lying helpless and terrified on ground traveled by predators. It had come upon her so fast this time, this awful disease with the inadequate name. She sat on the edge of the bathtub and sobbed.

Twenty minutes later she made her way to the kitchen. No longer able to keep down solid food in the morning, she had abandoned a lifetime practice of consuming a farmer's break-fast of bacon, eggs, and orange juice in favor of forcing down some awful milk-soluble powdered concoction containing essential vitamins and minerals.

The morning paper had also lost its flavor, seeming to be lit-tle more than a parade of horrors. Everything seemed to be crime or accidents or negativity of one type or another. She became the characters in the news accounts, the boundaries between them having collapsed. Even the stories that were supposed to be inspirational and uplifting seemed to arouse a sadness of horrible poignancy. She pushed the paper off the kitchen table into the wastepaper basket, poured the powdered drink into the sink, and got into her car for the drive to St. Paul.

Liddy's underground parking privileges had been eliminated in the first wave of cost reductions, forcing her to park in a municipal ramp halfway across town. In the morning she had to allow an extra twenty minutes for the walk, which wasn't so bad. But at night she left long after the flow of day-end traffic. The municipal ramp was almost vacant most nights by the time she got there. Only the people of the night were out.

She ducked around the protesters in the Lobby Court on the way to the back entrance of the S&L. She then passed by the entrance to the ornate hallway, flanked by tall marble pillars, leading to the offices of the Lindbergh Trust Company, the subsidiary overseeing many of the region's great fortunes. Clouded in secrecy to protect the privacy of its wealthy patrons, the Trust Company was housed separately from the more public consumer areas. As an employee working in the general vicinity, however, Liddy regularly saw prominent customers coming and going down this hallway as she passed by on the way to her office.

By this time she was starting to feel a small measure of emotional strength taking shape. Body chemicals, neurotransmitters, whatever, stimulated by the sounds and smells of the workplace, were providing a little energy and everyday courage. Casting a routine glance down the hall, she caught sight of a young man engaged in a parting handshake with a senior trust officer as they walked in tandem through the ten-foot-high cherrywood doors of the Trust reception area. Although dressed now in a tie and sportcoat, she instantly recognized him as the money launderer who had threatened her the previous week.

Why now? she thought as her heart started to race involuntarily. She had secretly prayed that he would never be identified, that the whole thing would just go away. For a moment she considered not reporting seeing him. A report now would almost surely result in his being identified and probably arrested. She'd be dragged into an ugly mess that she just wanted to forget. But if she backed away, failed in her duty, he would win; intimidation would have paid off.

She took a deep breath and made for the phone in the lobby. With her heart in her throat, she twice entered the wrong set of numbers before reaching Skeeter.

"Mr. McReynolds's office, Ms. Swenson speaking," answered Skeeter.

"Skeeter, this is Liddy. I've got to come up there right away," she said in a trembling voice, gasping for air.

"Whoa, Liddy, calm down. What's happening?" said Skeeter. Liddy had always been the controlled one, poised and focused, the one in college who drove the drunks home and calmly pleaded their case before the disciplinary committee. Skeeter was the excitable one. The sudden role reversal threw her off balance.

"I just saw that creepy guy Riley was asking me about last week. He's down here on the first floor—" her sentence was broken by an involuntary swallow, "—in the Trust Department." Liddy twisted in her chair, looking around restlessly like a person losing her place in line.

When Riley returned from a breakfast meeting with the company's outside auditors, Liddy and Skeeter were sitting outside his office.

Flashing a warm smile: "Hey, you two, what is this, a class reunion? The sacred and the profane?" Liddy raised her head, showing a face like a frightened animal's. Skeeter's look was quizzical and worried.

"Come on in," said Riley, switching automatically to the soothing, reassuring tone he had used hundreds of times when meeting with crime victims in connection with a prosecution.

Liddy sat in a brown sidechair in front of a panel of bookshelves, to the left of a massive and ancient window. Skeeter grabbed a chair from around the conference table and sat next to her, her chair pulled so close that their bodies touched.

Liddy looked up at Riley. "I saw the guy we talked about last week—you know, the money launderer." She took a deep breath as though deprived of oxygen. "He was meeting with Harry Callinan at Trust."

After hearing the brief update Liddy had to offer, Skeeter accompanied her downstairs and stayed long enough for Liddy to calm down. Riley placed a call to Harry Callinan, pulling him out of a staff meeting.

"Harry , this is Riley McReynolds up on four."

"Hey, Riley, how ya doin'?" he said. He didn't get many calls from the fourth floor.

"Fine, Harry, just fine. Say, I need the name of the guy you were escorting out of the Trust reception area about twenty minutes ago."

"Sure, that was Brad Crosshaven, one of Ward Crosshaven's sons. You know, Woodward Vinehill Crosshaven himself, owner of Crosshill Enterprises." His voice contained a touch of pride. It gave him pleasure to drop the name of a Crosshaven, the family that was, by any measure, the company's largest and best customer. Every officer in the company who interacted with a Crosshaven was known personally to Buck. Should Ward Crosshaven pass on a kind word, an officer's career could undergo a meteoric rise.

"What does young Crosshaven have going at Trust, Harry?"

"He's a beneficiary of a whole series of trusts set up by his parents, and he was in looking to make a withdrawal from principal."

"Did you allow the withdrawal?"

"No, we didn't. His father has let us know that he doesn't want the kid to have uncontrolled access to the funds, apparently because of some drug problems in the past. Hell, he's twenty-five and has been in and out of trouble several times. He likes cocaine quite a bit. His father's worried about funding his habit." Harry's voice changed noticeably in the middle of the last sentence as he realized that he was talking freely about one of the most confidential subjects in the Trust Department. He naturally assumed that because Security reported to Riley and because Riley was thought to be close to Buck, there was no problem in laying out this information. But when he grasped how far he had gone, he started choking on his words. He abruptly cut off the conversation, referring any further questions to Buck's office.

116

Not wanting to put Harry on the spot and figuring he had what he needed anyway, Riley thanked him and hung up.

Walking through the Sacristy to Buck's office, Riley approached Gladys, who was busy making veterinary appointments for Buck's dogs, Butch and Fifi. They were having some air sickness problems.

"Is Buck in, Gladys?" asked Riley.

"Nope," replied Gladys, a woman of few words.

"Where is he, Gladys?" asked Riley in an exaggerated but unfailingly polite voice.

"Someplace where he can't be reached," said Gladys, tilting her head and squinting her eyes as if to say that try as he might he was never going to find out.

"Can you reach him and have him call me?"

"Nope," said Gladys. "He's inaccessible."

"I have something important, Gladys. When's he coming back?"

"If you have something important, Riley, go see Erving Russell. You know that's where you'll end up anyway." She said this in a slow, read-my-lips kind of voice.

"This matter has to be taken up with Buck, Gladys. When is he coming back? Is he returning for tomorrow morning's board meeting?"

"Yup," said Gladys as she picked up the ringing phone to talk with the veterinarian's office. As he walked away, Riley heard her say, "That's right, air sickness! Can't you understand plain English?"

Wally was watching a Charlie's Angels rerun when Riley turned the corner and popped his head in the door of his small office. The angels were working undercover at a massage parlor. "Where's Buck, Wally?"

"Fishing in Oregon," said Wally. Without taking his eyes from the TV screen, he shook his head longingly and said, "My God, Riley, would you look at those tits."

11

_____

F riday was a sunny day. The unseasonably cool air invested the landscape with added clarity as Riley drove to work. He arrived at 6:45 A.M. in order to see to last-minute details in preparation for the meeting of The Lindbergh Board of Directors scheduled for later that morning.

Turning on the overhead lights in his office, he spied a plain brown envelope propped up on his desk chair. On the flap of the envelope were the words: "From a Friend." He frowned with curiosity as he placed his briefcase on the desk and picked up the envelope, tearing it open as he sat down. Inside was a confidential memo from Gar to Buck, which someone had secretly copied and sent on to him:

MEMO
To: J. Buckley Montrowe CONFIDENTIAL
Fr: Field T. Blaisdahl
Re: Riley McReynolds

Chief -
This memo is in confidential follow-up to my recent comments to you. To underscore the seriousness of this issue, I wish to dialogue further and to background you on a few facts that I consider important. I firmly believe that one

118

NON-TEAM PLAYER, irregardless of his ability, can ruin the great advancements made possible by your splendid leadership.

You know me well enough to know that I believe in confronting facts and people head on, calling a spade a spade right out in the open. Therefore, I feel badly talking about a fellow executive behind his back, but I bow to your wise council to not publicly raise this kind of issue. I have spent more time gathering my thoughts and believe that Riley McReynolds is a negative force in the company because of his overly moralistic attitude. He is a man that feels life is some kind of "fairness" crusade, and never tires of advising you and I on what we should and shouldn't do. No matter what the technical accuracy of his criticisms may be, he obviously has no appreciation of the practical distinctions between high-level executives and ordinary workers, and why those distinctions justify, indeed mandate, that people in our positions not be bound by corporate policies designed for the rank-and-file. As you, with your super-incredible way of getting to the heart of a matter, have said on more than one occasion—he just doesn't get it!!

As one example of the problems someone like this can create, he recently openly interfered in my disciplining of a receptionist, making it impossible for me to carry out a carefully devised managerial strategy with respect to the aforesaid employee. Because the receptionist was one of the low-level employees he's always chumming around with, he decided to intervene in a matter completely outside his authority, which is something that high-quality executives know never to do! This is a totally unique situation in my experience. Because McReynolds reports to you, and I therefore have no authority over him, I haven't been able to do anything, and I haven't (until now) wanted to distract you from your single-minded mission of leading this Company, a job that absorbs 150% of your time and energy.

But the time has come when my loyalty to you requires that I warn that McReynolds's high-minded attitude could cause us big problems down the line.

The affect of his actions is the appearance of confusion and lack of solidarity among the senior executive ranks, all

119

because of one moralizing nay-sayer who has become like a giant mosquito bite that we have to constantly itch. I also believe that whatever steps are taken to address this problem should be embarked upon carefully, as he is popular with the lower and middle ranks. Without any notice to him, McReynolds's personnel file should be incrementally annotated to reflect his attitude problems.

Let's hope this situation can be resolved without to much trouble. As always, I stand ready to boldly address any situation you might assign to me. I am convicted that if anyone has the skill and wisdom to get the job done it is you!

P. S. - After reviewing my comments, please convey them straight to the fourth floor shredder!!!

Riley examined the handwriting on the envelope to see if he could identify the Friend who had managed to get a bootleg copy of the memo to him. The list of candidates—persons in the immediate vicinity of Gar and Buck—was fairly short unless someone in the interoffice delivery system had intercepted a copy, which was unlikely. And the handwritten notation was in block letters, almost like a child's printing. Nancy Park was the most likely suspect, but that seemed too obvious. And too risky for her personally.

He sat back in his chair for a moment, absorbing the implications of this cowardly attack. While it was true that Buck's arrogance had grown along with the increasing stock price and he was getting testier about some of Riley's recent criticisms, it was surprising that he'd entertain this kind of crap.

He postponed judgment on that larger question, feeling a small rush of glee at finding himself so squarely in opposition to Gar Blaisdahl. When on the opposite side of any issue from Gar it was hard not to succumb to moral and intellectual pride.

With a naughty smile he took pen in hand and marked up his copy of the memo for return to Gar:

MEMO
To: J. Buckley Montrowe   CONFIDENTIAL
Fr: Field T. Blaisdahl
Re: Riley McReynolds

Chief -

This memo is in confidential follow-up to my recent comments
to you. To underscore the seriousness of this issue, I wish to *also not*
dialogue further and to background you on a few additional facts *a verb.*
that I consider important. I firmly believe that one NON-TEAM
PLAYER, irregardless of his ability, can ruin the great *Not even*
advancements made possible by your splendid leadership. *a word.*

Not a verb.

You know me well enough to know that I believe in
confronting facts and people head on, calling a spade a spade right
out in the open. Therefore, I feel badly talking about a fellow *You talk badly,*
executive behind his back, but bow to your wise council to not *you golf badly,*
publicly raise this kind of issue. I have spent some time gathering *and, God knows*
my thoughts and believe that Riley McReynolds is a negative force *you write*
in the company because of his overly moralistic attitude. He is a *badly, but*
man that feels life is some kind of "fairness" crusade, and never *you feel*
tires of advising you and I on what we should and shouldn't do. *bad.*
No matter what the technical accuracy of his criticisms might be,
he obviously has no appreciation of the practical distinctions
between high-level executives and ordinary workers, and why
those distinctions justify, indeed mandate, that people in our
positions not be bound by corporate policies designed for the
rank-and-file. As you, with your super-incredible way of getting to *Did you*
the heart of a matter, have said on more than one occasion -- he *really say*
just doesn't get it!! *Lighten up on these !!!* *this?*

Counsel

who

me

As one example of the problem someone like this can create, he
recently openly interfered in my disciplining of a receptionist,
making it impossible for me to carry out a carefully devised
managerial strategy with respect to the aforesaid employee.

121

Because the receptionist was one of the low-level employees he's always chumming around with, he decided to intervene in a matter completely outside his authority, which is something that high quality executives know never to do! This is a totally unique situation in my experience. Because McReynolds reports to you, and I therefore have no authority over him, I haven't been able to do anything, and I haven't (until now) wanted to distract you from your single-minded mission of leading this Company, a job that absorbs 150% of your time and energy.

How would you know?

No degrees of uniqueness.

I'm surprised to hear you say this. Your wife says that at home you refer to Buck as "Mr. No-Show"

But the time has come when my loyalty to you requires that I warn that McReynolds's high-minded attitude could cause us big problems down the line.

Really?

effect (automatic "F")

The affect of all this is the appearance of confusion and lack of solidarity among the senior executive ranks, all because of one moralizing nay-sayer who has become like a giant mosquito bite that we have to constantly itch. I also believe that whatever steps are taken to address this problem should be embarked upon carefully, as he is popular with the lower and mid-level employees with whom he is always fraternizing. Without any notice to him, McReynolds's personnel file should be incrementally annotated to reflect his attitude problems.

Scratch

Is this double-secret probation?

Let's hope this situation can be resolved without to much trouble. As always, I stand ready to boldly address any situation you might assign to me. I am convicted that if anyone has the skill and wisdom to get the job done, it is you!

too (another automatic "F")

You may be convicted. The audit of your expense reports so far shows $67,000 in unexplained items, including $1,800 in personal phone calls.

PS - After reviewing my comments, please convey them straight to the fourth floor shredder!!!

after reviewing my comments, please convey them straight up your ass.

Garfie — There's a course in remedial English being offered over at Vo-Tech. If you can get your nose out of Buck's fanny long enough, you might want to enroll.

Your Pal, Riley

Giggling like a schoolboy, Riley sealed the interoffice envelope, addressed it to Field T. Blaisdahl and placed it in the inter-office mail basket.

Heavy curtains of a steel-wool consistency flanked the borders of the giant leaded-glass windows in the newly renamed J. Buckley Montrowe Room, where the monthly meetings of The Lindbergh Board of Directors took place. Stationed at the receptionist's desk outside the board room was the beautiful and well-spoken Renee Douglas. Judy Goodrich, who had been reinstated the previous afternoon on the unchallenged instructions of Riley, had been banished to the back room by Gar Blaisdahl in order not to befoul the scenery on board day.

Twelve white men with resumes to choke a horse gathered in clusters, sipping coffee and fruit juice, enlivened by each other's company and the power—ordained by law but rarely exercised—possessed by them as a group. As with all publicly held corporations, these directors had the legal authority (and formal legal duty) to determine the course set by the company, including all significant managerial issues. In spite of this clearly defined power—and in step with the vast majority of . their peer companies—once the board had chosen a chief executive officer, most directors saw their continuing role as largely pro forma. As a practical matter, they viewed their principal remaining duty to be to monitor the company's stock price, adhering generally to the reductionist principal that, in the absence of outright fraud by management, an increasing stock price meant management was doing a good job, and a decreasing or even flat stock price meant just the opposite. To achieve nominal compliance with their legal duty to manage, or at least direct management of the "business and affairs" of the corporation, they relied on the senior officers of the company—the very people they were charged with supervising—to see to it that a documented paper trail was created to evidence, or at least suggest, that they had given careful consideration to a long list of items relating to proper board oversight, such as responsible stewardship of corporate assets, observance of applicable laws and regulations, and fair and lawful dealings with customers and employees.

The Lindbergh Board was not exceptional in its attitudes or practices. There existed throughout corporate America an unwritten understanding that, unlike their British counterparts, American boards would have little to do with the detailed management of a company's affairs. Directors of domestic corporations by and large owed their board seats to the chief executive officer, and to offend the reigning CEO by leveling criticism in the face of a healthy stock price was considered not only bad form but risky in terms of losing one's board seat and the roughly $100,000 a year compensation package that went along with it.

The yawning gap between a board's legal accountability and the nominal time expended (approximately six hours a month during ordinary times) was nevertheless not a cause of anxiety for most directors. And reliance on the single measurement of stock performance was to a large extent well placed. Shareholders and regulatory agencies tended to settle into a contented mindset when earnings were high. They became aggressive and unfriendly only when poor performance threatened to inflict financial loss or some form of embarrassment on them personally. So far in the tenure of Buck Montrowe, the stock price had undergone a hefty increase, thereby inoculating him against much in the way of director criticism.

For his part, Buck viewed the board with deep ambiguity. On the one hand, they were the people who set his compensation and to whom he owed at least nominal accountability, but on the other hand he had trouble respecting a group so easily manipulated, especially the rank and file directors who seemed to have an almost unlimited capacity to absorb whatever line he chose to put out. Still, he knew he had to deal with the three or four directors who formed the board's core leadership and who were generally willing to tolerate his more questionable practices.

Though Riley was initially surprised by the indifference of the board as a group, he did not regard them as lazy or disreputable but rather as people who had other, more important, things to do in their own companies and who were following a generally accepted corporate formula. He felt confident that for all the mischief to which the core leadership was willing to turn a blind eye, they would not permit any serious wrongdoing to go unaddressed. That safeguard seemed to be the irreducible, core function of any legitimate board.

The mood was upbeat as the directors assembled. Clusters of two and three formed around the room with the largest group standing beside a long table on which were arranged coffee, rolls, doughnuts, and assorted fruits, all selected in accordance with the previously expressed wishes of the more fastidious directors. Railroad magnate and lead director William Henry "Hank" Wallstead, a tall man with stringy blonde hair, threw a major snit-fit a year earlier when the caterers switched from glazed to powdered-sugar doughnuts. That switch had been made in response to a health-related criticism leveled by director Charles Kleinwick, president and CEO of The Riverdale Soap Company of Central Iowa (known locally as the "Soap King of Des Moines"). Charles Kleinwick was not to be confused with director Charles Tallescher, a small man who headed a lumber concern in western Colorado and who did everything Charles Kleinwick told him to do. He was referred to out of earshot as Charles the Lesser.

Charles Kleinwick was a tall, stocky man with dark hair shot through with gray, and he wore cowboy boots under his suit pants. He was not a very nice man when dealing with people less important than himself, and he had lodged a series of phone complaints over the years to Riley. Apart from the doughnut controversy, he had weighed in on the temperature in the board room (too cold), the allocation of time for agenda items (too long), and the brand of liquid soap being used in the fourth-floor men's room (not Riverdale). Skeeter was the unlucky person to field most of these calls, and, believing the Soap King to be only human, she treated him with the good-natured irreverence she visited upon everyone. He, feeling that she was insufficiently awestruck by his rank and status, spoke to her during one call in an especially rude and patronizing manner. This in turn caused Skeeter to tell him he was acting like "a real dickhead." The Soap King had never been called a dickhead before, and he knew instantly that it was not a compliment. But something in Skeeter's voice, some inflection, some effortless spontaneity, some natural goodness, seemed to jar him out of his arrogance, at least when dealing with her. From that point forward, he would speak only to Skeeter. The big lug was crazy about her.

Gar Blaisdahl circulated through the room, working the director clusters, laughing hysterically at their jokes, thrusting at each the handshake that had catapulted him years before into the vice-presidency of his high school senior class.

The closing of the heavy, opaque curtains by Gladys (who entered the room for this sole purpose and spoke to no one) signaled the impending arrival of Buck, who had returned to town that morning from his fishing trip. Riley's head tacked in a southerly direction as he followed Gladys's hair clump across the room.

Prior to entering the boardroom, Buck preened before a full-length mirror in the private bathroom adjoining his office. He unbuttoned his shirt collar, loosened his tie until it sat at a careless angle, mussed his hair slightly, and tried on several facial expressions before settling upon one that he hoped would capture the look of a hardworking executive. At Gladys' desk he scooped up a pile of materials prepared for him by Erving Russell as a kind of cribsheet. He also instructed Gladys to have the company jet waiting for him after the meeting to fly him and Butch and Stud boy home to Boca Viejo.

The director clusters broke apart as Buck entered the room, the desultory talk stopping abruptly like the cessation of an orchestra's tune up. As he strutted across the broad expanse of the room, Buck had the air of a field commander taking time out from a back-breaking schedule at the front lines to brief the general staff back at HQ. The directors headed for their chairs, and the executive officers took their seats along the west wall under a formal portrait of Thaddeus Lindbergh, who had been the company's chairman in 1934. The portrait was partially illuminated by an overhead fixture missing a side panel, causing most of its light to spill uselessly onto the dark paneling, leaving half the former chairman's face in the dark. Several months before, Gar had proposed that the portrait be replaced by one of Buck and Eileen, but this was too much even for Buck.

Directors took their assigned seats around a large table, with Hank Wallstead seated to the right of Buck and Charles the Lesser to the right of Hank. On Buck's left was the retired major general, an unsmiling gray eminence sitting ramrod straight as though awaiting a Pentagon briefing. Across the table in a direct line from Buck sat Grant Sumter, a middle-aged, manufacturing CEO, who combined a quick business mind with a social conscience, making him somewhat of an oddity in the world of big business. He was the most assertive of a group of three directors who believed strongly that corporations in general, and The Lindbergh in particular, had wide-ranging moral and social obligations.

Joining Grant Sumter in this small circle of "bleeding heart wussies" (as Buck called them) were Aaron Herschel, CEO of a privately held food company, and Gil Chesterton, CEO of a natural gas company in Wyoming. Occasionally aligning themselves with the group were J. T. Cahill, professor of business at a local private college, and Frank Fulton, an elder in the Methodist Church. Because of their small numbers, the group posed little threat to Buck's views of how a business should be run. Though polite and deferring to them in public, he spent little time concerning himself with their idealistic and impractical opinions.

Seated immediately to the left of Grant Sumter was Buck's idea of the perfect director: Cosmo Towers. A large-framed, hard-of-hearing septuagenarian, he was the retired CEO of a rubber company in Lansing, Michigan, an important market territory for the company. Atop his head sat a toupee so chunky and artless that it looked like a stocking cap two dogs had fought over that morning. He was kept on the board for geographical diversity and because he was so far gone in the head he didn't make a fuss about anything. In fact, he slept through the bulk of each meeting.

In front of each director sat a loose-leaf binder of board materials for the day's meeting, assembled neatly in a dark green leather notebook, together with a copy of the newly published Lindbergh Annual Report, filled with glossy pictures of smiling models posing as contented Lindbergh employees sitting in the plush lobbies of company facilities. It was a beautiful site for anyone who couldn't read, for the printed text (as legally required) described the human slaughter that had taken place over the previous six months.

Riley took a seat next to Cole Girard, the head of human resources, making sure to select a seat upwind from Tom Arden, who had planted himself next to Gar Blaisdahl and was eagerly downing a bottle of highly carbonated mineral water in large, eye-watering gulps.

"Nice sunny day, huh, Cole?" remarked Riley, smiling pleasantly.

"Not in Gwat-tee-maala, it isn't," replied Cole a little indignantly.

"Gwat-tee-maala?" asked Riley, faintly confused. "What happened to Neek-hair-aak-waa?"

Cole shook his head in sorrow. "There are problems of poverty and violence all over Central America, Riley. You have no idea how bad it is." Earnestly narrowing his eyes at the thought of it: "Reactionary elements are in the ascendancy."

Riley leaned closer to Cole and lowered his voice to a whisper. "Yes, there is poverty and violence all over Central America, but what about the poverty and violence in North Minneapolis, Cole? You know about those folks, you see them every morning out the window of your Mercedes on the way to work. Some of them think the people in this room, including you and me, are reactionary elements in the ascendancy."

"That's different!" hissed Cole, pressing an index finger to his lips to signal the need for quiet.

By now the last few directors were taking their seats, with Buck enthroned in the high-backed chair reserved for the chairman, a nameplate on the table before him reading: CHAIRMAN, PRESIDENT & CHIEF EXECUTIVE OFFICER, a litany of titles he wore like the plume of a giant peacock.

By the time the opening gavel dropped, Gladys, Renee the Beautiful, and the caterers had scurried from the room, leaving an all-male group hunkered down to do a man's job. In a room containing twenty-two people, there was not to be found a single drop of estrogen.

Buck sat high in his chair and cleared his throat officiously. "Before beginning the meeting, I want to apologize for that gauntlet of protesters you had to walk through at the front entrance."

"Goddamn Reds," muttered Erving Russell from a seat behind Buck, shaking his head disgustedly.

"You bet your ass," said Buck, signaling agreement in Erving's direction. He then continued, "They think they're going to extort some money out of us for some homeless shelter and some other crap. But they're in for a surprise—they're not dealing with 'Minnesota Nice' with this guy." He said this in a husky voice while wiggling his thumbs at himself. "I had a few words with that overgrown broad leading the group. I laid a little charm—and a little warning—on her." A trace of the Look formed on his face.

"They don't know what they're in for messing with the Lion of the Lindbergh," said Hank Wallstead, laughing knowingly as though he felt sorry about the sad fate awaiting the protesters should they be foolish enough to tangle with the "Buckaroo." Several other directors fell in with the laughter, nodding their agreement.

Buck's chest expanded and the Look now reached full flower. "I can handle them with both hands tied behind my back," he bragged as he scanned his specially prepared copy of the written agenda, containing Erving's cribbed-in annotations designed to prevent him from making an embarrassing misstatement. Buck's familiarity with the detailed affairs of the company was roughly that of a sightseer in a foreign land who had given a once-over to the travel brochure. And like the sightseer, he knew at some level that important decisions were best left to others, such as that master of detail, Erving Russell. For his part, Erving was only too glad to run the company anonymously, ceding to Buck all glory and public credit for resulting successes. But he knew it was a dangerous game he was playing, for should it become known outside the company that Buck was largely a figurehead, that Erving was actually running things, nothing short of his removal would result.

After gaveling the meeting to order, Buck moved adoption of the minutes of the last meeting, the sole agenda item he was fully prepared to handle. Cosmo Towers, in the extra loud voice of the profoundly hard of hearing, screamed out "Seconded!" His neighbors on both sides jumped. The motion passed, without discussion, in a twelve to nothing landslide.

Buck then introduced the first substantive item, a review of operating numbers for the previous month. He turned the floor over to Erving, who walked the directors through a series of long and wide columns showing revenues, expenditures, capital investments, customer attrition, key accounting ratios, depreciation, and twenty or thirty other categories and subcategories, all depicted in contrast to previous accounting periods and anticipated future performance. Here and there Buck would interject a comment or anecdote unrelated to the technical information being presented. During the presentation on real estate mortgage revenues, for example, he let it proudly drop that he had formed a "close personal friendship" with the company's most profitable customer, Ward Crosshaven, a name well known to the other directors. Riley cringed inwardly at the mention, knowing that Buck would be discomforted by news of the complications created by Crosshaven's troublesome son and the fact that the company would have to identify him as a suspected criminal in a government filing. Riley also didn't look forward to being the bearer of this bad news, as Buck was not good at distinguishing between the messenger and the message.

When board members directed clarifying questions to Buck, he would answer in a self-confident, authoritative voice.

Given his general unfamiliarity with the facts, it was a tribute to the innate quickness of his mind that fully half his answers were accurate. When it was necessary to contradict a Buck misstatement, Erving would say, "Yes, that is an excellent point you have made," and then gently, artfully issue corrective words, spoken with such obvious affection for Buck that their complete negation of his earlier statement went almost unnoticed.

There was rarely much need for finesse in this regard, however, especially during the financial presentation, as a majority of the board had only a general notion of the matters under discussion. With few exceptions, they came to the board from wholly unrelated industries, knew little about the insurance business, and were there primarily for the status afforded by the position. As the avalanche of tedious figures, organized in accordance with accounting protocols peculiar to the insurance industry, were projected onto the giant screen on the north wall, Riley watched eyes of all shapes, sizes and colors, transformed from lively, sparkling windows to the soul into glazed, benumbed stares. It was as though ether had been pumped into the room through the ventilation system. Charles the Lesser's head bobbed, his eyes partially crossed, the lids at half-mast. Cosmo Towers, his energy reserves having been spent in seconding the motion to adopt the minutes of the last meeting, had gone sound asleep, purring contentedly in a bolt upright position, a plate of half-eaten fruit on the table before him.

Secreted behind the covers of his board book, Rick Snelling, the former fullback, was reading the latest issue of Sports Illustrated, his face alive with curiosity and pleasure, his shoulders giving off an occasional roll. Gar Blaisdahl had a napkin shielding his nose and mouth from the heavy barrage of incoming shit molecules issuing from Tom Arden's butt. Tom was looking straight ahead, feigning absorption in the finance presentation, now and then downing another gulp of sparkling mineral water.

In the midst of Erving's analysis of the loan loss reserve and with his eyes still closed, Cosmo Towers shouted out, "You know we lost Sparky last year?" Sparky was the Towers' family spaniel who had died the previous winter. Apparently he was still very much on Cosmo's mind, even in his dreams.

The proceedings came to a jarring halt. Grant Sumter patted Cosmo gently on the arm, causing him to come temporarily awake and loudly exclaim, "No thanks, Grant, can't stand raspberries. Those little seeds give me the shits." Sumter nodded tenderly, again patting Cosmo on the arm. Cosmo straightened his toupee and gave a milky, uncomprehending look at Erving's slide. He then closed his eyes and went back to sleep. Ted Colfax and Bryant Knox, who were attending their first board meeting, looked on with a kind of wonder.

After a decent interval in which Buck satisfied himself that Cosmo had gone back to sleep, he signaled for Erving to continue.

As Riley looked around the table at the lineup of distinguished CEOs he mused about how surprisingly ordinary they were. Very much like any other collection of people. Some nice, some mean. Some modest, some conceited. Most good fathers, adequate husbands. Of the twelve, four cheated on their expense reports, five cheated on their wives, and two cheated on their golf scores. One cheated on all three. In other words, they were like most of the rest of the world. And when the real turkeys had been culled, as well as the seat warmers, five or six honest, high-class gentlemen who took their responsibilities seriously remained.

Riley found them, with only a few exceptions, to be able and likable people. They were socially useful in their own way, certainly. Not like teachers or nurses or police officers or others who saw to the compelling needs of the human community, but important, nevertheless. Somebody had to be at the top of these big companies, and under the current system these guys were, by and large, well suited. Their principal distinguishing talent was a tremendous sense of pragmatism. In contrast to the popular myth of the business genius driven by a passionate belief in the capitalist ethic, they were bright but not brilliant, having rarely walked away with academic honors in school, and were, on the whole, devoid of any real commitment to a detailed economic system. On the contrary, they were adaptable to almost any situation called for by presenting circumstances. As to a majority of them, it could be said that if a socialist revolution were to occur in the country, they'd end up the commissars—if a fascist revolution, the reichsministers. Political philosophy and ideology had little real meaning for most of them, no matter what rhetoric they used on the cocktail circuit, no matter how big their checks to the Republican Party. It was fascinating to Riley how far removed the typical corporate director was from what was commonly supposed in the public imagination.

Following completion of the parade of financial numbers, Buck chuckled immodestly and said, "Well, we've done a pretty good job so far, I'd say."

"You're damn right, chief," said Erving Russell as he assembled his materials on the podium. Erving liked to call Buck "chief" when in the presence of the board. It went a long way toward sustaining the illusion that Buck, rather than Erving, was running the company.

Buck then consulted his agenda and announced the next item of business. Suzanne Penn, a vice president in the operations division, entered the room to explain the company's strategy for converting the widely disbursed customer service network to a centralized service center that would rely heavily on a sophisticated voice message network. Suzanne, a tall, well-dressed, mid-level executive, was heavy with child. She took to the podium and set about explaining in plain, understandable English, purged of all corporate-speak, the workings of the newly inaugurated system. She moved with dexterity back and forth from the podium to the screen, notwithstanding being in her eighth month of pregnancy. She was sporting a belly of awesome size. Riley thought it a wonder that she could stand up at all.

Riley had watched Suzanne swell to her current magnitude over the last several months and was always reminded of Betsy's pregnancy with Teddy seven years before. Like Suzanne, Betsy had been older than the typical expectant mother, and when they went to birth classes recommended by the family obstetrician ("Shared Childbirth for Modern Couples"), their classmates looked like teenagers at an all-school mixer. One young woman who couldn't have been more

133

than twenty-two leaned over to Riley at the first meeting and told him that she "had already pushed out two puppies before this one." A peppy obstetrical nurse named Jane ran the classes from the front of a large room, the floor of which was covered with carpeting that looked and felt like Astro-Turf, on which the expectant couples were sprawled at random, clutching pillows and blankets, giggling nervously at everything Nurse Jane said.

One couple was customarily selected to stand at the front of the room to illustrate anatomical features (such as the position of the baby at various stages) and demonstrate labor techniques (such as deep breathing). Joking lightly that "age has its privileges," Jane had Betsy and Riley join her at the front of the room for the first demonstration. Her lecture and slides involved a lot of formal biological information that no boy should ever know about, starting with the coarsening and shedding of the uterine lining to prepare for the implanting of the fertilized egg and degenerating rapidly into really unmentionable stuff like "engorged linings," "sodden tissues," and "milky fluids." As Betsy uninhibitedly gave herself over to the role of poster child for middle-aged procreation (having instantaneously bonded with the entire class), with each new gross biological term Riley swayed more unsteadily on his feet, perspiration forming on his forehead and upper lip, blood rushing from his extremities to wherever it goes when the brain thinks the body is about to blow lunch. Diverting his eyes from the graphic slides showing the exquisite manner in which Mother Nature engineers human reproduction, he struggled to turn his mind to baseball, sky-diving, the fluctuating prime rate—anything but the moist, untidy processes taking place in the ladies' department.

Through sheer will power he managed to stabilize himself as the lecture passed through the second trimester (at which time Betsy lifted up her maternity blouse and showed a room full of complete strangers the funny thing that had happened to her belly button), but when Nurse Jane flashed on the screen a giant color slide showing a massive, gelatinous, multicolored globule that looked like the monster loogie out of hell, and announced to the class that, "We are now going to examine the Mucous Plug," the three-time central city junior-welterweight contender, the crack prosecutor of the state's most dangerous criminals, and the man who had bitten the ear off Mad Dog Moriarity, went down like a California Redwood, landing face first at the feet of a surprised Nurse Jane.

Of the birth itself he could remember almost nothing, for he had again fainted in the delivery room after suffering a series of excruciating labor pains. The nurse and doctor were both attending to the fallen Riley when Teddy made his first appearance. Even Betsy had directed most of her attention to Riley, almost jumping out of the stirrups, fearing that he might have died. When the doctor informed him that "it" was a seven-pound baby boy, he could remember thinking that he didn't care if it was a seven-pound insect so long as he could get the hell out of that room.

And so it went with the glorious experience of Shared Childbirth for Modern Couples.

Rustling papers around the table signaled the end of Suzanne's formal remarks and returned Riley's consciousness to the present moment. After answering several questions relating to her topic, Suzanne collected her materials and waddled out of the room, exchanging a furtive smile with Riley. He looked up at her with admiration, knowing that every man in that room, starting with him, would have long ago taken to his bed, pleading for round-the-clock nursing care, were he in her circumstances.

"Great little gal," said Buck as Suzanne left the room.

"You betcha, one of the best gals in the company," joined in Gar from his seat behind Buck. Several directors nodded their heads in agreement.

What was all this "gal" shit? thought Riley. It sounded like they were talking about Dale Evans. This was one of the brightest and most competent people in the company, not some chick off the rodeo circuit.

"Cute little gal, all right, but it looks like she forgot to cross her legs," cracked Charles the Lesser, rocking with self-congratulatory laughter. Buck howled helplessly at this display of searing wit by the chairman of the committee that determined how much money he made each year.

In addition to his other board duties, Charles the Lesser had chaired a blue-ribbon board committee that drafted gender equity guidelines for the company. His was an interesting choice given a checkered history with women in the workplace, having been accused the previous year of unwelcome sexual advances at his company's Christmas party. It seems that a highly festive Charles had put a bear hug from behind on an attractive member of the support staff. His defense to her indecent liberties charge was that he thought she was choking, and he was merely applying the Heimlich maneuver. That he had grabbed and squeezed her breasts rather than her diaphragm was put down to a misunderstanding of the maneuver's proper execution, a mistake anyone could have made.

Buck introduced the next agenda item: "Downsizing Status Report." Turning of pages and clearing of throats were heard randomly around the table as Cole Girard took to the podium armed with his slide presentation, exchanging collegial nods with Erving as they passed in the aisle. Having said very little for the previous twenty-five minutes, Buck felt obliged to register his presence. "We have made substantial progress since our last meeting in workforce reduction. Fifteen hundred jobs were eliminated, and another five hundred have been identified as non-essential, and will be taken out in the next round." This statement was being made just as Cole flashed on the screen a slide showing that in fact eleven hundred jobs had been eliminated in the last go around, with two hundred additional positions identified as nonessential. Cole issued a gentle correction (a maneuver at which he had become expert) stating: "What Buck was referring to were the numbers for the last two downsizings, with the numbers you see here relating to status changes since our last meeting." As he said this Cole nodded agreeably in Buck's direction, with Buck replying, "Right . . . that's what I meant to say."

"Right, " said Cole.

"Right," said M. Bryant from his seat along the wall, nodding supportively.

"That's exactly correct," came Gar's muffled concurrence from behind his napkin.

Cole used a pointer to emphasize specific numbers illustrating the numerical impact, both in dollar savings and headcount, affecting all major business lines. He sought to humanize the pain underlying the stark arithmetic by describing elaborate, state-of-the-art protocols followed by the out-placement specialists hired to support the affected employees. He introduced the vice president of the out-placement consulting firm, a lipless little man in the back of the room with the permanently startled look one normally associates with escaped mental patients. Riley thought he bore a striking resemblance to Rudolph Hess. Sitting in the shadows against the back wall, the consultant twisted a rubber band around his bony fingers like Madame Defarge at her knitting.

Directors were invited by Cole to ask any questions concerning the handling of terminated employees. No questions were asked.

Buck, his face a mask of compassion, his voice moving from a quiver to a near blubber, said, "I review every single termination, and each one breaks my heart. I love these people"—his voice broke momentarily—"and they love me." The reactions around the room to this stupendous fib were interesting to Riley more for what they said about the peculiar assortment of personalities gathered at the table than about the speaker, whose theatrics he had come to accept, even admire on a primitive level. The two Charleses nodded sympathetically. Grant Sumter wore a poker face and maintained a gentlemanly silence. Hank Wallstead looked impatient. Aaron Herschel looked like he was going to throw up.

Ignoring Buck's display of manufactured emotion and looking directly at him, Hank asked, "What would a ten-year employee making fifty thousand a year in the Casualty Lines Division get in the way of severance and benefits in a job elimination?"

"Oh . . . we're very generous with them," answered Buck in a knowledgeable tone that also oozed compassion. It sounded as though this matter had been the subject of considerable thought on his part.

"But what are the actual numbers?" pressed Hank. Most directors seemed interested in this hypothetical, with the exception of Cosmo Towers, who was still in a deep sleep.

Buck stammered briefly before being rescued by Cole. "That individual would get six months of base salary and benefits plus one week's compensation for every year with the Company." Cole went on to describe the broad-based support for the current downsizing and cost-cuttings among the employee ranks, stating, remarkably, that morale had never been higher. Several senior executives seated along the south wall nodded their agreement in unison, not including Riley, who was gazing with fascination at the impassive face of Herr Hess, and Tom Arden, who was subtly raising his left butt cheek in the direction of Gar Blaisdahl, launching wave after wave of roving, free-range shit molecules of astonishing potency.

Cole then reported on the formulation and adoption of gender-equity and sexual harassment guidelines. This was a subject of great currency in the corporate world and affected the workplaces of every CEO in the room. As a visible symbol of its commitment to this important topic, the board had appointed a panel of senior directors to oversee the formulation of guidelines, which Buck privately referred to as the "Pussy Policies." The appointment of Charles the Lesser, of Heimlich maneuver fame, as chair of the committee was thought in some quarters to undermine the credibility of its work, but Buck dismissed that concern. Charles was joined on the committee by the kindly but somnolent Cosmo Towers and Todd Brookside, a real dumbbell with major sideburns, who was the CEO of a Midwestern restaurant chain, and president of three all-male social clubs.

Women employees of the Lindbergh knew through water cooler gossip of Charles' attempt to save the life of one of his employees by grabbing her breasts from behind, and as a result were distrustful of the committee's sincerity. It wasn't entirely accurate to say "water cooler gossip" inasmuch as Buck had had the water coolers removed as part of the last cost-cutting initiative, at the same time he ordered the doors removed from all bathroom stalls to ensure that employees didn't diddle away time in unproductive behavior when they should be working.

Charles the Lesser, flanked by Todd Brookside and a bleary-eyed, freshly roused Cosmo Towers, delivered an oral report (drafted word-for-word by the committee's lawyers) that recommended adoption of the guidelines and certified that after rigorous investigation no instances of gender inequity, discrimination, or harassment could be found at The Lindbergh. As the certification was being read, Riley studied the faces of the three committee members. They looked like tobacco company executives testifying that nicotine was not addictive.

Riley noticed that Charles Kleinwick wore a cynical expression, an expression that seemed to say, "I know we have to go through this drill, but give me a break." Kleinwick was an enigma to Riley; he could be gruff and dismissive, but he was also given to pronouncements about the importance of ethics in the workplace. He had even taken Riley aside after one committee meeting to tell him that he, Charles Kleinwick (he often referred to himself in the third person), knew that Riley was the senior officer most concerned with ethical compliance and that being in that position could be lonely and politically risky. He had gone on to say that if Riley were ever to feel that he was in need of board support he could call upon him—for he, Charles Kleinwick, a man of principle, knew what it was to be out there alone on a matter of conscience. Whether that was self-congratulatory rhetoric or a sincere offer of support, Riley didn't know. But he was glad for the offer and prepared to take him at his word.

The last regular agenda item was Gar Blaisdahl's summary of the Employee Awards Program, which had been held the previous week in the grand ballroom of the once-swank Island Side Hotel, with Buck giving the keynote address by phone hookup from Miami Beach, where he was holding down costs in an eighteen-hundred-dollar-a-night luxury hotel suite.

After arranging his typed notes carefully on the podium, a nervous Gar began, "We're very proud of our star performers in this company, and we feel it's important to have a tangible symbol of how much we appreciate them. Included in your

139

booklets is a three-page list of our Buckie Award winners for this year, which is the highest honor a regular employee can earn. You'll note from the list of eighty-five winners that there are a disproportionate number of gals and coloreds—ah, people of color—further proof of our equal opportunity culture."

"There's even a couple of homo's in there," interjected Buck with a mischievous chuckle, as if to wonder aloud what the world was coming to. Most in the room kept their eyes down in embarrassment. Grant Sumter glared at Buck, who didn't seem to notice.

"Anyway," continued Gar, "these folks were treated to a nice dinner and a fifty-dollar gift certificate, and each received a Buckie—an eighteen-inch bronze statue of Buck, modeled on the cover photograph from *The Gopher State Business Journal*, copies of which are also in your booklet."

Gar nodded in the direction of M. Bryant, who stood up and headed for the cabinet at the end of the room to retrieve a box full of Buckies, one for each director and executive officer. M. Bryant's wide butt failed to clear the handles of his chair, causing him to carry it as an appendage to his ass for several steps before it thumped loudly to the ground. Tom Arden let out a yelp of pleasure, simultaneously releasing another gaseous broadside in Gar's direction.

The Buckies were gold statues mounted on marble bases and looked like a cross between an Oscar and the Statue of Liberty. As one was placed before each director, Buck, now pink and swollen with greatness, shook his head in a gesture of modesty that disowned any part in the formulation of the award.

Gar continued, "We think this symbol really personalizes the bond we have with our high performers, and it leverages Buck's tremendous popularity with the rank and file." The absurdity of this last statement was lost on no one. Several directors cleared their throats to avoid laughing.

Riley looked around the table at a sea of bewildered faces staring slack-jawed at their Buckies as though gazing upon some unclassifiable artifact unearthed in an archeological dig. Even Erving Russell looked dumbstruck. Tom Arden, who had just reloaded his colon with an eight-ounce bottle of mineral water, was drawing pimples and a curlicue mustache on his Buckie. Rick Snelling drove a fist into his chest, muttering to himself, "Glory hog."

Buck was really too wonderful for words, thought Riley. How could you not have a grudging affection for a guy who commissioned a brass likeness of himself, decreed the image to be an official symbol of excellence, and then disowned any involvement in its creation?

Gar returned to his seat, patting Buck on the shoulder on the way by. The agenda now called for the outside directors to meet in executive session, with all members of management excused, to discuss matters relating to management's performance and compensation. Buck noisily collected his still-unread board materials and marched shoulder to shoulder with Gar, M. Bryant, and Erving toward the door leading to the Sacristy. They looked like a rugby scrum moving across the room. The remaining executive managers fell in behind. In the hallway Riley moved to the front of the pack and, with the Crosshaven problem on his mind, tugged on Buck's sleeve. "I need to see you for a few minutes before you leave the office." Buck responded that Gladys would call him later in the morning.

As lead director, Hank Wallstead now took over the meeting. He opened with a review of compensation recommendations for Buck relating to the fiscal year ending mid-July. "You have in front of you the comparative salary data for CEOs of insurance companies of comparable size and profile to The Lindbergh, together with the two-page written report of the Evaluation and Compensation Committee recommending a cash bonus figure, stock option award, and base salary adjustment."

Hank was a member of the Evaluation and Compensation Committee and expected this to be a rubber-stamp approval of the committee's recommendation, which included a two-million dollar cash bonus, options on two-hundred thousand

141

shares of stock at the current trading price, and an increase of ten percent in base salary (bringing that number to a moderate appearing $350,000, and enabling Buck to state publicly that he, like other employees, had a modest "salary").

As titular head of the Evaluation and Compensation Committee, Charles the Lesser chimed in, "We took a careful look at the compensation of peer-group CEOs, taking into account similarities and distinctions with The Lindbergh, and feel unanimously that this would be the appropriate package for Buck. Therefore, as Chairman of the Committee, I'd like to move approval of our recommendation."

Charles Kleinwick quickly seconded the motion, and Hank Wallstead called for a vote.

"Whoa, whoa," said Grant Sumter, his palms raised in the air in the manner of a traffic warden halting a fast-moving pack of schoolchildren. "I think we ought to at least have some discussion about this." Because Buck Montrowe sat on the Compensation Committee of the publicly held railroad of which Hank Wallstead was the CEO, Grant Sumter thought that it might be in everyone's best interest to do a thorough and independent review.

Hank Wallstead rolled his eyes in the direction of Charles Kleinwick. They shared a mutual disdain for Grant Sumter, the naive idealist.

"Sure . . . I guess," said Charles the Lesser, looking over to Charles Kleinwick for direction. "I thought everyone was already aware of these numbers."

"This is the first I've seen of them," said Aaron Herschel, paging through the surveys.

"Me too," said Gil Chesterton.

"Well, fine, but you should recall that the board assigned to this committee the obligation to look into the CEO's compensation," said Hank Wallstead, who seemed to have taken back the lead from Charles the Lesser.

"Yeah, but we didn't say that you could set Buck's compensation all by yourself. We didn't pass the corporate version of the Gulf of Tonkin Resolution," said Grant Sumter.

A handful of directors around the table, aroused by the change in tone, sat up in their seats and started rustling through papers in their director packages, looking for the comparable salary numbers. Hank Wallstead looked defensively about the table.

An audible snort emerged from what had been the steady hum of Cosmo Towers's restful purring, and a twitch of his left hand caused it to make contact with the glass sitting before him, spilling fruit juice across his board materials. Gil Chesterton dabbed at the spill with a handful of napkins thrust his way by several directors. Cosmo did not awaken.

Grant Sumter cleared his throat. "Now then, can somebody on the committee tell me why we're awarding two-million dollars in cash and huge options to a guy who's basically a salesman, an entertainer of customers. He's good at drumming up business with his endless fishing and hunting trips, but he doesn't do much else." Several directors looked uncomfortable.

"What's this about hunting and fishing, Grant?" asked J. T. Cahill, the business professor.

"It's a lot of cocktail party gossip, that's what it is," said Hank Wallstead, doing his best to maintain his composure.

"Well, I've heard it too, and not just at cocktail parties," said Aaron Herschel as he ran the fingers of his left hand through a head of wavy white hair. "And you saw Buck trying to muddle his way through the agenda during the meeting. My God, he's virtually clueless."

"An effective CEO doesn't sit in his office all day. He goes out and mixes the way Buck does," shouted Charles Kleinwick. He too was a member of the Evaluation and Compensation Committee, and had on his compensation committee at Riverdale Soap Company, Hank Wallstead *and* Buck Montrowe. Apart from a short entry in the proxy statement of each company, no further disclosure of this cozy arrangement was required. "And besides, look at this comparable data. Buck is paid no more than his peers in the insurance industry whose companies have had similar success. Look at the Lindbergh stock; it's gone up eleven dollars a share since Buck arrived."

Grant Sumter leaned forward, resting his arms on the table. "Look, gentlemen, we don't need to turn this into a quarrel, and we don't need to bullshit each other. There are a number of issues we have to face honestly here." Looking over at Charles Kleinwick, he went on, "It's no good to throw out clichés about how a CEO has to get out of the office to do his job right. No CEO can do his job if he spends most of his time on the golf course or hunting and fishing, dragging along some poor customer to use as a shill for his recreational activities. I know he's not the only one in town who does this, but we're putting out big dollars here, and we've got some responsibility to the shareholders."

Charles the Lesser's face was now glowing, and his hand trembled as he pointed across the table at Grant Sumter. "What do you care what he does with his time? The market capitalization of this company has increased over a billion dollars since he arrived, and goddamnit he deserves to be paid for that."

"There's an obvious answer for that, *Chas*," said Grant Sumter, who liked to call Charles the Lesser "Chas" when he thought he had made a particularly dumb statement. "First off, he's already been compensated for that increase in market cap through the thousands of options we awarded him at the time he was hired. Those options are already worth over two-million dollars. Beyond that I don't happen to believe that a coach who never shows up for practice should be paid when the team, on its own, has a winning season. I prefer paying the people who were actually responsible for the success."

Despite his contempt for Charles the Lesser, Grant Sumter now changed his tone and facial expression to one of conciliation. "But, look, let's just say for purposes of this discussion that Buck is doing just what a CEO should do—that it doesn't matter how he spends his time. Shouldn't we still be fair about this and distribute the compensation equitably among all employees?"

Sumter now fished through the handouts before him looking for the list of the two hundred fifty employees scheduled for option awards in varying amounts. Finding the appropriate sheet, he whipped his reading glasses across his face, in his enthusiasm nearly putting his eye out. "Look at this. We've got nine thousand employees in this company right now—two thousand fewer than we had ten months ago—and less than three percent of them are getting options in any amount. Three percent. And with this committee's recommendation, Buck will get more options than everyone else combined!"

Throwing the sheet back into the pile of materials spread in front of him and removing his reading glasses, he took a deep breath and continued, "How fair is that? There are thousands of employees working twice as hard as they used to. It's that effort which accounts for the increase in the stock price, and those folks don't get a penny out of the increase in market cap. If we want to make this a just system, let's take the available options and distribute them deep into the ranks, where the work is getting done. And while we're at it, let's do the same thing with the greater part of that two-million dollar cash bonus you're recommending that we pay to that professional fisherman we've got in the CEO's office. Shit, why don't we just hire Babe Winkleman and pay him two-million dollars to go fishing? At least he's a pro." He grabbed his Buckie by the throat. "This stupid-ass little trophy should be holding a fishing pole!"

Grant Sumter was an irritant to men like Hank Wallstead, Charles Kleinwick, and Charles the Lesser for two principal reasons: One, he was born and raised in a family of old wealth (very aristocratic, papers on both sides) causing the newly rich types to view his idealism as theoretical and disingenuous (also a do-gooder on the social front, he sat on half the non-profit boards in the area and even dished out food to the homeless in church basements), and two, they were irritated by his efforts to learn about and understand the insurance industry in order to make informed decisions as a director. That was considered butting in.

J. T. Cahill, the business school professor, now warmed and quickened to the topic, in part because executive compensation had become a hot item in the nation's business schools. "I agree with most of what Grant's been saying, although I don't know much about Buck's management style. I don't get to many country club cocktail parties."

Odd that the most educated man in the room should feel social inferiority, and odder still that he would give expression to it in a venue such as this, thought Aaron Herschel as he sat back watching the proceedings. Herschel, and his father and grandfather before him, could have bought and sold most of the others in the room but until the late 1970s had been denied admittance to the area's most prominent country clubs because of unapologetic anti-Semitism. When he finally was admitted, he was amused, even a little intrigued, that every long-time member to whom he spoke said he had consistently opposed the exclusionary policy all along. He chuckled at the thought of it. How such an invidious practice could have survived for over seventy-five years in the face of such overwhelming popular opposition puzzled him.

Cahill continued: "Well, look, set aside the question of whether Buck is just a high-paid sportsman, or the hard-charging guy we read about in the company's press releases. What I'm concerned about is that so many compensation dollars are being directed to any CEO." He spoke as though addressing a room full of graduate students. "If you take the compensation of our last three CEOs relative to the compensation of our average employee, you'll see that the current CEO's compensation is three times what it used to be, even after you adjust for inflation. And where's the money coming from? It's coming out of the hides of thousands of our regular employees through reduced pay and benefits. What the hell's going on here anyway? This is redistribution of wealth to the already wealthy."

Lacking the intellectual horsepower to joust with Cahill, Charles the Lesser, lifesaving giver of breast-level Heimlich maneuvers, simply shrugged his shoulders and retired from the conversation, leaving the affirmative to be argued by Hank Wallstead and Charles Kleinwick.

Part of J.T. Cahill's enthusiasm for this subject sprang from a deep-seated suspicion that this board, like most in the Fortune 500, was run, for all practical purposes, by a clique of powerful directors who displayed a polite but condescending attitude toward their fellow directors and a barely concealed scorn for him personally by reason of his no-count life as an academic. They took an almost pitying attitude toward him, and it made him burn with resentment.

Charles Kleinwick leaned into the table and looked over at Cahill with a smirk. "This isn't the campus, J.T. This is the real world. If you study the compensation data you'll understand the cost to hire and retain a first-rate CEO." His voice was dripping with condescension and his mouth was so twisted with scorn he looked like a stroke victim.

"Really?" said Cahill challengingly. "Why is the market for a CEO suddenly seventy times the compensation of the average employee, the ratio having quadrupled over the last twenty years? Fortune 500 CEOs are now making 400 times the pay of the average blue-collar worker in this country. How did all these ordinary employees get so horseshit so fast? Does anybody here seriously contend that CEOs are better now than they used to be?" He looked around the table daring anybody to take up the challenge.

J. T. Cahill had actually succeeded in sounding snottier than Charles Kleinwick. Every director in the room was now feeling the acrid tension passing across the table. Even Hank Wallstead seemed to be uncomfortable with the level of hostility that had developed.

Sounding more pedantic than a pissed-off college professor was no small feat, but Charles Kleinwick, the Soap King of Des Moines, did just that with his next remark. Accompanied by waving hands, he shouted, "Thank you for that high-minded lecture, Professor, but what the hell difference does it make what the ratios or multiples are? The marketplace has spoken, and in a free-market economy that's the end of the discussion."

Several around the table nodded agreement. Grant Sumter and Gil Chesterton puckered their faces as if to say, "It's really not that simple."

J. T. Cahill leaned into the table: "Free-market economy, my ass. Forgive me for saying so, Charles, but you wouldn't know a real marketplace if it ran you over on the first tee." Cahill's choice of metaphors was no accident. He had neither the connections nor the resources to join the clubs of which Charles Kleinwick was a member. "Just for your edification, Charles, this is a global economy, and European and Asian

147

CEOs aren't making anywhere close to these kinds of numbers. You don't have a true marketplace when you have a bunch of incestuous, fat-cat directors artificially bidding up CEO compensation each year in the board rooms of America. This isn't free-market capitalism, it's nothing but collusion. It's the moral equivalent of loaded dice."

"Now wait a minute," shouted Hank Wallstead, pounding his fist on the table. "The fact that Buck is on my compensation committee has nothing to do with what we're recommending here."

Hank's spontaneous outburst was greeted by an embarrassed silence. J. T. Cahill, a hint of a smile on his face, turned to Hank and said, "Gee, Hank, nobody said anything about you personally. But now that you raise the matter, why don't you and Kleinwick here tell us about your various interlocking directorships. You know, the ones that have no effect on your independent judgment."

Across the table, Charles Kleinwick's chest was heaving and his lips were moving, but no sounds emerged, his raging hormones having decommissioned his voice. His face was covered with dark red blotches as he struggled to speak, grunting and flapping like a beached whale.

"Okay, okay," said Grant Sumter, placing one hand perpendicular to the other in a time-out sign. He spoke now in a softer, more reasoned voice, hoping to vacuum the wounded egos out of the discussion. "This is a very rancorous way for grownups to do business. I didn't mean to provoke such a nasty quarrel. I'm merely pointing out that if we take our duties seriously, we have to confront the basic morality—or immorality, I should say—of squeezing the lower ranks to cut costs, while at the same time pumping up CEO compensation to keep up with the inflated numbers cooked up in these surveys—which, let's face it, will say anything the people who pay for them want them to say. These compensation consultants are the biggest whores in the world. Please, let's not buy into our own bullshit." Several directors nodded agreement.

"How are we supposed to retain Buck as CEO if we pay him less than the peer group? Will somebody please explain that to me?" said Charles Kleinwick, whose voice had now returned, though several octaves higher.

J. T. Cahill, luxuriating in the warm glow of having caused the Soap King of Des Moines to go to pieces moments earlier, answered calmly, "There are twenty, thirty senior managers in this company, starting with Erving Russell, who could run things just fine, and any one of them would work his or her ass off for half this package."

"Even if I agreed with that, which I don't, it wouldn't work for practical reasons," said Hank Wallstead. "We've succeeded in convincing Wall Street that Buck is responsible for the company's success. What do you think would happen if he walked away, and we had to tell a new story? Shit, the stock would tank."

"So in other words we're stuck with our own line of bull-shit?" said Gil Chesterton, his face lined with frustration.

"That's one way of putting it," said Hank Wallstead, banging the chairman's gavel. "But this discussion is over. I'm calling for a vote on the recommended package."

The motion carried seven to one, with four abstentions. Cosmo Towers, still asleep, was counted in the "yes" column.

The directors packed up their Buckies and went home.

12

Skeeter shouted from her desk, "Gladys says if you want to see Buck you'd better get down there in the next five minutes because he's leaving town."

Riley grabbed a notebook and headed toward the Sacristy, handing his "Buckie" to Skeeter as he passed by her desk. "Here you go, Skeets. I knew you'd want one of these for your bedside table."

"Oh, how sweet—I'll treasure it always," said Skeeter, as she dropped Buck in the wastepaper basket.

Gladys signaled with a tilt of her head for Riley to go into Buck's office. Buck was stuffing mail into a briefcase in preparation for his departure. He looked up with an air of mild disappointment, not offering a seat. "Yeah, what do you want, Riley? I'm in a hurry."

"Buck, we've got a Crosshaven problem down at the S&L," said Riley as he took a seat, uninvited.

Buck's attention turned from the briefcase to the conference table. "What'd ya mean, a Crosshaven problem?" he asked.

"That attempted money laundering I mentioned to you last week. Remember?"

"No, I don't remember, but go talk to Gar. I don't have time for this crap." In this approach Buck was modeling in one seamless maneuver two of the most important characteristics of the modern CEO: deniability and delegation. Delegate anything that can backfire and deny you ever heard about it.

Riley ignored the instruction to take the matter to Gar and went right on talking. "You'll want to know about this problem, Buck. One of Ward Crosshaven's sons is suspected of trying to launder fifteen thousand dollars in cash. When the teller told him there'd have to be a government filing he aborted the transaction and became threatening and abusive—said he'd get her if she turned him in. It sounds like he's either a nut case or a junkie, or both."

"So what's the problem? Nothing happened, right?" he snapped, chaffing uncomfortably at the subject matter.

"The transaction wasn't completed but we're still required to file a notice under these circumstances."

Buck smirked. "How does she know it's Ward's kid?" This subject was obviously making him nervous, and without realizing it his tone had become very nasty.

"We know it's Brad Crosshaven because the employee, Liddy Jonssen, saw him yesterday coming out of The Lindbergh Trust with Harry Callinan. There was no doubt in her mind. And according to Harry this guy's had drug and money problems in the past. It fits." Riley's tone was clinical, informational.

Buck turned abruptly in Riley's direction. "Harry Callinan told you that about a Crosshaven family member?" he snarled.

"What does that matter?" replied Riley, looking surprised. "We're all on the same side, remember? This kind of thing has to be handled by the book no matter who the customer is. We've got a duty to file a Suspicious Activity Report. And we sure as hell have a duty to protect an employee whose been threatened."

Buck was now shaking his head vigorously while pacing in a circle in front of his desk. "Who else knows about this?" he asked.

That seemed an odd question to Riley, but he answered, "Liddy Jonssen, the employee, and my administrative assistant, Skeeter Swenson." He hesitated a moment, looking at the ceiling as he searched his memory. "Dan Thornton knows about the incident . . . and so does Gordy Moorland in Compliance, but at this point they don't know who the suspect is. Harry Callinan knows I was inquiring about Brad Crosshaven, but he doesn't know why. So you and I and Skeeter and Liddy Jonssen are the only ones who know the whole story."

"Well, don't say another word to anyone," he shouted. "I'll talk to Ward and figure this thing out." He shook his head back and forth. "If I get on the wrong side of him, I've got big trouble."

Riley shifted in his chair while exhaling a deep breath, inflating his cheeks and letting out a small cautionary groan. "I don't have to talk to anybody immediately, Buck, but we've got to file that report within a certain time limit. And we have to let the employee know pretty soon what's going on. She's under a lot of stress. And whatever you do, don't tell Ward Crosshaven that Liddy Jonssen turned his kid in. This guy sounds like a real psycho, and we don't want him fixating on her."

Now back at his desk, Buck slammed his briefcase shut. "Okay, okay. You sound like some kind of social worker for this girl. Just keep quiet for now, got it?" He fixed his gaze on Riley, seeking confirmation.

Riley knew Ward Crosshaven was Buck's idol, but he was nonetheless surprised by the brittleness of this exchange. It just didn't feel right. "Okay, Buck," he said, tapping his fingers on the table next to Buck's Bible, "but we don't have a lot of options here. I'm just telling you."

"Don't worry," said Buck, "we'll do the right thing. I guarantee you the employee will be fully supported. And you won't have to violate your Boy Scout oath." That last crack could have been either a compliment or an insult. Riley wasn't sure which. He was the Boy Scout of upper management. Buck even referred to him publicly as the "voice of integrity." But that was when Riley was directing his criticisms at others, not at him.

When Wally appeared in the office door, Buck lifted his briefcase while scanning the desk for forgotten items. Finding none, he pitched the briefcase through the air to Wally, who fielded it like a veteran bellhop. Buck's expression now changed, and he slapped Riley on the back with one hand while tugging on his lapel with the other. Being taller, he leaned down to make level eye contact. His smile was that of a pal, a confederate. "Remember, not a word to anyone until you hear back from me."

Still a little perplexed by Buck's reaction to the Crosshaven news—his edgy defensiveness and demands for secrecy—Riley was replaying the meeting in his mind as he entered the parking garage at 7:10 that night. The stalls in the executive parking row were empty, save only Cole Girard's gray BMW, bearing a FREE TIBET bumper sticker, and Erving Russell's $75,000 Mercedes, signifying that Erving was still hard at work running the company. For Buck's part, after his meeting with Riley, he had departed the premises, photographer in tow, for a celebrity golf tournament in Ft. Lauderdale.

As Riley made his way toward his car, from behind him and to the right he heard the sound of uneven footfalls. Even before turning in the direction from which the sounds had come, he recognized the distinctive tapping as belonging to Kurt McBraneman, who, as a result of a leg wound in Vietnam, walked with an unusual gait. Though nearly undetectable to the eye, the slight pause and click of the right foot was unmistakable to the ear.

Riley turned and found himself face-to-face with Kurt. He smiled weakly and said, "What's with you and dark underground garages, Kurt? Couldn't we get together above ground sometime?"

A mysterious, slightly sinister smile crossed Kurt's weathered face. "You know me, Riley. I like to operate in the dark." This brief statement, notable for its economy of expression, was made with the cold self-confidence that had no equal in Riley's experience. Seeing Kurt standing there in his trademark greenish-brown combat jacket, deadly brown eyes peering like an animal's from within deep, hollow sockets, brought back a rush of memories.

Kurt McBraneman was the quintessential antihero, a man whose experiences in war had left him with a soul so badly damaged that it could thrive only in a subculture outside the bounds of conventional society and accepted morality. As a result of battlefield wounds and a plentiful supply of locally produced heroin, he had returned from Vietnam heavily addicted to narcotics and filled with rage against a political and social establishment that had slaughtered over fifty thousand of his comrades. Within twenty-four hours of his return, he murdered a camp counselor from northern Minnesota who had molested his younger sister more than eight years before. It had been his original intention, pre-Vietnam, to join the police force and arrest and prosecute the molester. But upon his return he modified the plan, dispensing with the constitutional technicalities in favor of a midnight visit to the guy's trailer, where he silently dispatched him into the next world. Although everyone in the area knew who had committed the crime, there was no evidence on which to base an indictment. Beyond that, the small rural police department didn't seem too interested in the case, in part because they thought Kurt had performed a public service and in part because they, too, were in no hurry to engage him.

Kurt then turned to armed robbery, mostly of local drugstores in the Twin City area. His own dependence raged unchecked, until cut short by a three-year prison sentence for armed robbery, where he was cellmates with Riley's old school pal, Chasbo Peytabohm.

Upon release from prison, Kurt became a non-using drug dealer. Affiliated with no gangs, cartels, families, crews, or other combinations, he was the consummate loner, working as an independent agent known for particular savagery toward those who opposed him or one of his small circle of friends—a circle in which Riley was relieved to be included. In spite of his line of work, Kurt rarely had problems with the law, for his violence was practiced almost exclusively upon other bad guys.

A study in contradictions, Kurt was versed in philosophy and literature, western and eastern, and held to a vague theological system entirely of his own making. He maintained a world view in which all others were rigidly categorized. Fanatically loyal to the small group he counted as friends, he was unspeakably brutal to those who gave him offense. He often described himself a character out of Dostoevski: "Raskolnikov without the failure of nerve," as he liked to put it.

"I saw you in the paper, Riley," he said in a flat monotone. "It looked like you were under a pretty nasty siege."

Riley paused for a moment, trying to think of what Kurt was referring to. He then remembered the picture of him in the newspaper being hit by a tomato. "Oh, you mean the newspaper. Those were just political protesters, Kurt . . . you know, social activists having some fun. I've been hit by things a lot harder than tomatoes."

Kurt lifted himself onto the trunk of Erving Russell's Mercedes, pulling his bad leg into a slightly elevated position. (Riley thought of asking him not to sit on Erving's meticulously maintained car but then decided against it). "You sure that's all it was, Riley? I don't like anybody fucking with my little friend."

"What d'ya mean 'little'?" snapped Riley.

Kurt paused, a frown taking shape on his face. "It's just a figure of speech, for Christ's sake. What the hell's the matter with you?"

"Never mind," said Riley, not wanting to discuss his shrinking height with the area's most feared drug dealer.

Kurt nodded, then smiled faintly. "So, buddy, who should I make a call on?"

This was what Riley feared. "Make a call on?" he said excitedly. "You don't make a call on anyone. Those protesters are real good people. They're just doing their thing. Don't scare me with talk like that." He then leaned forward for emphasis and said, "Is that why you called?"

Kurt tilted his head slightly. The dim ceiling lights of the basement garage reflected off his face, highlighting a scar just under his lower lip, the product of a prison-yard knife fight. The light striking Kurt's face at that angle brought to mind the strange rendezvous to which Kurt had summoned him years before at the unlikeliest of locations: the inside of the St. Paul

Cathedral. Riley had found Kurt in a side pew, his eyes closed, his head thrust backward in an attitude of subdued ecstasy, as a visiting boys choir practiced in the high loft at the rear of the church. The dark, cavernous interior of the cathedral vibrated with the voices of fifty pre-adolescent boys giving flight to the winsome lyrics of Panis Angelicus. Nearby votive lights flickered off Kurt's face then, too, as he recounted for Riley, without a hint of emotion or regret, the unspeakable things he had just done to one of his local dealers who had violated his rule against selling drugs to school children. Kurt had expected to be arrested later that day, and though he had no concern about ultimately being convicted (he was confident that upon release from the hospital the dealer would not be testifying), he wanted Riley to be on standby to arrange bail.

The eerie discordancy of that setting—the sweet, innocent voices of a children's choir mingling uneasily with the language of violence and evil—had caused Riley to go breathless and dizzy. He had wondered then what he was doing there in that great granite vault, surrounded by incense and the voices of boy-angels, giving legal advice to a man of such disturbing contradictions, a man of such frightening potentials.

Still, he had not been afraid then. Now, these many years later, once again in a dark, half-lit setting, as he looked upon that same raw intensity, that same iron will, he was no longer so sure.

Kurt leaned back on Erving's trunk and cocked his head in Riley's direction. "Yeah, that's why I called. I saw you in the newspaper and wanted to provide a little support. Thought you might need someone spanked." He laughed in a voice that was calm but menacing.

Riley threw his briefcase into the trunk of his ten-year-old black Ford, a car he retained in part, he had to admit, for the unholy pleasure it gave him to park its worn and battered carcass each morning close to Buck's Jaguar.

He slammed the trunk and looked over at Kurt. "Look," he said, "I don't want you acting as my champion anymore. I never did, in fact. And a few tomatoes might get you worked up, but they don't bother me at all. It's part of the game."

A heavy silence followed. Silence was always a little ominous when it was authored by Kurt McBraneman and even more so, Riley thought, when he was fixed in the grip of those dark, penetrating eyes—eyes that had seen things that no sane person even wanted to know about.

After an eternity of twenty or thirty seconds, Kurt laughed softly, nodding his head and flashing an incongruous smile that expressed disappointment at being deprived of another opportunity to pay down the debt he thought he owed. There was little doubt that from a purely clinical standpoint Kurt was insane. Not with the type of disorder that decreases function, quite the opposite. Rather the kind that results from a deadening of that part of the brain that in normal people equates conscience and morality with societal norms. That part had been decommissioned as a result of Kurt's life experiences, including complicity in what seemed at the time to be unavoidable atrocities in a war where children were used as decoys and combatants. Over the years there had been sporadic, nebulous talk about an orphanage mistaken for a Vietcong staging area. And grenades. And no forgiveness.

As he leaned on the car, Kurt wore his standard expression, a look that dared anyone within its range to move against him. Riley had always thought there was a death wish behind those dark eyes. That's what they had said at the state hospital where he had been evaluated after his second felony conviction.

"I like you Riley. I like watching out for you," he said, looking into the distance as he spoke. "But I do what I do because of my code. I don't expect you to understand it. But I don't need your fucking permission."

Riley nodded agreeably. It was best to agree with Kurt at moments like this. Riley shuffled his feet awkwardly. "But your code—as least as I understand it—doesn't involve violence toward a group of well-meaning social activists just because they got a little rambunctious." Riley's look invited confirmation.

"No, it doesn't, but don't get all huffy when I check into your welfare." Again he smiled inscrutably. With this he slid off

157

the car and stood upright. His face was only inches from Riley's when he said, "You wouldn't fuckin' be here if it weren't for me. Take my word for that."

Riley knew that was probably true, and the fact of Kurt McBraneman's saying it with such conviction made it an established fact. But he didn't want to think about that. "Never mind that, Kurt," he said. "Let's talk about something else. Do you ever see our old buddy Chasbo Peytabohm around?"

Kurt's expression changed. He put his hands in the pockets of his jacket as he leaned back against the car. Turning the discussion to their common friend seemed to have the desired effect. Kurt smiled. "Naw, I don't see much of him. He's gone completely straight."

Wanting to keep Kurt's focus off the protesters, and off spanking people, Riley asked the next question that crossed his mind. "Say, have you ever heard of a guy by the name of Brad Crosshaven?"

Kurt narrowed his eyes as though searching his memory. "Yeah, I do . . . but under a different name. He thinks nobody on the street knows who he really is. He's a sick-fuck junkie who likes to slum around in the drug world. Pushes coke to the jet set." He then looked up with an expression of curiosity. "Why you askin'? You got something going with him?"

"No, not really. I've never even met the guy," said Riley, "but his family does a lot of business with The Lindbergh, and my secretary's girlfriend is having some trouble with him." The minute that statement left his mouth he regretted it with every fiber of his being. His stupidity in using the Crosshaven name with Kurt made him so mad he had to fight for breath as he sought to appear casual.

"Is that right?" said Kurt darkly.

Realizing the enormity of his error, and badly rattled, Riley stammered, "Now wait a minute, Kurt. I don't want you involved in that. That's a Lindbergh problem. I'm sorry I mentioned it."

Kurt just stared.

Riley took a deep breath and moved closer, his voice trembling. "Promise me you won't lay a hand on that guy, Kurt. I mean it."

After a short silence, accompanied by an ambivalent half-smile, Kurt said, "Okay, buddy, relax. . . . I won't lay a hand on him." He seemed amused by the turn their meeting had taken. He was gently taunting his friend.

Wanting the conversation to end, Riley put his arm around Kurt's shoulder. "Here, let me walk you to the elevator."

Kurt pulled back; he didn't like being touched. "Don't bother," he said. "I can find my way out."

Riley watched as he disappeared into the darkness of the stairway. When he could no longer be seen in the shadows, the distinctive clicking of his uneven gait stopped, and Riley heard him say, "I'll be in touch, my friend."

13

———

Liddy drove toward Rochester on the four-lane, southbound freeway, a clean, bright sun penetrating the driver's window from the east, warming her face and neck. What a relief to have the week over, a week that saw nothing but tension and stress. There had been no further appearances by Brad Crosshaven, but she had gotten two anonymous faxes that day that said only, "I'm still watching."

Skeeter had called every day to lift her spirits, and Riley McReynolds had called on Friday afternoon to see how she was doing and to let her know that she could count on support at the "highest level" of the company—which she took to mean Buck Montrowe. She assumed that because a Crosshaven was involved, Buck had been brought into the loop. She liked and felt comfortable with Riley and was reassured by his call. Still, she told him nothing of the continuing harassment to which she was being subjected, in part because she thought it was bound to run it's course—and in part because she didn't want to sound like a cry baby.

By midmorning she seemed able to shake off some of the gloom and anxiety that enveloped her like a heavy fog in the early morning, a fog populated by unfriendly forces—some specific, some general. Now, this morning, she could feel the warm sun, look across the lush, rolling landscape, and listen to the soothing classical music coming from the radio. It felt for a moment as though she were on a vacation from the strain of recent weeks and months. It was a welcome respite. She was almost tempted to think it would last.

An hour out of town, she pulled off the freeway and drove through McDonald's for a cup of coffee. She still couldn't eat much in the way of solid food, but the coffee would taste good. Looking through the glass panels as she waited in the drive through line, she thought back to the time in college when she and Skeeter were bothered by some local toughs while eating lunch at this same McDonald's. Liddy had been picking delicately at a vegetarian salad while Skeeter wolfed down a Big Mac and a chocolate shake. Three boys in from the farm in their pickup truck had grown ugly when turned down for dates, calling Liddy and Skeeter "a couple of snobby college bitches." The girls bagged their half-eaten food and started to make their way toward the door, when one of the boys, a big guy with a scraggly goatee and wearing a John Deere cap, snapped his fist under the bag, sending food into the air and across the adjoining tables. Liddy remembered it as though it had happened yesterday, the humiliation and lack of control. She didn't treat people that way and didn't understand why anyone would do that to her and her friend.

Now sitting in the drive-through her heart sank at the memory, a reminder of how vulnerable to downturns in mood she was. Even events long past had the power to take her down. She felt anew the violation of her person, as though in a small way her soul had been ravaged. And she also recalled the difference between her reaction and Skeeter's. While she was burning with helpless rage, Skeeter threw a chocolate shake in John Deere's face and screamed so loud that he and his friends ran for their pickup truck. And the amazing thing was that Skeeter now barely remembered the incident, an incident that was burned indelibly into her memory. Liddy had brought it up recently when they were having lunch at the skyway McDonald's, and Skeeter had to strain to recall even the broad outlines of what had happened. It wasn't a defining moment

161

for her, one with existential implications, as it had been for Liddy. Skeeter hadn't generalized the experience. To her, it was just a handful of good 'ol boys feeling their oats. They just needed a dose of their own medicine.

Why did two human beings so alike in so many ways see the same events so differently, Liddy wondered as she sat in the car waiting for her coffee. Why couldn't she be like Skeeter, who blew right through such things? Was it a difference in brain chemistry or genetics? Was it her upbringing, or something that had happened to her as a child that she couldn't remember? Or, worst of all explanations, was she being punished for some nameless sin? These dark thoughts exhausted her, used up what little strength she retained. But she could not seem to stop them from playing over and over in her mind.

She pulled onto the service road and then south onto the freeway, where she accelerated quickly to fall in with the fast moving traffic. Continuing toward Rochester she looked in the rearview mirror every few minutes. It was probably her frayed nerves playing new tricks on her, but she had the feeling she was being followed. It was probably just her imagination, but an expensive green car seemed always to be a few vehicles behind her. That's all she needed now, a good jolt of paranoia.

The Holy Redeemer Lutheran Residence was a one-story brick structure spread in symmetrical wings in four directions, lush grass cuddling up to its stone walls. It looked from the high vantage point of the highway to be a giant cross laid peacefully on a bed of green. Even on the south side, paved over for parking and use by service vehicles—laundry trucks, ambulances, hearses—it looked so neat and tidy that it brought to mind the toy village she had played with as a child.

Making her way past a small reception desk tended by a gum-chewing teenager chatting nonstop on the phone with her boyfriend, Liddy turned right into the high support unit, which housed the residents unable to care for their most basic needs. The acrid smell of human waste smacked her in the face as she rounded the corner, causing her eyes to water and her breathing to go momentarily shallow. As she passed the laundry room, outside of which stood canvas receptacles holding bed sheets changed that morning, she unconsciously veered to the other side of the narrow hallway but had to resume a center course to avoid the shriveled, wasted body of an old woman propped up in a reclining chair, her body and mind strangulated by arthritis and dementia. Unfocused eyes and a toothless mouth were wide open, but the overall expression was a contented one, causing Liddy to consider the meaning of happiness. She couldn't know the state of this poor creature's mind, but in spite of her physical and cognitive limitations she seemed somehow content. Maybe it was a kind of vegetative well-being. It was strangely inviting.

Entering the recreation section of the north wing, she was immediately encircled by a flotilla of wheelchairs operated by old women who rolled in her direction like guppies toward freshly poured food. Several clutched at her sweater, pleading to be taken home. One reached into her purse, pulling out makeup and a bottle of aspirin, which spilled randomly to the four corners of the room. The activities director, a middle-aged woman with gray hair, clapped her hands loudly several times, and shouted, "Come on girls, back to our games." At the sound of the claps, the swarm of ancient Lutherans headed back in her direction.

In the hallway adjacent to the nursing station an elderly man in his wheelchair—one of the few men on the unit—was trying to get his hand up a nurse's skirt. "Oscar!" the nurse screamed, while leaping back from the wheelchair, "we talked about that yesterday, remember?" A naughty smile crossed Oscar's face as he pulled his hands back to his lap in a gesture of exaggerated contrition.

Margaret Jonssen's room was warm and dark, illuminated only by thin shreds of sunlight that managed to penetrate the narrow slits of the imperfectly closed blinds. In the adjoining bed was Margaret's roommate, a shriveled wreck of a woman who said nothing and rarely moved. Margaret sat in a wheelchair next to the bed, her left hand stroking her forehead in a kind of confused ritual. She looked up at Liddy with a pained expression and only a faint hint of recognition.

"Hi, Mom," said Liddy, planting a mechanical kiss on Margaret's cheek.

Margaret looked up, squinting. "Is that you, Liddy?"

"It sure is, Mom. How are you doin'?" Liddy started to open a package of cherry licorice, Margaret's favorite, purchased on the way down when she stopped to get gas. She handed a piece to Margaret along with a small Styrofoam cup of water.

"How are you feeling, Mom?"

"Oh, not very good, honey," Margaret responded weakly while looking up to inspect her only child. "Stand up straight, Liddy," she said, thrusting her own shoulders back in a feeble demonstration. Posture was very important in Margaret's family, and from the time Liddy was a little girl her mother had always tried to get her to stand up straight.

Liddy pulled up a chair facing Margaret, grasping her hands. "In what way don't you feel good, Mom?"

"Oh, I don't know . . . just not good," Margaret said, slurring her words. Her perfectly white hair surrounded a face ravaged by wrinkles and age spots but still possessing a set of dazzling, pale blue eyes. One could see that this southern Minnesota farm woman had once been a great beauty. And the resemblance between mother and daughter was unmistakable, the cheekbones and hairline nearly identical. Margaret's mouth had no doubt once looked like Liddy's too, but with the loss of fully half her teeth the lips had collapsed in on themselves.

"What room is Dad in? I want to see him," said Margaret with mild urgency as she lifted a piece of licorice to her mouth in a palsied motion.

"Dad's been dead for over ten years, Mom," said Liddy. She had delivered this sad news at least once a week for the last two years. Some days she wanted to just lie about it to spare her mother the repeat insults to this painful wound, but the counselors had advised her to be consistently truthful.

"Oh, no," gasped Margaret. "Why didn't someone tell me?"

"We did tell you, Mom. You were right there at the funeral."

"Ohhh," groaned Margaret as she returned to stroking her

forehead. "I have to know what I'm supposed to do. I don't know what to do here."

Today's conversation—to the extent it could be called a conversation—followed an established pattern. The same questions, the same answers. "You don't have to do anything, Mom. Everything is taken care of." Knowing the litany of her concerns, Liddy addressed each in succession. "Your care is all paid for; you have no financial concerns. This is your home now, and it's a Lutheran home; it's run by the church—you see Pastor Stensrud every few days. So everything is just as it should be."

Margaret nodded, but when the litany had reached an end she looked up with supplication. "But I want to come home with you, Liddy. Please take me home with you." A deep sense of loss was invariably called up by this plea, a plea that was made in every conversation between mother and daughter, whether in person or by phone. But until recently Liddy had been able to buck up and shake it off. Now she was powerless against the flow of warm tears, tears that came often, unbidden and out of nowhere. Sitting in a meeting the day before, she had been overtaken by a rush of unexplainable sadness and had to leave the room to avoid having her sobs witnessed. What in God's name was happening to her?

"You can't come home with me, Mom. I can't take care of you," she said with a wobbly voice. She felt responsible. Not just for this. For everything. For her mother, for suffering employees, for terminated employees—for all human suffering the world over. Whatever chemicals mediated guilt, were flooding her brain circuits. All she could do was weep. The brief interval of light that had shone through as she embarked on the ride down had been replaced by the all-told darkness from which recovery seemed less and less possible.

"What room is Dad in?" said Margaret, starting the cycle over, oblivious to time or space.

A nurse entered the room with a cart full of tiny cups containing the morning pills for the residents of the wing. "Hi, Margaret. How are you doing today?" she said in a kindly, practiced voice.

Liddy was in awe of these staff people, so patient and good-hearted. All day they worked with decaying human bodies and minds, changing bed linens and diapers, absorbing unreasonable demands, even insults. Yet she had never seen one of them lose patience. She wondered if it was the religious character of Holy Redeemer that accounted for this. Only religious faith, she thought, could enable ordinary people to carry out such works of mercy. She didn't know what had become of her own faith, the faith she had enjoyed, and taken for granted, her whole life. Until recently she had thought of that faith as unassailable, rock-solid. But if she truly believed in the core Christian message, in the reality of the heavenly hosts and the sovereignty of a benevolent god, if she truly believed in the joyful and certain inheritance of god's kingdom as promised in Sunday school, how could she be suffering such unrelenting torment, such sickness of soul? Physical pain and sickness she could understand, for rain falls on the just and unjust alike. But this was something else. Her mind seemed to be collapsing—not at the edges, but right at the center, where her soul resided. And that disintegration was to her utterly incompatible with the faith she thought she had possessed, an untested faith that must have been false all along. That was the only conclusion her logical mind would permit. But then logic was the last faculty to depart in people going mad.

Margaret looked up at the nurse and, pointing to Liddy, said, "This is my sister Carol. She's a farmer." The nurse winked at Liddy as she helped Margaret wash down the pills. Carol had indeed been a farmer, but she had been dead for over twenty years.

"No, I'm Liddy, Mom, remember?"

"Yes, I know," said Margaret blankly.

"You might wheel her down to the activities area," suggested the nurse, removing the blood pressure cuff from Margaret's withered arm. "She seems to track a little bit better when she's in a group. She loves to play checkers."

Liddy nodded agreement, taking a position behind the wheelchair. She leaned down closer to Margaret's ear. "We're going down to the recreation area, Mom."

"Yes, I know," said Margaret.

Outside the nursing station Oscar was trying to grope a passing nurse's aide, who let out a squeal as she cut to the other side of the hallway. The activities director was standing in the center of a vast circle of wheelchairs, tossing a giant beachball to the seated residents, fully half of whom were sound asleep. A Lawrence Welk tape played loudly in the background.

Every now and then a great scream would rise up from somewhere in the crowd. Several residents rocked back and forth, emitting sounds that would be taken for agony if issued by persons in full possession of their faculties. The staff went about their chores, as oblivious to these interruptions as if they were in a nursery full of newborns. As she gazed about, Liddy wondered about the histories of the physical wrecks strewn about the room. They had once been healthy, functioning human beings; some beautiful, some brilliant, all now just vessels of pain and confusion. And yet she would have changed places with any of them, believing that whatever their disabilities or limitations, they were less trapped than she in what felt like a walking nightmare. Even her brief moments of respite, of elevated mood, seemed a curse in their own way, for they were so short-lived and the re-descent so painful that it might be better just to stay on the bottom.

She sat motionless, unable to be present to her mother— unable to do anything but endlessly review her own stresses and misfortunes, now so greatly exaggerated. These stresses had become like cracks in her psyche, fault lines slowly spreading toward a point of merger where her mind would eventually lose its structural integrity and shatter into small pieces.

A large picture window bathed the recreation area in natural sunlight. Outside in the courtyard a birdfeeder sat atop a five-foot-high metal staff. Birds, mostly sparrows, fed lavishly upon a seed concoction, picking so aggressively with their tiny beaks that seeds were tossed in all directions. They looked like frolicking children having a pillow fight. To the left of the feeder, St. Francis of Assisi stretched his cement arms heavenward. As her eyes dropped to the ground, she saw a black-and-white spotted cat belonging to a neighbor sitting motionless below the feeder, its head up, eyes riveted on the feeding birds.

Without warning, the cat sprang from the ground into the air, catching a tiny sparrow in its claws and mouth, killing it instantly. Liddy gasped in horror while two janitors cleaning up a spill by the window gave out a congratulatory hoot and high-fived each other as though the cat had just sunk a forty-foot putt. They were only observing nature as it was. She knew that. But nature to her didn't seem noble; it seemed cruel. And her psychological boundaries had crumbled so completely that she identified with that sparrow with an awful poignancy.

Outside in the parking lot, from a distance of fifty feet she saw that both front tires of her car had been flattened. Watching the AAA-dispatched serviceperson—a young man with oily hair, who told her the tires had been slashed—she unsuccessfully fought off the thought that Brad Crosshaven had done this.

Back at her house, with the sunset ushering in darkness and the shadows long across the living room, there was a voice message from Skeeter inviting Liddy to join the Swenson family for a Sunday picnic, one from a local department store notifying her that the skirt she had ordered was available for pickup, and one from her mother asking what room her father was in. Last in line, after two silent hang-ups, was a deep male voice: "I heard you turned me in, you cunt. You'll be sorry."

14

A clear sky, blue and cloudless, made for perfect flying conditions as Riley, two mid-level executives, and the company's chief outside lobbyist arrived at Valley Field, where the Lindbergh's two corporate jets were housed.

The midlevel executives were in charge of the company's relationships with casualty agents in small rural areas throughout the twenty-state region in which the Lindbergh's business franchise was principally located. In response to a full-court press by the commercial banking industry, there was pending before Congress legislation which, if passed into law, would greatly increase the competition faced by the company's affiliated agents in locations outside major urban centers. The insurance industry, in turn, had launched a counteroffensive through its professional lobbyists and political contacts to stop, slow down, or at a minimum frustrate the passage of any legislation that would expand the power of banks to underwrite and sell insurance products beyond their present capabilities.

The outside lobbyist, Beth Gleason, was a former high-level staff person in the office of Congressman Danamore "Dan" Cleveland, chairman of the house committee through which any such bills would have to pass before reaching the floor. Bright, beautiful, and charming, Beth had been to Dan

Cleveland advisor, conscience, scold, uplifter, and supplier of intellectual horsepower. She was the ideal person to spearhead the Lindbergh strategy of suppressing bank competition through legislative fiat.

Beyond the broad picture window of the terminal waiting area the larger of the two Lindbergh corporate jets could be seen taxiing in from the main north-south runway, its great gleaming bulk turning ponderously like a majestic ocean liner. It was a Challenger 604—sixty-eight feet long and nearly twenty-one feet in height. It cost the "no-frills" Lindbergh a cool nineteen million dollars. It was Buck's favorite toy, his home away from home.

Riley and his small group of fellow travelers emerged from the building and made their way toward the jet, which was returning from Boca Viejo with three passengers entered on the flight log as "Mr. B. Setter," "Ms. F. French," and "Mr. S. Boy," disguising the true identities of the Montrowe family dogs (Butch and Fifi) and Buck's foul-mouthed parrot, Stud Boy. As the plane rolled toward the passenger pick-up area, Fifi could be seen gazing out one of the starboard passenger windows with an awestruck, wide-eyed expression, as though she were seeing Paris for the first time. Butch was sniffing Fifi's personal areas, which according to the steward he had been doing since they passed over Atlanta.

As Riley approached the plane, he could see Sonny Clinton, chief pilot of the Lindbergh flight team, unloading dog luggage from the plane's cargo area, and muttering to himself, "Those goddamn mutts! I'm not a pilot. I'm a zoologist."

Slamming shut the luggage door, he turned to see Riley making his way toward the plane a few paces ahead of the rest of the group. "Oh, hiya, Riley, how ya doin'?" he said. Without waiting for a reply, he continued, "Hang on a minute. I gotta clean up a pile of crap next to the fridge. That goddamn Butch—every time we get above seven thousand feet he takes a shit."

Sonny lowered his voice as the remainder of the group approached the plane, and bending his face closer to Riley's, he whispered, "I'll tell you something, Riley. I didn't fly sixty-seven combat missions in Korea and Vietnam to end up in the animal transport business. That goddamn parrot, Stud-Boy, kept telling me to 'go fuck myself' the whole three hours we were in the air. Why should I take that kind of shit from a bird?"

Not knowing the answer to Sonny's question, Riley just shrugged and nodded sympathetically.

Sonny now looked in both directions as though he was worried about being overheard. He then looked at Riley and said, "I don't know what's worse, transporting those fucking animals or transporting fucking Buck Montrowe. That prick thinks he's the Shah of Iran or something. And that official boot-licker of his, Wally, is just about as bad."

Riley looked around to be sure Wally, who was out at the airport to pick up the pets, wasn't within hearing distance. Should Sonny Clinton's attitude, let alone his words, get back to Buck, he wouldn't last a day. Riley liked Sonny and didn't want to see him get fired, but he had to admit that he was a little worried about somebody this agitated flying an airplane that went really fast. And had him on it. He was relieved to find that the copilot would be doing the driving this trip.

As the plane's steward carried Stud Boy's cage past the group, the bird screamed, "Douche bag!" at one of the mid-level executives, causing him to flinch in surprise.

Fifi, a pink bow tied to the top of her head, jumped compliantly into the backseat of the company car Wally pulled up to the tarmac. Butch took a quick sniff of the items removed from the luggage compartment before lifting his leg and pissing on his own suitcase. When Wally shouted rudely (in a tone he never took with Butch when Buck was around), Butch ran in a tight semicircle and dove headlong into the backseat of the car, face-first into Fifi's crotch. Wally and the Montrowe pets then disappeared down the terminal service road.

Riley shook his head and headed for the plane. He ducked slightly as he entered the cabin, more out of habit than necessity, for the six-foot-two-inch clearance was more than sufficient to accommodate his dwindling height. The forward part of the passenger area contained a conference layout of a large table (which could be dropped to make a double bed) and side

171

chairs covered in tan velvet across from a four-seat couch. Seating for an additional six people was spread on both sides of a center aisle covered in rich green carpeting. On the grass-cloth-covered bulkhead hung an expensive oil painting of a distinctly modern character, depicting through the use of grotesquely misshapen birds some kind of inner struggle that no one but Buck claimed to understand. Using the grim calculus of the downsizing, Riley ran the numbers in his head and determined that the acquisition of that pretentiously silly painting ($78,000.00) had cost two people their jobs.

Down the aisle, across from a second couch, was a wetbar stocked with every imaginable alcoholic beverage. Above the bar, between two gold sconces giving off a pale yellowish light, were two framed photographs: the first a wide-angle shot of Buck's Boca Viejo home (a sweeping, three-story structure of Italian design known locally as Castle Montrowe) and the second a head-and-shoulders color photo of Butch sitting upright in an almost human position. The photographer must have dangled a dog biscuit high in the air to get Butch to strike that pose. He looked like a canine J. P. Morgan.

Nineteen-million dollars to buy this plane, mused Riley as he looked down the long center aisle, an aisle that finally ended in a bathroom with wall-to-wall mirrors and gold light fixtures above a marble sink. Nineteen-million dollars. That would translate into about two hundred jobs. Two hundred human beings tossed out on the street to pay for this airborne obscenity. To relieve his mind of this repetitive and useless exercise, he pulled out a book on genealogy and forced himself to read it until they arrived in Washington.

Awaiting the group at Dulles Airport were two limousines, one of conventional size (as limousines go) and the other the length of a small football field. As they deplaned the jet, a tall man with black hair, dressed in a double-breasted top coat, identified himself as "Andre." He wore a uniform that made him look like an aide-de-camp to the last czar. He gave a snappy salute to Riley while opening the back door of the stretch limo.

The smell of rich leather upholstery permeated the cab of the limousine. A wet bar, two sixteen-inch TVs, and two built-in telephones (one for outside calls and one to communicate with Andre up front) were within easy reach.

"This is disgusting," said Riley to Beth Gleason, looking around the expensively appointed cab of the limousine. "Who made these arrangements?"

"I don't know," replied Beth. "Gladys probably did. This is the set-up for every trip I make to Washington on Lindbergh business when there's a senior executive in attendance."

"Well, I guess I'm the senior executive in attendance, and I don't want any part of this. I just fired a bunch of nice, competent people in the name of expense control, and look at the money that's being pissed away here. It's sickening." Riley picked up the internal phone and called the driver. "Say, Andre, we won't be needing this limousine. We'll just grab a taxi at the terminal."

"But, sir, the service has already been paid for," said a surprised Andre as he peered into the rearview mirror, trying to identify the author of this strange request. His dark, beady eyes darted back and forth between the roadway and the mirror. His elaborate chauffeur's cap looked like it belonged on a German field marshal.

Beth Gleason seemed to be having fun watching Riley's discomfort.

As they turned right out of the airport, Riley noticed that the shorter limo was directly in front of them, as though leading a procession. "What's with this car in front of us?" he asked Andre.

"That is the escort vehicle, sir," said Andre matter-of-factly. "It is driven by my colleague, Jean-Paul. These are the standing arrangements put in place by Mr. Montrowe's office."

Riley looked over at Beth Gleason disbelievingly, then said into the phone, "Well, Andre, tell Jean-Paul to vamoose. I'll be damned if I'll be seen in a multicar motorcade, whether it's been paid for or not." Vamoose was the only foreign-sounding word he knew that meant "go away," but he knew it probably wasn't French.

"Excuse me one moment, sir," said Andre as he picked up his other phone and dialed back to limo headquarters. After a short, muted conversation, Andre slid open the glass partition and handed the phone to Riley. A syrupy voice with a trace of a French accent said, "Good morning, Mr. McReynolds. This is Pierre, and I understand you have a question concerning the ground transportation."

"Yes I do, Pierre," said Riley in a controlled and reasonable tone. "I'd like you to tell Jean-Paul *hasta la vista*, as our group does not wish to be part of a make-believe presidential motorcade." Damn, *hasta la vista* wasn't French either.

"But, Monsieur, these are the arrangements we make for Mr. Montrowe whenever he is in town."

"That's fine, Pierre," said Riley, "but Mr. Montrowe is not aboard this trip, and we insist that Jean-Paul drop out of this procession pronto." Pronto? Shit! Foreign-sounding words were cascading through his mind, but to his frustration none sounded French.

"Very well, sir," said an obviously irritated Pierre, sounding like a waiter in an upscale restaurant who has just been asked for a bottle of ketchup.

The turn signal on the lead limo blinked, and Jean-Paul disappeared down a side street.

After a twenty-minute wait in Chairman Cleveland's anteroom, a large, balding man with flattened features and a florid complexion entered the room flanked by two male aides fresh out of law schools located in his congressional district. The Lindbergh party sprang from their seats, ready to extend personal greetings to the chairman. He gave only perfunctory nods to the men as he headed in a beeline for Beth Gleason, on whom he laid a ferocious bear hug that was somewhere between avuncular and salacious. When all were seated and Beth had glided through a brief, fact-filled update concerning her career and family, she launched into a remarkably concise and intelligent description of the Lindbergh position on the pending legislation. Several minutes into her remarks, she glanced in Riley's direction, saying, "And Riley McReynolds can summarize the constitutional difficulties with this piece of bad legislation."

Riley sat forward in his chair and cleared his throat. "Mr. Chairman, our attorneys have taken a careful look at the pending bill, and they believe that subdivisions four and five—"

174

Cutting him off midsentence, the congressman said, "Put it in writing and send it to one of these young geniuses here," pointing dismissively toward his twin aides without looking in their direction. He never took his eyes off Beth, who continued to smile at him with an expression one might use on a rich uncle with a bad heart.

Precisely eleven minutes into the meeting and pursuant to prearrangement, the chairman's administrative assistant entered the room and loudly informed him that he was due in the Speaker's office in five minutes. The nameless aides rose as one from their seats, taking positions on each side of the congressman, as though forming an honor guard.

Laying another mauling bearhug on Beth, he said, "By God, I don't know how I survive without you, Missy. I've had a broken heart ever since you left."

"Come on, Mr. Chairman, don't lay that political charm on me," replied Beth, giving him a gentle punch on the arm. But she knew he meant it, knew he had been as hopelessly in love with her as it is possible for a decaying old man to be with a twenty-seven-year-old woman. So in love that he hadn't dared risk an amorous advance, for fear that a failed attempt would deprive him forever of her friendship.

Back in the limo, Riley turned to Beth. "That sure was short. Did it do any good? It seemed like a waste of time to me."

"Believe me, it did a lot of good," she said. "It's not about the length of time spent with him. It's about our being willing to come halfway across the country to see him, to pay homage to him. And he now associates the Lindbergh position with me—symbolically, spiritually, physically. Those two little snots who will do the analysis and workup on our written submission and make changes to the pending bill know from his behavior that he will have a strong visceral bias in favor of our position. And they always try to trim their analysis and recommendations to his prejudices. Just like all you corporate types do for your CEOs." She delivered this last crack with a mischievous smile, winking at him. But what she had said was the truth, and they both knew it.

Riley looked out the window. "The whole business makes me hungry. Let's whip through Wendy's on the way back to the airport." He believed out-of-town travel was an exception to his diet, a standing dispensation.

The rest of the party gave indifferent nods.

"What may I ask is Wendy's?" stammered a caught-off-guard Andre when Riley slid open the glass partition and announced the group's lunch plans.

"You know, Andre, the fast-food joint. We can shoot into the drive-through and eat on the way to the plane," said Riley. Beth put a hand over her face and laughed quietly. She was a veteran of Pierre's limousine service, having accompanied Buck on several trips to Capitol Hill.

Several minutes later, Andre opened the partition and without a word handed his car phone back to Riley. "Monsieur McReynolds," came Pierre's effete, soprano voice, "allow me to make reservations for you at the most exclusive restaurant in Washington. It is where Mr. Montrowe dines when in town. It is very tony. You will be pleased with it."

"Tony? No thanks, Pierre. We're in kind of a hurry, and just want to grab a burger on the way out of town," said Riley. Beth Gleason, peering through the fingers of her left hand, was now rocking with suppressed laughter.

Riley had begun to sense that his culinary and transportation preferences were at odds with the corporate elite. As the product of a semi-privileged Midwestern upbringing, he had been raised to regard this type of vulgar excess as the exclusive province of the newly rich. Such demonstrations were virtually nonexistent among those of established wealth or high educational achievement where he was raised. The cultural example with which he had grown up, combined with the disdain with which his father had viewed elitism in any form, accounted for his visceral uneasiness in surroundings such as these. Added to that was the horrific disparity between the garish flaunting of privilege in which he was now encapsulated and the desperate circumstances of those on the other end of the economic spectrum, many of whom could be seen through the tinted windows of the limousine as it rolled through the slums of Washington. Beth Gleason came from a similar upbringing, endowing her with common sympathies. But she possessed enough common political sense to keep her mouth shut. And so long as Riley was impolitic enough to criticize these absurd practices, she could sit back and watch the point be made. It was at least a partial liberation from her own discomfort.

"Pierre, we are not interested in a tony restaurant, whatever that is," said Riley firmly. "We are interested in a couple of grease bombs. Please tell Monsieur Andre to motor over to the closest Wendy's."

"I'm sorry, Mr. McReynolds, but I will not allow the most beautiful motor creation found anywhere in the world, with my coat of arms on it, to be seen driving through a fast-food restaurant. It is *too* monstrous."

Pierre's snobbish tone was almost laughable, but Riley couldn't help but feel a little sorry about the very real discomfort that lay beneath the major hissy-fit he was throwing. "All right, Pierre, we don't wish to cause you any embarrassment. Have Andre pull up a half block from Wendy's, and I'll go in and get the burgers and bring them back to the car."

Now almost in tears: "Mr. McReynolds . . . we cannot have the odor of cheap and vulgar food seeping into the upholstery of our vehicles. I am sorry—it is the restaurant I have recommended or nothing at all."

"How about if we get chicken sandwiches and Frostys. They don't smell too bad," said Riley to an almost out of control Pierre. As he spoke, he looked directly at Beth, who was now nearly hysterical, tears flowing from her eyes, her face buried in her lap.

From the front cab, Andre could be seen shaking his head in disgust.

"Mr. McReynolds," said Pierre, the pronunciation drawn out to twice its normal length, "you don't get it, do you?"

Ah, there it was! It had to come sooner or later. Now he felt at home. That stock reference to the ineffable, esoteric body of knowledge available only to certain special, select individuals like Pierre and Buck and Garfie. People who wouldn't be seen in regular cars, at ordinary places like Wendy's because of some innate superiority they possessed over the great unwashed mass of ordinary people. After all, what good was their wealth and status if it couldn't be used to lord it over other people?

"Look, Pierre, I'll compromise," said a very hungry Riley. "We'll go instead to McDonald's, and I'll go in and get the food."

A long silence, and then: "You, Mr. McReynolds, are a pig!" shouted Pierre in a near falsetto, slamming down his phone.

"Pee-air, such hostility," said Riley, bewildered by the intensity of the reaction he had provoked. He held the now-dead phone off to one side and glanced over at Beth with a hurt look. "He hung up on me."

Beth Gleason, gasping for air, laughed so hard she wet her pants on the leather seats of the most beautiful motor creation found anywhere in the world.

Riley put the dead phone back up to his ear and for Andre's benefit said, "Au revoir, asshole."

15

R iley, darling, you are not getting shorter," said an exasperated Betsy in a voice one might use when talking to a child in crisis. The phone receiver was cradled between her shoulder and left ear as she scraped breakfast dishes and placed them neatly in the dishwasher. "At least not a lot shorter."

"Oh . . . so I *am* getting shorter! I knew it. Just like Grandma Carr," said Riley into his office phone in the ah-ha voice he had perfected during the cross-examination of hundreds of criminal defendants. "How fast am I shrinking? Tell the truth." Having gotten under way with his diet the previous week, he was filled with anxiety that the low-calorie regimen would accelerate the vertical shrinkage to which he was heir.

Rolling her eyes and shaking her head, Betsy said, "I didn't mean it that way. It's just that we all shrink a little over the years, and you're just like everybody else."

"Just like Grandma Carr, you mean," said Riley. He was sure he'd follow the course set by his grandmother and end up looking like Rose Kennedy, who at the time of her death was about a foot and a half tall.

Betsy poured detergent into the soap compartment while Tuffy licked food particles from the silverware. She said in a patient, reassuring voice, "I've had Skeeter set up a height chart in the coat closet, right next to the scale. She'll measure your height at the weekly weigh-ins for your diet. You'll see that your size reduction will be all horizontal. Now please go back to work."

"Well, wait, don't hang up yet," said Riley as he reached for a Milky Way in the middle drawer and tried to peel the wrapper off without being heard by either Betsy or Skeeter. He was amazed at how good he had gotten at this maneuver. He could remove candy wrappers almost soundlessly, even when he had to use his teeth to get started. And he figured he was probably the only guy in America who could do that. "Tell me what you've been doing today," he asked as he prepared to bite into the combination of creamy caramel and rich milk chocolate.

"Riley, you're just bored, so you want to keep me on the phone. I've got to get going," said Betsy as she looked at her calendar of activities for the day. "Go bug Skeeter, she gets paid to listen to you."

"No, no . . . I'm interested in what you're doing."

"Okay," she said wearily. "I got Teddy off on the bus at 8:32." She started wiping off the kitchen counter as she looked upward, trying to recall the sequence of her day. "By the way, I caught Teddy picking his nose and flicking it at one of the other kids. Did you tell him he could do that? He said you did."

Riley crunched his shoulders in a silent and unseen acknowledgment that he had asked one too many question. "Was the bus on time? It's been late recently," he said.

"Don't try to change the subject. Did you tell him he could do that?" "That" referred to flicking boogers, but Betsy found the word boogers so revolting she couldn't actually use it.

"No . . . not really," said Riley, like a man flagging a lie-detector test.

Betsy's counter-wiping stopped cold, her tone stiffened. "What do you mean 'not really'?"

"Well, I told him he could flick the crispy ones. You know, the kind you can fire at your buddies across the classroom. Chasbo Peytabohm and I used to launch about five an hour back at Sacred Heart when the air was really dry. He used to snag 'em on the back of Sister Nicole's veil when she was at the blackboard." He chuckled nostalgically. "But I told Teddy to stay away from the wet ones. You can't get any altitude or air speed with those. And sometimes if you try to launch a wet one it catches on the end of your finger and it's murder getting it off." By his routine, businesslike tone, one might suppose he had been instructing Teddy on the proper use of a lawn mower or an electric razor.

"Oh, no, you didn't really tell him that?" she gagged.

"It's a boy thing, Betsy. You wouldn't understand."

"I understand that most boys, of all ages, are gross. But I don't think fathers should teach their sons to flick bo—hoog." Her voice trailed off into a full-throated dry-heave.

Wanting to change the subject, he asked, "So what did you do after Teddy got off to school?"

Betsy swallowed hard to calm the gag reflex before yielding to the change of topic. "I made the mistake on the way back from the bus of making eye contact with Mr. Olson over the back fence and asking him how he was. That got him going full speed. He came in for coffee and talked for forty-five minutes about his gall bladder surgery last month."

"Why didn't you make up an excuse to move him out?" said Riley as he put his feet up on the desk and stuck his tongue out at Skeeter as she emptied the in-basket. She responded by giving him the finger.

Betsy continued, "Oh, he's such a dear old guy, I just love him. I couldn't bring myself to brush him off. He just adores me—says I'm the spitting image of his daughter in Vancouver." She now switched to the portable phone and moved upstairs to sort underwear from the morning laundry.

Riley thought about the irony of him sitting in a palatial office downtown discharging big-dollar responsibilities while Betsy sat at home sorting underwear. Back in grade school she was the class genius, and by any standard his intellectual, not to mention cultural, superior. In fourth grade they had taken her over to the university for those gifted-children tests, trying to figure out why some nine-year olds could understand differential calculus, while Riley was back at Sacred Heart flick-

181

ing boogers, writing Kotex notes, and biting people's ears off. At one point they were going to have him looked at by the university too but for a different reason. But she was happy with the choices she had freely made, and he was happy that she was happy.

At that Skeeter got on the extension. "Betsy, I've got to talk to you. Riley, get off."

Riley hung up compliantly.

As he started to page through a stack of regulatory reports, he could hear Skeeter laughing hysterically with Betsy, and though he couldn't prove it, he knew the laughs were at his expense. He felt like the boy in junior high who didn't realize his fly was open in a room full of giggling girls.

"Yes, right! . . . right!" shouted Skeeter, exploding in laughter. "Not an ounce," she screamed, followed by more ecstatic laughter.

They were talking about the diet. They had to be. Looking toward the closet outside his office, he could see that damn scale sitting in the corner. He knew this diet couldn't be a bust like the last three. The fourth-floor secretaries had organized a betting pool, essentially designed to reward those who thought he'd run true to form and actually gain weight this time around as he had in previous attempts.

His last try had been the Slim Fast Diet. He had a shake for breakfast, a shake for lunch, and a sensible meal for dinner. Then he had another sensible meal at eight o'clock, and another one at ten. He gained three pounds the first week.

But this vote of no-confidence from his friends was really too much. Did they think he had no will power, no self-respect? He'd show them. But what a frustration it was, this business of responsible eating. All his life he had been able to eat anything he wanted, even as an adult, so long as he kept up physical activity. But then something changed, a kind of a metabolic menopause, and he had to start watching calories or things got thick all over. This was grownup stuff, and he hated being a grownup. It was uncomfortable and boring.

What his tormentors didn't know was that this time around he had surreptitiously signed up with a weight-loss program on the other side of downtown, where he could be anonymous. It guaranteed quick and lasting results. Having enrolled by telephone, he didn't know what to expect at the newcomer's meeting, but was still surprised to be the only man among the twenty participants. There he was, crammed into a room full of fat women, most of whom started to cry when they gave their first name during the introductions. A blonde behemoth to his right named Darlene took up half his seat with her left thigh. This pushed him practically onto the lap of Tanya, a jumbo-breasted biker chick with a spiked-leather dog collar around her neck who stared lustily at him through eyes encrusted with dark blue eyeliner. Riley slipped on a pair of sunglasses and, for reasons he couldn't explain, introduced himself as "Duke." This served only to further inflame Tanya, who now had her hand on his knee.

The facilitator, Maxine, had the bleached, cadaverous look of someone who was once twice her present size—and would be again if she ate even one normal meal. "Well, Duke, it looks like you're the king of this class, eh?" she said with chopped, stacca-to laughter. Nervous giggling rippled through the room. Riley smiled shyly, adjusting his sunglasses, while trying not to look to his left where he could feel Tanya's steamy eyes upon him.

Fourteen first names and buckets of tears later, Maxine began explaining the weekly weigh-ins, support group meet-ings, and the tasty array of nutritious and reasonably priced food items available in the display room next door. In the mid-dle of her remarks, from the back of the room came heavy shuffling and wheezing and the sound of a door opening, through which passed a man the size of a small Zamboni. He was a slam-dunk four-hundred pounds, maybe more, his fea-tures barely discernible under the massive folds and fleshy deposits of his face.

"Ah, hello, Willie," Maxine shouted to the back of the room. "Welcome back. It's good to have another man around the house." More nervous laughter. "This is perfect! You and Duke can pair up under our buddy system."

When Riley turned to look at the spot from which the shuf-fling and wheezing had come and caught sight of Willie, he nearly jumped into Tanya's arms, being suddenly drawn to strong, protective women.

His reminiscence was interrupted by the sound of the intercom on his desk. Skeeter would normally have answered it, but she and Betsy were still busy making fun of him.

"Riley McReynolds," he said as he put the receiver to his ear.

It was Nancy Park, filling in for Judy Goodrich at the front desk. "Hey, Riley, I heard you're on a diet again. Good thing, too. Skeeter says your ass is getting really big." Nancy thought this crack was hysterical, as she went weak with laughter, nearly dropping the phone.

It was nice that these administrative assistants were able to give shit to at least one senior executive who wouldn't fire them on the spot. The human resources people told Riley he was too casual with the "lower ranks," and that he should make them keep a respectful distance. He told them to get a life.

Riley smiled wanly, his face turning an embarrassed pink. "Yeah, you're really funny, Nancy. You'll all see when I win the betting pool," he said. "Don't you have anything better to do than make fun of me?"

"Actually, I called for a legitimate reason." She now lowered her voice to a whisper. "You've got a strange looking person out here asking to see you. Says the name is Tenzie Dunseth. I think it's a woman, but I'm not sure."

"Sure, that's Tenzie—a tall woman with frizzy hair, right?"

"Yup, that's her. What do you want me to say?"

"Tell her to come on back. She's an old friend of mine."

"Oh, geez, I'm glad I called you," said Nancy. "I almost pushed the security button when I saw her get off the elevator. We don't see many people who look like that in the Sacristy."

"Send her back. There won't be any problem."

"Okay, whatever you say," said Nancy in a voice that disclaimed responsibility for what might develop.

Tenzie ducked under the archway separating the west side from the Sacristy, stooping slightly to clear her six-foot-three inch height and the high pompadour of salt-and-pepper hair standing straight in the air, in the fashion of Don King. Her

230-pound girth was confined uneasily in a pair of enormous bib overalls.

"Hey, Riley! How they hangin'?" yelled Tenzie as she passed Skeeter's desk, a large strap slung across her shoulder, at the end of which hung a canvas sack full of handbills cataloging the social and economic sins of The Lindbergh. At the center of each handbill was a grainy, head-and-shoulders photo of Buck, next to which were emblazoned the words: WANTED— FOR CRIMES AGAINST THE PEOPLE.

Tenzie handed a flyer to Skeeter while leaning over her desk. "What's it like working for this little fascist?" For the first time in her life Skeeter seemed speechless, transfixed by the sight before her.

Riley met Tenzie at Skeeter's desk, extending his hand, smiling warmly. "How you doin', Tenzie? Long time, huh?" She seized his hand in a soul-brother grip while slapping his ass with the other hand. Riley jumped a little, breaking into an abashed smile, nodding his head up and down. Skeeter thought this was very funny.

"How'd you get up here, Tenzie? I can't believe you smooth-talked the security guards into giving you a safe conduct pass," said Riley, as they walked toward his office.

"Naw, I used the freight elevator to get up to the third floor and then switched over to the regular elevators to get to four." She dropped her full bulk into a side chair, which let out a groan. "I know the union steward on the loading dock. He was happy to sneak me up. Jimmy Wadsworth—remember him from the Selma March? Played guitar but only knew three chords. He's still a good citizen. Didn't sell out like you."

Color rose up the back of Riley's neck and into his ears. "I didn't sell out, Tenzie. I'm the same person I always was. I hated discrimination, and I hated the Vietnam War—the War for a very personal reason as you may recall. But I didn't think cops were pigs, and I didn't hate the country or the government or anyone who had an opinion different from mine, like those phony revolutionaries you used to hang around with." He stopped abruptly. This was where they had left off nearly thirty years before, and he could see that she was amused that she could still get him so irritated and defensive with just a few words.

He felt foolish. She had always had fun with him, the frat boy in the tan khakis and penny loafers, who got mixed up in the movement; the one who refused to wear the uniform of the New Left or spout the sayings of Chairman Mao or throw bags full of shit at the ROTC building.

But they had been pals, nevertheless. There was no one in the world he had admired more. For her it was a kick to have a real live Republican as a comrade on the barricades. A Rockefeller Republican, to be sure, but there were lots of them in the old days, before the parties were delivered without a struggle into the hands of the special interests of the right and left.

Riley took a deep breath and settled back, while Tenzie smiled silently across the table.

He reached for a Milky Way to calm himself. "Want one?" he said.

"No, thanks, they give me zits. I have to watch my cover girl complexion." She brushed her hair back like a fashion model preparing for a photo shoot.

Riley smiled as he reached across the table for a handbill. "What's this crap, Tenzie?" he said. "Let's see here: 'Lindbergh Life & Casualty Company—Slum Landlord; Environmental Criminal; Racist/Sexist Employer; Exploiter of the Poor.' Geez, Tenzie, that's a lot of bad stuff. How'd we come in for all that name-calling?"

Tenzie shrugged as she leaned back in her chair. "You're no worse than a lot of other fat-cat companies in town. You're just vulnerable to bad publicity because of your downsizing. You can't stand more negative stories right now, so we're going to help you do your social duty, or"—she tapped a surprisingly well-tended, graceful index finger on the Wanted Poster picture of Buck—"I'm goin' to personally rip this guy a new asshole."

Riley studied the grainy photo of Buck on the wanted poster and wondered where they had gotten it. He looked like he was trying to pass a hard stool. Scanning the six-count mock indictment, he asked, "Why are we slum landlords, Tenzie?

186

The only residential properties owned by The Lindbergh are the ones we get back on mortgage foreclosures, and those are put up for immediate resale. The only stuff we own by choice is commercial property, like this building."

She cocked her head to the side and gripped the sides of her chair. "So what?" she said with an uncompromising smile. "Those are just details. The Lindbergh is part of a corrupt business establishment that exploits the poor day in and day out. It deserves to be held up every now and then for the good of the people."

"But doesn't it bother you that these specific charges are untrue?" asked Riley.

"Same old Riley," she groaned impatiently, "always wanting to apply morality at the micro level. Just like the old days when we'd make up inflated atrocity figures in Vietnam and you'd get all upset. Get over it, my boy. When you're fighting powerful institutions, you can't fight fair. We were up against the Pentagon then—the biggest pack of liars who ever lived—and now we're up against a stone-cold business establishment, the second biggest pack of liars who ever lived. And they've got a lot more power than we do, so we take our shots where we can get them. And believe me, we're on the moral high ground, even if we have to fudge a few facts here and there." She held forth with the concentrated certainty of true believers everywhere. For all their superficial differences, she had more in common with Buck Montrowe that either of them would care to admit. They were both about fudging facts: Tenzie for the good of humanity, Buck for the good of himself. The social altruist and the social Darwinist. Riley didn't like their methods, either of them, but at least he admired Tenzie and the devotion with which she pursued objectives that he considered worthy.

Several fourth-floor personnel had gathered outside Riley's office, hoping to get a look at the strange visitor. Riley walked slowly to the door and gently closed it from the inside. "Why the wanted poster of Buck, Tenzie? Isn't that a little personal?"

Tenzie shook her head. "In the end, all life is personal. This one man can cause The Lindbergh to fund a homeless shelter

187

with a wave of his hand. And for all the millions he makes each year he should be able to take a little heat."

"Yeah, I hear you delivered a little heat his way the morning of the board meeting, when he tried to make his way to the elevators."

"Yup," she smiled. "Caught him with that little twit who carries his briefcase. I don't know which one looked more scared. Buck tried to turn on the charm. What the hell's wrong with his face anyway? Right out of nowhere he got this goofy look, like he was having a seizure or something."

Riley laughed involuntarily, covering his face with the wanted poster. He turned without comment to another subject. "So what do you want, Tenzie? What do you need to take the Red Guards someplace else, like over to The St. Paul Companies or First Bank?"

Tenzie gave him an I-thought-you'd-never-ask-look as she pulled a legal pad from her satchel. "The Lindbergh owns a seventy-unit apartment building on Rice Street that's damn near completely empty." She turned the page to a set of figures on a spreadsheet. "It's worth about eight-hundred thousand dollars—pretty run down. Buck Montrowe could get a lot of good publicity for himself by donating the building to the Homeless Empowerment Council. He could jack up the price for tax purposes and then write off the gift. It would cost the company very little. We'd then issue a press release about what a great progressive humanitarian he is. We'll give the piece of shit an award or something. The newspapers will all cover it. He'll look great." She adjusted her weight in the chair and leaned into the table. "Otherwise, we'll let the local community know about his real social views. You know, on poverty and race and gender and that kind of stuff. And believe me, we know all about him. He's a mean-ass, brain-dead reactionary, and that won't play too well around here."

Riley took a few notes as she spoke, then said, "Isn't it a little duplicitous to accept money from a guy you consider to be a hopeless redneck?"

She ran the fingers of her right hand through the mound of wiry hair exploding from the top of her head. "You don't get it,

Riley—for a large enough money contribution to a good cause I'll kiss his ass on the front steps of the State Capitol and give him the film rights. It's fine with me if the public thinks he's something he's not, so long as a good cause is served. People accuse me of all sorts of things, of being a radical and a degenerate, even a 'poverty pimp.' I'm none of those things. What I am is a pragmatist who sees suffering and injustice and tries to fix it by any means necessary. I can be charming and agreeable or I can be confrontational and intimidating—and I've got a costume and a personality for either mode. And, yeah, I can be completely disingenuous if that will get the job done. My test is how many people who have been screwed all their lives get helped not how many closet rednecks I expose."

Riley sat in silence, bewildered by yet another thing he didn't get. He was sure Tenzie wouldn't have struck such a cynical bargain in the old days—a deal that involved so much insincerity and manipulation of image. She would have demanded and gotten money for her causes, sure, but she never would have kissed up to someone like Buck. Not even the social justice movement, it seemed, had survived the eighties with its principles wholly intact.

After a moment of awkward silence, Tenzie's face broke out in an impish smile as she raised her enormous bulk from the side chair. She looked down at him affectionately and patted him on the cheek. "Poor Riley. You never did quite get it. You never really grew out of your schoolboy idealism."

"Funny," he said, "other people have been telling me the same thing."

"Anyway," said Tenzie, pointing once again at the picture of Buck, "people usually end up seeing things my way, even ones who fly around in big-ass private jets. Your man Montrowe better think about this. We're not going anywhere 'til this company engages in a little good citizenship. If he turns us down, he won't like Act II."

She broke the mood by smiling broadly and giving a sweeping look around Riley's office. "Damn, Riley," she said, "you don't belong in a place like this. You should be on the barricades with me. I don't know if I'll be able to save you from the justice of the people when the revolution comes, but I'll do my best." She laughed so enthusiastically he could see her tonsils. Just like the old days.

"Thanks, Tenzie, but don't you know that the first people the revolutionaries shoot after the revolution are the liberals who helped them? You'll be the one in front of the firing squad, and these captains of industry you hate so much will be the new commissars. I'm afraid I'll be working for the same people I'm working for now."

"You've been reading too many counterrevolutionary historians," she laughed, punching him on the arm so hard he was propelled backwards. "Besides, you used to be a socialist, too—remember?"

"Yeah, for two weeks," he admitted. "But I was also a Republican."

In the hallway outside the office a plainclothes security officer was leaning against the wall, pretending to read a newspaper. He looked as out of place as Dashiel Hammett. Tenzie stuffed a handbill in his coat pocket on the way by and said, "Why don't you get a real job, you little pimp."

The guard bristled but said nothing. Skeeter interrupted her typing to ask Tenzie, "How'd your meeting go with the little fascist?"

"Aw, he's a cute little guy," replied Tenzie, putting a suffocating bearhug on Riley, nearly lifting him off the ground.

"What do you mean 'little'?" snorted Riley as he straightened his crumpled tie.

"I don't know," said Tenzie quizzically as she stepped back, looking him up and down. "You just look shorter than you used to."

16

HEY BUCK—YOU SUCK!" . . . "HEY BUCK—YOU SUCK!"
came the sound of three-hundred angry voices shouting
in nearly perfect harmony, the vowels and consonants
bouncing off the high rafters and cold steel of the Lobby Court.
From an acoustical standpoint, the enraged mob might as well
have been in Buck's office with the assembled Lindbergh crisis
team, consisting of Gar Blaisdahl, Riley, Security Chief Dan
Thornton, and the Lindbergh's community-affairs officer, Liz
Bridge.

Buck had rejected out of hand the idea of donating an
apartment complex to the homeless and declined repeated
invitations to sit down and meet with protest organizers. Riley
and Liz Bridge had recommended in a memo that the donation
be made, but making the case for social action to a man who
had yet to come to grips with the income tax or women's suf-
frage proved to be more than they could put across.

Buck wanted no part in any "cave-ins," monetary or symbolic, to what he called "this assortment of rabble." For a man
who grew up poor and loved to brag about it, Buck was a
tremendous snob when it came to the underclass. His determination not to be found in the same room with these people
was beyond discussion, saying without irony that he wouldn't

give the sweat off his balls to a bunch of loafers who didn't work hard at a job every day. Gar and Erving enthusiastically supported Buck's rejection of Liz and Riley's harebrained recommendation, with Erving noting that history showed beyond any question that appeasing communists proved to be a mistake in the long run. He cited as an example the Hungarian Uprising of 1956, an event that had escaped Buck's notice.

The crisis-response team had convened in Buck's office to formulate a reply to the disruptive and publicly embarrassing demonstration downstairs in the middle of the customer areas. Buck, noticeably rattled by the ugly turn of events, talked a mile a minute while pacing about the office, his hands fanning the air. Riley declined a seat next to Liz Bridge to avoid the great likelihood that they'd get the giggles if they were in close proximity to each other. He had known Liz since college, long before they found themselves as joint retainers in the dysfunctional court of Buck Montrowe.

"Let's blast them out of there with fire hoses," said a serious Gar Blaisdahl, sounding like George Patton racing toward Berlin.

"Yeah," said Buck. "That'll teach 'em a lesson."

Dan Thornton rolled his eyes and shifted in his chair.

"That's really not a very good idea, Buck," said Liz, speaking with a calm authority.

Riley looked across the table at Gar. "Don't be an idiot, Gar. You do that and we'll be all over the front pages and end up paying out millions of dollars in civil judgments for assault and battery, not to mention the customers we'll lose."

Dan Thornton, whose uniformed security officers would have to take on stormtrooper duty should Gar's suggestion be implemented, sat silently in his chair, his eyes fixed on Riley, an is-this-really-happening expression on his face.

The cries of HEY BUCK - YOU SUCK! had grown in volume and hostility with each new chorus, until the meeting participants had to raise their voices just to be heard within the office. A wild, deranged-looking man in his midthirties, with a red bandanna tied around his forehead, a ring through his nose, and the tattoo of a snake spread across his left cheek,

192

had managed to scale halfway up the tiered south wall of the Lobby Court. He suddenly appeared at the glass wall of the office, glaring insanely at Buck while shouting ugly and untrue things about Buck and his mother. Handfuls of stones, scooped from the garden display in the center of the Lobby Court and thrown skyward, pinged against the glass wall of Buck's office, followed closely by deafening cheers from the assembled mob.

Riley looked up to see how Buck was reacting to all this, but the space he had occupied only seconds before was now empty. At the site of the tattoo-faced social activist, the company's alpha male had made a mad dash for the executive bathroom.

"Come on, Buck, let's go down and meet with these folks and hear 'em out. They won't kill anybody—honest," shouted Riley in a voice loud enough to be heard through the bathroom door.

"Yeah, come on, Buck. Folks are just folks," joined in Liz Bridge, winking impishly at Riley.

"Is he still out there?" came Buck's thin, high-pitched voice. It sounded as if he had retreated all the way into the shower stall.

"He's gone, Buck," called out Dan Thornton. "Two of my guys just pulled him down."

All looked expectantly in the direction of the bathroom.

After an interval of embarrassed silence, Buck's voice, which had gone weak and reedy, issued from behind the door: "You meet with them, Gar, so that we can retain executive flexibility. I'd love to go down there and teach them a lesson, but we'd lose flexibility. Flexibility is very important in a situation like this." His words were spoken in short, choppy segments, punctuated by frequent swallowing. "And you're a good negotiator from all those books you've read. You have full authority to make any deal you want. This is your baby. It'll be good for you to fly solo. I can't always be there. At some point a mentor has to step back, and provide . . . ah, provide flexibility."

The word "frightened" doesn't begin to describe the look that now came over Gar Blaisdahl's face. In a heartbeat he had been transformed from General Patton into Chicken Little, beads of perspiration condensing on facial skin drained of all color.

Liz fought back laughter. Riley leaned over to Gar, his eyebrows arched in mock commiseration: "What'd you expect, numb-nuts?"

"Well . . . you bet . . . that's fine with me," stammered Gar, hands trembling, mouth twisted in a gesture of counterfeit bravery.

"Right, that's the best way to handle it," came Buck's barely perceptible voice from deep in the caverns of the executive shitter. "I'm only sorry I can't get a crack at 'em."

After a brief discussion of timing, Liz Bridge volunteered to carry the meeting proposal to the protest leaders. Dan Thornton called upstairs to Security to advise uniformed personnel of the change in strategy. On the way out of the office, the group shouted their good-byes at the bathroom door.

"Bye-bye now," came the barely audible reply.

At 2:30 P.M. the customer conference room off the Lobby Court, just adjacent to The Lindbergh Trust Company, was ready to receive the Lindbergh delegation, consisting of Gar Blaisdahl, Liz Bridge, Riley and Lindbergh Foundation head Rick Snelling, all of whom had made their way through a gauntlet of screaming protesters.

Buck had gone on the lam, beating a hasty retreat through the sub-basement like a medieval prince fleeing an enraged peasantry. Gladys explained that Buck had just remembered a pressing engagement in Boca Viejo. At the airport, four mid-level executives from the Casualty Division, who had just boarded the plane for a meeting in Hartford, were unceremoniously yanked from their seats and left standing with their suitcases on the open tarmac. They barely caught sight of Buck as he shot into the plane without so much as a nod. He settled back limply into his seat, and after exhaling a deep sigh of relief, shouted at the copilot: "Who took a shit in here?"

By the time Tenzie Dunseth opened what would turn out to be the shortest and most one-sided negotiation in the company's history, The Lion of the Lindbergh had soared to the safety of thirty thousand feet.

Representing the SASI Strike Force was president Tenzie Dunseth, Homeless Empowerment Council president Maney Thies, and from the Inter-Religious Social Action Council, Sister Sarah Keel, freshly released from a five-year confinement in a convent in northern Minnesota. They were joined by several unintroduced people, including a tall, well-muscled transvestite and a shabbily dressed man with that loner-with-a-history-of-mental-illness look so often seen in the lobby of public libraries. The group was anchored by a well-groomed man in his mid-forties, incongruously dressed in a sleekly tailored three-piece suit, French cuffs with gaudy gold links protruding from the neatly pressed sleeves of his suit jacket. One by one he sneered at the Lindbergh delegates, rolling his shoulders, shifting from one foot to the other and straightening the knot of his blue silk tie in the style of a Brooklyn wiseguy.

During the round of introductory handshakes, Sister Sarah's face emanated a cozy goodwill as she bowed gently to the Lindbergh delegation. "Bless you, my child" she said to each, even though she was the youngest person in the room. Sister Sarah was twenty-seven years old and without a dash of makeup was possibly the best-looking woman Riley had ever laid eyes on.

When Gar extended his moist, trembling hand to Tenzie, saying in a quivering voice, "I'm Gardahl Blaisfield," she slapped him on the ass and chuckled, "Lighten up there, hombre. You'll get outta here alive."

Gar took a seat at the large rectangular table in the center of the room, flanked by the Lindbergh representatives on each side and directly across the table from Tenzie, who was leaning back in her chair, the legs of which were creaking and groaning under the unreasonable burden. She was in battle dress: army combat jacket over bib overalls.

"Well," said Gar nervously, his many cowlicks pointing skyward like the teased hair of a grunge rocker, "before we get started, I think we should lay down a few ground rules."

"Ground rules, my ass!" roared Tenzie, falling forward in her chair, hands and forearms crashing onto the table. She had gone into attack mode and was now wearing the Frau Himmler face Riley had seen so many times in years past. "Are you going to donate the fucking building or aren't you?" she shouted across the table.

"Yes, yes—I am," blurted Gar in a please-don't-hurt-me voice.

It occurred to Riley that Gar had failed to reread *Getting To Yes—Negotiating Agreement Without Giving In*, which expressly warned against folding on any point early in a negotiation.

So delighted was Tenzie by the quaking jellyfish across the table that she decided to press out beyond the Strike Force's original demand list. "And we need a hundred thousand dollar cash contribution to the South City Daycare Center," she growled.

"You goddamn right we do!" exclaimed the snappy dresser in the corner, shifting his weight from one foot to the other.

"Okay, Okay," agreed Gar as he scanned the room in frightened confusion. He looked as though he might have soiled himself.

"Bless you, my son," said the dazzling, knockout nun, now sitting directly across the table from an admiring Riley, who was fighting off a rush of forbidden images, high on the list of sacrilege, as he looked upon her remarkably beautiful face. Back at Catholic school impure thoughts about anyone, including yourself, were grave sins—impure thoughts about a nun were straight-to-hell material.

Liz Bridge scowled disapprovingly as company assets hemorrhaged across the table. She hurriedly scribbled a note to Gar. "Slow down, stupid. You're giving away the whole company."

A nervous Rick Snelling, amidst a flurry of shoulder rolls and chest poundings, sought to ingratiate himself with the protesters by describing the "many Negroes he had played football with back in college." Liz kicked him under the table, but not before Tenzie took that as her cue to up the ante a little further. "And another hundred thousand for St. Jude's Center," she shouted.

"Okay!" came Gar's instant reply.

Sister Sarah let out a cry of religious ecstasy, while the transvestite and the snappy dresser suppressed a snicker. The loner with a history of mental illness stood staring at Gar.

Feeling an urgent need to put a stop to this expensive burlesque, Liz jumped from her seat, forcibly lifting Gar by the elbow. She said in a peremptory voice, "Well, there we have it. The necessary transfers will be made in the next several business days."

"Wait a minute, we're not finished," said a ravenous Tenzie, barely able to strike a serious tone.

"Yes we are!" commanded Liz with steely finality as she led a befuddled Gar toward the door, where she gave him a shove into the hallway.

Tenzie winked at Riley as he made his way to the door. He shook his head and smiled weakly but said nothing.

In the narrow hallway outside the conference room, several members of the protest group stood in reserve, making casual conversation like actors between scenes. Included in the group was the tattoo-faced climber who had scared Buck out of five years of growth less than an hour earlier. He was talking to an enormous woman decked out in an all-leather outfit topped off with a spiked collar.

"Tanya?" Riley sputtered in surprise, looking about nervously to see whether he might have been overheard.

"Duke?" she replied in a voice reserved for loved ones. "What are you doing here, Sugar?"

Ducking his head turtle-like into the collar of his suit jacket, and looking about nervously, he whispered, "I'm . . . I'm just a customer passing through who got caught up in the crowd. And don't call me Sugar!"

Tanya cozied up closer, rubbing against him provocatively. "Let's go have a chocolate malt, Sweetie. What do ya say?"

Riley rolled his eyes in embarrassment. Then in a collegial, supportive voice he didn't intend to adopt, said, "You can't have a malt, Tanya It's not on our program." He sounded like an AA sponsor.

"Neither are Milky Ways!" she shot back defensively.

Riley flushed red. He couldn't believe he was standing in the hallway of his employer conducting a sensitivity session with a 240-pound lovesick biker chick. "We'll have to talk about this another time," he said as he broke into a gallop to catch up to Liz, who in the style of a nursing home attendant was guiding Gar into the elevator .

"Come on in, Duke," she said without a change of expression, using a voice that promised a lifetime of ridicule.

17

I n hopes of shaking off the thin crust of exhaustion that had settled upon him, Riley canceled his appointments for the remainder of the week, opting to get away briefly from the office and its mounting unpleasantries. "Take over, will you Skeets?" he said with trepidation. "And try not to call anyone a dickhead."

"Hey, boss, don't give it another thought. I'll handle everything," said Skeeter with an angelic look on her face. It was a look he knew well, and one that did not inspire confidence.

He exhaled deeply after filling a briefcase with unread industry materials. He looked around the room at nothing in particular. "Okay then, I'll see you in a few days."

Without looking up from her work: "See ya, dickhead."

Crossing the lobby to the garage elevators, he passed Gar Blaisdahl's secretary, Nancy Park. She was bound for the dry cleaner with a sack of laundry. Nearly as big as she was, the sack was slung oppressively over her rounded back, forcing her face into an alignment almost parallel with the ground. She looked like a figure out of the stations of the cross.

"Hi, Riley," she grunted, straining her neck to look up.

Riley switched the briefcase to his left hand and reached with his right to support the bottom of the laundry bag. "Let me help you with that, Nancy"

"No, thanks. Once I get going in a straight line I've got to keep rolling 'til I get to the dry cleaner." But it was too late. In grabbing the bottom of the bag, he had redistributed the weight, throwing off her equilibrium. The canvas bag dropped to the marble floor with a thud, nearly taking Nancy with it. She stood upright with both hands at the base of her back, a grimace on her face. She expelled a painful groan.

Riley gave off a small sympathetic groan of his own. "Why don't you take your laundry to one of those drive-through facilities so you don't have to lug it around?" he asked.

Nancy looked at him with unbelieving eyes. "This stuff isn't mine! It's Gar's. I'm taking it to the dry cleaner. Then I have to drop off a check at his stockbroker, then I go over to the courthouse to pay another one of his tickets for parking in a handicapped space—they finally caught him for using his grandmother's handicapped permit. God, I loved it when he got nailed." She laughed wickedly. "Then I have to come back and write checks for his personal bills." She was counting off the list of chores on the extended fingers of her right hand. "Then I type his son's term paper and fax it to him at that snotty prep school they sent him to get him out of the house." She shook her head in weary disgust. "Half of what I do is personal stuff."

"Gee, last time I checked, the company was paying your salary to do official business, not to act as his maid. Sounds like Gar's engaging in a little corporate larceny," said Riley.

"What?"

"Never mind," he said, reaching for the drawstrings of the canvas bag. "Let's get this stuff over to the laundry."

"No, no," said Nancy, grabbing the bag out of his hand. "I could never live with myself if I made you carry Garfield's dirty laundry. Gallantry has its limits."

"You've got a point there. I might just pitch it off the skyway."

"Say, you seem thinner there, big guy," said Nancy, looking him up and down. "You better not make your weight. I bet against you in the diet lottery." She said this almost as a boast, indifferent to the fact it might hurt his feelings.

"I have nothing to say on that subject," said Riley cryptically. He had in fact lost seven pounds during the first week of the diet, winning a gold-star lapel pin at the official weigh-in. It occurred to him that he might have inadvertently fallen into the diet discovery of the modern age: four Milky Ways, two Pepsi's, and a chunky vitamin pill each day, and nothing else. He had a stomach ache the first few days, but he attributed that to the emergence of a long-simmering colon cancer, which his body had been able to throw off. Maxine, the program facilitator, said she didn't think the Milky Way diet was healthy, that the body would go into a hoarding mode once it figured out what was going on, and if he kept it up long enough he'd probably die of malnutrition. But Riley was not deterred.

At the first week's weigh-in, he had won the grand prize. Cheering weight-loss coordinators dressed up to look like nurses delivered serial hugs as a siren sounded and his numbers were put up in bright lights on the honor roll above the scale. Most of his fellow dieters, predominantly female, sobbed as their numbers were read off.

Tanya, who was right behind him in line, had gained two pounds. "Screw that shit!" she yelled for all to hear when the tally was read, storming from the room. "Go after her, Duke," said Maxine in a velvet voice, as though urging Ryan O'Neal to go after Ali MacGraw. "Screw that shit," said Riley as he headed in the opposite direction.

Nancy tossed the laundry sack over her shoulder, staggered in a tight semicircle under the swinging load, and headed off toward the dry cleaner.

Driving west out of St. Paul, toward the Minneapolis suburbs, Riley looked forward to this mental-health break. The timing was perfect. Betsy was going to a friend's lake cabin for a few days. He could hold down the homefront and at the same time save the cost of an all-day babysitter for Teddy. His daughter, Lizzie, would ordinarily cover the babysitting duties, with the help of some young hunk from the football team who'd wear Teddy out with tackling drills and wrestling matches, but she had signed up to be a student counselor at a girl scout camp that week.

In the driveway at home Betsy and her lifelong best friend, Sissy McCambridge, were piling provisions into the back of

Sissy's van: tennis racquets, golf clubs, tape decks, hot rollers, hair dryers, and so many books and magazines that Evelyn Wood couldn't read them in the time allowed.

Between hacking coughs that sent particles of sputum flying into the air, Sissy gave Riley a big smooch on the lips. Pretending to be distracted by a passing car, he turned his head and wiped the uninvited saliva, teaming with microorganisms, from his mouth. Visions of a tuberculosis sanitarium flashed through his mind.

Betsy came around the car and, putting her face up to his, said emphatically, "Be sure to feed Teddy and the pets, Riley. And water the plants, especially the two in the living room that need water every day. And bring in the mail. "

"I know, I know," he replied impatiently, a little wounded at the implication that he was not up to handling simple domestic tasks. He thought of himself as highly competent in that area.

Riley watched Betsy and Sissy pull away, thinking of how pretty they both still were. Although she feigned indifference to such classifications, it secretly pleased Betsy to hear Lizzie say that the boys in her class thought her mom was a "real babe." That is until Lizzie went on to quote the captain of the football team as referring to Betsy as a "MILF." "What's a MILF?" asked a smiling Betsy as she peeled potatoes one night before dinner. "Moms I'd Love to Fuck," replied Lizzie non-nonchalantly. Betsy let out a sound that fell somewhere between a scream and a dry heave, throwing a potato across the room at Lizzie. "That boy should have his mouth washed out with soap," she shouted. For her part, Lizzie was thrilled that she had made her father laugh so hard he almost choked. Thereafter Riley called Betsy "Milfie" until she threatened to divorce him.

Riley and Tuffy went inside where the interior of the house was immaculate, kitchen counters sparkling, carpeting showing the fresh strokes of the vacuum cleaner. It was a clean, orderly scene, reflecting the symmetry and optimism of its creator. An oasis amongst the mild chaos of the surrounding world; a retreat from the conflicts and dilemmas of The Lindbergh Life & Casualty Company.

After dinner that night, Teddy went to bed early and Lizzie went to Mall of America to hang out with a bunch of other teenagers. Riley was adamantly opposed to this activity, giving his grudging and long-withheld permission only because all her friends were allowed by their parents to go. After two years of tears and pleading and threats to run away, he had finally let her go at age fifteen, openly expressing worry that she'd fall in with bad types.

When she'd returned from that first trip, he nervously had asked how it had gone. "It was great," she'd said. "I scored some drugs and lined up a really good pimp." She thought that was very funny. But he could tell that she was grateful that she had been allowed to go and maybe even a little sorry for the argument they had had on the same subject the previous spring, in which she had called him "a dictator and a douche bag." Although surprised to be labeled this way (he had never thought of himself as a douche bag), he couldn't help but be impressed by her alliterative skills. As he had watched her stomp toward her room, he thought in stunned silence what his father would have done if his sister had said something like that. She would have been sent off to a nunnery in Switzerland. But these were different times. And he had seen other men, men so tough in business and in life that most of the world was scared stiff of them, get browbeaten like naughty puppies by their daughters. There was just something about fathers and daughters.

He had thought of grounding Lizzie after the douche bag incident, but instead he sat down and wrote a poem entitled "The Mischievous Miss McReynolds." It was not a good poem, but it was full of love.

Riley hadn't realized how bone tired he had become over the last several weeks—how much he needed this break. But exhausted as he was he slept fitfully that night, having an unusually vivid dream. Even after he got up and went to the bathroom, the dream recommenced as soon as he was back in bed. In the dream he and his sister and three brothers were sitting in the dining room of their family home, their father seated at the head of the table. John McReynolds was telling his children that he had just left a business partnership that would have made the family wealthy. He had left, he said, because he had refused to cover up some unspecified misconduct. As he talked, his father looked sad in a way Riley had never seen before.

Had the dream images not been so insistent, and had his heart not been pounding so forcefully when he awoke, he might have forgotten the dream. Instead, it stuck in his mind throughout the day. He felt its presence wherever he went.

Down in the kitchen he prepared a healthy breakfast for the newly awakened Teddy: toast-a-waffle, bacon, and orange juice. In accordance with his own weight-loss program he consumed a Milky Way and a multiple vitamin. The kitchen TV was placed on the counter next to the stove so he could watch "Good Morning America" while cooking. An occasional bacon-grease missile launched itself from the pan and stung his face. It had been a long time since he had cooked bacon. He didn't remember it being quite so painful.

When the TV screen went to static and he wasn't able to achieve a clear picture by manipulating the stubby, broken aerial extending from its flank, he took a coat hanger from the hall closet and inserted it into the hollow of the broken stem. The TV ceased its wheezing and the host snapped back into focus. He was proud of how cleverly he could shortcut his way through household tasks like this one. Betsy thought his self-confidence in this area to be absurdly misplaced, cracking that between him and his brothers there wasn't enough mechanical aptitude to set an alarm clock. "Worthless" was the word she kept using.

But Riley was unfazed by this criticism, confident in his own mind that few problems would fail to yield to his mechanical skills. The kitchen TV was only the latest example.

His meditation was ended by a loud, piercing screech from the hallway ceiling. The downstairs smoke detector had come alive when it smelled burning bacon. Closing the door separating the kitchen from the hallway, he mounted a chair and pushed what he assumed was the on-off button. When that didn't work, he placed his hand over the small grid he took to be the sensor. When that didn't work, and he thought his ear drums would burst, he ripped the front panel of the fixture from its mooring, exposing a fanfare of wires and circuits, which he pulled at indiscriminately. The screeching dropped an octave with each pull, descending into a low, anemic whine before trailing off altogether.

Another problem solved, he thought proudly as he brushed dust and a thin coat of ceiling plaster from his shirt.

The noise had awakened Lizzie, who sat, bleary-eyed, on the top step. "What did you destroy this time, Dad?" she asked calmly in a tone that bespoke long experience with her father's household adventures.

"I've got it all taken care of, honey. Don't give it another thought," boasted Riley as he stuffed a handful of now useless wires and circuits into the detector's body cavity and forced the bulging panel cover shut.

Lizzie pulled a mass of thick hair back into a giant pony tail. "God, I hope we never have a fire around here. We'll all be barbecued."

Riley started to say something, but she interrupted in a sing-song voice: "I know, I know. Don't tell Mom."

After getting Teddy off in the day-camp carpool, Riley returned to the house, which was now completely quiet. Lizzie had made a hurried exit, with a donut hanging from her mouth and tennis shoes in her hands as she jumped into the backseat of a friend's open-air Jeep. Riley settled into a chair of soft cushions, adjoining the bright white bookshelves covering the living room's west wall. He felt relaxed.

Long shafts of luminous sunshine crossed the room, coming to rest on the bindings of symmetrically arranged volumes of the Encyclopedia Brittanica sitting on the bookshelves, calling out the crisp, brilliant reds and blues of the leather coverings. The family birds gave off happy sounds from the next room.

Tuffy slept peacefully in the warm luxuriance of a full-bodied sunbeam piercing the east windows. A movable feast, his naps were chosen in reference to the location of these shafts of sunshine, sleeping east in the morning and west in the afternoon. Tuffy was blissfully, enviably happy, able to think only of food and sleep and smelling fire hydrants and rough-housing with Teddy and humping the guests. He didn't know about lost jobs or office politics or any of the bad news of the day. He didn't even know that his balls were missing.

Riley sipped coffee from a mug with the Lindbergh logo emblazoned on its side, and scanned the morning paper, reading all the headlines and about every third story. No surer way existed to reenter the real world than the morning paper, that running account of the previous day's controversies and heartaches. Crime and political corruption were given special prominence.

In the family section he came upon a large color photo of the Woodward Vinehill Crosshaven family, eight children surrounding Ward and his wife, who were seated in high-backed wing chairs. Ward looked smug and arrogant. His wife, the mother of the encircling brood, looked as though a sob was about to break through her broad, practiced smile. The photo was accompanied by an article filled with self-serving statements made in response to softball questions from an adoring reporter, who wrote as though he were auditioning for a job as director of communications for the Crosshaven business empire, an empire founded seventy-five years before by Ward's father, Vinehill Crosshaven. Deep in the text was a quote from none other than Buck Montrowe, CEO of The Lindbergh Companies and close personal friend of the Crosshaven family: "Ward Crosshaven is one of the finest men it has ever been my good fortune to know. He embodies the best of American values—hard work, unflinching honesty, faithfulness to God and family and community. And his children display those same unshakable qualities."

Riley looked back at the family portrait and from among the brood of eight siblings had no trouble finding Brad Crosshaven, formally listed as Bradford Vinehill Crosshaven, the only unsmiling face in the picture. He had a hard and cruel look. His well-oiled, slicked-back hair exposed a birthmark just below the hairline. No wonder Liddy had remembered him. That face would be hard to forget. In fact, it looked strangely familiar to Riley. It was the type of face he had seen on countless occasions in the criminal courts, but he didn't think it was probable that he had encountered him there, for it was unlikely that with his father's influence Brad Crosshaven would have had a criminal, or even an arrest, record.

He lifted the paper and looked again, closer this time. The green Jaguar that almost hit him on Tenth Street! That was it. What an asshole. Reckless, irresponsible, intimidating. Lucky he's got his family's protection. Maybe it will get him past the investigation that will follow upon the filing of the Suspicious Activity Report, and maybe it won't.

As he folded the section containing the Crosshaven family tribute and tossed it on the floor, he thought about the power of spin, the power to create and sustain a public image utterly at odds with the real truth. Brad Crosshaven looked like a solid citizen—a favored and gifted son of an old and privileged family. A family known for its generous philanthropy. But Riley's father had always said that the test of generosity is not what you give; it's what you have left. By that standard, the obscenely wealthy Crosshavens were little more than skinflints, giving away amounts that, though princely sums for most people, represented a trivial percentage of their own wealth. Giving until it hurts was clearly not part of their philosophy.

Riley dismissed further thoughts about the Crosshavens. To catch a ray of sunshine, he shifted his body a quarter turn and opened a volume of Yeats. Halfway through the first poem he fell fast asleep and started to dream.

A few minutes later the telephone rang. The first ring integrated itself into his dream as a whistle blowing on the playing field across the street. The second ring brought him awake and out of his chair, Yeats spilling rudely to the floor.

"Riley McReynolds," he slurred in a voice half awake, not quite realizing where he was.

"Riley, sorry to bother you at home. Tom Anderson here."

Riley looked groggily about the kitchen, adjusting to the unusual daytime surroundings, unaware of how long he had been asleep. He looked at his watch while straining to marshal enough consciousness to coherently greet Tom Anderson, a senior supervisor in the Trust area. "Oh, hi, Tom. No problem.

I was just taking a little nap." He didn't like the way that sounded, but it was out. "What's up?"

Just then the mailman pushed a handful of postal items through the slot in the front door, causing magazines, post-cards, and letters to spill haphazardly across the marble floor of the hallway. Tuffy ran for the door, letting out a series of ear-splitting barks.

"Oh, you on the corporate jet?" said Tom dryly.

Riley laughed involuntarily at this irreverent observation. "You know about that, huh?" he said.

"Hell, everybody knows about it, people start growling under their breath whenever Buck walks through. Which isn't very often, by the way."

Riley shook his head. "I don't want to hear any more."

"Yeah, if Buck thinks his abuse of the corporate airplane is a secret, he's barking up the wrong tree!" roared Tom, nearly overcome by his own wit.

"Come on, Tom, why'd you call?" asked Riley, not having the stomach for this troubling subject.

"I hear you fired the wrong person the other day," said Tom, his voice now winding down to a friendly chuckle.

Riley felt color rising in his cheeks. "Good God, everybody in the company seems to be having fun with that one. I hope to hell you didn't call me at home just to give me more grief."

"No, no, I've actually got a business purpose for the call," he said, his voice turning serious. "I'm trying to tap the grape-vine to solve a little mystery we've got down here."

Tom was not one for gossip, so Riley paid attention as he took a seat at the kitchen table, pushing aside a plate con-taining the remains of Teddy's half-eaten breakfast. "What mystery is that?" he asked.

"Do you have any idea why Harry Callinan was fired?"

The question congealed in Riley's stomach, sending a wave of nausea up into his throat. "No—I don't. I didn't know he had been fired," he replied haltingly. "When did that happen?"

"We don't know. He was here on Friday, and everything seemed normal. Monday morning we came in and his desk was cleared out and there was no trace of him. I called him at home. We've been friends for a long time, but he wouldn't even talk to me."

Riley started to ask who had succeeded Harry Callinan as administrator of the Crosshaven trusts, but not wanting to place anyone else in harm's way he choked off the words before they were spoken. Ruining the career of one nice man in a week was enough; he didn't want to end up getting Tom Anderson fired, too. He felt a little sick. Like the feeling that comes when witnessing cruelty to children. "I can't help you with this, Tom, I'm sorry," he said as anger began to thicken his voice.

He hung up and immediately called Buck's office, getting Gladys's voice recording. After the tone he recorded a message saying that he knew Buck was not in town, but wanted to leave a call for him to call Riley's home number when Gladys next heard from him.

He settled back into his chair and, in an effort to shake off the unwell feeling that had come over him—the feeling of responsibility for Harry Callinan's demise—he plowed back into Yeats. Before he had completed two lines, the phone rang again. He headed for the kitchen, rehearsing on the way what he was going to say to Buck.

"Hello," he answered in a voice more stern than brave.

"Is this Theodore McReynolds's father?" asked the day camp nurse in a flat, medicinal voice.

Shifting gears: "Yes, it is."

"Theodore has a stomach ache, and you'll have to come pick him up." Without waiting for questions, she continued, "Do you know where we're located?"

"Yes, I do, nurse," he replied compliantly, lapsing automatically into the respectful tone he had been taught to use with Nurse Quigley back at St. David's Military School, where he had been sent for four years of high school. His parents thought that after the incorrigibility he had displayed at Sacred Heart, a military school would be just the thing for him. What they didn't take into account was that Chasbo Peytabohm's parents had the same idea, thereby teaming Riley with the one influence in his life guaranteed to stunt, if not totally arrest, any further emotional development.

Nurse Quigley, practically the only woman at St. David's, was a mean old bag who never smiled during Riley's four years at school even though during each of his many visits to her office he brought candy and a little joke, in hopes of lightening up her life. This had worked with Sister St. Lillian, who in spite of all her better instincts succumbed to his good-natured ways, even telling him in his last year at Sacred Heart that when all was said and done she couldn't help but love him a little bit. But not so with Nurse Quigley. And she was especially hard on Chasbo, to whom she meted out record-setting demerit totals, thereby depriving him of promotions (which he didn't care a whit about) and passes from the dormitory (which he cared a lot about). Chasbo exacted his revenge by throwing up on her every chance he got.

On the way home from day camp, Teddy slumped in the front seat, looking a pale shade of green, his mouth hanging open ominously. Riley carried him into the house and gently put him down on the den couch.

Before he could sit down to comfort Teddy, the phone rang. It was Buck's secretary, Gladys. "I listened to your voice message for Mr. Montrowe, Riley. He is not accessible, but you will be able to catch up with him next week."

"But that's four days from now," Riley pointed out. "What I'm calling about is important, Gladys. Can you tell me where he is?"

"Nope," she said rhythmically as though the word bounced off his question. "Talk to Gar Blaisdahl or Erving Russell if you need immediate attention."

"Nope," replied Riley in a slightly snotty imitation of Gladys' voice, which he immediately regretted. "When you talk to Buck, please tell him I'm requesting a call at home concerning the matter we talked about late last week. It's very important. He'll know what I'm talking about."

They exchanged chilly good-byes.

He'd have called Wally to determine Buck's whereabouts, but he knew Wally had accompanied Buck on this trip, no doubt carrying his suitcases for him. Besides that, he was growing tired of playing hide-and-seek with a full-grown man.

If all this time away was really justified, as Buck claimed, why did he go to so much trouble to cover it up?

Riley went back to the den to check on Teddy. But having undergone a remarkable recovery, Teddy was now upstairs playing in his room. Riley turned on the TV but was almost immediately interrupted by a crashing sound from the next room. He walked into the kitchen, where Tuffy had pulled over the garbage pail stored under the sink, secreting the choicest morsels to other parts of the house. As Riley stood fuming over the mess, he could see Tuffy out of the corner of his eye scooting up the steps, a cylindrical ice cream carton almost as big as he was being carried in his teeth. He had to hold his head at a sharp angle to keep the container from dragging on the ground.

Chasing after Tuffy would be pointless; he was probably already under Teddy's bed. So Riley got down on his knees and started picking up rotting fruit, piles of coffee grounds, waffle fragments, and other detritus left by a family of four over a three-day period. God, he thought, this staying at home was starting to suck. The office was looking better with each handful of organic waste.

"I wouldn't come down here if I were you, Tuffy!" he shouted angrily in the direction of the stairs. No matter how hard they tried to get Tuffy to obey, no improvement ever occurred. Riley had once enrolled him in dog obedience classes, prepaying six weeks of nonrefundable tuition only to have him expelled during the first class for what the trainer called "inappropriate sexual behavior." When asked what that meant, the trainer said only that Tuffy ran around the whole session in a state of obvious arousal, occasionally trying to hump the girl dogs. Riley tried to explain that Tuffy had no balls and therefore really didn't pack much of a wallop. The instructor patronizingly countered that the girl dogs didn't know that and pointed rudely to the exit.

When the floor was clear of garbage, a sonic boom-like thump came from Teddy's room directly above the kitchen, followed by the splattering of a large chunk of ceiling plaster on the freshly cleaned floor. Riley raced up the steps, and found

Teddy jumping to the floor from the top of his bunk bed. In the corner of the room Tuffy's head was buried in the ice cream carton. To lick the walls of the container he had to twist his head, causing his body to do a full roll-over. He finally collided blindly with the wall. Riley pulled the carton off Tuffy's head, exposing whiskers caked with melted Pralines and Cream. Rather than being grateful for his liberation, Tuffy growled belligerently, chasing after Riley, humping his leg.

The phone then rang. Riley picked up the receiver while simultaneously trying to shake Tuffy off his leg.

"Hey, Riley, how's it going at home?" asked an upbeat Skeeter.

"God, Skeeter, get me out of here. I'm losing my mind."

Skeeter laughed triumphantly.

Trying not to betray his desperation, he asked, "Say, could your sister come over and baby-sit? I should really be at the office." Skeeter's younger sister, Gretchen, was a professional baby-sitter (ten-hour minimum) and got most of her business from Lindbergh families.

"Not a chance, you wuss," said Skeeter. "You're going to stick it out at home, no matter how tough it gets. You'll see what the moms of this world go through every day."

"But things must be really backing up down there."

Skeeter was emphatic. "It's not backed up at all. You have only one external call. The timing of your little break was perfect. You can lose yourself in the bliss of homemaking." She gave out another full-throated laugh.

As Riley continued his talk with Skeeter, Tuffy came over and sat attentively on the cushioned bench of the breakfast nook, his ears moving up and down in sympathy with the rhythms of Riley's voice. When Riley made eye contact, the pace of Tuffy's tail-wagging accelerated. His eyes left Riley only long enough to give an occasional lick to the spot where his balls had once been.

"You haven't heard from Buck, have you?" Riley asked. "I left a message for him to call me."

Skeeter gave off a faint chuckle. "Ah, no—Buck hasn't called me, or you. In fact, there hasn't been a Buck-sighting all week. I don't think you need to hang real close to your phone."

"No, I suppose not." He felt a renewed jolt of nausea as the thought of Harry Callinan's firing passed through his mind.

"I heard the alpha male skipped town when the protesters were closing in," said Skeeter.

Riley smiled. "Well, he didn't exactly cover himself in glory, but I don't want to talk about that. Anything else going on there?"

"You had another call from your buddy Kurt McBraneman. He was real friendly this time. Said he had talked to you."

"Did he leave a number?"

Skeeter chuckled. "No, I don't think he leaves numbers with anyone. By the way, how does he know about Liddy's problems?"

Riley paused. "What do you mean?"

"Well, when he called, he asked how my friend was doing, the one who was having trouble with the Crosshaven kid."

Oh, shit, thought Riley, here we go. "What did you tell him?"

"It sounded like he knew all about it," said Skeeter a little defensively. "So I said 'Do you mean Liddy Jonssen?' And he said 'Yes.'"

"Oh, no," said Riley. "He just conned you out of her name. I've got to get hold of him."

Skeeter now seemed concerned. "Is that bad?" she asked. "Is he dangerous?"

"Not to Liddy," said Riley. "And he promised me he wouldn't . . . well, never mind, but if he calls again, tell him I have to talk to him. Give him my home number."

Changing topics, he asked, "Has anybody stopped by since I've been home?"

"The only person to come by was Liz Bridge, and she was only here to rifle through your desk for a Milky Way."

"How many did you let her take?" Riley asked possessively.

"Just one. She needed a little sugar fix and knew right where to get it." Skeeter's voice was lilting but now turned quiet and conspiratorial. "And I'm not supposed to tell you, but she recalibrated the scale in the closet so it runs three pounds heavier. I've never seen anyone so giddy. She's determined to win the weight-loss pool."

Riley nodded, puckering his mouth into a pained smile. "God, I can't wait until this damn diet is over. I'm an object of ridicule everywhere in the company."

"Hold on," said Skeeter, "I've got to grab an incoming call. Maybe it's Buck."

As he waited on hold, Riley gazed out the kitchen window at a small band of shirtless roofers across the street tearing shingles from the neighbor's roof. They looked like they belonged in a line-up. Waiting for Skeeter's return, he found himself repeating the lines to "The Itsy, Bitsy Spider," which seemed to intrude on his mind whenever he thought of Liddy Jonssen.

Skeeter returned. "You still there?"

He choked off his recitation. "Yup."

"I've got a guy named Willy on the other line who says he's your 'weight-loss partner' and needs to talk to you because he ate a full side of beef last night and wants to share his feelings." She recited these words as though reading from verbatim notes. She paused. "Geez, you've got some weird friends. Do you want to talk to him? I can patch the call through."

"Hell no, I don't want to talk to him! Tell him I retired and moved to Arizona with no forwarding number. He can share his feelings with you."

Skeeter expelled a loud laugh as she conjured up the image of Riley and his 400-pound weight-loss partner sharing their feelings. "Why don't we just stay on the phone and visit until another one of your strange friends calls in."

A thin, muscular roofer with tattoos spread across his naked torso dislodged a large section of wood shingles, sending them hurtling over the gutter and into the neighbor's garden, where they flattened a clump of daisies.

Turning his attention back to Skeeter: "While I think of it, how is Liddy doing?"

Skeeter paused briefly, and in a voice now reflecting concern said, "I don't think she's doing very well. I had lunch with her this week, and I can usually get her giggling, but now she just seems flat—kind of on a different wave length. I took it personally at first, thinking maybe she was mad at me about something. But that wasn't it because a couple of girls from Accounting stopped by our table and she could hardly force a smile. And she couldn't seem to eat anything."

Riley could hear a ring in the background on Skeeter's end. She broke off to answer the phone. Returning: "That was Judy Goodrich asking me to help her out at the front desk, so I've got to go pretty quick. But, anyway, I'm worried about Liddy— I've never seen her so sad. Her eyes filled up with tears right out of nowhere when we weren't even talking about sad things. A woman at the next table yelled at her little girl in a mean voice because she had spilled ketchup on her dress. I thought Liddy was going to go to pieces. You'd have thought the mother had beaten the child."

"What do you think's wrong? Maybe she has mono," he said. Mononucleosis had been the standard diagnosis for any kind of fatigue when Riley was in college, and he had had what he regarded as a life-threatening case.

"I don't think she has mono," said Skeeter dismissively. "I think the overwork and so much tension in her unit is getting to her. She wants to make everybody happy, and that's not possible during a downsizing. And I think this sicko who's threatening her is still a problem, but she wouldn't talk about that."

"Why won't she talk about that?" he asked, now concerned.

"You know, she doesn't want to appear weak. She likes to make people think that she's always calm and in control, but in spite of that I've always known that she's a very vulnerable person. She's an only child, and her father's dead, and her mother has gone senile. All the supports have been pulled out from under her."

Riley was paying close attention, sitting down to make a few notes. "Has she actually heard from Crosshaven again?" he asked.

"Yeah. But I don't know, like, how much or anything. But I think it's a big part of what's going on with her."

"I'll try to get Buck to authorize some security for her, but I can't do anything about the management problems she's having; just about every manager is going through the same thing—it's part and parcel of the downsizing. In fact, I can't even talk to her supervisor because it's a sensitive customer issue, and Buck has ordered me not to." In truth, Riley shouldn't even have told Skeeter who Crosshaven was. He looked vacantly out the kitchen window where a couple of young mothers were walking their children in baby strollers, but his eyes were unfocused as he considered what he was hearing. "Maybe if she'd apply for a stress leave she could get a couple of weeks off."

Skeeter was emphatic. "No chance. She'd have to say she couldn't cut it, and she'd die before she'd do that. People would say she can't take it because she's a woman."

The phone rang again in the background. "That's probably Goodie, so I'm goin' to have to go. But why don't you just ignore Buck's instructions and notify Security yourself to watch out for Liddy?"

That was telling it like it is, he thought. Typical Skeeter. But it wasn't that easy. Buck would go nuts if he disobeyed his instructions, and a little while longer probably wouldn't do any harm. He had to admit that he was reluctant to get Buck too mad at him.

"I can't do that, Skeets, but I'll keep after him so the situation isn't allowed to go too far. Buck's in a tough spot with the company's biggest customer."

"Okay," she said. "But I'm scared for Liddy, and I think you should be too."

"I know you are, and I'll move as fast as I prudently can. You know how Buck is."

"I suppose so, but you're not Buck, and you have to remember that," she said. "Anyway, I've got to go."

"Talk to you later," he signed off.

He sat at the kitchen table feeling conflicted. Putting too much pressure on Buck too soon could cost him his job, could end the gravy train—the big money and the perks, the power and the status. At the very least it would spell banishment from the inner circle, an end to the influence and access he now enjoyed—access that allowed him to affect policy in a humane and constructive way for all employees.

He struggled to balance the downside risk to his career against the likelihood that a little delay—a little time to finesse Buck—would make any difference to Liddy's situation. He reasoned that, soon enough, the matter would come to a head on its own because of the filing deadline on the Suspicious Activity Report. He would never allow that deadline to be ignored, which would be a deliberate violation of a government regulation. And in the meantime he could monitor Liddy's situation through Skeeter.

There, he had logically established why his present course was the right one.

So why did he feel a little sick.

Riley and Teddy and Tuffy spent the evening watching TV. Ten minutes into a sitcom re-run, Teddy went sound asleep, flopping rightward onto his lap. Under his free arm, Tuffy also slept soundly, his feet in the air. At nine o'clock Riley carried Teddy upstairs and, clearing away a pile of baseball cards, placed him in bed, planting a gentle kiss on his warm, moist forehead.

He then went into the master bedroom and climbed into bed, feeling strangely unwell. Tuffy jumped onto the other side, sniffing and scratching for Betsy, finally curling into a tight, fluffy wad against Riley's body, where he expelled a surrendering breath.

Riley awoke the next morning at 5:00 A.M., seized with an undefined worry, the kind that can overtake a troubled sleeper in the early hours of the morning. He felt the sort of strange desperation normally associated with missed appointments and forgotten exam dates. His thoughts were of Liddy Jonssen and seemed to issue from a pressing sense that, in spite of all his rationalizations, she faced a danger more real than previously thought.

Unable to stop his racing mind, he leaped from bed and took several deep breaths. It's just the early hour, he told himself, or maybe something he ate before going to bed. After he was up and around the upset would subside, he was sure of it.

Despite six hours of sleep, he was as tired as when he had gone to bed. In the shower the lines to "The Itsy, Bitsy Spider" repeated themselves in his head. He tried unsuccessfully to stop them.

He stood at the bathroom mirror staring at his own image, an image that seemed more than ever to be aging before his eyes. He could see that more gray hair was emerging, and not just at the temples. His father had retained a head of thick, dark hair into his midfifties, when in the space of nine months it turned brittle and nearly pure white. And then three months later, sitting quietly at the dining room table, John McReynolds died, one year to the day from that sunny May afternoon when Father Longville and an army captain, resplendent in his dress uniform, rang the front doorbell and announced the death of his first-born son, First Lieutenant James Carr McReynolds, at a place with an unpronounceable name in central Vietnam.

Jamie was dead, and what was left of his precious body—a body on which his father could point to the smallest mark of every injury he had suffered from birth to an appendix scar at West Point—was returned in a gray box to the O'Halloran & Murphy Funeral Home in St. Paul.

That day the boy went out of his father, and through his own frightening grief Riley watched the man he had thought invulnerable, the man with the strength and wisdom of ten, who had honorably faced every problem that life had sent his way, set aside his work and his books and all else he cared for, and fade out beyond the reach of his family to a place where he could will himself from this vale of tears. Few words passed his lips save only a daily prayer of forgiveness for Lyndon Johnson, the man he believed had killed his beloved boy. Not even the coaxing of a now-elderly Saul Rosen, the benefactor and preceptor of his youth and the person in life he admired most, could pull him back from the abyss.

With Jamie gone, and his two older brothers away at college, it fell to Riley, in the company of an uncle, to appear at the hospital where the body of his father lay on a cold slab. The young doctor who had signed the death certificate was warm but formal. The attendant in the hospital morgue was cold and mechanical as he turned a brown envelope upside down, and his father's ring and watch and billfold tumbled out onto the table before them. He stared numbly at the wallet, from which he had been allowed as a boy to take a few dollars for a school project or busfare, or as a reward when he had gotten "A's" on his report card. That was what was left. He stood there dazed and wordless, hardly able to breathe, until his uncle put an arm around his shoulder and whispered that he should sign the inventory.

There was nearly a full house for John McReynolds' funeral that rainy afternoon at Sacred Heart as Father Longville stood at the back of the cathedral and recited the prayers of Christian burial. Riley was stunned by the size and variety of the crowd that had assembled, feeling for the first time the full measure of the esteem in which his father had been held by the many people he had touched in his lifetime. Sitting uneasily between a congressman and a justice of the state supreme court was an aging gangster with whom John had run as a boy, whose friendship he had refused to disown in later life. Day laborers and derelicts, some of whom Riley recognized as shadowy figures who had over the years appeared at their back door and even at their dinner table, knelt in the back pews, weeping along with everyone else as the soloist sang the sweet and mournful lyrics to "Danny Boy."

The McReynolds family lived on, surviving their double-barrel grief arm-in-arm, a great platoon of uncles and older cousins from both sides of the family flowing across the wound, closing and sealing its jagged borders. But their lives would never be the same. Vietnam and the arrogance of brilliant and ruthless men in Washington had inflicted two needless and awful casualties on his family.

And though life would move on for Riley after his father's death, within the cloud of benumbed loss there lived a sense that some secret had been left untransferred, some code of manhood known only to this one man.

A small tear formed on his cheek as he looked at himself in the mirror. He wiped it away and wondered what the hell was going on.

* * * * *

Downstairs the sound of the TV could be heard from the den, causing Riley to wonder if he had left it on the previous night. Passing through the kitchen, which had developed a strange and objectionable odor originating somewhere in the pile of unwashed dishes he had allowed to collect in the sink, he could see Teddy lying in front of the TV. He was propped on his elbows, his head resting on the palms of his hands, intently focused on the TV screen, which appeared to contain nothing more than a rolling list of text entries. Having gone to sleep at eight o'clock the previous night, Teddy arose at 5:30 A.M. and headed straight for the TV.

"What are you watching at this time of the morning, Teddy?" Riley asked, straining to read the screen.

"'Jobs Galore,'" Teddy answered, not taking his eyes from the screen. By his tone one would think he had said Masterpiece Theater.

Riley sat down and tried to focus. He read the parade of entries passing vertically across the screen:

Clerk-Typist. 65 words/minute.
Partial benefits. Competitive Salary.
Respond: Box 1683

Waitress-Waiter. Training provided.
Evening hours. Minimal Benefits
Respond: Box 1840

Over-the Road Trucker - 18 Wheeler
Prior experience and all licenses req'd
Respond: Box 1097

After the third entry Riley transferred his glance to Teddy, who stared zombie-like at the screen. "Why are you watching this?" he asked.

"There's nothing else on yet," said Teddy. "But I'm getting kinda bored of it."

"I should think so," said Riley as he lifted cushions from the couch, looking for the channel changer. Most of the other

220

channels were occupied with sales promotions and religious services, including a bejeweled TV preacher shooting invisible healing rays out of his fingers at a group of sad, overweight people with ambiguous illnesses. As he thrust his ray-gun hands at the afflicted, they fell backwards, as though hit by a firehose, into the arms of waiting deacons. Except, he noticed, for the few who were not paying attention. When the rays hit them they just stood there like stumps.

He pressed on through the cable menu, looking for suitable viewing. The best program, a group of singing and dancing children, was in Spanish, and neither he nor Teddy could understand a word being said. He passed through a music video, which was borderline pornographic, to a professional wrestling match of startling vulgarity with a crowd that looked like it belonged at the Nuremberg Rallies. And then more over-dressed, overcoifed televangelists leaping about the stage with their throbbing, warbling voices superbly trained to sound as though they were talking and crying at the same time. Next in line was a group of valley-girls testifying to the spooky accuracy of a phone bank of "certified psychics," followed by a talk show where every few minutes the women got up and started beating the crap out of each other.

Oh, my God, thought Riley, this was appalling. He dropped onto the couch, dumbfounded by what he was seeing. Was life always full of this much manipulation and superstition, this many charlatans? he wondered.

He finally came upon a cartoon that seemed suitable for a seven-year old, and made a deal with Teddy that he would watch for one hour only.

Friday and Saturday were uneventful: a series of shuttling between baseball, summer hockey, soccer, and birthday parties.

Saturday night was given over to watching two rented videos after Riley carefully checked out Lizzie's date for the evening, a towering, flaxen-haired youth from the basketball team who kept bowing at Riley and calling him "Sir." The bowing didn't fool Riley for one minute. He stared suspiciously at the horny giant as he and Lizzie made their way to his car.

At ten o'clock Betsy called. "Have you been doing your jobs?" she asked fearfully.

"Sure," Riley lied, never taking his eyes off the video.

"Did you feed the birds?"

"Yes."

"The dog?"

"Yes."

"The fish?"

"Yes."

"The turtle?"

"Yes."

"The salamander?"

His attention veered from the video. Did they have a salamander? He didn't remember seeing one—didn't know if he'd even recognize a salamander. Oh, well.

"Yes."

"Did you water the plants?" she asked with emphasis.

"Yes," Riley answered as he scanned the parched and lifeless remains of Betsy's favorite plants in the living room, offering a silent prayer that they were revivable with a good dousing of water.

As they continued talking, he moved into the kitchen to fill a water pitcher from the sink.

Betsy confirmed that she'd be home by noon on Sunday and implored Riley to clean the house before her arrival. She asked to talk to Teddy, but he declined. Riley couldn't tell if he was pouting about his mom being gone for so long or if he was just absorbed in the cartoon.

On early Sunday morning a gagging Riley set about cleaning the kitchen as Teddy watched The Midwestern Ag Report. He donned a pair of rubber gloves and waded into the forbidding swamp of the kitchen sink in search of the offending odor, which had by then permeated the back of the house and advanced into the den and living room. His search revealed that a kitchen sponge used to clean up a milk spill on Friday morning was what accounted for the odor, not the nearly four days of dirty dishes, which really didn't smell that bad. He then fed the menagerie of starving pets, less the salamander, which

222

he couldn't find. A few laps with the vacuum cleaner, and things looked presentable, though far from the pristine condition in which Betsy had left them.

At church Riley struggled to listen to the sermon while Teddy fidgeted in his seat and Lizzie exchanged less-than-prayerful looks with a boy across the aisle. Riley finally gave up the struggle to pay attention, and instead paged through a pamphlet that had caught his eye entitled, *God's Help With Chronic Illness*.

Back at home, Betsy was pulling into the driveway as they rounded the corner. Sounds of great joy escaped her lungs as she delivered suffocating hugs to all present, with Teddy clinging to her neck, and Tuffy humping her leg. She and Sissy had experimented with new hairdos at the lake, leaving Betsy's head covered with tight, spongy ringlets that looked awful.

"You look great," said Riley as he kissed her on the cheek.

She made her way into the house. "What smells?" were her first words as she crossed the threshold.

Riley grimaced. "You should have been here this morning."

Betsy shook her head as though she regretted having returned home. She then let her suitcase and athletic gear fall to the hallway floor, just under the smoke detector, which, aroused by the commotion, chose that moment to burst open, disgorging its overstuffed contents into the air. The now useless wires hung above her head like chicken entrails.

"What happened to the smoke detector?" she asked despairingly.

Before Riley could offer an explanation she caught sight of her two favorite plants in the living room, which had failed to revive after apologies and a good soaking from Riley. He didn't understand plant talk or bird talk or the other forms of mystical communication that came naturally to Betsy. In fact, there were many areas of human communication and interaction, verbal and nonverbal, that Betsy understood in ways he never would. She had wider frequencies, more channels.

"Oh, Riley darling, you are so worthless," she said in a forgiving, I-should-have-known-better voice, followed by a kind of keening over the deceased plants as she picked at their withered leaves. And to make matters worse, in protest at not being allowed to go to church Tuffy had done a giant dump in the middle of the living room.

With Betsy's return came relief from the domestic duties of the previous days, freeing him to turn to the pile of in-basket materials Skeeter had sent to him from the office on Friday afternoon and then again on Saturday morning. He retreated to the upstairs study and happily reentered the affairs of the office.

Working his way through memos received since his departure, he made margin notations on some (returning them to the writer for further action), dictated formal responses to others, and tossed into the wastepaper basket a growing number on which he had copied for the sole purpose of inoculating the writer against claims down the line that he or she had failed to keep senior management informed of some problem (the classic cover-your-ass memo so common during downsizings).

He read the weekly company publication, *The Lindbergh Lantern*, which addressed a broad range of company matters. It was the house organ and main communication vehicle with company employees. This week's issue contained a lengthy article on changes to the employee health plan, including the sorrowful news that employees would be required to sever longstanding relationships with pediatricians, family physicians, and other healthcare providers in favor of a series of discount clinics. This step was portrayed as necessary to keep costs down.

A cost control it clearly was, but in what respect it was "necessary" was not explained. The company was now more than stable financially, and its stock was trading at a healthy premium. Riley knew that these kinds of takeaways, which cut to the heart of an employee's loyalty, were for the sole purpose of increasing earnings per share, thereby greatly increasing the value of stock and options, the latter being held in massive amounts by the CEO and other executive managers, including himself. Employee-alienating steps of this kind were nothing more than the reallocation of corporate wealth from employees, who actually generated the revenues, to shareholders and, perhaps more tellingly, to option holders. The common employees who suffered most from the gutting of benefit programs like health insurance were given no opportunity to share in the success made possible by such cuts because they were not eligible for stock options. They consistently got the short end of the growth formula: longer hours, reduced healthcare, and countless symbolic absurdities like being charged admission to their own appreciation dinner, while at the same time having no chance to participate in the mechanisms designed to reward success. Call it modern capitalism, Riley thought, call it shareholder-friendly, call it Darwinian management, call it anything that can even remotely be tortured into an honest statement—but for God's sake stop calling it "fair and necessary" as these ruthlessly dishonest company publications regularly did.

At the back of the *Lantern* was the "Ask Buck" column, a forum of such astounding chutzpah that one couldn't help but feel a perverse admiration for its creators, who in defiance of Abraham Lincoln's maxim believed that you could fool all the people all the time. Without rival, it was Riley's favorite read of the week. And not just Riley. Roars of bitter laughter exploded from the offices and work stations of corporate headquarters on the morning of the *Lantern*'s arrival. The editors would sift through employee letters received in a given week, pull out (or create) several that contained topics needing political spin, and work up draft answers. Buck played little part in the formulation of the responses, but where matters of political sensitivity and employee morale were involved, he would have the responses read to him in advance of publication.

Friday's column lead with a query by "Doris," an employee in the Life Underwriting Division:

> Dear Buck: Why is it that the company maintains luxurious corporate jets in the midst of dramatic cutbacks in employee benefits?

> Dear Doris: There is a widespread misperception about the corporate aircraft, with some people holding the mistaken belief that the planes are luxuries

for company executives. Nothing could be further from the truth.

As you know, Doris, our great company does business across a wide trade territory. In order for our executives to arrive quickly at emergency situations that arise we maintain two fairly modest aircraft to improve customer service and efficiency. While private jets may seem like a luxury, you have my word that they are not, and that I personally monitor their use to be sure there is no abuse.

Thanks for your question, Doris, and congratulations on being a Buckie finalist this year! You are an inspiration to all of us as we sacrifice together in order to be able to share together down the line.

Your partner in progress,
Buck

Riley had read countless falsehoods of this type over the last five months, but rather than growing numb to them, he was finding that the cumulative effect left him with the psychological equivalent of chronic fatigue syndrome. No matter how harmless others regarded these "white lies," to him they were just plain shabby and immoral. Beyond that, on a purely practical level, they were insulting to the employees and therefore harmful to morale.

Early on, he had gone to the communications people to naively point out what he assumed were inadvertent factual errors, only to be told that any issues of that type should be taken up with Mr. Blaisdahl inasmuch as he finalized all responses with Mr. Montrowe. When contacted, Gar suggested that Riley confine himself to his own duties and not worry about things that were none of his business. When Riley called it to Buck's attention, he was snappishly told to deal exclusively with Gar. A tidy Catch-22.

The remainder of the in-basket backlog consisted of unread correspondence received during his break, including a letter from the company's principal outside law firm analyzing the legal requirements for filing a Suspicious Activity Report when grounds existed to suspect an attempted money laundering. The outside firm had been supplied with the essential facts (without names) as reported by Liddy Jonssen and made an analysis independent of the one previously conducted by the in-house legal department. Like the in-house conclusion, the letter reported that the filing of a notification was mandated under the applicable laws and regulations. Among other things, it advised that the notification must provide the identity of the person under suspicion, where known.

Without disclosing the identity of the suspected wrongdoer or the acute sensitivity of the matter, Riley had indicated to both the inside and outside lawyers that if there were a legally permissible way to avoid a filing or, in the alternative, to make the filing without identifying the suspected individual, he wanted to be expressly advised of that fact. But the lawyers, inside and out, were of one mind that given the factual information in the possession of the company the filing had to be made in its entirety, including an identification of the suspected individual.

This was the advice Riley had expected to hear, but he was nevertheless disappointed that there was no room to maneuver. Whether or not criminal charges were brought, the filing would result in embarrassment to the Crosshaven family and gravely damage Buck's (and the company's) relationship with its most profitable customer. And Brad Crosshaven might seek revenge against Liddy should he confirm beyond any question that she had turned him in.

But, for all of that, there was only one thing to be done. The filing had to be made. And from his standpoint the company's top priority was to take such steps as were necessary to keep Crosshaven away from Liddy, including the physical surroundings in which she lived and worked. Riley felt sure that Buck would set aside all other considerations and do what was necessary to insure the safety of a loyal and valuable employee, who by following company procedures and simply doing her duty found herself in an ugly and potentially dangerous situation. But still the contours of a suspicion, dark and insistent, were taking shape in his mind.

227

He fought back sympathy for Buck, who would be seen by his hero, Ward Crosshaven, as a betrayer, someone who put technicalities above friendship. Buck would be trading in the fiercely longed-for social acceptance, reflected glow, and borrowed status that came from Ward Crosshaven's friendship for hostility and ostracism. For Ward Crosshaven was known to be an unforgiving man, especially in matters relating to his family.

Riley closed his briefcase and turned his mind away from business as he headed upstairs for what he hoped would be a good night's sleep. Betsy was in bed, surrounded by books and writing materials, reading and taking notes. He cleared away the debris, got into bed, and before turning out the light lay still for a moment, his eyes resting on the ceiling above him. The piece of cardboard he had taped over the hole where the ceiling fixture had once been had broken loose of its restraints and was now hanging completely open. A scratching sound that seemed to come from the attic could be heard, at first faint and then louder as it migrated toward the center of the ceiling. Riley initially entertained the implausible thought that the sound was a water pipe, but as it grew louder even he was able to eliminate that possibility.

Betsy set her book on the bed and removed her reading glasses. "That sounds like a mouse," she said, looking up at the ceiling flap.

Tuffy stared upward, tail straight in the air, nose twitching excitedly, a steady rumbling coming from deep in his throat.

"That stupid piece of cardboard you taped up there is just hanging by a thread," Betsy said in a tone of unconcealed irritation.

With that a large black bat with a wing span that seemed the width of a football field dropped through the hole into the bedroom airspace, flying frantically between the corners of the room, occasionally dive-bombing the bed.

"Wow," said Betsy calmly, "That is one huge bat." She looked over to check Riley's reaction, but he was nowhere to be seen, having ducked under the covers at first sight of the winged intruder.

As the bat made a dip toward the bed, Betsy and Tuffy joined him under the covers, Betsy screaming with laughter and Tuffy barking so hysterically he filled the dark, tent-like space with coma-inducing dog breath.

"This isn't funny!" yelled Riley, nearly paralyzed with fear. "Those damn things carry rabies!" This caused Betsy to go into a laugh fit so earsplitting that Tuffy jumped on her head.

"Get the tennis racket and swat the damn thing," she instructed after recovering her voice.

Nearly overcome by Tuffy's breath, Riley answered, "You swat him with your racket. I've got tennis elbow. And it's well-known that bats are much more likely to bite people with fair skin."

Betsy's shrieks awoke Teddy, who was making his way into the room, rubbing his eyes with his fists. Only the prospect of his first-born son being attacked by a rabid bat galvanized Riley's courage sufficiently to propel him toward the door under the protection of the bedspread, which was spread tent-like over him and Betsy, with Tuffy crawling along the ground between them.

They slept that night in the den, the door to the bedroom having been firmly secured. In the morning Riley declared his weekend stewardship of the household a success of which he was justly proud. He left for work secure in the knowledge that Betsy would figure out a way to exterminate the beast in the bedroom, patch up the ceiling, revive the plants, and locate the salamander.

18

Monday found Buck back in the office, tan and rested after a four-day respite in Boca Viejo, where he replenished vital resources expended in last week's exhausting run of three successive days of work. The last round of downsizing had been completed during his absence, sparing him the unpleasantness that invariably accompanied mass bloodlettings.

The protesters, having secured ownership of the sought-after apartment building plus a good deal more, had departed the Lindbergh premises, migrating back to their special-interest constituencies to await Tenzie's call to regroup for the next engagement.

So it was a lighthearted Buck who surveyed the broad expanse of his corner office, breathing deeply and stretching his arms widely as he contemplated several days of ribbon-cuttings and newspaper interviews at which Erving Russell and Liz Bridge would sit on each side of him, spring-loaded to put a sock in his mouth should he depart from the remarks they had carefully prepared for him. Early in his tenure he had given a spontaneous, unsupervised interview to a reporter that resulted in a string of post-interview corrections, clarifications, and apologies that ran twice the length of the original story. That was the last time Buck was left alone with the press.

Buck also was scheduled to attend one or two gatherings of charity and business associations for which he served as honorary chairperson. These community positions were arranged by Liz Bridge in an attempt to manipulate Buck's image to fit the Minnesota culture, which carried a long tradition of citizen involvement in community and charitable affairs. Buck stood still for all this image making, apparently realizing at some level that it was in his best interests to appear to fit into the local cultural landscape, notwithstanding his private contempt for just about everything those groups stood for. Buck was a social Darwinist, believing that only the fit should survive and that all this community bullshit was a lot of leftist nonsense so typical of Minnesota, a state and culture for which he was privately contemptuous. Knowing his true feelings and fearing that those feelings might seep out if left to his own devices, Liz secured from him a commitment never to depart from her approved remarks.

And Buck lived up to that commitment, at least in public. At the recent annual shareholders' meeting, for example, he read the script almost flawlessly, inadvertently omitting only one short paragraph, which went unnoticed by an audience that had long since lost interest in the proceedings. As had the elderly director, Cosmo Towers, who, sitting on stage with the other directors, fell fast asleep on Hank Wallstead's shoulder, leaving an oil slick of wide diameter on Hank's Armani suit jacket.

Also contributing to Buck's upbeat mood today was an afternoon golf date arranged by his idol, Ward Crosshaven. It would be an interesting round, for included in the foursome were Bayard Van Studdiford and Tad Wiresbury, the two old-money patricians who had excluded Buck from a prestige seat at the Charity Ball earlier in the year. At Ward's request, Wiresbury and Van Studdiford had agreed to play golf with Buck so long as he didn't try to join their social set or date one of their sisters. For his part, Buck said he harbored no resentment against them for their earlier snub, but as he had taken to privately referring to Van Studdiford and Wiresbury as a couple of "quiche-eating fairies," Riley didn't believe that the wound had completely healed.

Ward Crosshaven had expressed appreciation for Buck's keeping him privately informed of the ruckus caused by his favorite son, Brad, who was admittedly high-spirited—but certainly not a bad kid. And he genuinely appreciated Buck's assurance that no embarrassment would come to the Crosshaven family name.

Buck settled back into his commodious desk chair, causing the headrest to expel a tuft of stuffing high into the air, where it was picked up by a stream of cool air from the vent above the credenza and then wafted across the room, where it did a tight somersault before floating slowly to the ground. As he scanned the day's calendar, Buck noted a nine o'clock debriefing with Cole Girard and the downsizing consultant, who would tell him far more than he wanted to know about the previous week's firings. Then Riley McReynolds was slotted in for twenty minutes. Two do-gooders in a row by midmorning, thought Buck wearily, as he let out a deep sigh. Well, at least Cole would come around when Buck laid down the law. He was not a man who liked arguments.

But Riley, that was something else altogether. A nice enough fellow, he supposed, and a good guy to have around during a crisis. Useful in keeping company managers on the straight and narrow—sort of a one-man detox unit. And he was well established in these parts, connected on both sides of the law. But he was surprisingly naive about the world of big business and could be a real nuisance, harping about double standards and a duty of care toward employees and all that other crap so typical of Midwesterners. He didn't seem to understand that there *were* two sets of standards: those for the elite and those for the masses. There it was. You had to pretend they didn't exist, but everyone knew they did; that's the way the real world operated.

Riley was a typical Irishman, thought Buck. They were all a little nuts, by turns sentimental and hotheaded, cooperative and confrontational—and always stubborn. But members of that strange race could be loyal and helpful when the more fainthearted types headed for the tall grass. And he had to admit that Riley had guts. Good god, some of the things he was

232

willing to say. It might be called courage, he supposed, but with the Irish it was more the courage of stubbornness than any real nobility. With the exception of one summer in Savannah back in high school, when he had caddied at a country club overrun with Irishmen, Buck had known almost none or, for that matter, Catholics of any nationality, until he got out of college and went to work with an insurance company that did business with Yankees. His father, the Reverend Mr. Montrowe, had taught him and his siblings that the pope was the anti-Christ, and all Irish were papists—so there you were. In his confusion, the young Buck had wondered if Catholics were part of the international Jewish conspiracy his father had also fulminated against. There were so many godless, degenerate conspiracies his father warned about—Jews, Freemasons, papists, communists, homosexuals, race-mixers, the World Council of Churches. He had had trouble keeping track of them all.

But Buck had spent his whole adult life charming people of all viewpoints and nationalities into playing their proper supporting roles, even hard-case Irishmen. He would explain some of the practical complications associated with the Crosshaven matter and, once explained, Riley would become a loyal ally as he had in countless other cases. Deep down he was one of the boys, a team player. He was just used to the black and white of the court system. A little mentoring would help him understand how business operated.

At 9:45 Riley took a seat outside Buck's office, next to the angry alligator. He apologized to Gladys for the crabby voice he had used on the phone the previous week. She blushed like a schoolgirl, patting and smoothing the borders of her beehive hair bun. She could be cold sometimes, it was true, but he liked her. And she liked him. He knew that, just as he knew as a child that this or that mother of a friend or some teacher liked him in a special way. Sort of like a crush. Maybe that was why when he grew up he liked the world back and almost always gave people the benefit of the doubt. And why it took a lot for him to judge anyone harshly. Take Buck, for example: egotistical and selfish, yes, but not evil. He had had a tough childhood as the son of a backwoods religious fanatic. That would screw anyone up. Face to face with ordinary people Buck wasn't a mean guy. It was only from a distance that he could preside over so much pain. That wasn't much to celebrate, he supposed, but it was a lot better than those sadistic managers in some companies who actually enjoyed the dirty work.

As Riley sat deep in thought, arms folded across his chest, M. Bryant Knox passed by on his way to a ten o'clock meeting with Tom Arden, something he always dreaded. M. Bryant never knew when Tom was serious and when he was making fun of him.

Bryant flashed a smile of unusual warmth, accompanied by a comradely wave. "Riley, how you been?" he said with great ardor.

"I'm doing fine, Bryant," said Riley cautiously. M. Bryant was known to be a major suck-up; taking a backseat in that department only to the reigning champion, Gar Blaisdahl. But Riley could not retrieve from his memory any precedent for Bryant's being so genial toward him. He could feel the thick vapor of politics in the air, so thick he thought it might congeal on the walls and slide down and stain the carpeting.

M. Bryant came closer. "Say, Riley, do you suppose I could get on your calendar later in the day?" His velvety voice, honed during long sessions in the Dale Carnegie program, was carried on a cloud of smoker's breath.

Riley eyed him furtively while leaning back in his chair. "I suppose, Bryant. What do you want to talk about?"

M. Bryant pinched his face in the way small boys do when deferring further discussion to the tree fort or the back yard clubhouse. "I'll fill you in later," he said, winking.

Riley looked at his pocket calendar. "How about two o'clock?"

"Fine, I'll see you then," he said with another wink.

Cole Girard and the Rudolph Hess lookalike downsizing consultant emerged from Buck's office, walking backwards in the style of medieval courtiers leaving a royal throne room, with Cole timidly expressing concern that Buck viewed the current severance guidelines for terminated employees as too generous.

Gladys, who was writing monthly alimony checks to Buck's two ex-wives, looked up and signaled for Riley to enter the office.

"Hey, Buck, how ya doing? Nice tan," quipped Riley.

"Thanks," replied Buck, missing the implication. He landed an affectionate slap on Riley's back. "How the hell you been, Riley? How's Betsy doin'? What a fabulous girl she is."

Uh-oh, thought Riley. This is not good. What's he up to? Why all this chummy sociability? This was the nicest Buck had been to him since that time a few months ago when a deranged employee had gone postal on the executive floor and threatened to kill Buck. Riley had been able to calm him down long enough for Buck to slip out of the building, and Buck had been very grateful.

They took seats across from each other at the conference table. The morning sun poured through the windows and reflected brightly off the highly polished mahogany of the table. The room had a stale, unlived-in feel, like that of a rarely used lake cabin. Buck flashed a broad smile and stretched his arms widely. "What can I do for you, my friend?"

Riley rearranged the ashtray and coasters on the table, then looked up. "What happened to Harry Callinan, Buck?"

Buck did not stiffen as Riley expected, but rather, after a brief pause, leaned in Riley's direction, creating an air of greater intimacy. "I meant to talk to you about that, Riley, but I wanted to do it in person." He then launched into a lengthy commentary about the proper handling of blue-chip customers, followed by a rambling, largely inaccurate, account of the multigenerational relationship between the Crosshaven family and The Lindbergh.

Watching Buck's face closely, Riley could feel the Look being cranked up for his benefit. And, sure enough, several minutes into the discussion it made an appearance, the mouth curling sharply downward, the right eyebrow reaching nearly to the hairline.

Riley gave an embarrassed smile, an instinctive reaction to the Look. It was a curious thing; he actually felt himself a little seduced by the dog-and-pony show being enacted for his benefit.

He refocused, cleared his throat, and then looked across at Buck. "So what about Harry?"

"Yeah, I was getting to that," said Buck, his expression turning earnest as he leaned back in his chair and broke eye contact. "We just can't have people around here who leak information."

Riley looked puzzled. "Leak information?" he asked incredulously. "Harry was talking to me, a senior officer of the company. It isn't as though he was blabbing secrets at some bar after work. He was responding to a question from a colleague with responsibilities that often require customer information."

Buck paused briefly to let the silence speak for him, a look of fatherly tolerance on his face. He joined his outstretched fingers in an almost prayerful arrangement, causing his clear nail polish to gleam in the morning sunshine.

"These are matters you don't need to concern yourself with, Riley," he said in a tone that was at once collegial and threatening. "You do a great job and I've got big plans for you, my friend. The sky's the limit. But there is much you don't understand about how business operates. Don't risk a fabulous career with unlimited advancement by messing where you don't belong. I want you to become a wealthy man someday as a result of your association with me." He paused briefly and then tapped his fingers on the oversized Bible sitting before him on the table. With a gooey smile he said, "And Jesus wants you to be wealthy, too."

Even when measured by the peculiar standards of Buck Montrowe, this was a strange pitch and more than a little embarrassing. The Jesus of Riley's upbringing was a Jewish carpenter's apprentice of modest means, with a radical love of the poor and dispossessed. And while the scope of his love was doubtless broad enough to embrace the rich of the world, the weight of the evidence on the subject suggested that, as a class, they were not his favorite people.

As he sat watching Buck's saccharine smile peering at him across the table, Riley felt the full force of the cultural divide that separated them, and flattered though he was by the line of unsubtle bullshit about his "unlimited advancement," he was not buying that either. He had witnessed this contrivance, this conversational trickery, being practiced by Buck on others. It was a fleshed-out version of the You-Don't-Get-It ploy, with the added threat of demotion or worse.

After a brief hesitation, and not wanting to enter into a fruitless theological debate, Riley pressed on. "Then help me understand, Buck, what is it about Harry Callinan that justified the termination of a twenty-two year career for such a small infraction?" They were both growing a little uncomfortable, a little nervous. Buck didn't like having his bluff called. And, truth be told, Riley didn't much like putting his career on the line.

Buck's interlaced fingers tightened, his knuckles growing white. "Never mind what went into that decision," he said. "There were compelling factors."

Riley knew this was pure jive. He could tell it from the strain on Buck's face. For all his vanities, Buck had some decent sensibilities; he was not a born liar. If you knew him, as Riley did, you could usually tell when he was lying. And it was also clear that his temper was rising at Riley's unwillingness to just get on board with the surface explanation, even if he didn't actually believe it. That's what a team player would have done.

Buck was not yet ready to abandon Plan A and move into his hard-ass routine. Too early for that. Winning Riley's cooperation in this dicey matter was highly desirable. In some ways Riley was perfect for this situation; he was used to dealing with tricky stuff, things that required street smarts, and he apparently had the confidence of the employee who was the one and only witness who could identify Brad Crosshaven. He could use his influence to get her to withdraw her identification. That would relieve the company of its obligation to name him in the government filing, and everyone could go home happy.

A friendly countenance now returned to Buck's face. "Look, Riley," he said, "you don't need to bother with the reasons for the judgments I'm making here, and I guarantee you that

Harry Callinan has been well taken care of." The Look was now in full flower, the corners of his mouth reaching almost to his chin line. And, by God, if Riley didn't feel the spell of it, just a little. It actually projected a certain ineffable charm when focused directly on a person.

But it was not the conversation stopper that Buck had planned. Riley nodded acknowledgment that the Harry Callinan part of the discussion was over. "All right, Buck, but we've got to talk about how to accomplish the filing of the Suspicious Activity Report, and about the employee who had the run-in with Brad Crosshaven."

Buck straightened in his chair, a touch of panic breaking through his sunny manner. "The employee hasn't been talking about this has she?"

Riley looked down and shook his head, as if to say "Is that all you care about?" "No, she hasn't," he said. "That's not the issue. She's having a problem with this guy. He's harassing her. The son of a bitch is dangerous. That kind of stuff has to stop immediately."

Shifting uncomfortably in his chair, Buck said, "I've talked to Ward about any trouble for the employee. Take my word for it, that won't be a problem. And as to the Suspicious Activity Report, you know there's always a way to get around those filing requirements."

"I'm sorry, Buck, but there isn't a way to get around filing and identifying Brad Crosshaven as the suspected wrongdoer. I've checked anonymously with both inside and outside counsel and specifically asked for any scenario where we could meet the requirements of the regulation without making the filing or, in the alternative, without identifying Crosshaven. There's no way under these facts that it can honestly be done."

Buck grimaced. "There's always a way when something's important enough, you know that!"

"No, Buck, I don't know that," said Riley calmly, shaking his head. "I've checked it out thoroughly."

"Yeah, but you're a real goody two-shoes when it comes to this stuff. This isn't the time for your Boy Scout routine," Buck's anger was now quickening his words. He had always given Riley free reign to see to it that the company met its obligations so long as it concerned regular employees, but this was something different. Why couldn't he understand that?

"No, I'm not overly conservative, Buck," said Riley, surprised and a little offended. "I'm not splitting hairs here. If this were a marginal call I'd go along with a self-serving interpretation because I know what's at stake. But it's not a marginal call. All the elements that trigger this kind of filing are clearly present here. There's no honest way that we can avoid filing. I'm sorry—I know this puts you in a bad spot."

Buck was now out of his chair, leaning over the table. "A bad spot? That's the understatement of the century! I guaranteed Ward there'd be no problem, and he assured me that his kid would go nowhere near what's-her-name." The veins in his forehead were swollen and throbbing. The collegiality of a moment before had vanished.

Torn between sympathy for Buck's distress and irritation at his rashness in making that kind of commitment to a customer, Riley took a deep breath and counted to ten. "Buck," he said in a firm but cool voice, "you shouldn't have done that. Number one, we can't commit to violate a government regulation, no matter who the customer is; and number two, Brad Crosshaven hasn't left Liddy alone. He blames her for turning him in and he knows she's the only witness. He's threatening her. Apparently Ward doesn't have as much control over him as he thought."

Buck started to interrupt, but Riley stood up and signaled that he wasn't through talking. "And like you agreed in our last meeting, our principal duty is to our employee. It's time to end the secrecy and get our security people involved on her behalf, and if they can't put a stop to it, we should file a criminal complaint for stalking and terrorist threats."

Buck's face darkened to a deep scarlet and his hands began to tremble. He took a long breath. "Do you know how many millions of dollars of profit we'll lose if we anger Ward Crosshaven on this?"

"No, I don't, Buck. And I don't care. The money has nothing to do with our legal or ethical obligation, let alone our duty to that employee."

What the hell was going on here, Riley wondered. Had he completely misjudged Buck—he was coming apart at the seams right in front of him. Riley knew there were profits at risk, but was there more to the Crosshaven relationship than he realized? He briefly entertained, and then fought off, the idea that Crosshaven had Buck compromised in some way.

Riley continued, "And like I just said, other company officers should be brought in on this."

"Nobody can know about this," shouted Buck. "You hear me? Don't say a word to Security. And stop acting like you're this girl's social worker."

Remaining calm and lowering his voice almost to the kind of whisper one uses when talking a jumper back from a ledge, Riley said, "I'm not talking about going public with the information, Buck. But inside-people like Cole Girard and Gar Blaisdahl should be involved here, just as they would if it were any other customer and employee."

"Cole Girard and Gar Blaisdahl?" Buck snorted disdainfully, as though Riley had suggested that Curly and Mo get involved. "Those two are not to know anything about this, you understand?"

"Look, Buck," said Riley, shaking his head, "don't take my word for it. Talk to someone on the board of directors. If you don't, you'll force me to. The company can't knowingly violate the law and our own policies. That's just the way it is."

Gladys appeared at the door, pointing to her watch to signify that the allotted twenty minutes were up. Buck waived her off rudely, and then closed the door. Riley sat back down.

Moving toward the south window, Buck inhaled deeply, allowed a short silence, and then in a calmer voice said, "We need to take another look at this, Riley. Let's sleep on it. And I'll talk to Ward about his kid staying away from Lonnie."

"Liddy," Riley corrected. "L-I-D-D-Y."

"Right . . . whatever." Buck seemed now to be someplace else, his eyes unfocused. He picked at his crotch as he stood by the window, staring out at the state capitol. Some people nurtured creative thought by twirling their hair; others doodled; still others sat in the lotus position. Buck scratched his nuts.

After a short interval, he turned to Riley and in total disregard of the known facts, said "Isn't it probable she misidentified Brad Crosshaven? Couldn't it have been someone else?" He arched his eyebrows, searching Riley's face for a sign of concurrence as though they were a couple of buddies working their way through a common problem.

Here was Riley's chance and he knew it. He could climb on board with a simple "yes," a little lie that would never be discovered, one that would relieve the company of the filing obligation and take all pressure off Buck—and advance his own career astronomically.

After a moment of silence he took a deep breath and looked over toward the window. "No, Buck, she got the right guy—right down to a little birthmark on his forehead."

Buck looked over at him sadly, shaking his head. "How do you know? You weren't there," he said.

"Buck, you're grabbing at shadows. This identification was much stronger than hundreds of others we've filed notifications on. There's no serious question here. And, besides, if it wasn't Brad Crosshaven, why is his father saying he'll keep him away from Liddy?"

"Ward never confirmed to me that it was his kid—he only said he'd have a talk with him. She could be wrong." He now began pacing like a playwright in the midst of creation. "And we all know how hysterical women are. They imagine things. Maybe she's a little nutty. Maybe she's obsessed with Brad Crosshaven—you know, in love with him. Maybe she's a fortune hunter. Or maybe she has PMS. Who the hell knows? You don't know. And I don't know. Do we?"

Riley was incredulous. He hadn't expected even Buck to go this far, hadn't expected him to be this desperate. "Buck, think about what you're saying . . . and what you're doing here. And why you're doing it." He held his hands out before his face in a gesture of bewilderment. "This isn't harmless wishful thinking—this is malevolent. You're smearing a decent person with all this crap because you're trying to avoid offending an important customer. But you're doing it at the expense of a loyal employee."

241

Buck wheeled sharply in Riley's direction and through clenched teeth he shouted, "Answer my question! You don't know, do you? You don't know everything all the time, do you? Just because you're one of my favorites doesn't mean you're going to get your own way all the time. You can be pretty arrogant about a lot of things. I'm not the only one to notice it."

Riley leaned back in his chair, ignoring the personal insult, which he knew to be a conversational gimmick informed by the juvenile scheming of Garfie Blaisdahl, and one that was calculated to get him to back down. "Buck," he said in measured words, "I don't personally *know* that Elvis is dead, either, but I think the evidence is pretty strong, certainly strong enough to meet the level of probability required by this regulation." He got up out of his chair. "And Liddy Jonssen is no hysteric. She's a solid, long-term employee. And a person we've got an obligation to support. You've got an obligation to support! For God sake, do your duty."

Buck just stared out the window, to which he had returned after his attempt at intimidation had failed. His lips moved rapidly but no sound could be heard. He was obviously in an act of composition.

Riley took a calming breath and continued. "Look, Buck, we can wait for a short while, but in the meantime please at least authorize a secure parking stall for her downstairs, so she'll feel a little safer and feel supported by the company."

Buck looked toward the conference table, but avoided Riley's eyes. "No way. We can't be making exceptions for her. I'd be giving credibility to her story. I've got a better idea, though. Let's reassign her, maybe to a spot over in Minneapolis."

That was an upside-down solution, thought Riley. Why should the blameless, under-siege employee have to move? She didn't do anything wrong. "No. We should be providing protection, not banishing her to a branch office," he said.

But Buck was paying little attention now, his mind focusing on the script he was drafting. His eyes took on a new texture, like an animal who hears a sound in the distance. Riley could tell that some revelation had come to him, some new theory.

Buck finally looked in Riley's direction. "Let's sleep on it. I'll talk to you in a couple of days." He then slapped Riley on the back in a fraternal gesture as though no harsh words had been exchanged moments before. "I'm sorry to scream at you, partner. But I expect you to understand teamwork. I don't blame you for not seeing the broad picture yet. You're pretty new to big business. You're going through a passage, a transition. You've got to trust my judgment on tricky matters like this and not take any steps without my say-so."

Riley knew that any further argument at this point would be useless. He just looked him in the eye until Buck broke contact. Then he turned and walked out of the office.

Returning to the west side, Riley encountered Skeeter, Liddy Jonssen, and Judy Goodrich taking a coffee break around the circular table in the copy room. With Goodie present he couldn't bring up the Crosshaven controversy, but observed in Liddy a starkly changed person from their first meeting. Her eyes—now surrounded by dark, grainy circles—stared out at the world with a drained and frightened look, and were set in a face that seemed to have lost all tone. She looked ill and exhausted.

After the others had left, Riley, grasping at straws, asked Skeeter, "God, Liddy looks awful. Is it possible that some physical sickness is accounting for her decline?" But, now, not even he could believe that.

"No," said Skeeter, a little irritated. "Every problem in the world is not caused by physical illness, Riley. You're so naive about some things. What you're seeing is depression. It scares me to death. I've got a cousin who's a lot like Liddy—bright, perfectionist, overly conscientious—whose life has been ruined by depression. Liddy promised me she'll go to the doctor soon, but she keeps putting it off. And I know how this kind of disease works—it takes on a life of its own and it can go completely out of control."

Riley accepted the scolding. He was naive about a lot of things. But now, for the first time, he knew that what he was

243

seeing in Liddy was something terrible and frightening, even if he didn't fully understand it.

Skeeter didn't want to dwell on the subject any longer. It was too upsetting. She thrust an armful of long-delinquent department budgets at him and pushed him into his office. "You've got to approve these by the end of the day. Don't come out until you're finished."

Getting current with office paperwork was especially important this week because he was leaving Wednesday night for the Executive Management Annual Offsite Conference in Boca Viejo lasting from Thursday to the following Sunday. The trip included spouses, so Betsy was coming along, which helped make tolerable the prospect of four days behind locked doors with the senior executive group, most of whom would smile politely for Buck's benefit, while secretly plotting each other's destruction.

At two o'clock sharp, M. Bryant Knox appeared in Riley's doorway, looking like a fraternity pledge seeking an audience with the chapter president. Such humility was uncharacteristic of M. Bryant, normally a man of swagger and self-assurance.

Looking up from the spreadsheet he was reviewing while talking on the phone to the accounting department, Riley switched the receiver to a position between his neck and shoulder and silently waved the visitor in with his free hand. After concluding his phone conversation, he replaced the receiver and laid the spreadsheets on one of the floor piles surrounding his desk. "Can I get you anything Bryant? Would you like a Milky Way?"

"No, thanks, Riley, I'm good," he said nervously while opening a file folder and removing several pages that looked to be from a manual of some sort, highlighted here and there in bright yellow. Also in the file was a legal pad bearing a series of handwritten notes, which Riley could not make out.

M. Bryant smiled nervously and stroked the arms of his chair as he prepared to state his mission. He seemed to be searching his mind for the right words.

What was it that accounted for such congeniality on the part of this self-impressed man? Riley wondered. He could hardly wait to hear the pitch. "What can I do for you, Bryant?" he asked again.

M. Bryant crossed his legs, placing the two printed pages under the legal pad. His expression became earnest. "I've got kind of a sensitive issue, Riley, and I thought maybe I could get your advice," he said, flashing an insipid smile that seemed out of place.

Riley had been around long enough to know that when a man of Bryant Knox's conceit asked for "advice," what he really meant was that he wanted you to save his ass. About the only good thing that could be said about M. Bryant was that he despised Garfie Blaisdahl and all his works and rarely missed an opportunity to intrigue against him. In this instance he said with considerable understatement that he'd have taken the as yet undescribed "sensitive issue" to Gar, but that "he's such a goddamn butt-licker he'd have turned on me and used it to ingratiate himself with Buck at my expense."

It takes one to know one, thought Riley as he smiled across the desk at his guest.

Most of the authority built into Bryant's power outfit— starched white collar against blue background, dark tie with tiny dollar signs forming a striped pattern, bright red suspenders, gold cuff links, and hair so lacquered it looked like a patent-leather flight cap—had been drained of its potency when removed from the bravado of the trading floor. His silver-buckled pumps appeared especially ridiculous.

In the midst of his introductory remarks, M. Bryant caught sight of his image reflecting off a silver coffee server on Riley's desk. Turning his head slightly to get a better view of his profile, he pulled a comb from his pocket and swept back a lock of well oiled hair from his forehead. For an essentially homely man, M. Bryant was remarkably vain. It never occurred to him that others might find this small ritual of self-adoration offensive.

Riley winked inwardly at the picture of Sir Thomas More hanging on the north wall of the office, then transferred his gaze back to M. Bryant. "What 'sensitive issue' have you got, Bryant? I have a lot to do today."

Bryant puckered his lips as though preparing to commence a sermon. "You know, Riley, Buck loves to make a deal and will do almost anything to get one done?"

Riley gave a short, silent nod, not returning the sheepish, buddy-buddy smile spread unattractively across Bryant's face.

Bryant continued, "Well, anyway, I was out with him recently with a public finance consultant who advises a bunch of municipalities on underwriting and distribution of their tax-exempt securities—you know, municipalities we do business with. So this guy's in a position to recommend us to his clients in a big way, and that translates into nice revenues each year." He shifted in his chair, recrossing his legs and looking at Riley as if to say: Have you heard enough?

Riley leaned forward. "Yeah? So what? You haven't described anything that's a problem."

Riley knew that M. Bryant hoped the conversational momentum would change, that Riley would take the initiative and ask questions, draw him out a little, kind of take ownership of the problem. But that wasn't going to happen, not today, not for this asshole.

"Well, let me go on," Bryant continued. "This consultant was talking about a nonprofit corporation that his daughter runs—she's the executive director and gets paid a bundle of money in salary. And about how that nonprofit is having a cash flow crisis and could really use a bridge loan of some kind so they could meet payroll."

"So?" said Riley a little impatiently, irritated at Bryant's indirectness and apprehensive about being forced to take on yet another matter where Buck had to be reminded of right from wrong. Some CEOs appreciated being protected from their own folly, but Buck was not one of these. Like most people who bragged about how open they were to criticism, he loathed being told he was wrong about anything.

"There's more, just hang on," said Bryant. "This guy is carrying on about the problems of the nonprofit right during the pitch Buck and I are giving him to recommend our broker-dealer to his public finance clients." With that M. Bryant's eyebrows shot up in a gesture of grave concern, which he fully expected Riley to share.

But Riley continued to play it deadpan. "I still don't see what the great sensitivity is. You haven't described anything that Buck has done wrong."

Bryant let out a sigh. He couldn't believe he would have to go on the record criticizing Buck, the guy who could—and as a result of this situation very possibly would—break his career like a match stick. He obviously wanted to just drop a few hints and toss the whole thing in Riley's lap. He would have just looked the other way at Buck's mischief but for the fact that he was personally in the stream of liability as a principal in the broker-dealer.

He took a deep breath and continued, "Well, I'm told that Buck cut out the normal underwriting process and authorized a sweetheart loan to the nonprofit. I'm worried as hell that the securities regulators will consider that to be an undisclosed benefit paid to the financial advisor, you know, a quid pro quo—the kind that's not kosher. Not to mention the difficulties that could arise on the bank side."

Riley opened his side drawer and pushed aside some Tootsie Pops left there by Liz Bridge as penance for the Milky Way heist she had pulled off the previous week. He extracted a legal pad on which to make a few notes. "Bryant, this is just Buck being unacquainted with the rules and a little careless. He's not deliberately doing anything wrong. Just explain to him why these things can't be tied together and why he has to follow the established loan procedures."

M. Bryant was now shaking his head and looking desperate. "That would kill the deal, and there'd be hell to pay. And I tried to talk to him about this ten days ago, but he got out of town on me," he said. "He had a golf game set up with Ward Crosshaven and a couple of other swells on the day I was scheduled to meet with him. When it started to rain, he piled the foursome onto the company jet and flew to Las Vegas where it was nice and dry."

He raised two fingers in the air in a scout's honor sign. "This is no shit, Riley. He actually commandeered the plane from a bunch of middle-managers so he and his buddies could head south for a nice dry round of golf. Can you believe that piece of shit?"

Riley didn't answer. He was disgusted but not surprised. Buck's arrogance seemed to be spinning out of control. But Riley was not about to have a discussion concerning Buck's tasteless practices with M. Bryant Knox. He adjusted himself in his seat and brought the conversation back to the subject at hand. "Well, he's in town now, isn't he?" he said. "I just left him. Why don't you go down and see him about this?"

M. Bryant shook his head and scanned the ceiling nervously. As far as he was concerned, if he challenged Buck on something like this, he could kiss his ass goodbye. He smiled enigmatically, disclosing rows of uneven teeth discolored by years of coffee and cigarettes. "What I was thinking, Riley, was that because you seem to be able to give him bad news without a lot of political damage, that maybe you could talk to him about this problem. I'll support you, of course—you can count on that—but I thought it might be best if you carried the ball. He seems to listen to you."

Carry the ball, Riley mused to himself. *Most of the ball carriers in this company had been purged long ago. Ball carrying was a very dangerous activity.*

After toying briefly with the idea of just telling Bryant Knox to kiss his ass, to get some balls and do the right thing, he realized his only choice would be to look into the story and, if it turned out to be true, carry the water for this overdressed little coward sitting across from him. If Riley didn't take up the problem, M. Bryant would never have the guts to say anything, and the company, with Riley's knowledge, would stumble headlong into a violation—in which case Buck could rightfully say that he hadn't been properly advised. He didn't want to get involved in this, didn't care to have his courage tested yet again, especially on top of the Crosshaven problem, but he had no choice. As his father used to say, "Heroes aren't born, they're cornered."

"All right, Bryant," he said dryly as he put the legal pad down on his desk. "Anything else?"

248

M. Bryant's eyes lit up with relief. He let out a long sigh, like a condemned man whose hanging had been called off. The swagger began to reemerge and a healthy color returned to his face, highlighting the lighter-colored skin just below his nose, where a winter mustache had recently been shaved off. Last March Buck had grown a closely cropped mustache that he thought added dignity to his face (Riley thought it made him look like an obscene phone caller), and within days Gar, M. Bryant, and several others followed suit, with mustaches sprouting on the fourth floor like a fast growing rash. M. Bryant's mustache was bushy and colorful, while Gar's consisted of widely spaced tufts of yellowish corn silk. When Buck tired of his mustache, finding it too hot for the Florida climate, it was shaved off by his barber. Within forty-eight hours all facial hair on the fourth floor had likewise disappeared, leaving a series of pale upper lips. You could spot the butt-kissers by their skin tones.

"Hey, thanks, Riley, I really appreciate it," said M. Bryant, his confidence restored as he made his way to the door, waving a good-bye to Skeeter and swaggering down the hallway.

"See ya, dickhead," muttered Skeeter under her breath.

19

A cloudless blue sky greeted the Lindbergh executive team and spouses as they landed in the company jet at the Boca Viejo Airport, where the temperature stood at a mild seventy-three degrees on way to a daytime high of ninety-two. They were conveyed in rented limousines to the newly opened Hernando Cortez Plaza, a four-hundred-room edifice of such surpassing vulgarity that it might have doubled as the Jim and Tammy set.

Driving the limousines were chauffeurs outfitted in the battle garb of Spanish conquistadors, including giant metal helmets with feathers sprouting from the top. All embarrassments in Riley's life combined were as nothing compared to the experience of riding in the back seat of a stretch limousine driven by a man in a conquistador outfit.

A giant fountain surrounded by palm trees stood at the center of the drive-through courtyard of the Hernando Cortez Plaza. A doorman, also in conquistador dress, ran toward them.

"Wow, this gives new meaning to the word garish," said Mimi Colfax, Ted's wife, bending forward in her seat to get a view of the whole ghastly façade.

"I think I'm going to puke," said Gail Girard, Cole's wife, a petite blonde with lots of attitude.

"Behave yourself," scolded Cole. "Buck thinks this place is the Versailles of the New World." Gail curled her lip and shrugged.

For her part, Betsy was paying no attention to the buildings or the decor, her full attention having turned to the elaborate, steeply tiered flower garden surrounding the courtyard. She shot out of the limousine and sprinted toward the flowers, swooning with admiration. Riley saw the vivid, brilliant shadings and colors of the flowers and thought they were pleasant enough but experienced none of the ecstasy that overtook Betsy when in the presence of natural beauty. When the rest of the party had long since left the courtyard, Riley pulled her by the arm through the high-buttressed, marble pillars, arranged over a moat in which floated lifeless plastic swans and alligators, and into a spacious lobby of Italian marble, smoked glass, and plaster relief ceilings.

Off the main lobby opened a poorly lit bar from which calypso music escaped. Above the bar's Roman imperial entryway was a neon sign reading: HERNANDO'S HIDEAWAY. Beyond the lobby was an Olympic-sized swimming pool, surrounded by statues of ancient Greek athletes with rippling biceps, flat torsos, and large wieners.

The hotel staff radiated that special air of priggish self-satisfaction that seems always to accompany expensive bad taste.

On the way to their quarters, following closely behind a conquistador bellhop, they passed no fewer than three older men (bull-legged, gray chest hair protruding from open-neck floral shirts) in the company of women who looked to be in their twenties, causing Riley to wonder if the Hernando Cortez might not double as a high-ticket whore house.

In their assigned space, a large suite of three rooms and bath, was an expensive flower arrangement that set Betsy to swooning anew and a giant basket containing fresh fruit, cheese and wine. The suite went for $750 a night.

Not being a golfer, Riley spent the afternoon returning phone calls and reviewing materials faxed down by Skeeter, leaving only once to buy a newspaper at a corner bookstore filled with old men wearing those mid-calf Bermuda shorts so beloved by elderly retirees. Betsy and Mimi Colfax sat in the sun and went for a tour of local flower gardens. The evening was taken up with an undistinguished musical presentation at a local dinner theater.

The following morning, the first session of the executive business meeting convened at 7:30 A.M. in the Cortez Room. Sun poured through the east windows, bathing the participants in its warm glow and turning the lenses of Buck's high-fashion eyewear a deep purple.

Erving Russell opened the meeting by delivering a long and tiresome financial presentation, through which Buck and one or two others slept intermittently.

"Super job," said Buck as Erving passed by on the way back to his place.

"Well, it's a pretty encouraging picture," said Erving as he sat down.

"You bet your ass," said Buck, wiping sleep from his eyes.

That completed, Cole Girard, wearing a T-shirt bearing a blown-up image of the Dali Lama, moved to a table in the corner of the room on which sat a stack of blue loose-leaf booklets containing the profiles of seventy-five key Lindbergh employees, arranged according to the divisions in which they worked. To maintain confidentiality, Cole had personally assembled the booklets. The face page of each certified that the printing had been done on reclycled paper by an equal-opportunity employer using soy-based ink.

Tom Arden, wearing a T-shirt listing the last twenty Grateful Dead concerts, leaned over to Riley and grunted, "What the fuck is soy-based ink?"

"Beats the shit out of me," answered Riley.

The other executives, all dressed in casual clothing, shuffled in their chairs and sipped coffee as they paged through their booklets. M. Bryant Knox, his hair down about a quart of oil, was from habit trying to hook his thumbs into nonexistent suspenders. Riley was surprised to see that in its unlarded state Bryant's hair appeared clean and fresh. And he had never seen him in a tightly fitting sports shirt. He looked like he could use breast reduction surgery.

Bobby Morestad, his corn-crop hair plugs growing with a vengeance, was wearing a pale-blue, button-down shirt tucked neatly into a pair of tan khakis.

Cole stood with his booklet open before him on the podium. "We've tried to include salient information on each employee under review, but you should feel free to add to the list. We are actively looking for feedback if you've had personal interaction with the employees or heard anything about them."

A large photo of the employee under review would be projected onto the flat west wall of the room. Riley couldn't help but note the irony as he watched Cole Girard, crusader for offshore social justice, standing just underneath a large color portrait of General Cortez, the explorer best remembered for having killed most of the natives of Latin America when they didn't see things his way.

Gar Blaisdahl, one-time president of his high school audiovisual club, worked the projector.

Cole opened by saying, "If you will turn to page four of your binder, we will begin with Jack Wincrest from Bryant Knox's division, who manages the distribution of our mutual funds in the Midwestern region." He gave a coordinating nod to M. Bryant.

At that a giant image of Jack Wincrest appeared on the wall, with Jack striking a Rhett Butler-like pose. M. Bryant cleared his throat and began, "I think all of you know Jack, but listed on your sheets are his educational credentials and work history, together with his salary and bonus for last year. He's been an "A" level performer from my standpoint and has basically doubled his duties since the downsizings commenced, without complaining. I consider him to be a candidate for big things in the future." He then looked around the table for input from others.

"Super guy," said Rick Snelling, rolling his shoulders. "Played some ball back at Edendale Junior College in the early eighties. Hit like a fucking bulldozer."

Tom Arden looked up scornfully from *The Insurance Times*, which he had commenced reading the moment M. Bryant started to talk. He said nothing.

"Very bright guy," said Erving Russell.

"Yeah, he is, isn't he?" said Buck, straining to place the face on the wall. He had no recollection of ever having seen or heard of Jack Wincrest.

"You bet, he is," said Cole Girard, from the podium, "and he's a real self-starter."

"Yeah, he dances to his own drummer," agreed Bobby Morestad, tossing his head back to sweep a shock of transplanted hair off his forehead. Not only had the plugs taken root in their new location, they had grown at a furious pace, like grass over a septic tank, leaving him with a two-tone head.

"Hit like a fucking bulldozer," repeated Rick Snelling, still gazing admiringly at Jack Wincrest's picture on the screen.

After a short interval of silence allowed by Cole for insertion of any further comments, he clicked the slide button, bringing forth the image of Bruce Browndale, a midlevel manager in the investment securities side of the business.

M. Bryant ran through the data relating to Browndale and offered the assessment that he too was a "star," one from whom great things could be expected in future years.

Another described a good experience he had had working with Browndale, and still another pointed out that Bruce had been a Buckie finalist that year. Buck studied the photo on the screen, trying to place the face, his curiosity apparently aroused by the Buckie reference.

"Super guy," said Ted Colfax. "Helped out one of my most important customers last month. Smoothed over a service problem."

Buck continued his visual examination of the photo on the wall, his eyes narrowed in concentration. Suddenly he bolted forward in his seat. "Isn't this guy a fruitcake, a member of that group that tried to get us to sponsor some gay event last year?"

"No, no!" injected Cole Girard hurriedly. "He's not gay."

M. Bryant joined in. "You're thinking of another manager in that unit who works closely with Bruce."

"Let's not tar him with the same feather," cautioned Bobby Morestad.

Gar looked across the table at Buck with an expression of shared concern, a We-have-to-get-to-the-bottom-of-this look on his face. Erving Russell, ever the cautious politician, kept his eyes down, not daring to scold Buck, but also not wanting to get on board with his social views.

Rick Snelling shook his head as he looked up at Bruce Browndale's photo. "No gay could run that fast. Bruce can run like a fucking deer."

Riley felt a sensation of mild despair pass over him, a feeling that he had come to know well over the last five months whenever Buck's social views came to be expressed. He was feeling a nagging discomfort at being a collaborator in the effort to manage Buck's image, an image designed to portray him as a progressive, enlightened, and hard-working leader—an image dishonest right down to its core. Press releases and speeches prepared for industry groups were one thing, he supposed. But this was something different; flesh and blood were involved here. Careers of real live people were made and destroyed at these meetings. A negative or even a careless word from Buck, no matter how sophomoric or misinformed, could ruin a person's future with the company.

He took a deep breath and sat forward in his seat, glancing past Tom Arden to the head of the table, where Buck was seated. "There are two problems here," he said. "One is we've got to be careful about labeling people inaccurately; and the other is we can't let personal views on lifestyle, gender, race, and that sort of thing determine personnel decisions. That wouldn't be right." Though the message was fairly clear, Riley delivered it with an inflection that removed most of its sting, almost as though he was stating a proposition to which Buck fully subscribed but had momentarily lost sight. This approach had worked by and large in the past, but as the Lindbergh stock price soared, Buck had grown less and less tolerant of criticism, more and more certain of his own biases, no matter how antediluvian they were. And he had actually come to believe the public-consumption stories that the company spin doctors, including Riley, had been putting out about him. Riley fought to suppress the growing notion that he was an accomplice to a fraud. A fraud that might claim real victims after all.

"Well, I'll tell you this, traditional family values are the most important thing in the world to me," said the thrice-wed Buck. He looked over at Gar. "And this crap has its limits."

Cole Girard, a man without social prejudice, a man who knew better, stood bowed at the podium, choking on his own soul-blighting silence.

Tom Arden passed a note to Riley: "Drop it. It won't do any good."

Riley felt disapproval descending upon him from the other end of the table but was strangely indifferent to it. However unpleasant it might be, no matter what the political consequences, it was trivial when compared to the self-loathing that would take hold in the wake of silence.

To break the tension, Cole pressed the slide button and brought up a new photo. Shuffling papers at the podium, he mumbled in a voice hardly audible at Buck's end of the table, "Well, it might be best to move on to the next slide."

Buck cupped his ear with the palm of his hand to signify that he hadn't heard Cole's last statement. Cole repeated himself, this time more loudly.

Buck then mumbled something in return in a loud but deliberately garbled voice.

"What?" asked Cole, leaning into the podium toward Buck, straining to make out what he had said.

"I said 'jacking off makes you hard of hearing!'" Buck shouted in triumph, laughing so hard he succumbed to a coughing fit.

Cole gave an embarrassed "touché" nod. Gar laughed appreciatively at Buck's cleverness, giving him a high-five.

When the merriment subsided, Cole reached for the slide clicker and said, "We now say good-bye to Bruce Browndale—who is not a homosexual. Not that's there anything wrong with being a homosexual."

The next image projected onto the screen brought forth a qualitatively different response from those that had preceded it, namely, a wolf whistle from the south end of the table, giggles from the corner closest to the large picture window, and a few strokes of Buck's fist over his lap, accompanied by an eyebrow-wiggling grin. Even Tom Arden temporarily suspended his reading to gaze up at the three times life-size image of Julie Newton.

Several of the group, including Cole Girard and Erving Russell, squirmed with discomfort at the burlesque atmosphere that had now overtaken the room. Some of them had grown daughters who were working in business and industry, and they cringed inwardly at the thought of one of them being treated, even in absentia, in such a degrading way. To Riley, what was happening here argued for the prompt addition of at least one woman to the Executive Management Group. The whistlers and eyebrow-wigglers would not—no matter how retrograde their social views—dare act this way in the presence of a woman. But when he and Cole had made that suggestion barely two months before, it had been summarily vetoed by Buck. Try as he might, Buck couldn't bring himself to take any woman seriously outside a domestic or sexual context.

Julie Newton's history as a college-age beauty queen may have marked her for especially salacious treatment, but she was, in Riley's direct experience, an exceptionally bright and hard-working employee who, like so many other talented people found in the middle ranks of the company, contributed to the success of the enterprise all out of proportion to the recognition (financial and nonfinancial) that they received. When emergency projects were thrust upon the company, when all-night sessions in distant outposts had to be endured, it was these people who answered the call—not the elite and pampered executives who were now passing judgment upon them.

Ted Colfax, Julie Newton's supervisor, turned to his section of the binder and on signal from Cole Girard took over the lead. "Julie is one of the great people in our division, the kind who make me proud of what we've accomplished."

Buck gazed lustily at the photo. "She makes my dink hurt," he said with gigglish delight.

This comment had the sycophants in the room rolling in the aisles. Gar laughed so hard it looked as though he might choke.

"God, does she have a rack on her," boomed M. Bryant.

Buck leaned forward, squinting at the picture. "I don't think she wears a bra. They really flop around a lot."

Cole dropped his head onto the podium, as though he was about to break down and sob.

Ted Colfax, who seconds before had sounded the consummate professional, now luxuriated in the role of supervisor to the company employee who made Buck's dink hurt, the expression of seriousness and dignity on his face transformed into the lewd grin of the high school quarterback who had just scored with the head cheerleader.

But for the fact that she was a personal friend, Riley might not have had the guts to say anything. But Julie Newton was a person of great competence and dignity, and a friend who had done him many good turns during his time with the company. He felt like his sister was being made fun of. He took a deep breath. "I've worked with Julie a lot. She's exceptionally competent and energetic about her work. She doesn't deserve this kind of treatment."

"I agree," Bobby Morestad hurriedly joined in.

"She should lose the earrings," said Buck, "they're too big."

"I think she's good," said Erving Russell.

"I don't know. I hear she's kind of a bimbo," said Gar Blaisdahl.

Riley's face reddened, and his voice became husky. He glared down the table toward Gar. "What do you mean a 'bimbo'? Define that term for us," he said sharply.

Gar looked surprised, caught off guard. An expression of smug superiority formed on his face. "I think everyone here knows what that term—"

"No, they don't, Gar. You're talking about Julie's career here. You've got an obligation to be clear. What do you mean, 'She's a "bimbo"'? What exactly is a bimbo?"

The initial playfulness now stopped cold, leaving Gar isolated against a backdrop of silence. A forced, insecure laugh escaped his throat as he strove to cloak himself in an air of nonchalance. "Well, I'll explain it to you later, Riley."

"I don't think she's a bimbo," said Ted Colfax, at long last awake to his responsibility as Julie's sponsor and advocate before this group. Two or three others in rapid succession weighed in favorably. A smile returned to Cole Girard's anguished face.

Buck felt the tension and didn't like it. For all his tough talk, he couldn't stand confrontation. He signaled for Cole to move on.

Riley returned Gar's look of hatred with a warm smile. He seemed a lonesome, pitiful figure down there at the end of the table.

A long series of unremarkable reviews followed, with the attention span of the participants dwindling as the morning wore on. Midway through the review of personnel in the non-insurance consumer-products group, most of whom reported up through Bobby Morestad, Riley was struggling to stay awake when on the screen appeared the face of Liddy Jonssen. The photo had been taken a year earlier and showed a strikingly young-looking face, flushed with eager self-confidence, a broad smile spread below sparkling eyes. Riley looked up at the lovely face on the wall, the face that had belonged to Liddy a year ago. This was the relaxed and happy Liddy described by Skeeter on so many occasions, the one who existed before the ugliness of the downsizings and the Crosshaven matter had taken its toll. The smiling face and dancing eyes in the picture betrayed no hint of the agony that awaited her.

Stunned by this unexpected visual encounter, Riley sensed again, this time more strongly, how profoundly and dangerously affected Liddy had been by recent events. It was no wonder Skeeter was so worried.

Bobby Morestad began formally: "Liddy Jonssen is thirty-three years old, a graduate of St. Olaf College, and until recently has been one of our star performers. Although she has continued to work at a grueling pace, she seems depleted of the kind of energy that characterized most of her tenure with the company. The downsizing was hard on her, especially firing people in her own unit, and we can legitimately ask whether she's fit for the new culture—whether she can take the faster, harder pace."

"She's been a great employee whenever I've dealt with her," said Tom Arden, putting on a pair of reading glasses to review her resume in the binder. He seemed surprised by what he had just heard.

"Same here," said Ted Colfax, looking confused.

Trying to recover from his recent humiliation, Gar Blaisdahl, who knew nothing about Liddy, launched into a speech about how some people who did fine in the old culture were bound to fail when tested by the rigors of the new Lindbergh and about how it was sad but necessary to identify and weed those people out—for their own good and the good of the organization. Several people nodded.

Riley stared down the table at Buck, waiting for him to say something that would let Bobby Morestad and others know that Liddy's decline was in great part the result of harassment from the son of the company's most valued customer—his pal Ward Crosshaven—not from some personal shortcoming on her part. But Buck said nothing. He only nodded general agreement with Gar.

It dawned on Riley for the first time that maybe Buck wanted to get rid of Liddy under some kind of pretext, some claim of performance deficiency. That would get her out of the way, and no one would know the real reason. Could he be that devious, that unprincipled? Riley wondered. Until that moment he wouldn't have thought so.

Without taking his eyes from Buck, he said in a cold and exacting voice: "Maybe her recent change in performance has more to do with other things—things that have nothing to do with the new culture, things her managers don't know anything about. Let's not brand anybody unfit until we've heard all the facts." His burning stare had now caught Buck's eye. "Wouldn't you agree, Buck?" he said challengingly.

Buck seemed suddenly to come awake to the realization that Riley, in a gesture of misplaced gallantry, might be on the verge of blurting out the Crosshaven story. He sat upright in his chair, cleared his throat and said preemptively, "This is an exceptional case. She's fine. Let's push on to the next employee. We've got to pick up the pace."

Riley settled back in his seat. Others looked confused, and a little titillated by the mystery.

Liddy was replaced on the screen by the swarthy and unattractive face of Art Coolidge, the lending officer who had been swept off his feet by Buck's charm several weeks before when he visited the Sacristy for a signature on some loan documents. In contrast to his simian appearance, Art Coolidge was an intelligent and thoughtful man who was liked and admired by both customers and fellow workers. Ted Colfax lead the group through his vital statistics, including a description of his service in Vietnam, where he had suffered neurological damage from exposure to defoliants and war chemicals, which accounted for his palsied facial expression.

"It was ancient orange," said Bobby Morestad.

"Stood up in the fight against communism," said Erving Russell.

"Is he very smart?" asked Buck. "He doesn't look very smart."

"Actually, he is quite smart," replied Tom Arden. "He graduated with honors from college and came right to work for The Lindbergh. He's been in the lending division for almost eighteen years."

Technology chief Harold Westline, who had worked closely with Coolidge on several projects, put down the pipe on which he had been chewing and said, "Art is good at avoiding conflictualization of commodified traffic. On an outcome-based analysis, he has unalloyed access to his sublinguistic gifts."

Several around the table shook their heads in unalloyed, sublinguistic confusion. Buck leaned over to Gar and said, "Now is that a genius, or what?"

And so it went for five endless hours, broken only by delivery of lunch orders. Buck (and then Gar and M. Bryant in rapid succession) ordered corn beef sandwiches on rye. Cole Girard ordered an "en-chee-lada" from a Cuban waiter, giving him a Latino power salute that made the waiter laugh out loud. Riley had a Milky Way and a Pepsi.

Male employees under review were lauded for their "brass balls" and "scorched earth" attitudes, while the women, though great gals all, were faulted for everything from penis-envy to bad hair.

261

Friday morning was more of the same except that division heads became aggressive in criticizing the lieutenants of their rivals. With Buck forbidding managerial disagreements in his presence, all issues between divisional executives were forced below ground, where they ripened and festered, undermining any possibility of real cooperation. Given Buck's general absence from the workplace and his resulting ignorance of the malignant intrigues that infected managerial relations, it was not surprising that the major players turned their fire on the surrogates of their competitors. Lacking the sophistication to recognize and decode the complicated personal interactions being played out before him, Buck was in no position to provide leadership, and the sessions became little more than political theater.

After Friday morning's segment, lunch was served, buffet-style, on the open air deck of the Cortez's top floor. Large potted plants flapped in the wind, and a blazing sun beat down on the metal tables and chairs. No one seemed much interested in conversation, all intent on the afternoon recreational activities.

Standing at the deck railing, Riley scanned the surrounding landscape studded with golf courses and row after row of expensive homes. From behind him he could hear Buck regaling a group of admirers from his stock of off-color jokes.

To the north and west on the far horizon he could see distant fields with groups of migrant workers picking fruits and vegetables, whole families spread out in random bunches, streaming to and from older-model, decaying automobiles parked in careless and uneven patterns along the shoulders of adjoining highways. As he watched the small figures move about in the distance, he picked at his diet salad and thought back with nearly perfect recall to the summer after high school when he and Chasbo Peytabohm, still seventeen years old, hitch-hiked to central California to join a classmate who had been a boarding student at St. David's, on the promise of glamorous outdoor work in the San Joaquin Valley. It turned out that their buddy, one of several boys in a well-to-do

California manufacturing family, was on his father's bad side that year and could deliver nothing more glamorous than itinerant fruit-picking with large crews of migrant workers. And at that they had to work under false names because of laws prohibiting the hiring of minors. Riley and Chasbo had signed on using those favorite pseudonyms of all teenage boys: Dick Hertz and Jack Meehoff.

The wages were $1.00 per hour, plus fifteen cents per bucket of plums picked. For the migrant workers who chose to house their families in the dilapidated shacks maintained by the owners, twenty-five cents out of each dollar was withheld, leaving a pathetically deprived group of people barely able to pay for food, cigarettes, and cheap wine. Coming from a boy's military school filled with mostly overprivileged sons of prominent families, the experience of life from morning to night with people who could neither read nor write and who were aging from abuse and poor nutrition at a pace one could almost sit and watch was an experience that shocked the conscience. Riley had read and seen dramatized *The Grapes of Wrath* and other depictions of life among poor farm workers and felt as moved as one could feel from the comfort of a paneled school library but was wholly unprepared for what he was seeing and smelling each day in the vast plum fields of the valley. Not even the acting of Henry Fonda had prepared him for the ugly reality of this, the last example of indentured servitude in the second half of twentieth-century America. These people were not the Joad family or anything close to it. They were much worse off.

Driving to and from the fields each day in large trucks designed to haul cattle, Riley and Chasbo would visit with their fellow workers, forming a close friendship with a man who spent most of each day with a finger up his nose to the second knuckle, attempting to unclog nasal passages closed as a result of being bashed with a company policeman's baton as a youngster. He went by the unsurprising name of "Boogie." His parched skin and infrequent and unhealthy teeth caused Riley to estimate his age at a hard-worn fifty. He turned out to be twenty-three years old.

The picking crews were overseen by a corps of mean and humorless foremen with mirrored sunglasses reminiscent of the guards in *Cool Hand Luke*. They were assisted by the few workers who could add and subtract, the latter acting as "checkers" at evenly spaced stations where buckets of fruit would be poured by the pickers into large wooden boxes for removal to the central processing facility.

Nothing at St. David's, on or off the athletic field, had prepared Chasbo and Riley for the special stresses laid upon the body by the simple act of fruit-picking, an activity which from a distance looked almost effortless. Strict rules concerning placement of ladders, together with unreasonably high production goals, forced the workers to duck and stretch into unnatural positions, oftentimes exposing them to risk of great injury.

After two days of sweat and pain in the blistering California sun, Chasbo had had enough of the short end of the worker exploitation game and decided to test the system. The Checker—himself a picker just weeks before—was drunk with power and went about his work with theatrical excess. Each picker was assigned a number listed in a vertical column on a sheet of heavy paper attached to the Checker's clipboard. As the pickers filed past the central drop-off point, where the Checker sat imperiously on a camp stool, they would empty their buckets into the wooden container and recite their numbers for entry into the Checker's log. The Checker would then officiously shout out a confirmation and enter a check mark on the log, which was used at the end of each day to determine compensation. Chasbo was assigned No. 619 and Riley 620.

Feeling sure he could dramatically improve his compensation, Chasbo waited for high-traffic periods at the checking station, got in line, poured only a half bucket of plums into the wooden container, and shouted out "619."

"619, big boy!" came back the Checker's authoritative reply. This method doubled Chasbo's bucket count for the ensuing two days.

Not satisfied that he had exhausted his options, on the third day Chasbo picked no plums at all, but worked his way through the line ninety-seven times (each time kicking the wooden container to make the sound of tumbling plums) and yelled "619."

"619, big boy!" came back the military like confirmations, ninety-seven times.

Emboldened by the heartstopping stupidity of the Checker and bored with his frequent trips back and forth to the central station, Chasbo now took to sitting in his tree, picking only such plums as he could eat, and every time traffic got heavy at the checking station, shouting through the branches: "619!"

"619, big boy!" echoed the Checker. That day Chasbo was credited with 157 buckets, more than tripling his wages and setting the world's plum-picking record.

The following day a special foreman from headquarters was dispatched to monitor Chasbo. It did Riley's heart good to watch Chasbo give himself over to the picking arts, expending all resources at his command, bending and stretching like a carnival contortionist. He picked as though his life depended on it, and at the end of an exhausting day had racked up a grand total of sixteen buckets.

He was fired on the spot. Riley, as a known associate, was fired right along with him. On his way out of the headquarters building, Chasbo threw up on the general manager. When the ill-gotten gains were not repaid (Chasbo gave them to Boogie to get his nose fixed) a bulletin was sent to all company locations placing the names Hertz and Meehoff on a list of trespassers to arrest on sight.

The next day, lightly disguised in sunglasses and baseball caps, they went down the road to another fruit company and were promptly hired to pick grapes, this time as Hugh Jardon and Dick Goesinya.

By the time Riley's mind returned to the roof of the Hernando Cortez, Buck and his friends were rising from the table. Following Buck's last joke, Gar was doubled over with laughter, gasping for air, saying, "Oh, chief, you've got to stop. You're killing me with these stories."

Riley waited for the others to leave the area before joining Wally for an afternoon walk. Back at his room, he returned a call from Skeeter.

"Your weird buddy, Kurt McBraneman, called again," she said. "We're becoming pretty good pals, Kurt and I. I'm not even scared of him anymore."

"You're the only one who's not," said Riley. "Please tell me he left a number this time. I've got to talk to him."

"Of course he didn't leave a number. You know that," she said, "but he did say things are under control, and then laughed a little. I didn't ask what he was talking about."

Riley sat overlooking the Cortez pool five floors below, shaking his head nervously. "I don't know either, but I'm plenty worried about it."

On Saturday morning the business sessions focused on the company's most important customer relationships. A list of the one-hundred largest and most profitable relationships was handed out to each officer. Number one on the list was Crosshill Enterprises, the umbrella entity through which the Crosshaven family coordinated its financial activities, ranging all the way from its massive real estate and furniture manufacturing empires, established by Ward's father, Vinehill Crosshaven, to the individual trusts set up and administered by the Lindbergh Trust Company for and on behalf of Ward Crosshaven and his heirs. Just about every major operating division of the company had a share of the business, with the largest piece residing in the real estate lending-investment area. Each division head in turn described his area's slice of the Crosshaven pie, including an assessment of the Crosshill people who were his principal contacts. Riley listened with interest to this part of the program, which laid out the Byzantine complexity of the Crosshaven family interests.

And for his part the phlegmatic, uninvolved Buck of ordinary times showed a remarkable energy and detailed familiarity with every aspect, no matter how small, of the Lindbergh-Crosshill relationship. It was a dazzling display of what he was capable of when he had reason to become interested in a subject.

As the session broke up, Riley grabbed Buck and Bryant Knox for a quick caucus on the matter raised by Bryant in their recent meeting.

Buck looked at Riley impatiently. "Make it fast. I've got a tee time."

Pulling a legal pad from his briefcase, Riley started in: "There's an item that came to my attention which we have to be careful about, involving loans as a possible quid pro quo for steering deals to the broker-dealer."

Buck got a here-we-go-again look on his face. Turning toward the door, he yelled for Erving, who was just leaving, to join the discussion. Erving pulled up a chair in the small circle.

Riley continued, "We can't make undisclosed sweetheart loans for the benefit of a relative of a guy we're trying to get underwriting referrals out of."

"So?" demanded Buck.

"Well, a question has come up about written procedures having been suspended in order to make a special loan to a non-profit corporation, where the director is the daughter of a guy in a position to influence some public finance underwritings that we're bidding on." Riley looked over at M. Bryant Knox, who sat silent as a stone, his eyes fixed to the ground. The promised support was not exactly bursting forth.

Buck crunched his face into a look of restless irritation. "What's the matter with you?" he shouted. "Don't you know anything about the real world? Why shouldn't we benefit in this way? It's our money that's being loaned!" He now looked over at Erving. "God, I'm getting sick of this crap." Erving returned the look but without either concurring or disputing, for he knew that this was one more example of Buck's mischief and he was glad it was being surfaced by someone other than himself. He was only sorry he hadn't gotten out the door several seconds sooner so he could have ducked the issue altogether. He was secretly grateful to Riley but not about to provide any explicit support.

Buck sneered at Riley. "Why does every other company in the world get to do that sort of thing, and we don't? Tell me that?" He was nearly screaming.

"Every other company doesn't do it, Buck," replied Riley calmly, "and even if they did it wouldn't give us license to."

Buck turned sharply toward M. Bryant, giving him a penetrating stare. "It's your division. What do you say about this?" he asked in a voice that dared Bryant to disagree with him.

M. Bryant, now feeling the full force of Buck's passion on the subject, turned and glared across the circle at Riley. "Buck's right. Why the hell shouldn't we be able to do what everybody else does? Maybe you're wrong about this." He then looked back at Buck, giving a collegial nod.

For all the duplicity of the Lindbergh culture generally, and all the butt-licking hypocrisy of M. Bryant Knox specifically, Riley was not quite prepared for this little bit of treachery. The saggy-breasted little coward sitting across from him took the grand prize for trashing Buck behind his back, but that didn't stop him from doing a quick political analysis and, without a trace of shame, making a high-speed leap to the safe side of the issue. It was breathtaking.

For his part, Erving spoke not a word, but when his glance turned to Riley it expressed silent appreciation.

Whether in due course Riley would have called out Bryant Knox and exposed his double-dealing could not be answered, for Buck had promptly risen to his feet, and as he left the room snorted at Riley, "I'll issue instructions to call off the loan. Will that make you happy, Archbishop McReynolds?"

Riley said nothing.

As they walked out of the conference area of the Cortez Plaza, Riley asked, "Did I misunderstand our conversation last week, Bryant? I thought I was carrying your water for you, doing you a favor."

M. Bryant answered, "Right . . . right. I think it went real well in there. You did a great job, Riley. Boy, he's a real scumbag, isn't he?"

Riley felt dizzy. He stopped and looked Bryant hard in the eyes. "A scumbag? Not five minutes ago you were in there shamelessly sucking up to him. Now, behind his back, you're calling him a scumbag? What the hell's the matter with you?"

"Oh, come on, Riley, give me a break," he whined. "I was in a tough spot. You're much better at that stuff than I am."

"You're pathetic," Riley replied as he started down the hall. He then turned back in disgust: "There was only one scumbag in that room, and it wasn't Buck."

M. Bryant shouted after him, "You're an idealist, Riley—you think you have to like the guy you're working for. That's not the way the game's played, buddy. When you gonna grow up?"

Saturday afternoon was set aside for recreational activities before the gala Saturday night dinner. Buck, Erving, Gar, and M. Bryant played golf. Rick Snelling organized a touch football game. Cole Girard attended a Save the Whales rally. Riley rented a car and toured local cemeteries.

Cocktails were served at 6:30 P.M. in the lounge of Buck's favorite country club, a structure of serious architectural confusion built in the mid-fifties, its large low-ceilinged rooms boasting a series of light-green metal wings that looked like the fins on a '59 Cadillac. Faithful to its overall theme, which blended Eighteenth Century Spanish with post-World War II metal sterility, the interior defied categorization. Mimi Colfax thought it could best be described as "Early Hugh Heffner." But out beyond its broad picture windows lay a golf course of spectacular beauty, set out in full cooperation and simple harmony with the incorruptible beauty of Mother Nature.

Most of the guests, who looked tense and not altogether happy to be facing an evening of false joviality, were downing cocktails at a pace more akin to teenagers before the senior prom than corporate power-couples awaiting the arrival of the boss. Most of the men were dressed in blazers, worn over blue or white cotton shirts tucked into khaki or beige slacks. The women wore colorful but tasteful outfits tailored to emphasize or detract, as appropriate, from their varying body shapes and sizes, set off by jewelry that was snappy but not gaudy.

At 6:55 Wally opened the ornate double doors of the lounge, silently announcing the late arrival of Buck, Eileen on his arm. Eileen was wrapped in a brightly sequined, sleeveless dress that stopped well short of her shapely knees. Though young

269

enough to be Buck's daughter and still quite attractive, she was a long way from the blushing coed of their first meeting.

Marie Blaisdahl, already three drinks ahead of a very hard-drinking crowd, leaned over to Betsy and whispered, "Did she think this was a costume party?"

"I think she looks adorable," replied Betsy sweetly, a gentle reprimand in her voice.

Gar appeared behind Marie and, grasping her rudely by the arm, marched toward Buck and Eileen, a huge smile on his face.

The other couples in the room scrambled for places at the long, elaborately set dinner table, as far from Buck and Eileen as they could get. They almost tripped over each other in the stampede.

Buck, aflame with whiskey from a pre-dinner cocktail party that reunited old friends from the Wallace for President campaign, was now in his natural habitat, free of sartorial restraints. He was decked out in an ensemble that included white patent-leather shoes and belt, lime green double-knit trousers, and a pale blue, Day-Glo blazer. His body-fit shirt was open several inches down the chest, exposing a thick gold chain nestled upon a tuft of protruding chest hair dyed-to-match in a sort of tangerine color. His rust-colored hair, naturally curly to begin with, had been rendered more frizzie by an afternoon swim, giving him a slightly smurfish look.

"Oh, my God," said Tom Arden, more in sadness than in ridicule.

By the time Betsy and Riley made their way to the table, most of the places had been taken, leaving them seated across from each other, with the Montrowes on one side and the Blaisdahls on the other. Betsy, indifferent to company politics, was fine with the arrangement. On her right was Gar, who, totally ignoring her, turned toward Buck and proposed a toast to "the Chief and his lovely bride, for their sponsorship of this spectacular dinner." So worshipful was Gar's gaze that Riley thought he might lean down and kiss Buck full on the lips.

"Here, here!" joined in M. Bryant and Cole Girard, their wine glasses thrust in the air.

"Dipshit," mumbled Tom Arden, at the far end of the table, nipping at a bottle of mineral water.

Marie Blaisdahl, seated to Riley's immediate left, shouted "Down the hatch" and guzzled her entire glass of wine. Gar stared at her with the face of an angry headmaster.

Eileen, who felt herself unfairly judged in this group, seemed to relax after several minutes of conversation with Betsy. Unlike Buck, Eileen—a nice and perceptive person—could see through the flattery and gushing insincerity that Buck took to be authentic and well earned.

By the second course, Buck and Marie Blaisdahl had each downed another two martini's, making it hard to tell which one sounded dumber. With each drink the backwoods southern accent that Buck had worked so hard to eradicate in years of elocution lessons had become more pronounced until Riley thought he was listening to Gomer Pyle. When Buck began fulminating against affirmative action and accusing Riley of naiveté for not believing that Bill Clinton had personally murdered eighteen people in Arkansas, Riley decided that Marie might, after all, be the better conversationalist. Turning in her direction, he heard her responding to Gar's sanctioning look by sticking her tongue out and shouting for all to hear, "Blow it out your ass, Buster!"

Riley leaned down and whispered gently, "Why don't we have a cup of coffee, Marie?"

"You'd drink, too, Riley, if you were married to that tight-ass," she replied. She then wiggled the last digit of her index finger in front of Riley's face and said, "And he's got a pecker about that big."

For some reason, Riley found this observation to be so funny that he completely lost control of himself, laughing into his napkin until one of his contact lenses washed out. This caused Betsy to go into her own fit of giggles, though she had no idea what they were laughing at. Because Betsy had been talking to Buck at the time she started giggling, Buck assumed it was one of his many witticisms that had set her off, and this started him laughing along with her. Soon the whole table followed suit, laughing contagiously and uproariously at some unknown quip they thought had originated with Buck.

Marie assumed they were laughing at Gar's dick size, so she stood up and took a deep bow. Eileen, who apart from Riley was the only one to follow the true course of this mass hysteria, winked knowingly at Riley.

The gathering dragged on painfully for another hour, sustained only by the grit of the participants and the copious flow of alcohol. By nine o'clock Marie was face down on the table, and Buck was so shit-faced he had joined a conga line winding its way through the dining room from the main dance floor. Lost in a sea of leisure wear, Buck disappeared into the hallway as the line snaked its way back to the Cortez ballroom, where he and the other locals danced the night away.

Eileen rose from her chair, graciously thanked the assembled guests for their attendance, and headed out in pursuit of Buck.

With Buck's departure (and the onset of some pretty severe hangovers) all pretenses were dropped and the festivities ground to a merciful halt. Gar grabbed a handful of hair and lifted Marie's head off the table. He then raised her from her chair, picking a piece of parsley from her forehead.

"Oh, hi, pencil dick," she cracked, hoping to repeat her comedic triumph of earlier in the evening. She looked about in vain for an appreciative audience.

The ride back to The Hernando Cortez was on the grim side, standing in sharp relief to the madcap hijinks of the early evening. The alcohol that had worked such magic at dinner was now being exhaled into the cab of the limousine as a series of stale by-products. Against that backdrop some normally discreet people openly mocked Buck and Eileen, taking no care to avoid being overheard by the conquistador-outfitted driver.

The plane ride home was even grimmer, with the rival executives reassuming their roles as independent power centers, all weekend fellowship having evaporated with the exhaled alcohol. It was back to business as usual.

20

On Monday Riley made sure to get to the office before Skeeter's arrival in order to weigh himself on the official scale sitting in the closet across from her desk. After Liz Bridge's attempt to tamper with the scale's workings he had been alert to any signs of sabotage. All seemed to be in order for the eleven o'clock weigh-in, at which he would step triumphantly onto the scale and receive apologies and payoffs from those who had been fool enough to underestimate his resolve. What a pleasure it would be.

Slipping out of his shoes, he hopped on the scale for a dry run only to find, to his horror, that the reading was two pounds over the goal weight. How could this be? he wondered. He had cemented the weight-adjustment gauge in place after Liz's attempt to tamper with it, so he knew that couldn't be the problem. It must have something to do with the Florida climate or air travel or something else related to the trip that caused water retention. He resolved to go to the health club down the block at about ten o'clock to sweat off the fluids that were being mysteriously retained. That would put him in good shape for the eleven o'clock ceremony.

As he slipped back into his shoes he experienced an anticipatory gloat thinking about the crow that would be eaten by his many detractors, not to mention the money he'd be collecting.

His phone was ringing as he reentered his office. "Hello, Riley McReynolds here," he said cheerfully.

"Jesus H. Kee-rist, Riley!" bellowed Chief of Security Dan Thornton. "Do you have any idea who you were chatting with in the garage a while back?" Thornton spoke so loudly that Riley switched the receiver to his other ear. His eyes lit up with mischief, and a smile took shape on his face as though he were undergoing some private amusement. Dan Thornton, ex-hard-ass military policeman and the world's biggest cynic, had never, within Riley's hearing, sounded so intense, so focused.

Adopting a mock-quizzical tone, Riley asked, "What do you mean, Dan?"

"That guy in the garage," Dan yelled. "We go over the surveillance tapes every couple of weeks, and there on my screen is fucking Kurt McBraneman, fucking Public Enemy Number One! Jesus, even the cops are scared of that guy." Dan drew in a raspy breath and continued, "What the hell did he want? What was he doing talking to you?"

"Easy, big guy," said Riley. "Kurt's a friend of mine—a former client. He's no danger to anyone around here." Riley should have anticipated this call, should have known that Kurt would probably be recognized on the tapes. This wasn't the first time he had had a conversation about Kurt with a perplexed friend or colleague. There had been others—most notably fellow prosecutors—who couldn't believe Riley considered Kurt a friend.

Unable to resist the temptation to have a little fun at the expense of Dan Thornton, who had cruelly bet against him in the diet lottery, Riley said, "Look, I could tell Kurt that our Chief of Security Daniel J. Thornton doesn't want to see his ass around here anymore."

He could hear Dan's breathing accelerate on the other end. "You asshole—don't even think of mentioning my name around that guy. I don't even want him to know we've got him on tape."

"Believe me, Dan, he knows where every security camera in the place is located, and if he didn't want to be taped you'd have never seen him."

Dan could be heard taking a pull off his cigarette, talking through the exhale. "Come on, tell me really. How the hell do you know McBraneman? Did you send him up when you were prosecuting?"

"No, no. Just the opposite—I kept him from being sent up." Riley removed an armful of files from his briefcase and started placing them one by one in the out-basket as he went on talking. "How do you know about Kurt? He's never pulled any insurance scams as far as I know."

Dan chuckled quietly. "Through my friends on the police force. McBraneman is a legend among those guys—they're not sure if they hate him or kind of like him. But they openly admit that no individual cop is real anxious to try to arrest him."

"That doesn't surprise me. The reason they kinda like him is because the other dealers are scared shitless of him."

During the ensuing pause, Dan made a note on the company's standard security form. He then said, "I've just made an entry on the surveillance log that: 'A known felon was observed on the premises, with satisfactory explanation provided by a company officer.' I'm not even going to note the identity. Sometimes the FBI asks to look at these things."

Dan tossed the completed form into the appropriate folder in his desk drawer, and said, "Let's change the subject—how's your diet going?" He laughed mockingly, secure in the belief that he was in for some easy money.

Standing at his desk, Riley looked down at his hand as he counted off notches in his belt representing the midriff shrinkage. He patted his flattening tummy and said coyly, "You'll find out soon enough, sucker. Just plan on attending the final weigh-in outside my office at eleven o'clock sharp. And bring your money, big mouth." With the exception of the two pounds of fluid retention that he would shed presently, the breakthrough Milky Way-Pepsi diet had been a great success. Apart from some dizziness in the morning and a few canker sores, he had felt no ill effects.

In a voice devoid of the reverence normally shown toward one's boss, a cocky Dan Thornton said, "Don't worry, I wouldn't miss your final humiliation for anything. Just don't bring your buddy from the garage."

Riley hung up the phone and looked at his watch. It was 9:50 A.M., seventy minutes before the scheduled weigh-in. A full seventy minutes in which to drop two pounds of fluid.

"See you at eleven, Skeets," he said on the way out, "and don't let anyone near that scale while I'm gone." Skeeter chuckled, spreading her arms protectively across the door to the closet.

At 10:02, Riley stepped into the men's sauna at the Capital City Athletic Club and cranked the temperature up to the highest allowed setting. Within minutes he had to abandon reading the newspaper left on the sauna bench, as his eyes were burning with perspiration. Having regularly sweated off five or more pounds during vigorous tennis matches, he assumed that twenty minutes in the sauna would comfortably shed at least two pounds. It was a surprise, therefore, when twenty minutes into the bake-off he was only one pound lighter. Already dizzy and weak in the knees, he didn't dare go back into the sauna, and it was now 10:20, too late to take a diuretic.

Just when he had nearly despaired at the lack of options, he remembered seeing the local blood bank set up in the club lobby when he had passed through on the way to the elevator. There it was, the God-sent solution. He hurriedly dressed and made his way downstairs.

"Yes, sir, and how much blood would you like to donate today?" asked a perky nurse.

"One pound," answered Riley through dilated eyes set in a face flushed pink from twenty minutes in the sauna.

"Oh . . . no, sir, we measure blood donations in volume—ccs, pints, you know."

"How much does a pint weigh?" he asked urgently.

She gave a confused half-smile and took a small step backward. "I really don't know. I've never been asked that before."

"Well, I want you to drain at least a pound's worth."

The nurse looked uneasy, as though she might be dealing with a mental case. Moving over to the next station, she held a whispered conversation with a tall, bald man with a stethoscope around his neck. The man looked furtively over his shoulder at Riley while murmuring something to her out of the side of his mouth.

She then returned to where Riley was standing. "Apparently the average pint of blood weighs slightly more than one pound, sir," she said with a nervous laugh, not getting too close to this strange, overcooked man.

"Great, I'd like to give one pint," he said, rolling up his sleeve. "And please hurry, I've got an eleven o'clock appointment."

At 11:03 A.M. he wobbled unsteadily into the waiting area outside his office. A small crowd of about fifteen people had gathered and were sipping beverages provided by Skeeter. Even Gladys had made a rare trip out of the Sacristy to witness the much-awaited event. Liz Bridge was counting money and confirming bets. Only Judy Goodrich had bet on Riley, and she for purely sentimental reasons. She couldn't bring herself to bet against him.

Riley forced a weak smile as he swayed toward the scale, moving unsteadily through the small group, which had now parted to allow his passage.

Four smiling secretaries were hooting and doing the wave.

"Good luck, Fatso," said Dan Thornton in a last minute psych-out attempt, patting Riley on the ass as though he were about to take a free-throw.

Liz Bridge stood by the scale, clutching an envelope bulging with cash. "Hello, Duke," she said officiously, without smiling.

The sounds and faces of the crowd were a blur to the parched, anemic figure who now stepped falteringly into the closet. Skeeter held his arm for support as he kicked off his shoes and mounted the scale. The dial accelerated past a whirl of numbers, like fence posts out a train window, finally coming to rest on a cluster of three numbers that were too wavy for him to make out.

"One hundred eighty pounds exactly!" shouted Liz. "Atta boy, Duke!"

"Shit on a stick!" yelled Dan Thornton, tossing a folded newspaper to the ground. Judy Goodrich had a tear in her eye. Liz looked secretly pleased.

Riley turned to the crowd and with a woozy expression and the inflection of a man who had no idea where he was, said "Thank you all for coming" and passed out face-first into the carpeting.

21

Liddy finished the day's work at nine o'clock on Monday evening, packing her briefcase and purse and heading out for the twenty-minute walk to the municipal parking ramp. This time of night, after the distractions of the workplace had ceased, was the most difficult part of the day. The demons of anxiety and despair that had become part of her life were now most in play.

She waved at the private security guards tending the stations along the skyway as she made her way to the ramp. The skyway route took a little longer but felt safer. She relayed from one security station to the next rather than walking outside. It wasn't until she reached the ramp that she was completely on her own. Exiting the hallway into which the ramp elevators emptied, she headed for her car, which today was located on the far side of the ramp, the stalls closer to the elevators having already been taken when she had arrived that morning at six-thirty.

As she reached in her purse to find the car keys, she heard shuffling of feet near a row of cars off in the distance to her left. She turned abruptly in that direction, her overworked senses hyper-focused to any sign of danger. She stood still in the middle of the ramp, her heart pounding in her throat.

She stared intently in the direction of the unexplained sound and tried to decide what to do next. But what she was feeling was not the strength of fight-or-flight but rather the helplessness of temporary paralysis. The shuffling recommenced, and from between two cars emerged a man who appeared to be black, though in the shadows it was difficult to be sure. She felt a momentary relief—Brad Crosshaven was white. Closer now, she saw that the man wore the gray uniform of a ramp employee and carried a tool box from the workshed located in the corner from which he had come. He smiled warmly as he passed by. She gave a pained, tired sigh.

As she made for her car she scolded herself. How foolish she had become, how pathetic. She felt that her brain circuits were being rewired by what she was going through. She feared she would move through the rest of her life scared and helpless. To dispute her own fevered thinking, she reasoned that even brave people would have been alarmed by unexplained noises in a dark and empty parking ramp. But would they automatically assume the worst, as she had taken to doing, and slip into a stunned insensibility? Even false alarms like this one carried an emotional hangover that seemed to have no end.

She drove her car through the circular down-ramp, opening the driver's window just enough to pay the parking fee. Her hand trembled as she passed a five dollar bill to the attendant. Out on the highway, she looked in the rearview mirror through a film of tears and saw the wavy silhouette of a man in a car coming up fast on her rear bumper, his head and shoulders outlined by the headlights of the car behind him. His dark, featureless face seemed menacing. But then so did every stranger these days. The thick, pulsating despair that had originated in her midsection was now reaching up into her throat, where a permanent lump had formed. The whole world seemed to have gone dark. And it wasn't just the here-and-now. Even old, painful memories, long ago forgotten, were now rising in her consciousness like ancient spots on a carpeting. She felt caught in a living hell.

It was only a small relief when the car behind her turned off on a downtown exit, for she knew the next stranger would provoke the same reaction. Was she losing her mind? Was this what it was like to go mad? An all-consuming sense of loss washed over her. She was sure that some essential component of her mind was ruined, and that it would never be restored. That she would never again experience happiness.

When she arrived at her three-bedroom colonial in the far-south suburbs of Minneapolis, she entered through the garage door and turned the lights on in the downstairs hallway. As she set her purse on the counter just inside the kitchen, she thought she detected a sweet-smelling odor like heavy cologne, but her senses were playing so many tricks on her these days that she dismissed it. The day's mail was spread randomly on the floor just inside the front door. She crouched down to pick up the envelopes, sorting the bills from the junk mail as she walked back into the kitchen. After switching on the late news, she quickly turned it off when the lead story featured the arrest of a local stalker who had killed a former coworker two days after being served with a protective order forbidding any contact. Her defenseless mind could no longer distinguish between her troubles and those of others. As irrational as she knew it was, all of life's evils seemed to be closing in upon her personally.

The low-grade nausea that had become her regular companion prevented the retention of anything in the way of solid food, so in place of an ordinary dinner she gagged down a glass of Instant Breakfast, reasoning that it would keep her alive until her appetite returned. She had lost an alarming fifteen pounds in the last forty days, four pounds in the last week alone.

As she made her way upstairs, she noticed that the door to the bedroom, rather than being open as she left it each morning, was half closed. Inside the room a light was burning.

Though distracted and forgetful in recent weeks, she knew she hadn't left the bedroom light on. Her heart began slamming against her chest. She stopped for a moment and considered flight, but then thought the worst that could happen was that she'd be killed, and that seemed almost a welcome alternative. At least then the torment would stop. Passing through the doorway, she saw written in lipstick on the mirror above her dresser—at first faintly and then more clearly as she drew closer—the words: YOUR TIME IS COMING BITCH—I'LL BE BACK.

She raced through the house looking in closets and behind couches to be sure no one was still in the house. With trembling hands she locked the doors and windows, pushed a large bureau in front of the door to her bedroom and vomited up the glass of Instant Breakfast. She then got into bed, and after a long period of heart-pounding silence, slept in short, choppy segments filled with chaotic and frightening dreams.

In the darkness of the alley across from Liddy's house, a well-dressed young man put heavy binoculars back in their carrying case, expelled a sadistic laugh from deep in his throat, and pulled a late-model, dark green Jaguar forward onto the street toward the freeway leading to Lake Minnetonka.

From a place deeper in the alley, a midsize Oldsmobile with its headlights turned off crept out of the alley and onto the same street. From the driver's window protruded the soiled sleeve of a green combat jacket. The Olds fell in behind the Jag at an undetectable distance as they both made their way west on Interstate 494.

22

---

uck wants to see you in about a half hour, so don't go
anywhere," said Skeeter on Tuesday morning. "Gladys
will call us when he's ready." She was in the copy room
assembling the original and three copies of the Suspicious
Activity Report drafted by Riley, which outlined the circumstances surrounding the attempt of one Bradford Vinehill
Crosshaven to convert fifteen-thousand dollars of cash into a
monetary instrument twenty-nine days earlier, at the teller
window tended by Lydia Ingrid Jonssen. Suspicious Activity
Reports were normally filed by the Lindbergh Security
Division, but, trying to meet Buck halfway, Riley had pulled
the filing from normal channels in order to reduce the number
of internal people aware of the Crosshaven involvement.

"Okay," Riley yelled back, not looking up from the handwritten notes he was making in his private file, notes which
documented the steps taken to comply with the regulatory
requirements. He then attached those notes to photocopies of
the written opinions received from inside counsel and the company's outside law firm advising that the filing was mandatory
under these circumstances. The completed file was then
placed in a locked drawer.

Deep in concentration, he had failed to notice that the copy room across the hall had fallen silent and was, therefore, surprised when, turning toward the door of his office, he saw Liddy Jonssen standing there. Skeeter, who looked as surprised as he was, stood beside her. Liddy's countenance was that of a cornered animal, her eyes set in exhaustion and unrelieved agony. A look of terrified resignation had taken over her once-lovely face, the face of a year ago—the face on the Cortez Room wall. Riley jumped from his seat and took a position on her other side, and together they sat her on the couch.

Skeeter kept repeating, "Liddy, Liddy, Liddy," as she took a seat next to her, large tears forming in her eyes.

"That awful man violated my house," came Liddy's trembling voice.

"Crosshaven?" asked Riley almost in a whisper as he pulled up a chair across from her. He was afraid that if he spoke any louder she might shatter like glass.

"Yes." Then a long pause. She turned and stared deeply at Skeeter, and in the voice of a drowning child, said, "I don't like it like this anymore."

She seemed disconnected, and unlike the occasions when Riley had seen her before, she had taken no care in her appearance. It was as though she had risen from a sick bed.

As they sat not knowing what to say, an uninvited shadow cast itself across the room, causing all three to turn toward the glass panels where a window washer was being lowered on a large scaffolding. His shadow spread its darkness across the thick carpeting, passing cleanly between Riley and Skeeter and coming to rest directly on Liddy. Riley squinted toward the window, eerily disturbed by this intrusion upon their space. The window washer, whose face was obscured by the sun at his back, seemed not to move. From within the shadow that surrounded her, Liddy looked up slowly at the dark silhouetted figure but showed no surprise. Her expression was one of resignation toward him or whatever it was he represented.

Riley walked to the window and closed the curtains. When he returned to his seat across from Liddy, he raised his hand to her stricken face, brushing aside a tear that had formed on her trembling cheek. She lifted her eyes to his with an expression of deep but hopeless gratitude.

Skeeter, stroking Liddy's shoulder, turned to her and said, "You're coming home with me, Liddy, until this awful stuff is over."

But Liddy's eyes had once again gone vacant and unfocused, looking past them as if into another world. "It won't make any difference," she said weakly.

In a voice intended to convince her that others would now assume the burden, Skeeter said, "Just meet me downstairs. I'll bring my car around and pick you up in front. We're going to my house." Skeeter looked up at Riley as she spoke, obtaining a ready confirmation.

Liddy forced a weak smile, and said, "I have my car downtown. I'll drive home and get my things first and then go to your house."

Riley went back to his paperwork but couldn't concentrate. He was frightened and angry that things had been allowed to go this far—that he had allowed things to go this far.

After three distracted phone calls on unrelated matters, he was no better. He got up from his desk and headed for Buck's office.

"He's not ready for you yet" said Gladys, looking over her reading glasses, as Riley moved directly through Buck's open doorway.

In the far corner of the room a portrait artist stood before a large canvas. He was dressed in a smock and beret and held a pallet in one hand and a brush in the other. Across the room from him Buck sat astride a large wooden sawhorse. He wore formal riding gear: red jacket with black felt collar and a single row of gold buttons running down its front, and a white silk ascot protruding from the neck. A riding crop rested casually upon white jodhpurs tucked into high leather boots. On the shelf behind him, and also being painted into the picture, stood an oversized Buckie, placed in a shrine-like recess, illuminated by a single, low-watt light bulb.

As a result of the last downsizing and a general run-up of stocks in the industry, Lindbergh shares had jumped $5.00 in the previous week alone, earning Buck another two-million dollars in option gains, and costing eight hundred and fifty hardworking people their livelihoods. That the stock run-up was an industry-wide phenomenon having nothing to do with the company's individual performance did little to slow the orgy of self-adoration that had come to dominate Buck's world.

Buck had finally surrendered to Gar's suggestion that he sit for a formal oil portrait, and the unveiling ceremony was scheduled for mid-July in the Lobby Court, to be followed by a late-summer, Monet-style tour of Lindbergh branch offices.

"That will be it for today," Buck said to the artist as he dismounted the sawhorse.

He then turned to Riley, and with a cold aloofness, pointed to his conference room. "Get in there. I want to talk to you."

He unbuttoned his riding jacket as he made for the conference room. He walked to the head of the rectangular mahogany table, and sat down. "What's that?" he demanded, pointing rudely to the file jacket under Riley's arm.

Riley opened the manila folder and pulled out the completed Suspicious Activity Report and two copies and handed them across the table.

Buck read only the caption before tossing them dismissively back at Riley. "This has all been taken care of. Tear those things up!"

Riley did not reach for the forms, which were now spread randomly about the table. "What do you mean, 'all taken care of?" he asked.

Buck sat like a coiled snake at the end of the table. He lifted his riding crop onto the table surface, gripping it hard as though struggling to resist giving Riley a good thrashing. "I took this matter, as you call it, to Channing & Hollis in Washington, D.C., the best lawyers in the country—not like those second-stringers across the street who you think are so great." He waved his hand dismissively in the direction of the building housing the company's principal outside law firm. "Wells Channing tells me that you're all full of crap, that no form has to be filed with the government. So that's the end of this subject. I'm only sorry I don't have people around here whose heads are in the right place. Now, tear those things up!"

Riley gave Buck a sideways glance of incredulity. "What did you tell Wells Channing to get him to say that?" he asked.

Buck shouted, "I told him the facts! Don't you get it? This matter is over; there will be no further discussion. And don't you dare have any contact with Channing & Hollis on this subject."

Shopping for agreeable legal opinions was one of the oldest games in the long, sad history of jurisprudence, and this was a childishly transparent example. But there was no point in arguing further with this overwrought equestrian. He was wound too tight. Reasoned discussion was not possible.

Riley reached for the scattered forms, straightened them into a neat pile, and placed them in the manila folder. "Now we're going to talk about Liddy Jonssen, Buck."

Buck pinched his face in mock sympathy, and whined, "Whaaat's a matter, is life tooo tough for the little baby?"

In the silence that followed, the image of Liddy's drawn and pain-wracked face flashed through Riley's mind. Good God, he thought, maybe Buck was the monster people said he was. Maybe the countless times he had defended him, had called him "misunderstood" and "fundamentally decent" when others inside and outside the company trashed him behind his back, had been grotesquely misplaced. He felt his skin crawl. And he hated being talked to in this tone of voice—the voice of the playground bully. The voice of Mad Dog Moriarity.

Riley leaned forward in his chair. "Listen, you cold-blooded little bastard, that psychopath Crosshaven is terrorizing her, and we're not going to debate this anymore. I'm going to do what you should have done a long time ago. I'm going to order our security people to watch her day and night until he's been dealt with, and I'm going to do my damnedest to get her to swear out a complaint with both the downtown and suburban cops for breaking and entering and aggravated stalking—and I don't give a shit if the newspapers hear all about it." Without taking his eyes off Buck, he shifted in his chair. "And I'll tell

287

you what else, I'm going to the board with this whole sorry tale."

"Are you crazy?" Buck shouted, now out of his chair, waving his riding crop hysterically. Then suddenly, as he turned toward Riley, his expression turned from hostile to conciliatory. "I'll call Ward Crosshaven again and put a stop to any more contact. I promise."

"The last time you said that he broke into Liddy's house."

Buck now resumed his seat. His breathing became labored, as though the air in the room was too thick. He squirmed and his eyes darted from corner to corner, never meeting Riley's. He then said in a voice so disingenuous it caused momentary pity on Riley's part, "I couldn't get a hold of Ward before. He was in Europe . . . or, um, Africa. But I did consult with Charles Kleinwick from the Board, and it was his decision not to take any other steps. He and Hank Wallstead think that we can't afford to offend Ward Crosshaven. So the board is already involved. Kleinwick made the final decision and he specifically said you should butt out and start following orders."

Riley just shook his head. The lie about not being able to get a hold of Ward Crosshaven didn't even pass the snicker test. The board part, maybe, but he didn't want to believe it. He'd call Charles Kleinwick, the director who loved to talk about ethics and who had offered himself up to Riley as a port in a storm.

Leaning forward in his seat, Riley said, "I don't care how important the business relationship is, it's nothing compared to Liddy's safety. I just told you what has to be done. I don't care what anyone else thinks. I just hope it's not too late for her."

Next came a very uncool rendering of the Look, all twitchy and spastic. "Just give me another day. I guarantee he'll get the kid out of town."

"And then what?" asked Riley. "Is he going to be banished for the rest of his life, or the rest of her life?"

Buck now took a calming breath and started caressing and stroking the leather Bible on the table before him. A suitable period of silence was allowed to pass, after which his expression turned smarmy and ingratiating and his Southern accent returned. He gave a syrupy grin and said, "Remember what the Good Book says, Riley—we are all sinners and we should not be judgmental about others."

Riley thought he might actually lose his breakfast over that one. But it had to come sooner or later, he supposed—the corruption of Scripture to suit his own twisted purposes.

"Sorry, Buck," he said. "That trick isn't going to work either. I've searched the Bible from cover to cover and I can't find a single word in support of laundering drug money and stalking women."

Buck reared back in his chair and his expression again turned angry. He moved from preacher-supplicant to drill sergeant, and the thin row of pockmarks lining his chin started to glow white against his hypertensive face. Pointing the riding crop across the table almost in Riley's face, he shouted, "I'm ordering you to follow my instructions on this. If you don't, there will be serious consequences."

"Serious consequences, Buck?" said Riley dismissively. "Who're you trying to shit? The only serious consequences will come if anything happens to that young woman."

Gladys popped her head in the door, partially breaking the tension in the air. She announced that Eileen was on the phone from Boca Viejo and wanted to talk to Buck immediately.

As Buck started to rise from his seat, Riley asked, "Say, Buck, what would you do if this guy was after Eileen?"

"Shut up," snarled Buck as he made his way to the phone.

Concluding that there was nothing more he could say to change things, Riley left the office when Buck started his phone conversation.

"What'd he say?" asked Skeeter as Riley approached her desk.

"He issued three orders," replied Riley, "not to call Channing & Hollis, not to tell Security about Crosshaven, and not to file the Suspicious Activity Report." He then leaned into her desk and spoke the words she longed to hear: "I'll call Dan Thornton. You get Wells Channing on the phone."

Within five minutes Dan Thornton had been located and briefed on the whole sordid tale. "As your immediate supervisor, Dan, I'm instructing you to provide round-the-clock protection to Liddy Jonssen, starting as soon as you can get someone out to her house, where she's packing some personal things to move over to Skeeter's for a while. That's all you need to know. If there's any political fallout, you'll be clean— you're just following instructions. I'll get you a confirming memo if you want."

"Fuck the politics. This'll be fun," said Dan.

When Riley hung up, Skeeter was standing in the door. "Wells Channing is on line two."

After telling Skeeter to get director Charles Kleinwick on the phone next, he picked up the line on which Wells Channing was holding. "Wells, I'm short on time, but I just wanted to check with you quickly on the advice you gave Buck Montrowe last week about when a Suspicious Activity Report has to be filed."

"Sure, Riley, I assumed he was just confirming what he had been told by your inside people, that in order to trigger an SAR filing there has to be reasonable suspicion that an attempt was made, and that if the identity of the suspect is known it has to be disclosed."

"How did he describe the facts of this case?" asked Riley in a routine, nonchallenging tone.

There was a brief pause. Wells Channing was a man who could smell political trouble fifteen hundred miles away and usually succeeded in ending up on the side with the winners. But the survivor instinct in this case was trumped by fear of professional censure for giving false advice on a topic of this importance. It wouldn't be the first time he had been used by a client to accomplish some nefarious scheme. "Buck said that an unstable woman with a history of hysteria handled a transaction at a teller window and gave a weak identification of a good customer of the company for whom she had some kind of sexual or romantic fixation."

"Okay," said Riley, "that's about what I thought. Tell me, what would your view be if the facts involved an attempt to convert fifteen thousand dollars in cash into a monetary instrument, with an identification that was unequivocal and from a long-term employee with a flawless record and no ulterior motives?"

Now there was no pause. "There's no question in that case: a filing would be absolutely mandated. And if you didn't file you'd have your tit in a wringer." Riley could visualize Channing furiously making CYA notes in his file.

Skeeter came in and handed him a note saying that Charles Kleinwick knew why Riley was calling and refused to talk to him, referring all contacts to Buck. Riley shook his head in disgust—most of it disgust with himself for having misjudged the character of yet another highly placed person, this time the self-described man of principle, a man "who knew what it was to be out there alone on a matter of conscience."

He reached for the blue pen in his shirt pocket and signed his name in large and legible handwriting on the original and two copies of the Suspicious Activity Report and handed them to Skeeter for immediate posting.

Liddy took the long way home, leaving the freeway several miles before the normal exit. She drove past the parks of the far southwestern suburbs, along rolling residential streets, flanked on both sides by homes of quiet dignity, and past small lakes on which ducks of all sizes glided silently, through neighborhoods with large, gracious trees, past sidewalks cluttered with tricycles and lemonade stands tended by boys and girls not yet ten years old. It took her back to her childhood, a blissful time, a time before she knew anything of the mean side of life. And before she knew anything about her own emotional vulnerabilities.

The terror of the last twelve hours, the fatigue and despair of recent months, had given way to her first moments of peace in a long while. The doctor she had seen the week before without telling anyone would probably say that the blue pills and white pills he had prescribed were now starting to help, bringing back her focus and ego strength, whatever that was. But she knew that pharmaceuticals had little to do with it. The decision that had been ripening in her mind over the last twelve hours had now been taken.

As she turned into the driveway of her house, a pleasant breeze blew through the trees, and soft, friendly raindrops began to appear on her windshield. Down the block, a neighbor was trimming his neatly manicured lawn. She pressed the automatic door opener and crawled slowly into the single-car garage. Without turning off the ignition, she pressed the button again. The door closed, sealing off the nearly airtight compartment.

23

Dan Thornton and two Lindbergh security officers found no signs of activity when they drove into Liddy's driveway a little after noon. While his two associates hurried to the front and back doors, Thornton went to the window at the side of the garage. It seemed to be frosted over with a condensation of some sort, making it hard to tell if there was a car inside. Placing his hand on one of the panes of glass, he felt a faint vibration, from which he concluded that there was a car in the garage and that its engine was running. Unable to raise the sliding door in front, he returned to the side and with the butt of his pistol broke the window pane closest to the inside lock. He entered the garage and opened the driver's door, where he found the peaceful and lifeless body of Liddy Jonssen.

The Shepherd of the Hills Lutheran Church, a white clapboard structure with a tall steeple pointing heavenward, sat modestly but confidently on a small hill overlooking fields of grain and corn waving in the gentle breeze for as far as the eye could see. Located just a mile from the farm on which Liddy had grown up, it was the church from which she was now being buried.

In accordance with company social customs, a large floral wreath had been sent to the church with an attached sympathy note bearing Buck's signature, forged by Gladys. Buck had taken no notice of Liddy in life, but her death had seized him with a panic such as he had never before experienced. He had fled to the safe and familiar surroundings of Boca Viejo moments after hearing the distressing news. Several calls he had placed to Riley had gone unanswered.

Riley and Betsy sat in the pew behind Skeeter, who upon learning the awful news at the office had given up a wail so pained and mournful, and so out of character for her, that those within hearing joined involuntarily in her tears.

Jonssen cousins from throughout Iowa and southern Minnesota, most of whom Liddy had barely known (having seen them only at weddings and funerals), made obligatory appearances to see off the only child of Gunnar and Margaret, the child whom they remembered for her sweetness and good looks. Margaret, who had suffered a second and more serious stroke just ten days before, was not present; and had not been told of Liddy's death.

Pastor Stensrud, who had baptized and confirmed Liddy and was normally an undemonstrative man, wept openly throughout the homily and conceded that after forty years of theological study he had no idea why such cruel things were allowed to happen.

Filling the remaining pews of the plain wooden chapel was a vast array of people Liddy had loved and helped in her short lifetime, but to whom she was unable to appeal when her own need was greatest. In the back pew, off to one side, sat Jeannie Kelley, her face buried in her hands, her shoulders heaving uncontrollably.

Still knowing nothing of the horrors to which Liddy had been subjected at the hands of Brad Crosshaven, a kneeling Bobby Morestad shook his head in confusion, wondering what could have brought such a gifted and promising young woman to this end. The yellow chrysanthemums on the far side of the altar had been sent by Bobby with a handwritten card reading: "With dying gratitude for your wonderful service."

Following the liturgy, the mortal remains lay in a gray metal casket suspended on a scaffolding of canvas straps above a great cavernous hole in the ground, next to a simple stone marking the grave of her father, Gunnar. Betsy, who had neither met nor heard the name Liddy Jonssen before the previous Tuesday, cried softly at the graveside, her makeup running in wide patterns across her face. She had viewed the photographs of Liddy, from infancy to her last promotion at The Lindbergh, displayed on the bulletin board at the back of the church, and by the time they had made their way to the far end of the church graveyard, she understood more about Liddy than Riley could have discerned in a lifetime.

As the casket was lowered into the ground, the rich baritone voice of Pastor Stensrud, his vestments blowing in the wind, called out the final prayers. Children bored with the service ran in and out of nearby tombstones, and a pair of dogs chased each other playfully around the sole mausoleum in the graveyard. Skeeter collapsed in her sister's arms.

The following day Riley accompanied Skeeter, who was designated in the will as executor, to Liddy's small suburban rambler to help sort through papers, identify insurance policies, and marshal Lindbergh-related documents, including work in progress in her briefcase. True to the habits of a lifetime, Liddy had neatly arranged everything in clearly marked folders. Even the work in progress was annotated in her small, legible handwriting to ease the transition for her successor. Thoughtful to the very end.

Likewise her clothing and other personal items were meticulously arranged about a modestly appointed bedroom, sparkling clean except for a reddish film spread like fingerpaint across the mirror above her bureau.

Atop the taller dresser across the room was a small picture gallery, enshrining her happiest memories, including a group picture of her confirmation class, a photo portrait taken upon her graduation from college, and a backstage snapshot of her and Skeeter standing on each side of Neil Diamond, the two of them snuggling up to their song-idol with grins so wide and toothy that they were hardly recognizable. The remaining pictures were of her mother and father during happy times, including a formal black-and-white of her father, just returned from World War II, glorious in his dress uniform.

Knowing that Liddy would wish it, Skeeter, with Riley in tow, had visited Margaret Jonssen the day before. Mercifully, Margaret knew nothing of Liddy's death. The recent stroke had added greatly to her confusion and she mistook Skeeter for Liddy and Riley for her late husband, Gunnar, to whom—judging by the picture on the dresser—he bore a striking resemblance. When he saw that picture he understood for the first time why Liddy had looked at him so strangely at their first meeting, and why she had been so trusting toward him throughout these last horrible weeks. He didn't think it was possible to feel worse, but suddenly he did.

Skeeter and Riley had both played along gamely with Margaret's delusion, Riley even enduring a warm, wet kiss on the lips. He shook like a leaf, but couldn't bring himself to shatter Margaret's belief that Gunnar had returned.

In the top drawer of Liddy's bedside table was a book on how to deal with elderly parents during their declining years and below that a small red spiral notebook, noting in her handwriting a series of threatening phone calls received from Brad Crosshaven over the preceding three weeks, none of which she had reported to Riley or anyone else for fear of being perceived as a weakling in the muscular, survival-of-the-fittest culture of the new Lindbergh.

Riley felt his throat tighten and his hands shake as he read the detailed account of the sick, twisted ravings of this over-privileged bully. To his anger was added the frustrating recognition that these handwritten notes could not form the basis of a successful criminal prosecution, that it would be impossible to establish beyond a reasonable doubt who the unidentified caller had been, never mind the hearsay and foundation problems associated with Liddy's death. Even Crosshaven's ham-handed money laundering attempt could not now be charged, inasmuch as the only witness was gone, and the security cameras had been turned off to reduce costs.

His face and neck burned as blood rushed upward. With hands shaking with rage—a rage so fierce and concentrated that he hardly recognized it in himself—he slid the notebook into his jacket pocket.

Walking to the car, Skeeter turned and looked up at him. "Please don't take this the wrong way, Riley. I wouldn't hurt you for anything. But didn't you know what was happening? What she was going through? Liddy thought you were somehow going to be her savior. Maybe it was because you looked so much like her father or because she thought you sensed her vulnerability. She thought you were kind and . . ." Her voice broke, and her eyes filled with tears.

Riley stared at her, his own eyes now awash in tears. His throat closed up and he couldn't speak. He had gone weak and hollow and could feel only an exposed, bone-aching pain. Skeeter had verified his own worst self-accusations.

He drove to downtown Minneapolis in a quiet stupor, pulling mechanically into the parking garage of the Ramsay Inn Hotel. He made his way slowly to the grand ballroom, where a consortium of Twin Cities community groups was holding an award ceremony for good corporate citizenship. A table near the dais had been reserved for the ten senior officers of the Lindbergh. Also at the table were directors Charles Kleinwick and Hank Wallstead. Charles Kleinwick, who had refused Riley's call the morning of Liddy's death, avoided his eyes as he sat nervously across the table.

To enhance Buck's image as an altruistic and enlightened leader, he had ordered several grants to be made by The Lindbergh Foundation to carefully selected community groups specified by Tenzie Dunseth. In fulfillment of their end of the bargain, the consortium of community groups had announced that Buck would be awarded the Sibley Humanitarian Award. This honor was granted each year in recognition of the honoree's personal sensitivity to the needs of those who had experienced hardship and discrimination, including minorities, gays, and women. Local newspapers uncritically reprinted the

"Portrait of a Self-Made Man" profile compiled by the Lindbergh public relations department, complete with an account of Buck's deprived childhood and a series of staged photographs showing him hosting a picnic with child actors posing as inner-city minority youngsters.

Although it was intended that it be hung behind the podium at this event, in a hideous coincidence the formal oil painting of Buck had been defaced by a disturbed former employee who had somehow gained entry to the fourth floor. Thus the portrait, originally intended to celebrate Buck's fame and glory, was consigned forever, grotesque and unseen in the fashion of Dorian Gray, to a remote and lonely storage room.

The Sibley Award itself was presented to Buck by a smiling Tenzie Dunseth, conservatively dressed in the uniform of the day: a double-breasted blazer with a carnation in the lapel, her hair pulled severely back in the style of an upscale fashion editor. Gone were the bib overalls and combat boots so fitting to another occasion. Only the practiced eye noticed Tenzie's polite refusal to shake hands or otherwise touch the honoree.

Riley sat slumped in his chair, his face a study in dejection, unable even to acknowledge Tenzie's wink. He stared as though through a fog at the wavy, surreal figure of Buck who, standing at the podium, spoke in a voice thick with studied emotion of his own impoverished childhood and his lifetime sensitivity to the needs of those less fortunate than himself. Every few sentences his voice caught, and he suspended his words to allow for full emotional effect, appearing to blink back tears.

Riley struggled to recall if he had contributed to the formulation of this pack of lies also—if he had been an accomplice here, too, an accessory to yet another desecration of the truth. He couldn't remember. His mind was so choked with grief and remorse that it was barely functioning. He looked over at Charles Kleinwick, who refused to meet his gaze, his own sad eyes resting heavily on the plate of uneaten food before him.

Riley's eyes roamed aimlessly around the garishly appointed ballroom—to the imitation satin wallcovering, to the gold-colored sconces that contained no gold, to the sparkling silverware that contained no silver, to the recipient of the Sibley Humanitarian Award who was no humanitarian.

Back at the podium, Buck reaffirmed with mounting passion his "long-standing personal commitment to a diverse workplace, one in which all employees are valued, respected and cared for as individuals." On his face was a look of such tearful sincerity that one would have had to scour the airwaves of religious broadcasting to find its equal.

Riley felt sickly fluids forming in his midsection, and his mouth filled unnaturally with moisture. His vision became blurry, as though he were looking through a warped lens. All he could see was Liddy's coffin being lowered into the ground and that beautiful face entombed inside a satin darkness. He rose hurriedly from his place and moved on hollow legs to the men's room, where for ten minutes he threw up so violently that a blood vessel in his eye burst, as his body sought to purge itself of complicity and shame.

The massive Crosshaven estate looked down with graceful arrogance upon the most scenic bay in Lake Minnetonka, its large white pillars seeming twice their actual size when viewed from the steep angle of the lakeshore two hundred feet below. The house was similar in appearance and grandeur to the Lee Mansion in Arlington, Virginia. Thick woods sheltered the main house on three sides, with only a narrow, unmarked driveway providing access from the highway.

The house and surrounding property had been purchased in the 1920s by Brad Crosshaven's grandfather, Vinehill Crosshaven, a real estate tycoon who originally established the estate as a summer retreat before the Lake Minnetonka area was overrun with old money, and then new. Using the foresight for which he was famous, he had bought enough surrounding, thickly wooded land to buffer and protect the mansion on all sides other than the lake. Which explained why Kurt McBraneman, dressed in black clothing and a ski mask, entered the grounds by sea rather than by land. He made his way in the darkness up the far edge of the steep embankment leading to the house and attached eight-car garage. Climbing through a back window of the garage, he ducked between vehicles until coming upon the dark-green Jaguar, sitting regally in the middle row closest to the house.

The air in the immaculately kept garage smelled only faintly of oil and gasoline. There were no sounds other than the whir of a boat engine on the far side of the lake and the playful bantering of its teen-age occupants out for a late-night joy ride.

With his gloved fist Kurt smashed both tail-lights and the light above the rear license plate of the Jaguar. He then pulled from his jacket a transparent package containing a thick white substance and taped it to the underside of the driver's seat, where it protruded slightly from under the seat. He then silently made his way down the hill and away from the estate.

24

Riley sat in his den looking out at the row of closely sculpted evergreens standing along the property line separating his yard from the neighbor's. On the table before him sat the unread morning newspaper and a half-consumed cup of an exotic tea that was supposed to help settle the stomach. Tuffy slept cozily on his lap, blissfully unaware of recent events. The perfect symmetry of the evergreens, so proud and sensible, drew him into the agreeable but fraudulent notion that human beings can fashion their lives and circumstances into safe and predictable patterns.

In spite of repeated attempts to chase it away, the haunting image of Liddy kept taking shape in his tired mind. He struggled to discipline his emotion-charged thoughts into some kind of rational sequence. An impulse to make a list was felt, thinking that that might help tame the chaos. But thoughts just continued to cascade through his mind.

He thought of how, without warning, Liddy's world had unraveled through a series of blows that were beyond her control, such as the massive downsizings by the company and the criminal activities of a complete stranger.

Through the prism of her image, Riley now viewed the surroundings in which he had previously thrived in an entirely new light. The corporate culture that had given rise to the grievous developments of the last thirty days—the culture of macho slogans, of disinformation to trusting employees, of compensation distributed in grotesque disproportion to the efforts expended and results obtained, of kowtowing to high-status customers at the expense of loyal employees with whom a sacred covenant was supposed to exist—was wholly man-made. It was made by Buck Montrowe, a man he had misread to an extent he would not previously have thought possible.

But, try as he might, not all the blame could be laid off on cruel fate and Buck Montrowe. Nausea washed over him as he thought of the part he had played, of his own cautious inaction and silent complicity. He could have triggered the standard security procedures early on, and though it would have cost him his job, it also would have saved Liddy's life. And while it was true that he was appallingly ignorant of the illness that had come to possess her, he knew, or at least suspected, that something was terribly and dangerously wrong. His strange anxiety and early morning wakenings of recent weeks had been a summons he had failed to obey. Rather than acting on these warnings, he had naively and self-servingly gone along with Buck's flimsy representations that he would do the right thing.

Too late it was clear to him that the poisonous mixture of greed and indifference, of status-seeking and self-protection so manifest in the company's leadership was bound to have produced an evil result. People don't have to be evil to work evil. Just the suspension of a standard, a self-serving lie, an indifference to the welfare of the human beings placed in one's care, will eventually yield a host of faceless victims.

His insides shriveled with humiliation as he recalled following orders from a man who had from the very beginning intended to protect a rich pal at any cost. Buck's insincerity might have been more obvious to someone less enamored of his own status—someone less willing to believe that all would end well in what only months before had seemed such a benevolent setting.

Now, at long last, after nearly a half-century of life, the idealism of his youth, of home and school and catechism and courtroom, had collapsed before a reality that carried with it terrible and irrevocable consequences. He now got "it"—the "it" that Buck and Ward Crosshaven knew about instinctively.

Those two—Buck and Ward—would walk free of their sins, the price having been paid by Liddy. Somebody had to pay, and in the modern corporation it was usually some innocent person down in the ranks.

Worst of all, the odious Brad Crosshaven would escape into his family's wealth and privilege, avoiding altogether responsibility for the ruination of a human being he was not fit to live in the same world with.

Just then Riley's meditation was broken by a large taffy-colored cat that emerged from between two manicured shrubs, quietly stalking a rabbit that made its home under the backyard playhouse. Tuffy, who was coming in and out of sleep, sensed the presence of the invader and sat stiffly upright, trembling as though he had been placed in a paint mixer. Riley got up from the chair—careful not to let the badly outmatched Tuffy run into the yard—and quickly stepped out the French doors and onto the lawn between predator and victim, sending the cat on a high-speed retreat.

He fell back into a nearby lawn chair and looked up at the clear blue sky. A gentle smile appeared on his face as he congratulated himself on this small gesture of risk-free valor. He had acted with the simple purity of instinct. No political or career considerations, just the natural impulse to intervene between weak and strong.

His mind then turned wistfully to his father, John McReynolds. He could see his face, weathered by hardship but dignified and ruggedly handsome, nodding encouragement to him and the resolution that was now taking shape in his mind, just as he had when as a boy Riley mastered some new skill, like riding a bike or going off a high-dive. The voice of his father seemed to be whispering that against the ethic of Buck Montrowe and Ward Crosshaven, against the "it" that Riley had so long failed to get, stood a different reality, one for which the backyard scene was a simple metaphor. A reality that, impractical though it might be, was a worthier design for life.

He took a deep breath and exhaled it slowly, and as the air left his lungs a calm certainty took shape in his mind. A certainty that no matter how great the monetary or status rewards, no matter how many friends he left behind, he could have no further association with people so ruthlessly indifferent to the consequences of their acts upon other people.

And at that moment he was delivered forever of the allure of the corporate suite.

"I think I'm being real grown-up about this," said Betsy as they sat in the kitchen later that day. "You just told me you're walking away from one of the best jobs in town, a job that pays gobs of money—a job you once loved. And I haven't cried or anything. But couldn't you at least tell me why? It has something to do with Liddy Jonssen, doesn't it?"

"I can't go into that, darling," he said as he looked at her sadly. "But I know it's what you'd want me do if you knew the whole story." He then quickly transferred his gaze to the window in order to avoid her eyes. If she cried, he would too. That had always been the way it was, even when they were small children.

Propped up on his desk chair the next morning was another interoffice envelope from his nameless "Friend" containing a memo and attached photographs, which together told in more detail than he cared to know the seedy story of Buck and Ward Crosshaven as joint patrons of several young women who saw to their needs on the hunting and fishing trips they regularly took together. It seemed that Buck had been looking for love in all the wrong places. In one photo, taken through the smoky haze of a rustic hunting lodge, Buck and his girlfriend were raising a toast to Ward. Off in the corner one could see the sullen, unsmiling face of Brad Crosshaven, looking every inch the procurer that he was, his signature birthmark barely visible in the hazy lighting.

Poor Buck. He traded a life to protect such an unworthy enterprise. Riley felt nothing but pity as he tore the contents of

304

the envelope into small pieces and gave them a well-deserved burial in the copy room garbage disposal.

Returning to his office, he was confronted with the unexpected and unwelcome presence of Buck, with Gladys tagging closely behind, giving directions. Apparently unsure of where to find Riley's office, Buck was at some risk of getting lost. After greeting Riley, Gladys headed back to the Sacristy.

Buck's buoyant good spirits seemed a little forced this morning as he looked about Riley's office. His eyes were puffy and lined with dark circles. His face seemed bloated, the skin stretched to a shiny consistency. "Pretty nice setup you've got here, buddy," he said as he moved to the window to check out the view. "I don't get over to the west side very often," he added unnecessarily. His manner was uncomfortably chummy, collegial. Obsequiousness didn't become him.

"Have a seat, Buck," said Riley, directing him to a spot on the couch directly below the portrait of Sir Thomas More. He didn't know what Buck was about to say but figured that the Man for All Seasons, a guy noted for his honesty, would probably get a kick out of it.

Riley took a seat in a side chair toward the end of the couch, crossing his legs, his head resting on the palm of his right hand. "I'm in kind of a hurry, Buck. What can I do for you?" he asked flatly.

Buck was apparently counting on more small talk, more clubby fellowship, before getting to the point, and he seemed a little put out by Riley's directness. Nevertheless, he tried to crank up the Look, but the skin around his lips had tightened and his right eyebrow was twitching involuntarily. He shifted his body into a more casual pose, and draped his left arm over the back of the couch. "Ya know, Riley, I've given some thought to that poor girl from downstairs, the one who gassed herself in her garage. I know you had taken an interest in her, and while I don't want to say that I told you so about her being flaky and unstable, I do want to offer my support to you. It's really part of being a good CEO to emotionally support your senior managers." He sat forward on the couch, and what had been a neutral expression now turned to one of fatherly concern. "These things can be hard, but I want to be sure that you don't take on any of the blame. I know a lot about psychology and human dynamics—heck, that's a big part of my job—and I want to see you put all this out of your mind. A good manager never gets sentimental."

Riley fixed his eyes on the row of books standing in the built-in shelves near the tall, leaded-glass window, admiring the attractive binders of the ten-volume set on the history and organization of the insurance industry, paying little attention to Buck's filial musings. He could hear the sounds of the monologue in the background but was absorbing none of the words. He periodically glanced over to see the range of facial poses being acted out for his benefit. It was a strange, surreal experience, almost like watching an overacted silent movie. Stripped of accompanying words, Buck's facial expressions seemed more than normally absurd as his lips moved rapidly and his head bobbed expressively. But for the thin film of facial perspiration that had condensed onto the lenses of his designer eyewear, now glowing a bright purple in the morning sun, it would have been impossible to detect the fear he was experiencing.

Somewhere along the way, his lips ceased moving, and his expression took on an expectant, questioning quality, causing Riley to come out of his fog. "I'm sorry, Buck, what did you say?"

Buck cocked his head and smiled broadly like a father who had just handed the keys to a new Corvette to his son. "I thought you might be a little stunned," he chuckled. "I said, 'you're getting a two-grade promotion and a one hundred thousand dollar raise.' What d'ya think of them apples?" His smile was now ear to ear.

Riley didn't know whether to laugh or cry. In the end he just shook his head, and said softly, "All that pain and destruction just to cover up a little whoring by two old rich guys. God forgive you."

It was as though someone had pulled a cork out of Buck's ass and all the blood had drained down and out. A terrible panic spread across his face. By the time he had recovered his voice and begun to speak, Riley had risen slowly to his feet and, standing at the door, gestured for Buck to leave his office. "You can stuff your promotion, Buck—I'm declaring myself an 'outbound unit.' Now get out of here so I can finish packing."

Buck looked around the office, wiping perspiration from the palms of his hands onto the slip covers of the couch, noticing for the first time a series of partially packed boxes spread on the floor around the desk and credenza. He sprang nervously from the couch and hurried toward the door. "No, no, wait a minute, Riley—I'm offering you the moon." It seemed to have just dawned on him that in this wildly unbalanced environment a large hole might be left by Riley, not to mention that it might start a herd of departures among the more decent members of the middle ranks, who looked to him as the sole voice on the executive council willing to tell Buck the things he needed to hear. Or maybe he was just plain scared. Or maybe, just possibly, the small core of decency buried under layers of vanity and greed was being heard from, and the sins he had committed against his better nature were beginning to eat at him.

Whatever the reason, it no longer mattered to Riley. Whether his own inaction had made him an enabler or an outright accomplice, he wanted nothing more to do with the culture of cold indifference to other people, of routine dishonesty and poisonous vanity. Of sycophancy and shit molecules. Of anything to do with Buck Montrowe, a man he had once liked and tried so hard to admire.

Buck was trembling with frustration at Riley's unwillingness to acknowledge the practical necessity of the strategy he and Charles Kleinwick had adopted. He frantically renewed his pitch as he passed into the hallway, talking rapid-fire like a panicky child.

Riley looked him in the eye and in a soft, nonrecriminating voice said, "You don't get it, Buck." Then he gently closed the door in his face.

Making his way across the Lobby Court later that morning, Riley was approached by Gladys, who emerged from behind a pillar, where she seemed to have been waiting for him to pass. "Good-bye, my friend," she said softly, looking up at him with pale, liquid eyes.

25

———————

July 20, 1996. Now, eight weeks from the start of it all, Riley was driving back from Rochester, back from Margaret Jonssen's. The afternoon sun had started to burn the side of his face, but so deeply engrossed had he been in his memories he hardly noticed the discomfort.

He took a deep breath and stretched his arms widely, using his knees to steady the steering wheel. It had been just short of three weeks since he departed The Lindbergh, turning over his keys and access card to a tearful Judy Goodrich at the front desk. In spite of the company's best efforts to obscure his departure in a cloud of silence, he had received many notes from employees, including a cherished one from a barely remembered low-level clerk in the accounting department whose job required her to regularly interact with fourth floor executives. The note read, "I will miss you Mr. McReynolds. You were the only one up there who was always nice to me."

The moment he left the building, a new lightness had come over him. He had forgotten what truly restful sleep, sleep unburdened by conscience, felt like. And the vivid blueness of the sky and the greenness of the grass had taken him by surprise. His posture had improved. Even his teeth had gotten whiter. And, best of all, he had stopped shrinking.

Riley took a real joy in visiting Margaret, in performing the only small act of atonement available to him. Saturday was regular visiting day at Holy Redeemer Residence, and in his role as Gunnar Jonssen, in what had now become a weekly ritual, he spent most of the morning with Margaret. They had visited, shared a bag of cherry licorice, and played a round of checkers.

"Stand up straight, Gunnar," Margaret had said as he passed through the doorway on his way out.

It was mid-afternoon as he approached the outskirts of Minneapolis. Shepherd of the Hills Lutheran Church was now far behind him, but its liberating touch, its effusions of grace, were still very much felt.

Being in need of fuel and a little snack, he stopped at a roadside gas station. After filling up the tank he went inside, bought a doughnut, and took a seat in a corner booth. As he nibbled on the doughnut, he spotted a folded copy of the morning newspaper on an adjoining table. He reached over and opened it to the front page, where on the upper left-hand column he saw the bold headline:

CROSSHAVEN HEIR ARRESTED
Facing 10 Years to Life for Crack Possession
Stopped for Minor Traffic Violation

MINNEAPOLIS, MINNESOTA—Bradford Vinehill Crosshaven, son of Woodward V. ("Ward") Crosshaven, one of the area's wealthiest and most socially prominent citizens, was arrested Thursday morning and charged in federal court with possession, with intent to distribute, of two ounces of crack cocaine. The charge carries a mandatory sentence of ten years to life in federal prison.

Minnesota Highway Patrol representatives released a statement late Friday saying that a late-model Jaguar containing Crosshaven and a female passenger was stopped driving north on Highway 101 at 1:35 A.M. for defective tail lights and failure to illuminate the rear license plate. While conducting a routine visual inspection of the car's interior, the arresting officer noticed, protruding from under the back of the driver's seat, a cellophane bag containing a chunky white substance, later analyzed to be crack cocaine.

According to the arrest report made public on Friday afternoon, Crosshaven, 27, became violent and threatened the arresting officer. Several backup units were called to the scene, and young Crosshaven was badly beaten in the ensuing struggle. Additional charges of resisting arrest and threatening a police officer were added to the drug-related charges. The report went on to say that Crosshaven accused the arresting officer of planting the drugs, a charge that was denied by the veteran trooper, who has accumulated six citations for bravery and maintained a flawless disciplinary record in his twenty years with the Patrol.

The United States Attorney's Office, which will handle the prosecution of the case, said that it will vigorously prosecute the charges without regard to the defendant's social or economic status. That office has recently been under intense criticism from the African-American Community for what it regards as discriminatory pretrial release practices and vastly disproportionate punishment relating to crack cocaine (a drug more commonly found in underprivileged and minority communities) and powder cocaine (a drug more commonly found in affluent white communities). Informed sources within the legal community state openly that the U.S. Attorney will be looking to make an example of the wealthy, white Crosshaven to help offset such criticism.

Crosshaven is considered a flight risk and is being held without bail. The unidentified female passenger was released at the scene and is not expected to be charged.

Riley put the paper down and looked out the window with a puzzled expression. There was no way, he thought, that an experienced dealer like Brad Crosshaven would have drugs in his car in open view. It just didn't make sense.

He shifted in his seat as he considered the unlikely possibility that Kurt McBraneman might have had some part in Crosshaven's misfortune. It seemed a little far-fetched. For one thing it lacked Kurt's signature violence. He resolved to dismiss the thought.

He got up and moved slowly toward the door, shaking his head as he walked, an involuntary smile now beginning to tug at the corners of his mouth. In the car he put on his seat-belt and, in an effort to redirect his thinking, turned the radio on high volume.

From the speakers poured forth the clear and crystalline voices of young children accompanying Carly Simon in a heavenly, triumphant rendering of "The Itsy, Bitsy, Spider."

Riley's smile grew wide and irrepressible as he looked up at the sky and winked. He then entered the freeway, merged with northbound traffic, and resumed his journey home.

- END -